Gate 76

Andrew Diamond

This is a work of fiction. Names, characters, and events are the products of the author's imagination. Any resemblance to actual persons or events is purely coincidental.

Cover design by Lindsay Heider Diamond, based on a photo by Adam Birkett on Unsplash.

ISBN: 0-9963507-6-4
ISBN-13: 978-0-9963507-6-1

The gates of hell are open night and day;
Smooth the descent, and easy is the way:
But to return, and view the cheerful skies,
In this the task and mighty labor lies.

—Aeneid VI, 126–129

1

SEPTEMBER 29

In the security line at San Francisco International, there's this woman: blonde hair with dark roots, blue eyes that are hard and bleary and a little bloodshot, like she's been crying, or up all night doing coke. She might be thirty, thirty-two. She wears a light-blue blouse and pale-green skirt, both wrinkled, like they came out of the laundry pile. She has a thin black sweater on top, and a silver crucifix on a silver chain around her neck. Her mouth is set in a stoic, immovable expression that says she will not give the man the pleasure of seeing her hurt or intimidated—the tall, tan-skinned man who hasn't let go of her elbow since she showed up here twenty minutes ago.

I know his type. Not the boss, but trusted by the boss to take care of idiot-grade tasks like getting the car washed. He wears a suit he'll never live up to. The fabric and the cut outclass him and only highlight his cheapness. This is the kind of guy the hookers want to turn down, and still he thinks they love him.

Her, I can't quite figure out. You'd take her for a victim at first glance, with that unhappy face of long endurance and that greasy goon clamped to her arm, but there's something else. A strong will, patience, determination. The same qualities I used to see in those fighters who kept getting up off the canvas no matter how many times I knocked them down.

They're a few feet in front of me now, so mostly I'm looking at their backs. She's got a canvas tote bag over her left shoulder and the guy's holding her left arm. In her right hand is a boarding pass and ID. I can't read the name, but I

5

recognize the colors and the layout of the license. Washington, DC. Just like mine. I wonder if they'll be on my flight.

When the line snakes around, I see them from the front. The guy's face is angular, with a wide jaw, pointy chin, jutting cheekbones, and thick black stubble over oily skin. She's slim, attractive, five seven or so. Her face is pale, but her skin is clear. No bruises or cuts. There are no marks on her hands, and her nails aren't broken. She has a small bruise on her left knee, just below the hem of her skirt. Other than that, nothing. When I glance up again, her eye catches mine for a second with the hard look of a woman annoyed at being ogled.

You hear people talk about love at first sight: "From the second I saw her, I couldn't take my eyes off her." Yeah, well, train wrecks are like that too. You can't look away. Love at first sight is a kind of premonition for people whose lives are on the golden path. They have a house and kids and a steady job coming down the pike, and they know right away who they're going to share it with.

I get premonitions too. But with me, it's like I see some guy walking down the street—never laid eyes on him before—and I just know he's gonna be beating the crap out of me in an alley before the day is over. Or I'm out of town on a job, and I check my watch, and—I don't know—just the way it says 12:33, I know my apartment's on fire.

So I got a premonition just now, a kind of sinking feeling in the pit of my stomach. I know I shouldn't be looking at her. Look too far into anything and you'll find something you're not supposed to know. And that's the first step toward getting involved. Funny I wound up in this profession, a guy like me who always told himself to mind his own business. But it's better than beating people up for a living. Sometimes.

I miss the crowds now and then, and the electric charge of the cheers when you land a good blow and your opponent starts to wobble. But then I remind myself that by this age, thirty-four, I probably would have been out of the sport anyway. The guys who stick around too long get brain damage. They keep moving you up to tougher opponents, and if the first thirty guys can't beat your head in, they'll find someone who can. If you're lucky, that's a million-dollar fight. That's a Saturday night in Vegas and a full payout for the thirty beatings you inflicted just to make it that far. But really, how many people in this world are that lucky?

Lucky, for me, is not slurring my words, is being able to string together coherent sentences and having a steady job. Lucky, for me, is running into Ed Hartwell and getting a second chance.

They're up at the front of the line now. The uniformed woman at the podium asks for their boarding passes. The guy doesn't even offer his. Just tightens his grip on the blonde woman's arm, pulls her toward him, and whispers some rough threat in her ear. Then he walks away. Just leaves the line and heads back toward the exit.

The woman doesn't look after him. She hands her boarding pass and ID to the TSA agent. I can't see her face, but the guy on the other side of security can. The short Vietnamese guy emptying the garbage can into his big rolling bin. He's not watching what he's doing. He's watching the blonde.

The agent shunts her into the line on the left. A minute later, I'm sent off to the line on the right. I lose sight of her as I'm filling my bin for the X-ray. Wallet, phone, belt, shoes. No carry-on this time. I paid the twenty-five bucks and checked it.

On the far side of the X-ray machine, I get my shoes back on and look for a place to eat. Every TV in the terminal is tuned to CNN. It's a slow season for news, so the coverage focuses on the gubernatorial elections in the few states that are still up for grabs. The whole country is sick of the promises and innuendo coming out of Florida, Ohio, Pennsylvania, and especially Texas, where that fat cop-turned-governor has a threat on his lips for anyone who doesn't see things his way, and an opponent he just can't get rid of. I find a bar where the muted TVs replay the baseball highlights.

Twenty minutes later, I'm halfway through a beer, thinking about the case I'm working and what I'm going to tell Ed Hartwell when I get back to the office. First I'll tell him, yes, the guy I followed out here from DC did go into a bank. Two banks. He has safe deposit boxes at both, but not under his own name. They belong to his parents, who are both in homes with Alzheimer's. I managed to persuade the bank managers to tell me what he put in them: tiny corpses wrapped in burial shrouds. So, yeah, he probably did steal the artifacts. Where he finds a market for ancient religious statuettes, I have no idea. But the Smithsonian will be glad to hear they're not lost. We'll have to get the Feds to look into the boxes, and then it's out of our hands.

I'll also tell Ed we should be upgraded to first class. Not that we fly all that often. But Baker/Watson, the law firm that gives us a big chunk of our work, represents the airline and the Baker/Watson guys always get bumped up to first. At my size, it makes a difference.

In four and a half years of work together, Ed and I have only had one case that directly involved the airline. They thought two of their baggage handlers at Dulles were involved in some kind of smuggling. The airline had their own guys watch them at work and then we watched them the rest of the time. Turns out there were four of them, and they were dealing, not smuggling. Their extracurriculars had nothing to do with their day jobs. Once the airline was sure they were off the hook, they fired the guys, and we turned the case over to the Fairfax County cops.

I see the Vietnamese guy with the garbage cart shaking out a clear plastic bag to replace the one he just pulled out of the can. He's got close-cropped hair and big ears that stick out from the sides of his head like radar dishes. He's looking down the terminal like he's on alert. I follow his eyes, and there she is, walking all alone, looking sideways into the shop windows and fingering the silver crucifix between her breasts. The bag looped over her shoulder has a big red apple logo on the side, like a target.

She goes into the newsstand and comes out again a minute later. The agent at gate seventy-six is making the last call for the flight to Honolulu. The Vietnamese guy makes his way toward her with some urgency. He passes a few trashcans on the way without checking them, but he keeps a good forty feet behind her so she won't notice him.

I leave my half-finished beer on the table and follow him. I'm not even on the job. It's just habit—like a cat following a mouse it doesn't want because it has instincts it just can't ignore.

She walks slowly to the back of the line at gate seventy-six and pulls her boarding pass from her shoulder bag. A few passengers file in behind her. I'm past the Vietnamese guy. Twenty feet in back of her. Too close. She turns and looks over her shoulder, right past me, and her eyes show an animal wariness as she surveys the terminal. The short, fat gate agent with the long black hair reads her boarding pass and then hands it back to her. Why didn't she scan it?

The tall bald guy, next in line, hands her his pass. The attendant puts her hand over the scanner and shakes her head. She reads the pass and hands it back to him and waves him through.

The blonde is on the gangway. The Vietnamese guy wheels his cart down past the next gate, past the next set of garbage cans, then just leaves it and walks on quickly. Looks like he's got his phone to his ear, telling whoever he's supposed to tell that she's on the plane.

The gate agent continues reading passes. There are five more people in the line. The other agent, the one who works the computer terminal and deals with the standbys, has already left. The twelve people on standby will have to look for another flight. Three more passengers in the line. Two.

One. None. The gate attendant picks up the phone and makes a call.

And then she pops out of the gangway. The blonde. She's looking in her bag, a little frantic, a little too dramatic. She's overacting. She makes like she's going to say something to the gate agent, maybe ask her to hold the plane for a minute. But when she sees the agent doesn't notice her, she just keeps walking and digging through her bag.

Did she leave her wallet at the newsstand? That seems to be where she's headed. But she walks right by it, and then she relaxes a little. She stops digging through her bag and goes into the bathroom. I stand there for a minute watching the women go in and out. Two minutes. The door at gate seventy-six is locked. She's not out. Five minutes. The plane is pushing back and the gate agent is gone. The standby passengers have all cleared out.

I'm about to walk away when a dark-haired woman comes out of the bathroom, wearing big dark sunglasses, a white blouse, black skirt, black heels, a little bruise on her left knee. Her straight black bangs are cut half an inch above the eyebrows. The canvas tote bag looped over her shoulder is turned inside out, so no logo shows. But she's still wearing the black sweater on top of the new blouse. Why? I move a little closer.

She raises her left arm to check her watch, pushes the sleeve back with her right index finger. Her left wrist is bruised all the way around. Dark purple. Her right sleeve cuff slides back half an inch. Same bruises on that side. She goes past me, eyes on her watch, and now I'm following again.

She's two inches taller in those heels that clomp like hooves along the polished stone floor. The undercurrent of strength and will I saw in her before is now on full display. She moves with speed, determination, and certainty. She knows exactly what she's doing.

She passes several gates and then turns quickly to the left, right into the back of the line for the Chicago flight. Last call, and she's the last passenger in the queue of three. No wonder she was walking so fast.

She takes her glasses off and fishes another boarding pass from her bag. At the counter, she pushes it straight to the scanner, like she's going to scan it herself. The attendant takes it from her hand mechanically and passes it over the glass, but the scanner turns red instead of green. The attendant looks at the paper, a little puzzled, and then separates it into two. There are two boarding passes. She's catching a connecting flight in Chicago. The agent scans the right pass and returns the papers.

The other gate agent is already kicking the wedge out of the door to the gangway so she can close it. The blonde, now brunette, takes one last look over her shoulder, and when her eye catches mine, there's the spark of recognition as she remembers me from the security line—the big guy who was examining her a little too closely. She starts, with a look of pale terror, then turns forward and disappears with quick, unsteady steps.

Normally, I wouldn't mention any of this. Troubled people and their troubled lives, I try to put out of my head. God knows I see enough of them. But this one got to me, I don't know why. Like I said, sometimes you get a premonition. Sometimes you just know a world of trouble is about to open up and swallow you, and all you can do is wait to see what happens next.

When I get off the plane at Washington Dulles, it's almost midnight. I take my phone out of airplane mode, and there's a message from Ed. "Call me as soon as you get this." He doesn't say what it's about, but he doesn't have to.

When I step into the terminal, my face turns upward, like the faces of every other passenger coming off that plane. Up to the monitor. To CNN, and the reporter on the beach with his wind-blown hair. The Honolulu flight that left from gate seventy-six broke into pieces and went down into the sea.

The reporter keeps saying the flight was full. Every seat was taken.

But it wasn't full.

2

SEPTEMBER 30

Six o'clock the next morning, I'm in Bill Watson's office on the eighth floor of the Baker/Watson building on Connecticut Avenue, about six blocks northwest of the White House. Bill Watson is a big, red-faced man with grey hair and a belly swollen from years of gin and beef. He sits calmly behind a glass desk, his hands folded together on his stomach. They go up and down when he breathes.

Ed Hartwell, my partner, sits in a black swivel chair beside me, while a VP from the airline named Buster Thompson paces in front of the plate glass window that looks out over Desales Street. Thompson is sixty or so, thin and agitated. "You've seen the video," he says. He's talking about the cell phone video that the news networks started showing a few hours ago of the plane breaking into pieces over Santa Cruz. It's a little white cross in the clear-blue sky, then there's a flash and a dozen fiery chunks trail smoke in sharp downward arcs, like the branches of a willow tree weeping into the sea. It all goes down into Monterey Bay, just short of the deep-water canyon that would have made the wreck impossible to recover.

"It was clearly a bomb. You can see the explosion in the midsection of the plane." Thompson stops pacing for a second and strokes his chin. Then he looks directly at Ed and says, "Two hours ago, the FBI hauled in one of our baggage handlers as a person of interest. A black kid from Oakland named Rashad Obasanjo. Muslim."

Ed writes notes on a white legal pad on his knee. He never uses a computer in meetings. It's always pen and paper.

Except for some colorful language now and then, Ed's about the straightest straight arrow God ever made, with his tailored suit, starched white shirt, and conservative blue ties. He has that lawman look to him: tall, strong, and ramrod straight. He keeps his hair cut close on the sides, and a little longer on top, just like in his military days. He grew up in Alabama, in the decade after the heyday of the civil rights movement, when the world stopped watching that state, and as he tells it, the whites went on treating him and his family the same way they always had.

He's not the type to be bitter though. His answer to people trying to keep him down was to go make something of himself. He spent six years in the army after high school, then four in college, and more than twenty in the FBI. He's in his fifties, but he never drank or smoked, so he looks fifteen years younger than he is.

He has a way of presenting himself that demands respect. Always in a suit. Always looks you in the eye and says exactly what he means. Growing up in that crucible of racial hostility toughened him up. Neither one of us had it easy. That's one of the reasons we get along so well.

I owe the guy a debt for taking me on in the first place. We met about four and a half years ago, when I was investigating an insurance cheat up in Rockville. This guy had a scam where he'd pull in front of a car on the highway, then hit the brakes and get rear-ended. He'd claim to have whiplash and sue. Twice he settled, with two different insurance companies. The third time, the insurers were onto him. They sent me out to watch him.

It was early spring, and the guy was mowing his lawn in front of a little run-down cinder-block house. I rolled by slowly and made a video of him at work. There was a pick-up parked at the curb in front of his house. I didn't know it at the time, but the guy in the pickup was Ed Hartwell.

I parked a block away, got out of my car and walked back, acting like I was just out for a stroll. I stopped to ask Mr.

Whiplash some questions. He shut the mower off so he could hear me. Ed Hartwell had his windows rolled down, dressed in a dark blue jumpsuit, like a plumber. He had a clipboard up on the steering wheel and was writing on it like a contractor writing up an estimate. I could tell he was listening to us.

The insurance cheat was a sloppy, balding guy, with a double chin and a beer gut. The cool spring wind made the wispy dark hairs of his comb-over stand straight up. I asked him how were the schools in the neighborhood. He said they were OK and asked if I was thinking about buying a house. I said I was. I told him my wife was pregnant and we needed something bigger than our apartment out on Rockville Pike. The mention of the pregnant wife and the tiny apartment perked him up.

One thing about these small-time crooks who can't think past a quick scam: they feel sorry for themselves. And it makes them feel a whole lot better when they meet a guy whose life is worse than theirs.

So he told me about the neighborhood and the schools, and I kept slipping in complaints about how tough things were at home, and how I was everybody's doormat. "I got a crappy maintenance job with Metro. I can barely afford to ride the buses I clean. And now my wife can't work. She's cranky as hell, throwing up every morning, and all of a sudden everything is *my* goddamn fault."

That got him. His wife never stopped being a bitch after the first three months of pregnancy. And that was six years ago. "You think money's tight now, wait'll your kid starts going to the dentist."

I let him go on for a while, and he had plenty to say, whining about all the projects his wife had him working on around the house. He said he had carried a new toilet into the house the day before, because he wasn't going to pay no damn plumber a hundred and ten dollars to install the thing. He had also been up on a ladder, cleaning the gutters, because the Salvadorans wanted fifty dollars to do it, and screw them.

Those shiftless drunks can go clean gutters in Potomac for that kind of money.

He seemed lonely, like no one had listened to him for a long time, and he was trying to get it all out now, while he had an audience.

I was recording the conversation on the phone inside my jacket. Not that we could use the recording in court, but it would make a good threat, and give me details to follow up on later. I gave the audio and the video to the insurance company's lawyer, who confronted him with it and threatened him with criminal fraud. He dropped the case, and they let him know they'd come after him if he ever bothered them again.

That's how it goes. Tomorrow, some other smart-ass will come along and try the same scam. Like no one ever thought of it before and the insurance companies aren't wise to it. For every dumbass you meet in this business, there are ten more waiting to crawl out of the woodwork. Stick around long enough, you'll get to meet them too. After a while, you can't tell one from the next. They all just merge into one universal loser.

I met Ed, formally, about a week after the interview with Mr. Whiplash, in the lobby of a building in Bethesda. The lawyers who kept me busy had offices on the third floor. The ones who kept him busy worked in DC, on bigger stuff. Ed told me the woman who rear-ended my insurance cheat broke her nose when the airbag popped out. She was rich and pretty, and a broken nose to a woman like that is unforgivable. Her husband was a big shot, paranoid and vindictive. He was a client of Baker/Watson, and wanted Ed to look into the guy. Was he sent by someone? Was he a stalker? A blackmailer? You get to a certain level of wealth and power, and you can no longer understand how small some people think. You just can't believe that some loser in Rockville was only after a few thousand bucks. Mr. Whiplash picked the rich woman's car because it was a Mercedes and looked well insured. That's all there was to it. Ed reached the same conclusion as me. The guy in the cinder-block house wasn't part of any larger conspiracy, and he wasn't worth worrying about.

"I was surprised how you got him talking," Ed said.

"It wasn't hard. He wouldn't have opened up to you though. You're too imposing. You look like the law."

"Yeah, I know it," Ed said. "But it works in my favor when I need it to." Then he said, "You know, I took you for a heavy. An enforcer type. Thought maybe you'd try to beat something out of him."

"In the old days, I might have."

Ed laughed. "The old days? You must be talking about grade school. You can't be over thirty."

"In the old days," I repeated, "I used to almost make a living beating the crap out of people."

He said, "Well it's a good skill to have, long as you know there are better ways to do your job. Who are you working for?"

"A place up in Rockville."

"You interested in something more challenging?"

"Well I don't need to spend my life jacking with these small-time assholes. You only have to meet two or three like that before you're sick of them."

"Well I can introduce you to some big-time assholes," he said. "They have lots of money and lots of problems."

That's how we got started. Since then, we've done a lot of corporate work. A company thinks someone's embezzling, taking bribes, selling trade secrets, they call us in. Sometimes they want us to investigate their own executives. Is he racking up gambling debts, having affairs, or being blackmailed? Sometimes they want us to get off-the-record info about a company they're about to acquire. That's part of due diligence.

DC has a few specialties of its own. If it's a government contractor putting in a bid proposal, and they think they can dig up something to disqualify a competitor, they'll set us on the case. If a political party wants to back a candidate, they ask us to dig up dirt on him before the press does.

In general, the white-collar criminals are craftier than the small-time cheats. They take a longer view of their work and put more thought into covering their tracks. It took me a while to get used to working in that world. But here I am.

The airline VP starts pacing again. "A year ago," he says, "one of our ticket agents at LAX raped his coworker on the job, in the office behind the main ticket counter. The guy had a record of sexual assault. We didn't know that, but a jury said we should have. He had applied for the job under his brother's name, with his brother's social security card and license. The victim's lawyers figured that out. It cost us a million and a half to settle that case and keep it quiet.

"Four months later," he says, "one of our flight attendants assaulted a passenger on a flight to Atlanta. Another passenger filmed the incident. You might have seen it on YouTube. Turns out our flight attendant had a drug problem and was seeing a counselor about bipolar disorder. We knew none of this until we got the results of a failed drug test three days *after* the incident. That was another lawsuit and some very bad publicity."

He stops pacing and looks over at Bill Watson, who's calmly twiddling his thumbs on top of his big fat belly. "Two months ago," the airline VP says, "we found out one of our baggage handlers in Chicago was responsible for a series of thefts that resulted in our insurer paying out over $200,000 in claims. This guy was taking things from people's bags and giving some of it to his supervisor to keep him from reporting it. The baggage handler had a couple of misdemeanor charges on his record. All of them had been dropped and were more than ten years old when he completed his job application. So we let them slide.

"Our insurer has not been happy about any of this. We've had three strikes in the past twelve months, and two of them resulted in costly lawsuits. Yesterday, one hundred and eighty-eight people died, including eight airline employees."

He looks at Ed and says, "You know what the average payout is for an individual death in an air crash if it results from the airline's negligence?"

Ed shakes his head.

"It's around three million dollars," Bill Watson says.

"And if it was *gross* negligence," the VP says, "like allowing an obvious security threat to load bags onto your plane?"

"Wait," says Ed. "Are you talking about Obasanjo? Why is he an obvious threat?"

"He's not," Bill Watson says. "But in a courtroom, it's easy for a lawyer to paint him as one."

Watson gives us some background on Rashad Obasanjo. He's twenty-two years old. He's from a rough neighborhood in Oakland. His father emigrated from Nigeria in the 1980s. His mother and his maternal grandmother were both members of the Nation of Islam. The guy posts on Facebook and Twitter almost daily about his faith. You can play that up in court as him being radical or him being devout.

"And it could play either way in the media," the VP says. "Our PR guys are trying to figure out how to spin this one. But when it comes right down to it, people will see in him exactly what they want to see."

Bill Watson cuts in and says, "The airline disciplined Obasanjo once this year after he got in an argument with a coworker about praying on the job. The coworker said passengers don't want to see terrorists bowing down anywhere near an airport. That set the kid off on a tirade."

Then Watson leans forward in his chair and adds, "Obasanjo also had a criminal trial last year on a battery charge. He claimed self-defense, refused a plea bargain, and was acquitted. You know the media will pick that up. They're going to be asking why the airline kept him in a position with access to planes and baggage."

The airline VP goes back to the money. "So three million per person for negligence, and a lot more for what plaintiffs' lawyers can easily portray as gross negligence. Then throw in some hot-button political issues, like a Muslim killing Christians. A black guy killing white people. No offense, Ed."

"I understand how the country works," Ed says.

"Most of those passengers were white, you know. Throw that to a white, middle-class jury and what's a death worth then? Ten million? Now multiply that by one hundred and eighty-eight bodies. We could be on the hook for close to two billion dollars, and that's enough to put us under."

"But if your guy did it..." Ed says.

The VP lets out a long breath and shakes his head. "Everyone who worked with the guy says he couldn't have done it. He just wasn't the type."

Bill Watson says, "Isn't that what the friends of most terror suspects say?"

"Look," says the VP, "to be honest, I don't even care about the kid. I do care about two billion dollars. We're going to proceed on two fronts. First, we examine all other possible suspects. The best outcome for us is if someone else did this. Second, we want ears inside the government's investigation because, frankly, it doesn't look good. We want you, Ed, in San Francisco talking to the investigators. Work your connections in the FBI, pull every bit of information you can out of them, and pass it back to our legal team so they can prepare."

I can see Ed doesn't like this. He let out a little breath just now, and his shoulders sagged. I don't think Watson or the VP picked up on it. You wouldn't notice unless you knew Ed well. But I know he does not like to call in favors from any of his friends within the Bureau unless it's absolutely necessary. He's opposed on principal to agents releasing information outside of official channels. But his face shows none of the discomfort that I know he's feeling.

Bill Watson says the legal team in San Francisco has already assembled to discuss strategy. "Your plane leaves from Dulles in three hours," Watson says. "So go pack a bag, get out there, and pull every detail you can from everyone you know."

"And me?" I ask.

"You're on desk duty," Watson says. "The passenger list from the Hawaii flight is in your inbox. You and Bethany and Leon go through it name by name. If anything catches your interest, pass it along to the FBI."

"Seriously? You want us doing background checks? What are we going to find that the FBI can't dig up in five minutes?"

The airline VP says, "Something, we hope." He's standing in front of the window with his arms folded across his chest and a big frown on his face. "With that much money on the line, somebody better find *something*."

"All right," I say. "We'll go through the list."

This is not the kind of work I like. Sitting at a computer all day bores the hell out of me. And with 188 people to look into, I'll be at my desk for three weeks.

The VP says to Ed, "Your ticket's waiting at the check-in counter at Dulles. We'll send an email with the names of your contacts in San Francisco."

I say, "Hey, Bill—" I want to tell him about that blonde in the security line.

"You mind excusing us?" Watson says and gets up from his desk to walk us out.

Ed gets up and slides his legal pad into his shoulder bag. He looks at me and says, "You ready?"

"Bill," I say. "I was in San Francisco yesterday. I was at the airport—"

He goes right by me and opens the office door and says, "Strange, huh? Being that close to something like that. Makes you wonder—what if it had been you?"

"Listen though—"

"We can talk later," Watson says. "I need some time in private with this guy."

He shuts the door.

Ed's already on his phone, talking to someone at the Bureau, saying he'll be in San Francisco later in the day. "Ed," I say. He looks at me and shakes his head. Then he says into the phone, "Let us know who our guys should contact if their background checks turn up any leads."

He's still on the phone as we leave the building. The thing is glued to his ear as he gets into a cab on Connecticut Avenue.

"Ed," I say.

He nods and says, "Later, Freddy." Then he shuts the door and off he goes.

I stand there for a second watching the cab roll down the street. Then I pull out my phone and check my email. I open the message with the passenger list and find the email address of our contact at the airline. I type out a quick message asking for any other documents related to the Hawaii flight, as well as the passenger list for the Chicago flight that left a few minutes later. *And if you can get any footage from the security lines before the Hawaii flight boarded, send that too.*

3

At 7:40 a.m., I'm in the gym trying to work off some frustration. The TV in the corner above the weight rack keeps showing that cell phone video of the plane breaking up over Santa Cruz. The skinny kid who's in here every morning trying to build his muscles, who follows me around like a stray dog, is sitting on a weight bench staring up at the screen. He asks me what I think of the crash. I tell him I don't like it.

Seriously, what kind of question is that? What does he think I think of it?

This kid hit the heavy bag all wrong when he first came in here a few weeks ago. I had to stop in the middle of my sit-ups and correct him.

"Straighten your wrists when you punch! What the hell's wrong with you?"

I showed him how to do it. I could tell he's the kind that gets picked on—a sensitive-looking kid with too much soul in his eyes and not enough meat on his bones. He comes in before school trying to bulk up, but it's not working. I showed him how to wrap his hands so he doesn't break them when he punches. I should have let him learn the hard way. Now he thinks we're friends.

I got off the phone with Ed about ten minutes ago. He called from the road with a list of names the airline singled out from the passenger list.

"There's guy from Idaho," Ed said. "Owen Briscoe. Used to belong to a white separatist militia and has a history of mental illness."

"Sounds promising."

"Yeah. And a combat engineer from Kansas, just discharged last week. He had access to explosives."

"All right," I say. "Sounds like a good lead for Bethany."

"And a guy from Dearborn, Michigan."

"What's his story?"

"He's Muslim," Ed said.

"Who isn't in Dearborn? Is that a crime?"

"No. But if a Muslim extremist took this plane down, the airline would prefer it wasn't one of their own."

"So what am I supposed to do? Pin it on the other guy?"

"Come on, Freddy. Just do some digging, and if you find anything, pass it to the FBI."

"You want me to go to Michigan?"

"No," he said. "You're on desk duty. The airline has their A team out in the field."

"Their A team? What the fuck is that?"

The A team, Ed explained, is a bunch of former federal law enforcement agents, all with twenty-plus years of experience and connections to people inside the FBI, the National Transportation Safety Board, and a number of other agencies.

I don't fit that bill, so I guess that puts me on the B team doing background checks. Ed knows I don't like computer work, so he tried to give me a little pep talk.

"Look, Freddy, the airline has everything to lose here. They're at the roulette wheel spreading their chips across every number, praying for one of them to pay off. I just sent you the names of your contacts in the Bureau. A guy named Errol Lomax, and his boss, Mitch Rollins."

"You know these guys?"

"I know Rollins," Ed said, "He's an old-timer. Just came off a corruption investigation with Lomax. Lomax was the first one at San Francisco International after the crash. He was supposed to be catching a plane back to DC but he wound up sticking around. He'll be back in DC tomorrow."

"All right," I said.

"And just between you and me, I think Rollins is burnt out. He's been at it way too long. I don't know Lomax, but you might have better luck working with him. I'll let you make that call. I'll set up a meet and greet so you know who you're working with."

"Yeah, Ed. Listen—"

"I got another call coming in," Ed said. "I'll let you know when I land in San Francisco."

He hung up.

I'm still stewing about that, and maybe I'm taking it out on the skinny kid. His questions annoy me, but I really don't need to be so rude.

I could have been on the A team if it weren't for some bad decisions I made a few years ago. When I left New York and started over, I wanted to be a cop. I had the skills and the drive, but after the background check, they said I was too volatile to carry a gun. They knew about DiLeo from the write-up that cop did in my hospital room. That's what did me in. I'm sure of it.

So now I'm a bench warmer on the B team, throwing weights around in the gym to work off my frustration.

I'm sitting on the end of the weight bench, getting ready to do another set while the TV keeps playing the video of the plane.

The skinny kid turns to me and says, "I watched your fight on YouTube."

"Which fight?" Like I don't already know.

"That one you lost to—what's his name? Perkins. The contender."

That fight.

* * *

It was a priest who first got me into the gym. I had moved to Brooklyn from Philadelphia and lived in a filthy little apartment with my father's father, who was a worthless drunk. He had once been strong, but a stroke left him unable to swallow solid food. So he mostly lived on beer and shuffled around the apartment. Out on the streets, there was no one to defend me but me, and I got good at it. I got a reputation, and people mostly left me alone.

This priest, an old Puerto Rican guy named Father Sanchez, kept telling me I was headed for trouble, and when I said I wasn't, he'd say, "Yeah? What's your plan, kid?" I'd say my plan was to stay out of trouble, and he'd say that wasn't a plan. Without goals and skills and timelines, it was just a hope.

He brought me into Jimmy Rizzardi's gym where this kid JoJo was working out against a trainer who wore body padding and big black mitts. JoJo glided around the ring like a dancer, moving side to side and popping out quick shots against the trainer's gloves. He had a natural grace and fluidity that was impossible to teach.

Sanchez, the priest, pointed up at JoJo and said, "The Bible says God made man in his own image."

Jimmy Rizzardi came up and asked what I thought of the kid in the ring. I said I could lay him out with one punch.

"You want to give it a shot?" Rizzardi said. "Hey JoJo? You wanna spar?"

JoJo smiled at me and said, "Hey Freddy, step on in." Then he laughed and added, "It ain't like on the streets. You can't do me like you do those other guys."

Rizzardi wrapped my hands and put on my gloves and headgear. He told me no hitting below the belt, nothing to the back of the head, and don't hit him if he's down or gets spun around.

JoJo had this big white smile on his face, and I was gonna go in there and wipe it off. Rizzardi said get to it, and JoJo's trainer stayed in the ring to make sure we kept it clean.

I went right at JoJo and swung and missed. He popped a short jab in my face, and then I didn't know where he was. The guy moved sideways like a crab. I went at him again, swung and missed. He popped me three times in a row. Nothing too hard, but it got me confused. How could anyone put three punches together that fast? I never even saw them coming.

I started getting frustrated, swinging harder and harder. Big, wide, winging punches. Sometimes I swung so hard, my feet came up off the floor and I lost my balance. Every time I missed, he'd hit me two, three, four times. None of them felt too bad, except for a couple I walked right into.

JoJo started talking to me. "Plant your feet, Freddy. A punch ain't nothing if your feet off the ground."

I kept missing, and I was getting winded. JoJo kept landing short, quick shots right up the middle, and he never looked tired.

After a few minutes, Rizzardi called a halt. He said, "You got a good chin, kid."

I said, "Chin? Did you see the bombs I was throwing? If I'd have caught him, he'd be dead."

"Yeah, but you didn't catch him," Rizzardi said. "You swing like you're expecting him to stand still."

When he took my headgear off and I saw myself in the mirror, I was surprised at how my face was marked up. That guy hit me everywhere. Rizzardi and JoJo and the other trainer were all looking at me, and Rizzardi said, "That really didn't bother you? All those punches?"

"No," I said. "Not really." That was nothing compared to what my dad used to do to me back in Philly.

"OK," Rizzardi said, "come over here and hit the heavy bag."

I took a few swings at it. The same wide, winging hooks I had been throwing in the ring. And each time, thwack! The bag would dance, and the chain it hung from would jingle. Thwack! Thwack! Thwack!

"All right," said Rizzardi, "now hit the speed bag." He took me over to the little black bag, shaped like a teardrop, that hung on a short chain about six feet above the floor.

I couldn't hit the thing. I'd smash it once and it would flail around so fast, I'd have to wait for it to stop.

"Don't hit it so hard," Rizzardi said.

"What's the point of tapping it?" I said.

"Look at your face," Rizzardi said, and he turned me toward the mirror. "Those taps add up."

Rizzardi taught me patience, persistence, and discipline. It took him years, but he taught me to take the long view instead of going for the quick win all at once. Pick a strategy, work through it, and give it time. When I look back on it now, I don't know what the guy saw in me or why he stuck with me as long as he did. But somehow, over time, he brought me around, and I started thinking through what I was doing, instead of just flailing away.

In my first twelve amateur fights, I went six and six. The six I lost, I lost for the same reason. The game plan didn't seem to be working in the first round. The other guy was faster than me, or he was moving in ways I couldn't figure out, so I abandoned the plan and started winging big knockout punches.

Rizzardi told me that when I quit on the game plan, it showed I didn't believe in myself. If I didn't believe in myself, why should he believe in me? He threatened to dump me.

The next few fights, he said, "I expect you to lose the first round without abandoning the plan. If I see you winging punches, I'm gonna throw in the towel." So I stayed patient, even when I was sure it was all going wrong.

I won twenty-eight fights in a row.

Whenever I got cocky, Rizzardi would make me spar against guys who were way out of my league, and he'd watch them beat the crap out of me. I was stubborn and couldn't admit someone got the better of me until I had a thorough thrashing. I had spent the first eight years of my life getting beat up by my dad, so my response to being hit was always just—I'm going to kill you. No one will ever put me in that position again. You even think about hurting me, and I'll fucking kill you.

That's the attitude Rizzardi spent years working out of me. He taught me to observe and think, to understand my opponent, to give my plan several rounds to unfold, to expect setbacks, and to stick to the plan even when things looked bad. I don't know why any man would spend that much time trying to instill discipline into such a stubborn, hardheaded kid.

But it paid off. I finished my amateur career with a record of sixty-four and nine. In the pros, I trained harder, I trusted my teacher, and I trusted myself. I won my first twelve fights by knockout.

For years, I worked in a fish market during the day and spent my mornings and evenings at the gym. When I didn't smell like fish, I smelled like sweat, and the girls had no interest in me.

When I was twenty-five, my pro record was twenty wins and one loss, with nineteen knockouts. I was fighting in front of crowds of a few hundred, and I had a little bit of a following up in New York. Not much, but a few dozen people knew my name and hung around to say hello after every fight. I wasn't making any real money as a boxer, but I thought I should have been.

Then along comes this new promoter named Mancuso. Everyone calls him Slim. He's got a few fighters, and he's getting them good exposure. He tells me I have the skills, and he can get me the money. He signs me to a contract and puts me with a new trainer.

This trainer... I couldn't figure out what the hell was wrong with him. He'd have me sparring, I'd take a couple hard shots to the ribs, and he'd just clap and say, "Good work. Keep it up."

Rizzardi used to yell at me when he saw me getting tagged like that. "How the hell'd you walk into that one? Look at your feet, Freddy. You're tripping all over yourself, walking right into his power. Circle the other way and keep the jab on him so he can't load up!"

The new guy didn't push me at all. I should have realized something was wrong.

On the promotion side, though, Slim knew his job. He got me six fights in eighteen months, and he was turning out big crowds. Four, five, six hundred people. That may not sound like much, but boxers come up the same way stand-up comics do. You spend years putting on your best show in front of a bunch of heckling drunks in some depressing little clubs, but if you do it well, word gets around and the crowds get bigger. Eventually you get the attention of the right people. That's the way it all seemed to be moving.

Slim had me fighting in front of the cameras, but I had these nagging doubts about the opponents he was putting me up against. I had fought some tough, highly skilled guys under Rizzardi, each one better than the last. The guys Slim was lining up for me were no better than second-year amateurs. They *looked* tough on camera, which is why Slim picked them. He made sure that when I knocked those guys out the highlights made it onto ESPN and Fox Sports. They started calling me The Wrecking Ball because of the way I was powering through opponents.

There was another heavyweight up in New York, a guy named Alvin Perkins, who was also getting some press. He had twenty-six wins and no losses, with sixteen knockouts. By then I was twenty-six and one with twenty-five knockouts. The promoters talked about the match for nine months before it came off. One of us would be moving up to bigger venues. Maybe Madison Square Garden. Maybe an undercard in Vegas.

The other thing I should have paid more attention to—other than that loser trainer—was Slim's main line of work. He wasn't a full-time promoter. I mean, he was good at it, but mainly he was a bookie and a loan shark. When he switched me to the new trainer, he also gave me a bodyguard. A big fat guy named Chuck DiLeo. I didn't need a bodyguard. I didn't

GATE 76

have enough fans to mob me and no one would bother robbing me because I had nothing to take.

DiLeo was a bottom-rung enforcer who collected payments from people who owed Slim money. He'd pick me up from the gym in his Camaro and we'd go get four hundred bucks off some college kid who cried when you twisted his arm, or eight hundred from an old man who couldn't pay until his Social Security check came in. Slim never trusted DiLeo with the tough cases. He wouldn't send him on a job that required a gun because he knew DiLeo was a coward. Even though he was six-six and over three hundred pounds, DiLeo wouldn't hit anyone unless he was sure the guy wouldn't hit back. It took me a while to figure out that I was DiLeo's bodyguard. I was the extra muscle he brought along to make collecting easier.

This was the team I had around me when I went into the fight of my life. I knew that lazy trainer wasn't going to get me in shape, so I asked Slim to put me back with Rizzardi. He said that couldn't be done. Those were his words. Couldn't be done. Like it was up to someone else. That was a bullshit answer, and I knew it.

So I took it upon myself to do the work. I went back to the principles Rizzardi taught me. I ran extra miles each morning. I wrote out a chart of what to eat at every meal for sixty days and I stuck to it. I doubled my sit-ups and strengthened my neck, so the punches wouldn't rock my head so bad. I snuck back into the old gym—Slim didn't like me going there—and found better sparring partners. I did all this on my own. I wasn't gonna let an opportunity slip by after ten years of hard work.

* * *

The skinny kid's still looking at me, waiting for my comment on the Perkins bout.

31

"Tough fight," I say. I stand up and grab my water bottle and walk away, but he follows me past the weight rack, past the TV that keeps showing the video of the plane.

"What happened?" he says. "It looked like you were winning."

"I *was* winning."

Leave me alone, kid. Don't you get it?

"Then why'd you quit? You had the guy. Why'd you stop punching?"

That's really the wrong question.

"I guess it wasn't my night," I say.

"What happened in your next fight?"

The kid has this luster in his eyes, like he's looking for a hero.

"There was no next fight. Drop it."

"But why would you quit after you—"

I pull up short at the entrance to the locker room. "What do you want me to say? That I gathered up my courage and bounced back and it all turned out OK? You want some fucking moral to comfort you? *Work hard. Put your heart into it, and it'll all work out.* Is that what you want to hear? Because that's not how it works.

"The way it works is a fucking airplane blows up and a bunch of people who don't deserve it die for no fucking reason at all. *That's* how it works. The way it works is somebody decides they need to get paid, and if they have to ruin a guy's career or kill a hundred and eighty-eight people, they don't fucking care. You understand that, kid? Because the sooner you get it, the less time you'll waste being surprised and disappointed."

All the shine goes out of those dark, soulful eyes. He looks like a dog whose owner just walked out on him.

Sometimes I fucking hate myself.

4

By 8:45, I'm in the office. Bethany and Leon are at their desks, digging through the passenger list from the Hawaii flight.

The office is a big room on the second floor of a 1980s building on M Street, with a light gray carpet, overhead fluorescents, and big windows that look out onto the newer buildings across the street. Attached to the main room is a private side-office for Ed. He keeps his door open when he's here, closing it only for private conferences.

Bethany brought in a few plants to make the place look less sterile. I'm not sure how much of a difference it made. Most of the time, I'm just staring at my monitor.

Bethany came to us a couple years ago from a public library in Silver Spring. She walked in one day, put a résumé on my desk, and said, "OK, let me tell you what a reference librarian can do for you. Do you know what kinds of records are scattered across our nation's libraries that have not yet been digitized?"

"What?" I didn't even understand the question.

"Google can't answer everything, you know."

She went on for a few minutes about how to find obscure bits of information while I sat there taking stock of her. She was in her midtwenties, a little above average height, with a thin curveless build, like a young boy. She had fair skin with light freckles, pale blue eyes, blonde eyebrows, and long straight strawberry-blonde hair that she kept pushing away from her face as she talked. You couldn't see her blonde eyelashes at all until she was right in front of you. Her lack of color and curves made her look like she'd been washed and ironed too many times, but she was earnest and animated, expressing every point with her whole face, her long arms and thin hands.

She had obviously done her research on us and what kinds of information we needed to dig up. She also had a folder full of résumés under her arm.

I interrupted her while she was saying something about the Homeland Security Digital Library. "Excuse me—how many résumés are in that folder?"

That stopped her in her tracks. "Um, what?"

I realized then that she had rehearsed the whole spiel. My question threw her, and she lost some confidence.

I asked again. "How many résumés do you have with you?"

"Ten. But I only have four targets today."

"What do you mean targets?"

She opened the folder and showed me a set of neatly printed pages listing information about each company, including what they did, who held key positions, who was responsible for hiring, what types of information they needed, and which online resources could help them. She even had notes on each company's history and culture.

"Where'd you dig all this up?" I asked.

"I'm a reference librarian," she said. "This is what I do. Only right now, they have me reading story-time to preschoolers, because they don't need a reference librarian."

She said she was a year out of school and couldn't find a job she liked. She didn't show well on a résumé, so she preferred to go looking for work in person. "It's impossible to stand out in someone's inbox against five hundred other candidates."

At the time, we were digging up dirt on political candidates in Virginia. I called Ed and told him we needed to hire this woman. We did, and she hit the ground running.

Leon is a different story. He's a tall, thin kid, about twenty-four, with a high-top fade and pants that never quite reach his ankles. He grew up in a part of Northeast DC that's become gentrified recently. Ed goes to church with his aunt.

Leon is comfortable around the computer and awkward around people. He spent most of his youth indoors, playing video games. How he got by in that neighborhood without getting beat up all the time, I have no idea. Maybe the other kids didn't think he was worth the effort.

Before he came here, he had drifted through a few minimum wage jobs. He tried delivering pizza, but that lasted just two days. You can't put this kid in front of customers, because he just blurts out whatever crosses his mind. Watching him interact with others can be downright painful. Like, "Have you been putting on weight?" is not the right way to open a conversation with a woman. I don't know why he doesn't get stuff like that, but he doesn't. He's also very literal about everything. If you say it's raining cats and dogs, he looks out the window and corrects you. "No, man. That's just water."

Leon's desk faces the wall, because he doesn't like to be distracted by people walking by. He likes to be alone with his computer the way most guys like to be alone with their girlfriends. He's tenacious when he digs for information, but he gets off track easily. He'll find some bit of data that interests him but has nothing to do with the case he's on— like changes in census data, or unexpected spikes in commodity prices—and he'll start digging into that. We know when he's getting off track, because he talks excitedly about the numbers. Bethany can usually rein him in. She can also hand him the most mind-numbing work, and he'll happily scan through reams of data that would make a normal person's eyes glaze over. He gets a little too into it sometimes. I've seen the kid get into a staring match with his computer and win.

Today, Leon's at his desk with his back to the room, running background checks, digging through social media profiles and local news accounts. He's got days of work ahead of him, and he seems to like it that way.

Bethany's eating a bran muffin.

"Hey, Freddy."

"Hey, Bethany. Find anything interesting yet?"

She shakes her head and explains how they triaged the passenger list: they're looking first at males traveling alone or with other males, followed by anyone under sixty-five traveling without children. Families and the elderly come last.

I find the list in my email. It shows the name, address, date of birth, and seat assignment for each passenger. It takes me five minutes to figure out that the blonde I'm looking for is Anna Brook. I saw her holding a DC license in the security line, and there were only two women on the flight from DC. One of them was forty-five years old. Her profile photo on LinkedIn shows a heavyset woman with dark hair and small brown eyes.

The other woman, Anna Brook... Well, it's funny about her. She doesn't have an online profile. Anywhere. All I know about her comes from a search of public records, and from the credit bureaus. She's twenty-nine. A little younger than I thought, but maybe a few years of hard living have started to take their toll.

She was born and raised in Staunton, Virginia. She worked in a bar in Richmond, Virginia, and then she moved to Baltimore, where she worked in a strip club. She moved to DC about a year ago, where she has no employment record. But she pays her bills, so she must have some money coming in.

I found a mobile number for her. She doesn't have a landline. I want to give her a call, but... take a minute to think this through, Freddy.

She's running from someone. Maybe whoever she's running from has taken her phone. If that's the case, I don't want them tracing the call back to me. They don't need to know a detective is looking for her. So I head over to the Metro station at Foggy Bottom and use the pay phone. Remember pay phones?

After six rings, it goes to voicemail. "Hey, this is Anna. Leave a message and I'll call you back." Her voice is smooth but a little high, tinged with a strain of anxiety. My mind flashes back to that image of her in the airport, looking over her shoulder as she boarded the flight to Chicago, when the strength I saw in her seemed to vanish all at once. This is the voice of a woman who's been looking over her shoulder for a long time.

I hang up without leaving a message. When I'm back above ground, I open the browser on my phone. The Staunton *News Leader* has an article describing the promising young woman who died in the plane crash. It's the usual stuff: good student, well-liked, bright future, et cetera. It also says the family will be holding a memorial service, time and place to be announced.

Anna Brook is survived by her mother and sister. The *News Leader* prints their names. Her mother lives in Staunton. Her sister lives in Richmond and works at a flower shop. In five minutes, I have both phone numbers, and I give them each a call. There's no answer at the mother's house, and the sister's line goes to voicemail after a few rings.

"Hi, this is Julia. I'm sorry I missed your call. Leave a message and I'll get back to you as soon as I can." She's a little more cordial than her sister. Their voices are almost identical, but where Anna's sounds burdened and anxious, Julia's is warmer, more carefree. I hang up without leaving a message. What do I have to say to her?

When I get back to the office, I find a new email from the airline with some information I requested this morning. Video footage from the TSA security line in San Francisco, the seating chart from the Hawaii flight, and a list of passengers on the Chicago flight that Anna Brook boarded. They asked why I wanted info about the Chicago flight. I told them I like lists.

I skim through the security video until Anna and her tall, greasy friend get to the front of the line. That's when they're closest to the camera. I freeze the video and take a screen shot. He's got her by the arm and he's leaning in to whisper something. I save the photo to a folder on my computer called *Gate 76*.

When I zoom in on their faces, the picture gets a little grainy but I can still make him out. His features are angular and sharp. And her... That face, with its mixture of strength, endurance, strain, and beauty. What kind of life produces a face like that? That's what haunts me about her. I know exactly what kind of life produces a face like that.

You get in with the wrong person at the wrong time, like my mom with my dad, like me with that bastard promoter Slim and that idiot DiLeo, like Anna Brook with this clown... Maybe they catch you in a moment of weakness, or maybe they catch you before you have enough experience to know better. Maybe they just know what you want, and they offer it to you in a way you can't resist. The whole downward spiral starts there.

* * *

Me and Alvin Perkins, the heavyweights, were the main event on Friday Night Fights, up at the Foxwoods Casino in Connecticut. I don't remember the walk into the ring, but if you watch the video, you can see my nerves were tight. My eyes were wild and glazed, and I was pacing back and forth before the opening bell like a caged tiger.

Perkins hit me with a hard shot to the jaw in the first five seconds of the fight. That woke me up and brought me right into the present moment. I hit him back a couple shots to the body, and then I was totally at ease, just kind of feeling him out, figuring out where the danger was and where the opportunity was. The guy kept his guard up so high, I had no trouble digging hooks in under his ribs. All he could do was hit me with jabs. But they were good jabs. Quick and sharp.

By the end of the first round, I knew he was in a different class than the last six losers Slim had put me up against. I also knew I could handle him. The work I had done with the new trainer was worthless, but all the years Rizzardi put into me were about to pay off.

Perkins was strong, fast, and solid. And I had his number. He spent so much time protecting his head, he neglected his body. I started working him over in the second round. More body shots in the third. He'd catch them a little on the elbows and take some of the snap off of them, but they were bothering him. I know, because in the third he started dropping his guard, trying to protect his ribs, and then I'd hook him to the side of the head. He didn't like that. I gave him more of the same in the fourth.

At the end of four, I went back to my corner, and my trainer was looking worried. "What's the matter?" I said. "I'm killing this guy."

"I know," he said, and he didn't sound too happy about it. He pulled my mouthpiece out and squirted some nasty sports drink in my mouth. It was clear like water, but it had a funny orange flavor. I never drank that stuff during a fight. In the corner, it was water only.

I spat the orange stuff onto the canvas. Then he tipped my head back and squirted in another mouthful. He pushed his hand up under my chin, forcing my mouth shut until I swallowed.

I didn't think about that at the time. Cornermen work on fighters the way pit crews work on racecars. They have less than sixty seconds to patch up whatever damage your opponent just did to your face, so there's no time for coddling. If your eye is swelling, the cutman pushes the lump back down with a bar of chilled steel called endswell. If your nose is bleeding, he'll shove a big cotton swab of adrenaline hydrochloride up your nostril and push it against the broken blood vessels. You get a gash above your eye, he'll jam a swab of epinephrine into it to reduce the blood flow, followed by

Avitene to coagulate the blood. While he's doing that, your trainer is dumping water on your head, into your mouth, even down your shorts to cool you off, and he's talking the whole time. You tune out all the physical discomfort and focus on what he's telling you.

"Any advice?" I said. A trainer always has a different perspective on the fight, seeing it from outside the ring. A good one will pick out opportunities and tell you something like, follow with the uppercut, or slide to your left after you throw that hook. But this guy had nothing to say.

"No?" I said. "Nothing?" He put my mouthpiece back in, I banged my gloves together, and went back to the middle of the ring to administer some more punishment.

At the end of the fifth, he pulled the same crap with the bottle. Forced me to swallow another mouthful.

"That stuff tastes like shit," I said. "Gimme some water." I didn't think he heard me.

In round six, I came out OK, but after the first thirty seconds, my stomach felt off, and this achy fatigue came over my whole body at once, like when you get the flu. I lost that round.

In round seven, I couldn't get my punches off, and Perkins kept popping that jab in my face. When I go back and look at the video, there's a noticeable difference in that round. I'm not the same fighter. It's like all the wind went out of me. You can see in the recording, right near the end of the round, Perkins hits me three straight jabs to the face, followed by an uppercut, and then he eases off and says something. I remember his exact words. "The fuck happen to you?"

At the end of the round, I told my trainer I was going to kill him. I even took a swing at him while I was on the stool. The cameras caught it and replayed it twice, with the announcer saying it looked like Ferguson's corner was falling apart under the pressure of a fight gone wrong.

"He had a plan when he came in here," the commentator says on the video. "But after a few good rounds, he just couldn't execute, and now he's taking it out on his trainer. This is not the mark of a quality fighter. This is a troubled fighter. He should be swinging at his opponent."

Now I happen to like that commentator, but when I watch the video and I hear him saying it was *my* fault, I want to punch him too.

Rounds eight through twelve, I got the crap beat out of me. I was plodding around flat-footed, getting hit with everything, and I could barely keep my hands up in front of my face. Any other trainer seeing his fighter take that kind of beating would have thrown in the towel. But my guy couldn't do that. If the corner quit, it would look too much like a fix. Slim, the bookie, needed me to lose convincingly. And I did.

I spent the final round clenching my ass, because whatever was in that orange drink was about to give me the runs.

Perkins saw how bad I looked, and in the last minute of the twelfth, when he had that round and the whole fight in the bag, he eased up. Like I said, he's a good guy. I'm glad he went on to do as well as he did.

The judges said I won the first five rounds and he won the last seven. After the ref announced the decision, the ESPN guy put the mike in my face and asked a few questions. Did I think I had him in trouble in those early rounds?

"Well, it's like chopping down a tree," I said. "You just keep swinging, and eventually it'll go down."

"What happened in the sixth?"

"I don't know. It all went to hell, that's what happened."

"Will you fight again?"

"Shit! Do I look *that* bad? Of course I'll fight again. I'm gonna be the champ one day."

Then I ran back to the dressing room, to the toilet, and let that nasty orange drink do its number on me. When I came out, my trainer said, "Tough fight, kid. Take some time off.

We'll pick up in the gym after you get some rest, and I'll see what Slim can line up for you."

"If I come back to the gym, it'll be to rip your fucking head off, you lowlife piece of shit."

"Take it easy," he said. "You'll win the next one. Slim knows he owes you."

The fight doctor checked me out and asked if I wanted to go to the hospital. I said OK. As bad as I looked, I didn't have a concussion, and my ribs weren't broken, though they sure felt like it. I was dehydrated, and my muscles were cramping. As I lay there in the ER soaking up an IV, I knew I had to get back to Rizzardi, the one and only person who could take me to the top.

My trainer, that bastard, he went back to New York.

When I got back home, I was bitter about the way it all went down. I made a mistake one day and let that bitterness get the best of me. And I regret that. I mean, Chuck DiLeo— I have no regrets about him. He had it coming from a long line of people. I just happened to be at the front of that line on a day when my heart was black and full of rage.

* * *

Looking at the photo of Anna Brook in that security line, I wonder what *her* dream was. If she ever had one, you can't read it on her face. She has the face of a survivor. The energy normal people invest in dreams, she puts into getting through the day.

I close the photo of her and open the second attachment in the email from the airline. The seating chart. It's a color scan of a paper document that was marked by hand. It looks like one of those diagrams you see when you book a flight online and get to pick your own seat, with the wings and the aisle and the exit rows all drawn to scale. I was expecting a computer printout, but this looks like it came from some stewardess's clipboard.

Right away, I see there's something wrong. Every seat on the chart is marked occupied. The marks come from different pens. The seats in first class are checked with blue ink. The coach seats are checked in black. Except seat 32B. Anna Brook's seat is marked in blue. I put in a call to my contact at the airline—a snippy, short-tempered woman.

"Where did you get this chart?"

"Excuse me?" I can hear she's annoyed. There's a lot of chatter in the background.

"This seating chart," I say. "Where'd you get it?"

"Who is this?"

"Freddy Ferguson. The investigator. You just sent me a passenger manifest and a seating chart."

"I got the chart from the main office here at SFO."

"When?"

"Five minutes before I sent it," she says with annoyance.

"Any idea who saw it before you got your hands on it?"

"I don't know," she says. "Is there a problem?"

"Who else has a copy of this?"

"You need to work on your manners, sir."

I can hear a keyboard clacking near the phone.

"Who else has a copy?" I ask again.

For a second, she doesn't respond. Then when the typing stops, she says, "Everyone. TSA, FBI, NTSB, the airline's own investigators. Everyone's combing through the same list."

"Can you find out who touched this seating chart before it was scanned?"

"What's the problem?"

"Well, for one thing, all the first class seats are checked in blue, and the coach seats are checked in black."

"So?" she says. "First class boards first. The first class attendant checks off her passengers and gives the clipboard to the attendant in coach."

"Don't they use an iPad or something for that?"

43

"They use the scanner at the boarding gate, when it's not broken. When it's broken, they use paper."

"All right, so why is one coach seat marked in blue?"

She lets out a little sigh and then speaks slowly and deliberately, like she's talking to a child. "The head of the cabin crew does the final pass for the seating chart. If anything's empty back in coach, she'll double check it before she gives the chart to the ground crew." Then she adds in a condescending tone, "Is there anything else I can help you with, Mr. Ferguson?"

"Look, I get that you're stressed out," I say. "I get that nobody's having a good day here, and I appreciate your help. So just bear with me for a minute, OK? I'm trying to get to the bottom of something."

She sighs.

"So maybe 32B wasn't in her seat when they did the first check," I say. "Maybe the first class stewardess did a second pass and checked her off with the blue pen."

"It's pretty common," she says.

"Then why doesn't the ink match?"

"Pardon me?"

"First class was all checked off with bright blue ink from a fat ballpoint. Thirty-two B was checked with dark blue ink from a thin ballpoint."

"I'm sorry, Mr. Ferguson, I don't think this is a good use of my time. We're trying to—"

"Can you find out who had their hands on this manifest before it was scanned?"

"No."

"What do you mean, no?"

"I mean no," she says. "It's a madhouse here. We're still running flights and we have investigators, reporters, lawyers, and a thousand other people coming and going. Try doing *your* job in the middle of all that."

She hangs up.

Now who would go and check off Anna Brook's seat on that chart? Why would anyone besides her want the world to think she was on that plane?

5

The passenger list for the Chicago flight is a whole other problem. Anna Brook's name wasn't on that list, not that I expected to find it there. If she was running from someone, she wouldn't leave such an obvious clue.

She checked in for the Honolulu flight under her own name, so when she went through security, she had an ID to match her boarding pass. That got her into the terminal, and once she was in, she could go to any gate, with any boarding pass, because they don't check IDs at the gate. As long as the boarding pass scans, you're good to go.

So on this list, I'm looking for a woman traveling alone, name unknown. I should be able to rule out three quarters of the passengers off the bat. Half should be male, and a bunch of people would be traveling with relatives who have the same last name, so I can tell they're not alone. The laws of probability say I should have, at worst, forty or so names to look into.

That's how the numbers *should* play out. But wouldn't you know it? 128 of the 159 passengers on that flight were women traveling alone. How the hell does that happen?

It takes a little bit of digging and a call to the airline to figure it out. It happens when a nursing conference with three thousand attendees ends that day in San Francisco, and all those nurses fly back home at once. Anyone going east of Kansas is going to connect through Chicago. Anna Brook sure picked a good flight to cover her tracks.

It gets worse. This flight had four Smiths, four Johnsons, three Joneses, two Browns, two Greens, two Blacks, and two Whites. The airline has all their addresses, but I'm going to have to look up every one of these names and rule them out one by one, if that's even possible. This is going to be a long day. Maybe a long week.

I put in another call to my contact at the airline.

"Who paid for Anna Brook's ticket on the Honolulu flight?"

"Excuse me?" There's that snippy tone again.

"Can you get me the name and credit card number that paid for Anna Brook's ticket on the Hawaii flight?"

"We don't have access to credit card numbers," she says with a tone that suggests she's happy not to be able to help me. I hear her clack away at her keyboard for a few seconds, then she says, "I might be able to get you the name and the last four digits on the card."

"OK," I say. "I appreciate that. Can you also give me a list of all the Chicago passengers who were not on a round-trip?"

"You mean, like—"

"I mean, most of the people on this flight were nurses returning home from a conference. That means they should have flown into San Francisco a few days earlier. Some of the ones who weren't nurses maybe lived in San Francisco, so they would be flying back a few days later, right? I want to know which passengers were *not* flying round-trip."

"I'm sorry. I won't be able to get to that for a few hours."

"I can wait."

The office is silent, except for the occasional tapping of keys and the muffled noise of traffic from the street. Bethany stares at her monitor and Leon stares at his.

I start slogging through the list because... what the hell else am I gonna do? I'll make a guess that I can rule out any woman on the Chicago flight who is an actual nurse. I just don't think anyone would be lucky enough to pick a name that happened to belong to a nurse, and then board a flight full of nurses. I know some people who have the opposite kind of luck. Like they call 911 because they were in a bike accident and then the ambulance runs them over.

* * *

At two p.m., I get a call from my ex-wife wanting to know if I can watch Lenny for a few hours tomorrow. I'm tempted to say no, just because it's her asking, but I happen to like the kid. And he calls me Daddy.

"What time?" I ask.

"Eleven to two," she says. "He naps around one. Just bring him back when he wakes up."

"I have work do to," I say. "I'll take him, but he might not get his nap."

"Thank you, Freddy. His daycare is closed, and I have a job interview—"

"You don't have to explain."

I wonder sometimes why the hell she married that guy if he can't watch her kid. And how could someone with so much promise turn out like her?

If I had been a little wiser a few years ago, a little less blinded by her charm, I would have figured her out pretty quick. See, here's an example. We're out on a date at a nice restaurant, a fancy place with white tablecloths and crystal that was way beyond what I could afford. This is our second or third date. She tells me about growing up in Baltimore, her parents, her brother and sister, the family meals and all that, and then she says, "How about you?"

"I was born in Philly."

"And?"

"And then I went to New York."

"Your family moved?"

"I moved."

"Without your mom and dad?"

"Yeah."

She could see I was getting uncomfortable, but once something piqued her interest, she just had to pry. It was maybe the only thing that annoyed me about her before I started hating her.

"Where'd your mother go?"

"She stayed in Philly." In a fucking coffin, where my dad put her.

"You ever talk to her?"

"No."

"What about your dad?"

"What about him?" I asked as politely as possible, through clenched teeth. He was a drunk, violent bastard who died of liver disease eight years into a life sentence.

"Ooh, you don't like Dad, do you?"

I slammed my fist on the table so hard the plates and the silverware jumped and the water sloshed out of the glasses. Everyone in the place looked over at us.

"Sorry," I said, and I had to take a couple of deep breaths to get a hold of myself. "My father passed away. How's your... your, um..."

"Lamb? It's good. You want a bite?"

I watched her make a mental note of my reaction and tuck it away for later. I didn't quite understand her type at the time, but I get it now. Growing up, I always had my eye out for what the guys might try to do to me—the bullies at school, the thugs on the corner, and the fighter bouncing on his toes across the ring. I thought I had it all figured out. I didn't know I had to be on guard against the girls too. But she taught me.

Yes, she did.

* * *

The phone rings. It's Ed calling from SFO.

I must not have answered very politely, because the first thing out of his mouth is, "What's with the tone? Something happen?"

"Just one of my moods," I say. "Listen, Ed. There's a guy who empties garbage cans at SFO. Looks Vietnamese, about five foot six, age thirty or so, smooth skin, head shaved on

the sides with plenty of hair up top. He's got big ears that
stick out. You need to talk to him."

"About what?"

"About why he was watching the passengers board that
Hawaii flight, and who he was calling."

Ed repeats the question like he doesn't understand it.
"Who he was calling?"

"The guy was watching the gate," I say. "And reporting
back to someone on the phone."

"How do you know that?"

"Because I fucking know, Ed. I was there."

"Watch the tone, Freddy. What set you off today?"

"Me," I say. "What the hell else sets me off?"

"So you were there when the Hawaii flight was boarding?"

"Yeah."

"But you were flying to DC."

"I know, Ed. But I see something that grabs my interest,
and I just start following it. You know how I am."

"What makes you think this guy was watching the
passengers at gate seventy-six?"

"I followed him. He waited till everyone boarded, then he
made a call. He seemed specifically interested in one
passenger."

"Who?"

"A woman," I say. "A blonde-haired woman named Anna
Brook. Find that Vietnamese guy. Unless you have some
better lead to chase."

"All right," Ed says. "What do you know about Anna
Brook?"

*Well, I know she's the one person from that flight who isn't dead. I
know she went through Chicago on her way to somewhere else. But I'm
not going to tell you that, Ed, even though I tell you everything. I got a
strange premonition about her and it's kinda personal. I can't explain it
and I'm not even going to try.*

"I'll send you a photo from the security line," I say. "She's with a guy I don't like the looks of. See if one of your buddies in the Bureau can ID him."

After we hang up, I crop the photo that I extracted from the security video, making one picture of the guy and one of Anna Brook. They go into the Gate 76 folder, along with the passenger list and the scan of the seating chart. I send the photos of Anna and her friend to Ed.

* * *

At six p.m., we're still in the office. Bethany picked up Thai food for everyone. I've looked at so many nurses from that Chicago flight, I've forgotten what I'm after. Bethany's looking at shoes online, and Leon is watching Fox News on his computer. They're starting to delve into the human angle of the tragedy, with short profiles of people who were on the plane. Ted and Stacy Mills, a pair of newlyweds from Sacramento. Quinn Paddock, a financial advisor from Phoenix who helped retirees manage their investments. Brandon Robertson and Manuel Martínez, a couple of Texas cops who had recently won awards for their good work.

I spend a minute watching the video over Leon's shoulder, then turn my attention back to my dinner, a box of Pad Thai that's too sweet. I click over to MSNBC on my laptop, where they're showing footage of a Coast Guard ship hauling in wreckage from Monterey Bay. You can see the shadow of the helicopter on the water. It's the same footage they're showing on CNN and Fox.

The MSNBC report includes a look inside the hangar where the National Transportation Safety Board and Boeing engineers are reconstructing the plane. They don't have much of it yet, even though they're working round the clock.

I click over to Fox, where they're talking about the "person of interest," Rashad Obasanjo, who they speculate may soon be an official suspect. They're interviewing some analyst whose credentials I missed. He says Obasanjo "fits the profile." I'm not sure what profile that is, but he says it like I should know what he means. They don't even have a decent photo of the kid. They're showing a picture of three smiling black guys standing in front of a picnic table loaded with food. The two on either side are dressed in white tunics with white skullcaps. They're darkened, while the guy in the middle with the short Afro, blue slacks, and blue button-down shirt is highlighted in an oval of light. That's Obasanjo.

After a few minutes, Fox switches to election coverage and the big states that are still up for grabs. With less than five weeks to go, the Democrats are pulling ahead in New York and California. The Republicans are opening a slim lead in Ohio, Pennsylvania, and Florida. Texas is still a toss-up. I close the browser window and drop my empty food box into the garbage can.

I'm on my way to the bathroom when Leon says, "Damn, this dude's crazy!"

"Who's that?" I ask.

Bethany and I walk over to his desk, and he points to his monitor, where a man paces in front of the windows at gate seventy-six in a clip of security footage just released by the TSA. The man wears a hood and keeps his head down as he shuffles back and forth. He moves slowly, wiping his nose now and then, and his feet never come up off the ground.

"Owen Briscoe," Leon says. This is the guy Ed mentioned on our call this morning, the one with a history of mental illness, who once belonged to a white separatist militia in Idaho. The CNN reporter says he was schizophrenic but had lately been sticking to his meds. He had been rejected by the Army several years ago when he tried to enlist. The state of Idaho revoked his gun permit after he assaulted a grocery store worker and his mental illness came to light. In a YouTube video from two years ago, he warned the president of Iceland he would be punished if he doesn't get his nation's volcanoes under control. The guy really was crazy.

The reporter says that federal investigators are interested in talking with Briscoe's associates.

At half past seven, I get a new list from the airline: the Chicago passengers who weren't flying round-trip. There are six of them. Four are women.

And the Staunton *News Leader* posted an update. Anna Brook's memorial service will be held at eleven a.m. the day after tomorrow, at the Presbyterian church in Staunton. That's a three-hour drive from DC.

6

OCTOBER 1

I sat in front of my computer until ten last night. This morning, I was back at it at six-thirty. I have to get up and move, and I'm looking forward to a few hours with Lenny. The kid is happy, messy, and completely irrational. I hope that doesn't change when he turns four. The only hard part of hanging out with him is the pickup and drop-off. His mom and I don't get along.

Back when we were married, on days like this when I had my mind too deep in work, Miriam would strike up a conversation and slip in some question about my mom or dad, or what we did around the house when I was a kid. It was a button she could push when she wasn't getting enough attention, and somehow I never saw it coming. Those are the blows that really get you. The ones you don't see coming. In a few minutes, she'd pull all those old emotions out of me, just to reassure herself I was still there. And then she'd soothe.

"Poor Freddy needs a little love."

Miriam did one thing very well, and it wasn't the kind of thing she wanted her partner to do by rote. She wanted the feelings right up on the surface, and she didn't care if it was anger or love or hurt, just as long as it was all pouring out of you. She could draw it out of a guy whenever she pleased.

Before she came along, I wasn't careful enough with women. And after... Well, I don't need anyone doing *that* to me again.

When Ed Hartwell hired me, he did a background check. I remember sitting in his office. He had printed out a few pages, and he asked me about the hospitalization in New York and the injuries. He knew what had happened between me and DiLeo. He had the report in his folder, but he wanted to hear me tell it.

After I told him, he flipped the page and I could see the Department of Corrections letterhead. It was something about my dad. He skimmed it, glanced up at me for a second, and then went on to the next page without saying a word. That's a thing I like about Ed. Even though he's a natural-born cop, an investigator who digs deep into everything, he knows when to leave things alone. A guy like that sees where another guy's line is, and he acknowledges it by *not* crossing it. A woman sees that line and she just *has* to cross it.

After Rizzardi, Miriam was my best teacher. She showed me what to watch out for.

She's a good-looking woman. Half Jewish, half Italian, and if her ancestors were anything like her, she's half twenty other things too. She was the girlfriend of a guy I was investigating back in my early days, when I chased insurance cheats and petty thieves. Lenny D. fell into the latter category. He worked for a company that installed heat pumps and furnaces. He had a side business, stealing air-conditioners and copper pipe from his employer.

Lenny D. was a real jackass. Four counts of grand theft, and he punched both officers who arrested him. That earned him two extra felony charges. He wouldn't take a plea deal no matter what his lawyers said. I was a witness at his trial. That's where I met Miriam. Like I said, a good-looking woman. Dark olive skin, dark curly hair, and dark-brown eyes that sparkled even in the low light of a fancy restaurant. She was a little full in the cheeks, with dark-red lips and white teeth that were just slightly crooked in this way that made you want to kiss her.

She was shy, or at least she acted that way. She wore dresses that were high in the waist to try to hide the extra padding around her belly and thighs, like she truly didn't know how much some guys like that. The trim ones are nice to look at, but when it comes to the one you keep, I like a woman who's built for comfort. Someone I won't knock off the bed when I roll over in the middle of the night.

We had three dates before our first real kiss. She was so shy, I couldn't even compliment her. She'd just smile and turn her eyes down and not say a word, so I got to feeling bad for making her self-conscious. I wanted to marry her after the first kiss.

She'd had it kind of bad. No one was beating her up or anything, but Lenny D. neglected her, treated her like an old vacuum cleaner that belonged in the corner. I thought she was something special, a hidden gem whose beauty the rest of the world just didn't take the time to notice.

The first time I took her to bed I thought I'd have to take it slow. Be gentle. Maybe hold back a little on what I was really feeling because she was so shy. I didn't want to overwhelm her.

I was wrong about that. Shy over dinner and shy about compliments does not mean shy in bed. Looking back, I should have known. I should have had the same feeling I had with that bum trainer Slim stuck me with. When there's that much of a mismatch between what you think you're signing up for and what you actually get, it should set off alarm bells. Funny how I can see some people for one second and my instinct tells me to be wary, and then I can sleep with a woman and even marry her and still not get it.

So we got married, and we had this little apartment up in Rockville, just a short bus ride from the Metro. Everything was humming along beautifully. I'd always told myself that whoever I married would never doubt—not for a second— that she was the most special person in the world, the one and only, the be-all and end-all. I would open every door for her, pull out her chair at dinner, hold her coat so she could slide her arms right through—all of that. She would never have to wait tables at some dive where the guys leered at her ass and the women complained that their orders didn't come out right. She wouldn't have to worry about the bills being paid or keeping a roof over her head.

That was the idea. Funny how life has its own ideas.

I saw myself as a knight in her world, but I was a pawn in the real world. I'd come home tired and stressed out at whatever hour I managed to make it back—sleuthing is not a nine-to-five job. She'd be angry and anxious because she'd been alone all day, and that wasn't what I wanted to come home to. Some of the sparkle went out of her eyes. I forgot to pull out her chair one night, and she didn't make a fuss about it, so I started forgetting that every night. Then the charge went out of the sex. Instead of dynamite every night, we'd have a firecracker now and then. I was out working overtime, busting my ass, trying to give her the things I thought she wanted, and she just resented me for not being home.

The long weekends and late nights and all the travel I was doing started to get to her. She complained all the time, calling me up in the middle of the night and nagging. Calling me on the road and nagging. I'd get off a plane and there'd be six messages from her.

"You're not making this any easier," I'd say.

"I want you home," she'd say, and I could hear she was smoking a cigarette.

"Baby, I just got off the plane. I'm going to be here three days, maybe more. You gotta buckle down, OK? Find something to do. When I get back, I promise—"

"Fuck you!"

"Seriously, I got work to do—"

"And I have *nothing* to do!"

"—and you're putting all this worry in my head. I gotta focus here. You know, like when I'm home, I focus on you. I give it all to you when it's *us* time. Don't I, Miriam? Don't I?"

Long silence. Puff of the cigarette. Exaggerated exhale. "Yeah, Freddy. I guess. I just feel like I go a little crazy when you're not around."

"Go out with your friends and have some fun. I know you don't like being alone. Go be around people and you'll find something to do."

She found something to do all right. When we were in the delivery room at Shady Grove Adventist Hospital and the kid came out, the place went dead silent.

The nurse said, "Um…" And then just stopped.

Miriam was panting and crying. "What is it? What's wrong? Oh my God, he's not dead, is he?"

The baby had dark skin—very dark—and a full head of tightly curled hair. The nurse laid him on Miriam's breast and said congratulations. Miriam looked at the baby, and then at me, and I knew. I think everyone in the room knew what the blood test later confirmed. He was beautiful, but he wasn't mine.

The day after the blood test, Miriam was in bed with the baby sleeping beside her. I laid the tray of eggs and toast and coffee in her lap, and I remember how nervous she was. She kept looking at me, trying to gauge my mood.

"Who is he?" I said. "Who's the father?"

She screwed up her eyes like she was trying to remember the answers to a history quiz. As she was thinking it through, she popped up one, two, three, four fingers. And then she put on her bravest smile and said, "I've already narrowed it down!"

Miriam didn't contest the divorce. At the time, I thought that was pretty decent of her. Then one night when she was drunk, she told me over the phone that she didn't want me spending money on a lawyer when it could just go straight to her. I had promised her a little cash to help her get on her feet, mainly because I was worried for the boy. That was fifteen thousand bucks I didn't need to spend.

Here's the thing about people like Miriam and her ex-boyfriend Lenny D. They find each other one way or another. It's not just luck. The misfits can always sense what kind of person they mis-fit with.

And then once in a while some new guy comes along and he thinks he's gonna rescue some poor, unappreciated beauty. He has quite an imagination, that guy. He doesn't get why his wife's better qualities aren't coming out, even after he's given her better circumstances. He thinks he's doing it wrong. He's just not working hard enough to bring out her real shine. All the way until the day he wises up, he thinks he's doing it wrong.

I still check in with her every week or two, mostly to see how the kid is doing. If I'd found her with some guy like my dad, beating her up, I'd have got rid of him. Or I'd try to take the boy.

Now she's married to this Serbian guy whose name I can never pronounce. Take the middle third of the alphabet, nine or ten letters, and remove all the vowels. That's his name. They live in Bethesda. I don't know if she still sleeps around, but if she does, that's his problem. The home is stable enough, and the boy is healthy and safe, but I think he's a little confused. He calls both me and Miriam's husband Daddy. I sometimes wonder if that's genetic. Her lover and Lenny's dad is whatever man happens to be around at the moment.

I always have to brace myself when I see her, because she'll get under my skin one way or another, even when she's not trying to. Standing on the front porch of their little blue house, I take a minute to collect myself before I ring the bell.

She opens the door, and there's little Lenny standing at her side, with a sippy cup full of apple juice and a big smile. His hair is a lopsided Afro with a giant dent in the left side, where he had been leaning against something.

"He needs a haircut," I say.

"He just *got* it cut," Miriam says.

"Nobody wears their hair like that."

"Colin Kaepernick does, and I think it looks good," she says. "Oh, and by the way, it's nice to see you too. How about starting with a greeting?"

She's wearing a high-waisted dress that's grey on top and black from the midsection down. Good for a job interview, but she's still too pretty.

"Sorry," I say. "The hair thing bugs me."

"You look good, Freddy. You really do."

"Yeah, so do you." I hate admitting that. I thought the attraction would go away over time, but it hasn't.

"Did you take him to the white barber?" I say.

"I'm not going to drive all the way to DC."

"Yeah, but the white guy fucks up his hair."

"Watch your mouth," she says.

Lenny has his arm around her knee. He keeps leaning forward, swinging himself around and ramming his face into her thigh.

"He doesn't know how to cut it," I say. "Look how lopsided it is."

"We just haven't combed it out yet. What are you two doing today?"

"Are we going to the zoo?" Lenny asks.

"Yes, we're going to the zoo."

"How did he know that?" Miriam asks.

"We talked about it a couple weeks ago. You ready, pal?"

"Yes," Lenny says. He's staring up at me with those big dark eyes, holding his Finding Nemo sippy cup in the crook of his arm.

Miriam hands me a shopping bag. "There's more juice in there, some Gummi Bears, goldfish crackers, cheese sticks, and raisins. Take the booster seat out of the car. I'll be home around two. He usually naps at one, but try to keep him going. I'll put him down when you guys get back."

At the zoo, we have a mission: find the lion, the cheetah, the panda, the elephant, and the gorilla, and give them invitations to Lenny's birthday party. I picked up the invites two weeks ago, when we planned this over the phone. Lenny wanted to be sure they all knew he was turning four.

The panda enclosure is a steeply sloped hill with grass, bamboo, and boulders, surrounded by high concrete walls. At the rear is the panda house with the plate-glass windows. The pandas aren't out today.

"Where is he, Daddy?"

"He's probably inside. You want to go in and check on him?"

He stuffs two fistfuls of Gummi Bears into his mouth and says something I can't understand.

I squat down in front of him and ask again, "You want to go inside?"

He just stands there wide-eyed, trying to chew. He can't even close his mouth all the way. It's like he has a baseball in there.

"How many Gummi Bears did you put in your mouth?"

He holds up two fingers as his eyes begin to water.

"Two? I think you have more than two in there."

Then he pulls two empty bags from his pocket and shows them to me.

"Come on, Lenny. You only need one or two bears at a time. You can't even chew that many."

He shakes his head.

"Why don't you take some out?"

He puts both hands to his mouth and spits out a blob of rainbow-colored goo that would barely fit in an adult's mouth.

"Hold this," he says.

"You know what's going to happen if I take that. You know it's going in the trash."

His eyes get wider. "No, Daddy!"

"What's the rule when you give me things you pulled out of your mouth? I thought we were clear on that."

Now he's in a quandary. Should he give away the sticky little treasure or try to force it all back into his mouth? He looks at the blob of goo with a mixture of longing and sorrow. It's that same thing we all feel when our heart's desire is right in front of us and we know we can't have it.

"What's a fair solution?" I ask.

"I'm going to eat the red part," he says.

For the next few minutes, he eats out the red bits and deposits the cast-off green and gold chunks in my hand. I used to wonder why parents of young kids always carried hand sanitizer. Now I wonder how I always manage to not have any.

Two pandas come into the yard while he's chewing. When I point them out, he drops the rest of his Gummi goo onto the pavement, pulls himself up onto the railing, and announces that both bears are invited to his party.

"Hey," I say. "The cards, remember?"

I hold up an envelope containing an invitation made out to "Panda." He takes it from my hand, says "Here," and tries to throw it into the enclosure. But the envelope sticks to his hand.

"No," I say, taking the envelope back. "That's not how we do it."

We go into the panda house and give the card to a woman wearing a National Zoo uniform.

We go through the same routine with the elephant, the gorilla, the cheetah, and the lion. Lenny wants me to drop him into the lion's enclosure, so he can hand-deliver the invitation. It takes me a while to persuade him to give it to a zoo employee instead.

At ten past one, we're finishing lunch at the restaurant near the lion's enclosure. There's a TV up in the corner tuned to CNN. Why? Why not cartoons? Who comes to this place besides parents and kids? Do we need all the problems of the world to intrude even here?

They're showing footage of the ship in Monterey Bay recovering wreckage from the plane. I seated Lenny facing away from the TV, but he still turns and looks now and then.

I send a quick text to Bethany saying I should be back in the office by three. She says there's not much going on there. Just her and Leon slogging through the list.

Lenny stuffs a French fry into his mouth and says, "I'm going to be a policeman when I grow up, just like you."

"I'm an investigator," I say, "not a cop."

"But you catch bad guys."

"Sometimes."

"I'm going to be like you."

No, I think. But you might be like Ed. Your road will be marked with hardship and disrespect. People will throw obstacles in front of you every step of the way.

When Ed tells me about some of the things he's had to put up with—the hazing in the military, having to prove himself a thousand times to colleagues and superiors who accepted the abilities of his white coworkers without question, all the little slights and insults he let pass without remark—I wonder if Lenny has the toughness for it. He's a sweet kid who thinks every man is his daddy and the lion wants to be his friend.

There's Obasanjo on TV again. It's that same photo of him smiling at the picnic, only they've zoomed in to a grainy close-up and cropped out the guys who were standing on either side. I can't tell what they're saying about him now, but I don't want Lenny to look.

He stuffs two ketchup-covered fries into his mouth and says, "Why are you sad, Daddy?"

Because no matter how much I want to protect you, I can't.

"I don't know," I say. "You want to do some police work?"

"OK."

I can see he's getting sleepy. He usually does after lunch.

* * *

Anna Brook has an apartment on Quarry Road in Adams Morgan, just off Columbia. Harvard Street comes out of the zoo parking lot and goes almost right to it. It's a two-minute drive, and Lenny's asleep by the time I find a parking space. I scoop him out of his booster seat and carry him to the entrance. His head is against my shoulder, and he never wakes up.

The building is a standard World War II–era apartment block: six stories, brown brick with a little courtyard in front and air conditioners humming in every window. Behind the glass door, the marble-floored lobby is tiny. Just a side table, a big mirror, a wall of silver mailboxes, and a pair of elevators. And no way in unless you have an electronic key fob or you can ring someone upstairs to buzz you in.

A. Brook's name is printed next to the button for apartment 204. I start hitting the buzzers for the top-floor apartments, and on the fourth try, I hear a little click and the door unlocks. I take the elevator up to the second floor and walk left down the narrow, carpeted corridor. Lenny's hair rubs against my cheek and makes it itch.

Apartment 204 is on the southeast corner of the building, overlooking the street. It's got a steel door, like every other apartment in the corridor, but the deadbolt doesn't match the others. It's newer, recently installed, and it takes one of those special keys with the divots in the side. The kind you can't duplicate at a hardware store.

I can see through the gap between the door and the frame that the deadbolt is locked. I knock a few times and listen, but it doesn't sound like anyone's in there. A door ten feet down the hall opens up, and a white-haired woman of eighty or so pokes her head out.

"Are you looking for Anna?" she asks. Her eyes move back and forth between my face and Lenny's.

"I know she's not here," I say. "I just couldn't help knocking."

"You heard the news?" She blinks her dark watery eyes at me with sympathy.

"I came to get her mail," I say. "And make sure things are in order. Her family will want to collect her belongings."

"Poor Anna," she says.

"Any idea what was troubling her? You know, she didn't look so good lately."

"Oh, it was that fellow," she says and shakes her head. "Such an awful, awful man."

"You know who he was?"

"No, but I could tell when she'd been around him. She wasn't right."

"Any idea when it started?"

"Oh, I couldn't say." She looks again at Lenny, then back at my eyes. "She always seemed a little troubled. She was too free with the men. Every night a date." She puts her hand to her cheek and shakes her head again. "I told her there's a kind of man who watches for women like her. He's always got his eye out for the girl who says yes."

"Well it sounds like he found her."

"Do you know she brought me food when I was sick?" She pauses to look for my reaction, then adds, "Every day for two weeks. She'd bring me breakfast in the morning, and I could tell she'd been out all evening. Imagine that. Coming in from a long night, and still you think about the old lady who's too sick to get her own breakfast. How did you know her?"

"I'm a family friend. Just picking up the mail."

She eyes me for a second and nods. "Well, the mail's downstairs. You walked right by it on the way in." Then she shuts her door and turns the deadbolt, and I hear the little chain slide along its track.

The sound rouses Lenny, and I say, "Hey, kiddo, I'm gonna put you down for a minute." I set him carefully on the floor, and he leans his head against the wall and shuts his eyes.

I take a toothpick from my pocket, stick it into the crack between the door and the frame and snap off a little piece. If I don't find that toothpick fragment sitting on top of the deadbolt the next time I come by, I'll know someone's been here.

* * *

I get Lenny back in his car seat for the drive home, but before I start the engine, I get a text from Bethany. It's a link to a story on CNBC. I click through and watch the video, keeping the volume low so I don't wake Lenny.

The anchorwoman is saying investigators from the National Transportation Safety Board dug a partially melted metal fragment out of an interior wall of the plane's cargo hold. They've identified it as the clasp of a metal ammunition box. Another fragment retrieved from the remains of a suitcase pulled from Monterey Bay shows the box was loaded with a military-grade plastic explosive called C4.

The news cuts to an image of the kid, Obasanjo, being marched out of a building near San Francisco toward a waiting car. He's wearing a white t-shirt and blue high-water pants that look like hospital scrubs. He's surrounded by guys in dark jackets from the FBI and the TSA. He looks scared as hell.

I call Ed, and before I can get a word out, he says, "You see the perp walk?" I can hear the anger in his voice.

"Yeah," I say. "He sure looks uncomfortable."

"Did you notice all the cops were white?"

"No, but now that you mention it—"

"You know what it looks like to me?" Ed says. He doesn't wait for me to answer. "A scared black man in chains being paraded in front of the cameras by a bunch of white men?"

"Take it easy, Ed. Don't let your emotions get the best of you."

"Usually the Bureau is a little more sensitive about scenes like this," Ed says, "And it can't be just Obasanjo. There's no way a metal ammo box could have gone through TSA security, unless someone wasn't doing their job. They have chemical scanners that specifically look for C4. Obasanjo, or whoever did this, had some inside help. Or someone in TSA screwed up royally."

"That's what the airline is hoping," I say. "If TSA's to blame, it gets them off the hook. Kind of sick, huh?"

"Yeah, Freddy. That is kind of sick," Ed says, "but unfortunately that's how it works. And while I have you on the phone, I'll let you in on a little secret. You remember that crazy guy from Idaho? Owen Briscoe?"

"Yeah. They find something on him?"

"Not him," Ed says. "But one of his associates: a guy named Delmont Suggs. He drove Briscoe from Idaho to the airport in Spokane. Briscoe connected from there to San Francisco."

"What was Briscoe doing on a plane?"

"Going to visit his brother in Hawaii," Ed says. "This guy Suggs is trouble. Former military, special ops. He formed his own militia up in the mountains a few years ago. It's mostly disbanded, but he still has a handful of followers. The guy's got a beef in his heart against just about everyone—especially the US government."

"You think he gave Briscoe a bomb to take on the plane?"

"I don't know, but we're trying to track him down before the news media connects the dots and broadcasts the fact that we're looking for him. He doesn't seem like the kind of guy who'd be too receptive to a visit from the Feds. The airline has a former Bureau member in Idaho keeping them informed of what's going on. Leon and Bethany are digging up what they can on him, but the Bureau has a fuller picture, and it's not good. I'll let you know what I learn."

"Thanks, Ed."

* * *

I pull up in front of Miriam's house a few minutes before two. Lenny wakes up and the first thing he wants to know is how long until his birthday party.

"Three weeks," I say. "Be sure to tell your mom which animals we invited. She'll have to get a big cake."

Just then, the front door opens and Miriam smiles.

"You ready to go in?" I ask.

"Yes, Daddy."

I get Lenny out of the car seat, and he runs into the house on his own. I carry the seat back to the porch, where Miriam is standing in the doorway.

"Your interview went well, huh?"

She shrugs, like it doesn't matter either way.

"What, you don't care?" I ask.

"I could see myself working there," she says. "And I could see myself not. If it's supposed to work out, it will." She pauses a second and says, "Hey, Freddy?"

I put the booster seat down. "Huh?"

"You seeing anyone?" She has a big, warm smile on her face, which I don't trust at all.

"What do you care?"

"I'm just asking. I think it would be nice if you had someone." The way she has her arm up against the doorframe—it's a seductive pose, and I wonder if it's on purpose.

"Yeah, well, I work a lot—"

"You work *too much.*"

"—and wives, you know, they don't do well with husbands who are out all hours of the night."

"It doesn't have to be a wife," she says. "Who do you talk to?"

She's probing again. "I talk to Bethany—"

"She's young." Miriam says.

And that sweet smile. I can't stand that smile, because at her core, she really is a decent person. "I know she's young," I say. "I talk to Leon."

"Leon doesn't count. He's like a computer."

"That's not a nice thing to say."

"What about Ed? Do you still talk to Ed?"

I tell her I talk to Ed all the time.

"No, I mean, like *really* talk to him?" She finally takes her arm down off the door frame.

"What, like a dinner date?"

"Well… yeah. You know, Ed had it hard growing up. All those stories about his family, and the treatment they got from the whites down there. It made them close. They had to rely on each other. Do you ever talk with him about that?"

"We don't talk about race," I say. "Unless it comes up in a case."

"Ugh! I'm not talking about race. Why are you so thick?"

"Then what *are* you talking about?"

"Freddy…" She has this pained look on her face that I can't stand, because it makes me want to comfort her. "I hope you find someone."

"I find people all the time. That's what investigators do."

"You know that's not what I mean."

"Then why don't you tell me what you mean?"

"Find someone to talk to." She's trying to contain her frustration. I know that look well.

"Like a counselor?" I ask. "Or a girlfriend?"

"Either one."

"What am I? Your pity case?"

"It's not pity, Freddy. You know I care about you."

"Yeah, well if you cared so much, you could have had *my* kid."

"Get out!" she screams as she shoves me back from the door. "Get the fuck out of my house right now!"

She slams the door in my face.

This is the kind of crap I used to deal with every day.

7

Back at the office, Leon and Bethany are staring into their monitors like they haven't moved since last night. Bethany looks up and says hello. She always makes eye contact when someone walks in. Leon's resting his chin in his hand, reading a news story about militias in Idaho.

"Digging into Owen Briscoe?" I ask.

"Guy's crazy," Leon says without looking up.

Bethany tells me that the other names that had been flagged on the Hawaii list are looking less and less promising. The Muslim man from Dearborn, Michigan, was as moderate as a Midwest Sunday school teacher. And the combat engineer from Kansas turned out to be a solid levelheaded soldier with a positive attitude and no grudges against anyone.

Obasanjo, however, is now an official suspect. The news channels finally got some new photos of him and now he's all over the Internet. The kid is twenty-two years old. His face has a gentle look. In his fourth-grade photo, his front teeth are too big and his skin reflects the shine of the camera lights. His smile is just like Lenny's. It pushes his cheeks out and makes them look too big. The photo from his airline ID has the unfortunate look of a mug shot. Head tilted slightly back, eyes a little narrow. And he's got a three-inch Afro that might remind some people of the radicals of the 1960s and 70s.

CNN says he's from a solid working-class family in Oakland, with a mother and father who are both steadily employed. His former high school classmates describe him as having a strong sense of justice. His battery trial arose from an incident in which he claimed to be defending two Muslim girls who were being harassed by a couple of white teenagers. The jury agreed and acquitted him.

I switch over to Fox News, where they're playing up the Islam angle. Obasanjo's dad, a Nigerian Muslim, is a naturalized citizen who's worked the same job managing a car rental office for the past twenty-two years, but they keep calling him an immigrant and suggesting he arrived with questionable papers. Obasanjo's mom, an Oakland native, is a cook in a neighborhood restaurant. CNN described her as a deeply religious "socially progressive Muslim," whatever that means. Fox has her pegged as "a child of the radical Nation of Islam."

And when Fox talks about the battery incident, they emphasize the fact that Obasanjo was arrested and tried for a violent crime. Not that he was acquitted. They keep his ID photo up on screen, the one that looks like a mug shot, while their experts talk about how small failures in the criminal justice system embolden criminals to commit heinous acts.

According to Ed, the FBI has been putting Obasanjo through round-the-clock interrogation. The kid won't crack. Ed told me on our call a while ago that Obasanjo was so scared during the initial questioning he lost control of his bowels. They had to find him a new pair of pants. I guess those were the ill-fitting ones he was wearing during the perp walk.

Meanwhile, the airline is getting desperate. They're flooding us with videos of passengers in the airport before the flight.

"I've gone through four hours of footage today," Bethany says. "And the airline has teams in Denver and Chicago poring over the same images."

"You find anything interesting?" I ask.

"A couple of clips," she says. "You want to see?"

"Let's take a look."

I pull up a chair at Bethany's desk, and she says, "OK, I'm going to just skim through this one, because it's twenty minutes of the same thing."

She shows me a video of a white guy in a hoodie pacing back and forth in front of the terminal windows at gate seventy-six.

"That's Owen Briscoe," she says. "The schizo, and he's on meds. See how he shuffles his feet?"

"Yeah, I've seen this clip. That might be suspicious activity outside of an airport," I say, "but that's not how a terrorist behaves. Those guys are trained *not* to draw attention to themselves. They're not going to show up early to the gate and pace around, looking unsettled. Plus, if the guy is schizo and he's on meds, he's going to have a hard time planning an attack like this."

"Right," says Bethany. "They also sent video of these two guys in the executive lounge before the flight."

She queues that one up and runs it.

Two men are sitting at a table in the VIP lounge with drinks in front of them. They're both around forty, wearing slacks and button-down shirts. One has a big beer belly and looks like he might be drunk. The other one is agitated and fidgety. He talks a lot and keeps wiping sweat from his brow.

"Who are they?" I ask.

"Sheldon Brown and Franklin Dorsett," Bethany says. "A couple of rich guys from Texas with huge frequent-flier balances. Brown owns a string of car dealerships. Dorsett's company leases drilling equipment to oil companies. They're flying first class."

"Why are we looking at them?" I ask. "Why would they blow up a plane?"

Bethany shrugs. "You asked if there was anything interesting in the video they sent. So far, this is as interesting as it gets."

"Don't waste your time on those clowns."

"I have eight more hours of this stuff to look through," she says. From her tone, I can tell she's not thrilled about that.

"Go back to the passenger list if you need a break from the videos."

As soon as I get to my desk, Ed calls with some inside information.

"You know baggage handlers go through security when they come in to work."

"Makes sense," I say.

"Well our guy Obasanjo went through a checkpoint manned by two TSA agents. One of them wasn't feeling well, had the runs, and stepped away to the restroom. Obasanjo went through before TSA got a second guy in to help. This was early in the morning, when the airport was dead. The sole agent at the checkpoint when Obasanjo went through was a guy named Timothy Welcher, and he's AWOL."

"What do you mean?"

"The last person to see him was his girlfriend, a few hours after the plane went down. She said he was a wreck."

"I could imagine. You have a job protecting people, and then something like that happens. It has to get to you."

"His girlfriend said he stepped out of the apartment to talk to someone, and he never came back."

"She know who he was talking to?"

"She didn't recognize the voice," Ed says. "But she said by the way they were talking, they knew each other."

"So you gonna have the A team look for Welcher?"

"*Everyone's* looking for him. TSA wants to find him before the FBI does. They don't want a rival agency debriefing their guy first. Oh, and that Vietnamese guy you mentioned. He doesn't work at SFO."

"Yeah he does. I saw him."

"I know you saw him," Ed says. "Surveillance cameras all over the airport picked him up. But he doesn't work here. He came through security with a backpack and a ticket to LA. Then he went into a bathroom and came out without the backpack, dressed as an airport employee. He went around emptying garbage cans for about twenty minutes, staying near gate seventy-six. Watched the passengers get on then made a call as he left the terminal."

"Any idea who he is?"

"The Bureau ran facial recognition on the videos and matched him to a social media profile. The guy has no record, but some of his friends do. They say he ran low-level errands for quick cash. You know—follow someone, deliver something. He was reliable and kept a low profile. Seems he's been sliding beneath law enforcement's radar for months now. Oh, and he's Cambodian, not Vietnamese."

"They know where he is?"

"Not yet," Ed says. "But they found the number of that phone he was carrying. They pulled his call records from Verizon. According to the security footage, he made the call just before four p.m."

"Who'd he call?"

"Someone waiting in one of the satellite lots."

"Who was it?"

"We don't know," Ed says. "It was a burner phone, bought used with a SIM card from God knows where. But your garbage man is now a person of interest. Keep that to yourself. The Bureau wants to pick him up before he knows they're looking for him. Oh, and that other guy. The one with the blonde in the security line?"

"The tall greasy one?"

"Petty criminal. Has a record down in Texas. Possession and disorderly conduct. That blonde he was with was one of the victims. Her name was Anna Brook."

"I know. I told you that, remember?"

"Sorry. It's been a long day."

"You learn anything about her?"

"She's of no interest to the investigation."

"How do you know that?"

"Because the Bureau already looked into her and wrote her off. We know she didn't bring the bomb onboard. She didn't even check a bag."

"What's the greasy guy's name?" I ask.

"Ramón Ramírez."

"Can you send me some info on him?"

"Yeah."

We hang up, and I spend the next few hours running background checks on passengers from the Chicago list. By eight o'clock, my eyes are red and burning, and I'm starting to think I'm wasting my time. Ed and the Bureau, with all their resources, are in the thick of things in San Francisco, and they're making progress. Me, I'm sitting in an office on the other side of the country, playing junior detective with a list of people from a different flight.

Miriam once told me that at her family's Thanksgiving dinners, the kids had to sit at their own table, away from the grown-ups. She and her cousins were stuck at the kiddie table into their twenties, and they all resented it.

When she first told me that, I didn't understand why she was complaining. She had a family. They ate together. There was warmth and tradition—things I wanted but didn't have. So what's the problem?

I get it now. The kiddie table. The B team. It's demeaning.

I'm getting frustrated with all these names. My head aches.

Even Leon looks burnt out. But Bethany—she's a trooper. She never complains.

"Why don't you two go home," I say.

"There's one more thing in this video," Bethany says.

"The Cambodian guy?" I say. "Emptying the garbage cans?"

"How'd you know?" she asks.

"The FBI has already ID'd him. Ed told me. Go home, will you?"

"I ain't done," Leon says.

"We'll never be done," I say. "The Feds will have a suspect and a case before we finish crossing all the names off this list. I hate to say it, but this is pointless. We're digging around on the off chance that we find a clue that gets the airline off the hook. We're duplicating work the Feds are already doing. In three days, or five days, or ten days, the airline will call it off and tell us to send them a bill."

"Thanks for the pep talk," Leon says.

"Sorry. I wasn't trying to bring anyone down. I appreciate your work, but don't kill yourself over this. Go get some dinner. Go home and rest."

Leon stands reluctantly and stretches. Bethany picks up her bag and says, "I'm meeting some friends for a drink at eight thirty. Either of you want to come?"

Leon says no.

"What about you, Freddy?"

"I have work to do."

"Come on," she says. "That's two hours from now. And you just told us to go home."

"I have work to do."

After Bethany and Leon leave, I get up from the computer and rub my eyes and think of Anna Brook, and that feeling comes back. You have a crush on a girl, and every time you think of her, you get this warm, giddy feeling. With her, it's the opposite. It's an unsettled feeling in a deep, dark part of me that no one ever gets to, and it fills me with dread.

I dreamed about her last night. She was swimming in a clear blue sea while I watched from the rocks above. Then suddenly, the sea darkened, and a whirlpool opened beneath her. I watched her get sucked into it, struggling against the current as she swirled down into the center.

She went round and round, her arms extended forward against the spiraling waters, her blonde hair flowing out behind her. Her body was long and lithe, and her strokes were graceful and determined. She didn't ask for help, but it was clear she wasn't going to make it.

I dove in after her, more out of compulsion than choice. I'm not a good swimmer, and I've always feared drowning. The coldness and the weight, the dark and the depths terrify me. But I went in headfirst and followed her straight to the heart of darkness.

And when we got deep into that swirling funnel, when the light of the world above was almost gone, and it was clear there was no point in resisting any longer, she turned her body forward and swam downward with the current.

In that moment, the dread I had felt when I first saw her grew into full-blown terror. I remember thinking she has some instinct I don't understand, and if I get too close, she'll pull me down with her.

She swam far out ahead of me, and I couldn't follow. I turned and began to swim back toward the surface, but I was powerless against the current of the cold, dark water. When the terror was overwhelming, I woke up gasping for breath in sweat-soaked sheets, like a drowning man.

* * *

At nine-thirty p.m., as I'm nearing the end of the Chicago passenger list, the office door opens and Bethany walks in.

"Why are you working in the dark?" she asks.

"Because I am."

"You want the lights on?"

"No. What are you doing here? I thought you were meeting friends for drinks."

"I left my bank card," she says as she walks to her desk.

"When you were buying shoes online?"

"You noticed that?" She laughs as she picks up the card.

She pauses for a few seconds, tapping the card on the desk and looking at me. Finally, she says, "Hey Freddy?"

"Huh?"

"Why are you still working?"

"You know me," I say. "I get on the trail of something and I just keep going."

"You find anything?"

"Just a tangent. A personal interest, I guess."

"The victims won't mind you taking a night off. They're all dead, you know." Then she sees my reaction. "Ooh, that got your shoulders up! You feeling a little defensive?"

"My mind's on the case, OK?"

"Why don't you join us for a drink? We're two blocks away."

"No thanks."

"Teresa's there. The one you said was cute."

"Yeah?"

"She asked if you'd be coming."

"I won't be. I'm working."

She sits on the edge of my desk. "I really think you'd like her. You only talked for five minutes last time, but you made an impression. She's asked about you twice."

I keep my eyes on the monitor. "Maybe I'll catch up with her some other time."

"No you won't. Whenever you say that, it means you'll never get to it."

"Well then maybe I won't."

She stands and runs her hands down her legs, smoothing out her jeans. "You can be really frustrating, you know that? You know what you look like right now? You're a silent, lonely face, lit by the glow of a screen in a sea of darkness. Outside those windows is a world of life that you keep choosing not to be a part of. There's more to life than work, Freddy."

"I appreciate your concern, but you take care of your life, and I'll take care of mine."

"OK, Freddy," she says as she walks toward the door. "Should I tell Teresa not to waste her time?"

"Tell her whatever you want."

She leaves, and the office is quiet again.

When I get through the Chicago list, it's close to midnight. There are four passengers I want to know more about—and two of them are also on the list of one-way travelers the airline sent me. Anna Brook could have traveled as any one of these people. Mostly, I want to know where she wound up. These are my four possibilities:

Melissa Edwards, age 33. No social profile, so I don't know what she looked like. No frequent flyer number either. She connected to Buffalo, but she lives in LA. How she got to San Francisco, I don't know. Maybe she drove.

Tanya DuPree, 29, connected to Philadelphia. No frequent flyer number. Never flew this airline before. No info about her anywhere, but the airline has her listed as a resident of Oakland. No return ticket.

Katie Green, 27, Dallas, Texas. There are 114 Katherine Greens in Dallas, four of them aged 27. She connected to Austin. Why would she go to Austin if she lives in Dallas? And who goes through Chicago to get to Austin from San Francisco? She does have a frequent flier number, but her address is a couple years out of date. No return ticket.

Betsy Renfro, 31, from Rocky Mount, North Carolina. Connected to Raleigh. Nothing on her. Just nothing.

Tomorrow I go to Staunton for Anna Brook's memorial service.

8

OCTOBER 2

This morning, I got up at five. It's a three-hour drive to Staunton without traffic, but the morning rush in DC is usually bad, so I figured I'd give myself time to review any new material that came in overnight before I head out. And it's a good thing I did, because one of Ed's buddies passed along some info about Ramón Ramírez—the tall, angular guy who was escorting my blonde friend through the security line.

He's got several arrests to go with his convictions for possession and disorderly conduct. The funny thing is, that misdemeanor possession conviction should have been possession with intent to distribute, which is a felony. The arrest report says he was carrying $3,000 worth of cocaine.

And he has a few other arrests that didn't lead to charges. One of the reports refers to a prior arrest for which there's no report. Two other reports are redacted. All of which makes me wonder if this guy is an informant.

Whatever he is, he's small time. Definitely not the kind you trust with a tough job, unless you're stuck and have no one else to turn to. He reminds me of a skinny Chuck DiLeo. The bottom of the barrel. A real loser.

I hit the road a little before seven a.m. Give myself an extra hour to get to Staunton, which turns out to be a good idea because traffic is heavy. It takes almost two hours just to get to 81, the southbound highway that runs through the Shenandoah Valley. I put the radio on and let my mind wander.

* * *

After that loss to Alvin Perkins, I spent a couple of weeks stewing about how it all went down. Then I went to see my old trainer, Rizzardi, to ask him to take me back.

Walking into Rizzardi's gym, I had the feeling I was home. I never had that feeling with Slim's trainer. Here, everyone said hello to me. There, they looked at me from the corners of their eyes, the way you might look at a stranger passing through, or a man on his way to the gallows.

Rizzardi was in his sweats, holding the heavy bag while this big, muscular kid was swinging hooks against it. The kid couldn't have been more than sixteen. Left, right. Left, right. Rizzardi had to hold the bag to keep it from swaying out of range.

"Keep your right up when you throw the left. Right hand up, goddammit! You're leaving your chin wide open!"

"Hey Rizzo," I said.

He said, "Hit this kid, will you? Show him what he's doing wrong."

The kid glanced up at me for a second, and kept swinging.

"I don't want to hit him," I said.

"You know what I mean," Rizzardi said.

The kid swung a left hook, and I gave him a quick, light, brushing slap on the cheek, just to show how easy it was to connect when he had his guard down. He jerked his head back in surprise, a little too late.

"That's what I'm talking about," Rizzardi said.

The kid smiled, feinted a left hook toward the bag, then popped a sharp jab at my face. I ducked it, and he smiled.

"You see that?" Rizzardi said to him. "A good puncher will drop you as soon as you throw that hook."

I said, "Hey, Rizzo, we gotta talk."

He said to the kid, "Take a break. I'll be back in five."

"We might need more than five minutes," I said.

He said, "No we won't."

We walked over to one of the benches by the empty ring in the rear of the gym and I said, "I need you to take me back. Slim isn't looking out for me, and that trainer is worthless. Did you see what happened to me?"

"I saw it," he said. "I saw it coming before it happened. But I can't take you back, Freddy. Did you read that contract you signed with Slim? He owns you. You'll win when he wants you to win. You'll lose when he wants you to lose. You want my advice? Get out of the sport. There's no future in it for you."

"You can't help me out?"

"I can't even talk to you no more. I don't like it, but that's how it is. We're not friends anymore, you understand?"

That I got. I understood the kinds of things Slim did to people when he didn't want them to be friends with someone.

Then Chuck DiLeo walked in, all 330 pounds of him, wearing his trademark dark-blue tracksuit and untied Air Jordans, sucking on a milkshake. Looked like a giant goddamn baby. How the hell did he know I was here? Was he following me?

He said, "Come on, Freddy. We got a job to do."

I told him to fuck off.

He said, "Come on, man." Like he didn't even hear me.

I don't know why I walked out of there with him. But what was the point of hanging around if Rizzardi wasn't going to take me back?

Me and DiLeo went out to his Camaro. The whole damn car rocked sideways when he got in, like a hippo stepping into a rowboat. We drove to the Bronx.

"Where we going?" I said.

"Collect on a loan."

We parked in front of Burger King, and DiLeo went in and got another shake. Didn't ask me if I wanted anything. Then we walked up the street, past the liquor store, past this wig place, and we stopped in front of a shoe repair shop. Looked like it had been there for a hundred years and no one had dusted the place since it opened.

He stood there looking in through the door. The sign said Open, but he was checking for customers. He didn't want to beat anyone up in front of witnesses. He kept sucking on his milkshake with a loud slurping sound. He pulled the straw out to lick it off, and some of the shake dripped onto his tracksuit. He started cursing, like he'd just ruined a damn tuxedo.

I wanted to hit the guy right then. Big fucking overgrown baby. Why the hell's he always wearing a tracksuit? Like he might break into a run at any minute. His fucking shoes aren't even tied. Fat bastard.

He slid the straw back into the cup and opened the door. We got inside, and there were no customers, just an old woman at the counter in back: skinny, with little librarian glasses and fake red old-lady hair. She couldn't have weighed more than a hundred pounds. As soon as she saw us, she called out, "Mort!" Her voice was high with fear.

The place had racks of shoes and boots that looked like the kind of crap people give to Goodwill. There was a register behind the counter next to the old lady, and behind her was a workbench with tools. A couple of boots that didn't match were mounted upside-down for re-soling.

DiLeo turned the deadbolt on the door, and flipped the Open sign to Closed. "Where's Morty?" he said.

Again, the old woman, scared, yelled out, "Mort!"

An old man came shuffling out of the back room. He was wearing a green plaid shirt, grey sweater vest, and little half-glasses perched on his nose with a string that looped around his neck. When he saw us, he let out a sigh. He didn't seem scared. Just kind of resigned. He opened the register, pulled out the drawer, and nodded for us to follow him into the back room. We went in, with the old lady trailing after us.

The guy sat down at a desk and put the cash drawer on top. DiLeo went and stood behind him, with his fat tree-trunk thighs framing the old guy's head. Mort unlocked a desk drawer and pulled out an envelope.

"Fifteen hundred," he said. "I think I have it all."

"Sixteen hundred," DiLeo said.

The old woman, who was standing right next to me, quietly wringing her hands, blurted out, "Fifteen hundred! It's fifteen!"

"It's sixteen now," DiLeo said, and he took a big slurp of his shake.

The old man slid a stack of bills out of the envelope and offered them up. "That's thirteen-forty," he said. "Count it."

DiLeo swatted him in the back of the head and said, "You count it, you little fuck." Big fat arm like DiLeo's probably weighs forty pounds. The blow knocked the old guy's glasses off, and the woman let out a little yelp and started toward her husband like she wanted to comfort him. But then she pulled back and looked at me with this plea in her eyes, like she was searching for something human in me, begging me to use whatever ounce of decency I might have left to protect her husband.

The old man put his glasses back on and started counting the money. He licked his fingers and peeled off the bills one at a time and laid them down on the desk. Twenty, forty, sixty, eighty. A wisp of his thin grey hair was sticking up, out of place from when DiLeo swatted him. DiLeo stood there slurping the milkshake real loud, like he was *trying* to annoy everyone. He leaned in on the old man, rubbing his crotch on the back of the guy's head, just to add an extra touch of humiliation.

"Two-hundred sixty, two-hundred eighty, three hundred." It was like me counting off sit-ups in the gym. The guy was so diligent in peeling off those bills, pinching every one, like he didn't want to let it go. Because how much work did he put into earning it in the first place? He was probably in his shop at seven every morning, the same time I was out running. And he laid those bills down just a little out of line, so the corners would show, so that fat slob DiLeo could see each one and know he wasn't getting cheated.

Four years as an amateur, and six as a pro. God knows how many hours I put in and how many blows I had to take. And in the end, I'm just a pawn in some lowlife's scheme to build up another fighter. This old man and me, this old lady, we do all the work in the world, we put everything we've got into every day, just so this fat, milk-sucking baby and his tribe of bullies can walk in at the last minute and take it all away.

"Pick up the pace," DiLeo said.

It took a while, but the old man counted out $1340. Then he started pulling bills from the cash drawer. He had $181 in there. That bought the total up to $1521.

He turned to DiLeo, handed him fifteen hundred, and kept the other twenty-one in his right hand. DiLeo threw his empty milkshake into the corner, took the fifteen hundred, and the twenty-one too, and said, "I said sixteen hundred."

"It was fifteen," the old man said, and DiLeo gave him another backhand to the side of the head. The old woman started again like she wanted to help him, but she held back.

"That's all I have," the old man said.

"Bullshit," said DiLeo.

I said, "Come on, Chuck. Let's get out of here."

He said, "Gimme the rest of the money. I know you fucking Jews got some cash hidden around here." He stuffed the bills into his pocket, lifted the old man up by the back of his collar, dug a hard right hook into his kidney, and then dropped him on the floor.

I could have told you this was coming. I could have told you the night of the fight, when I was lying in that hospital bed up in Connecticut, still awake at four a.m., wondering what the hell had just happened to ten years of hard work.

I knew I was gonna snap. It was just a question of when.

I said real calm and kind of cold, "You know that's not a nice thing to do, Chuck, hitting someone in the kidney like that."

He didn't get it. He pulled the money back out of his pocket and started counting. He had no idea what was coming. But the old lady did. There was this electricity running through my veins, and she felt it. She had the instinct. She started backing away from me, nervous and scared.

DiLeo just stood there, counting the bills.

In a calm, even tone, I said, "You ever been hit like that, Chuck?"

His lips moved as he counted.

"I asked you a question, Chuck."

He didn't even look at me. Just snorted a big rumbling wad of snot up his nose and kept right on counting. "Three-forty, three-sixty, they got more cash here somewhere," he said. "Start looking through the drawers."

I took a couple steps toward him, and BAM! I dug a left hook right into his liver. The money went flying, and he doubled over hard, right into my right knee, which was on its way up to break his jaw. He slumped onto the desk and I pounded the side of his head with four straight rights. I felt his eye socket crack on the last one.

He tried to straighten up but those blows to the head short-circuited his legs. He flopped right back onto the desk, and I started raining punches into his face and ribs. I don't know how many. You know that expression "blind rage?" Well, it's pretty accurate, because when you're that mad you don't really see what you're doing. When he hit the floor, I gave him a good hard kick in the nuts, just to punish his children if he ever had any.

For a minute I stood there with my hands on my hips, just kinda catching my breath. When you come back to your corner from a round where you've been throwing bombs, the first thing your trainer does is try to get your breathing under control. "Deep breaths," they say. "Deep breaths."

DiLeo wasn't moving, but he was breathing. And Christ, he was ugly. I didn't think the guy could get any uglier, but you turn someone's face inside out and he gets real hard to look at.

I started feeling nice and calm, like when the adrenaline wears off after you knock a guy out. It's just this calm, floaty feeling.

Then I saw the old man and the old lady. I had forgotten they were there. The man was propped up in a corner. His lip was quivering, and his eyes were leaky. I don't know how he got over there. Did he drag himself, or did his wife drag him? The old lady was standing beside him, wide-eyed and shaking.

I said, "Sorry for the mess, ma'am. You mind opening that door?"

I pointed to the door at the back of the room. She opened it quietly, and I dragged DiLeo across the blood-spattered, cash-strewn floor, through the door, and into the alley. I propped him up between a couple of dumpsters. He was still unconscious. Then I took the 1 train all the way down to Canal Street and had the first drink of my life.

A couple days later, Slim's worthless trainer picked me up off Kings Highway in Flatbush. He had two other guys with him I'd never seen before. They told me to get into the car. It was not a request. We drove a mile or so, turned into an alley, and stopped halfway down. The guy sitting next to me said it was time to get out. We went into the back of a restaurant, into a room filled with cleaning supplies. There was one high dirty window with grey light coming in.

And there was Slim Mancuso in a light grey suit, with a cream-colored shirt and blue tie. The outfit must have cost a couple thousand bucks. He wore wire-framed glasses and had short grey hair. He was trim and tan and manicured, like an old playboy who spends his mornings in the spa. The trainer was standing behind me with the other two guys.

Slim had this real calm demeanor. He was looking at me like he didn't quite know what to make of me. Not hostile or anything. Just curious. Then he said, "What the hell'd you do to Chuck?"

"Is he dead?" I said.

"No."

"Then I didn't do enough."

Slim said, "There will be no psychopaths in my organization." Before I could figure out what that meant, I felt a sharp blow from behind, right in the ribs. It shook my whole body and sent a blinding white light into my eyes. The next couple of blows, I only kind of felt. And then I was out.

I don't know what they did to me, but I woke up in an empty room and staggered out the door into an alley full of oily puddles. I remember thinking that it must have rained while I was out. I made it to the street before I passed out again.

In the hospital they told me that if the lung puncture had been any worse, or if it had been another hour before someone found me, I would have died. I had three broken ribs on the right side. You could see the imprint from a crow bar. One of the ribs punctured my lung. I had two hairline fractures in the vertebra of my midback, lacerations on my face and scalp, a bruised kidney, broken nose, and I don't remember what else.

But I didn't have to worry about DiLeo coming after me. My second day in the hospital was his first day out, and someone gunned him down. Nobody liked that guy. Fat fucking bastard.

That evening, two cops came by my hospital room asking about DiLeo. One of them was a real asshole. A white guy with close-cropped hair and the kind of accent people put on when they want to make fun of New Yorkers. He had big, thick weightlifter arms, and he liked to show them off. "You're lucky you were in this bed when DiLeo bought it," he said. "Because otherwise, you'd be suspect number one. We know what you did to him." This cop was the kind of guy I instinctively wanted to punch.

The other cop was older. A dark-haired Puerto Rican guy, kind of short, with flecks of grey around his temples. He pulled up a chair next to the bed and told his partner to leave us alone for a while.

I had a good talk with him. He wanted to know what happened with DiLeo, and he said right off the bat, "Look, the guy's dead. He's not going to press charges." At first I didn't want to tell him anything. The people I was working with didn't like anyone talking to cops.

He said, "Where was the shoe repair place?" I acted like I didn't know what he was talking about, and he said, "The cobbler shop where you beat up DiLeo. Where was it?"

He wanted to know because I'd left the money there, and he was worried about the old man and the old woman. "You guys didn't collect," he said. "That means they'll send someone else to get the money. And they're gonna be angry. You want those people to get hurt?"

Now that's a good cop, looking out for the right people. I told him everything, and he took notes. It all went into a police report that eventually found its way into Ed Hartwell's hands when he decided to look into my background.

The cop said, "Who else wanted to hurt DiLeo?"

"Lots of people," I said.

"Like? Come on, I got a murder case on my hands and I don't like leaving killers out on the street."

"If I'm gonna start giving you names," I said, "I'm gonna have to name a dozen people, and that's just gonna get me in trouble. I don't know who did it."

He said, "OK. You got anywhere to go besides New York?"

"No. Why?"

"Because you don't have a future here. Unless you want to take DiLeo's job and end up like him. But after what you did, I don't think Slim or anyone else is gonna want to work with you."

This was the same conversation I had just had with Rizzardi. Another version of "Get out while you can."

When I left the hospital, I wasn't gonna wait around to see if anyone was looking for me. I took a southbound from

Penn Station, and I paid a visit to my mother's grave in Philly. It was the only place I knew to go.

Most of my memories of my mother are at the breakfast table. It's always her filling my bowl with cereal and telling me what a great day we're going to have. A day that never came.

The memory that sticks out the most, though, is from a day when I was six. It was a Sunday, just past noon. The first thing I did wrong was I woke up my dad. But he let that slide. He got a beer from the fridge and turned on the TV. The Phillies were playing the Mets. I was jumping around the living room because sitting still for an hour in church had made me antsy. I should have been more careful. He had that look. Angry, irritable, eyes all bloodshot.

I accidentally knocked his beer off the table, just being clumsy, and he went into a rage. That was the scariest beating I ever got, and I'd had plenty by then.

My mom was at the grocery store, and the way he was going at me, I was sure I'd be dead before she got back. Then the door opened.

She couldn't stop him, so she grabbed me around the waist, pulled me toward her, and folded her body around me. I could feel the blows landing on her back. The shock came through her chest and shook my head. She took all of it, and didn't let go of me until he had worn himself out.

How could he have killed a person like that? How could anyone kill a person like *that*?

Over the years, the other memories of her faded and blurred. But that one is vivid.

When Miriam was pregnant and had family on her mind, she started getting more curious, prying into things about my past that she knew I wasn't going to talk about.

"Why don't you ever tell me things?"

"I tell you everything."

"You don't tell me how you feel."

"You can see how I feel. I don't hide it."

"You never tell me about your past."

"I told you about boxing."

"Why did you stop? It sounded like you were doing well."

"It didn't work out."

"Because you lost one fight? Come on, Freddy, I know you're not a quitter. Tell me what happened."

"I told you. It didn't work out. Why dwell on it?"

And that was just the beginning. When she wanted to ruin a date, she'd start in with this: "Tell me about your mother."

"My mother's dead."

"Tell me about your father."

"My father's dead."

"What were they like?"

"It doesn't matter. They're gone."

"What about your childhood?"

"It didn't work out, so I grew up."

"Well, aren't you a charmer? You want to write your autobiography? Here's a napkin. Feel free to use both sides."

Give me all the paper in the world, I couldn't explain to you the burden of the debt I owe to the one who brought me into this life, to the one who laid herself down and took all the blows that were meant for me. They say we all have our crosses, right? Well, try bearing that one. How could you ever repay a debt like that?

This is why I like to keep busy. Empty time isn't good for me. When I fought, there was always a purpose to what I was doing. The sit-ups and the running and the sparring would make me a little bit stronger, and the next day I'd work harder, just to get a minor fight. A little fight led to a bigger fight. It was all going somewhere. I knew it would take years to unfold, and I could put all my energy into it, day after day after day. It was big enough to absorb everything I had to give.

And this? What I do now?

Like I said, I'm thankful to be in good health, to have all my faculties, and a job and a place to live. I'm grateful to Ed for giving me a chance.

But when I have too much empty time, I start asking myself who I'm really helping. Insurance companies and corporations. Sure, they're getting ripped off. Sure, the people who are screwing them are assholes. But those companies have millions and millions of dollars. Do they really need my help?

The only reason I'm still in this world is because all those years ago in Philly, the right person walked in on me at the right moment. All those years ago in New York, the right guy took an interest in me at the right time.

I always wanted to pay them back. Somehow. Some way.

9

I park in front of the church fifteen minutes early. There's a Chrysler 300 with DC tags and no dealer markings parked in front of me. That's a Fed car. I wonder if it belongs to the FBI contact Ed mentioned. What was his name? Lomax?

When I walk into the church, an ashen-skinned elderly woman with a pinched face hands me a program. On the front is a photo of Anna Brook, looking younger and healthier than when I saw her. Beneath the photo is her date of birth, a dash, and the date the plane went down into the sea. September 29.

The vaulted ceiling inside the church has exposed wood beams. Not the rough kind you see in stripped-down restaurants that are trying to look hip and authentic. The beams are thick, finished, and stained. The dark oak pews on either side of the red-carpeted aisle creak when people sit on them. There's an organ behind the pulpit, to the right of the altar. Whoever built this place didn't take any shortcuts. They did it right.

It's been a long time since I've been in a church. That priest who first brought me into Rizzardi's gym, Father Sanchez, took a special interest in me when he found out my mother used to take me to a Catholic church in Philly. He wanted to bring me back into the fold, but I had no interest in returning to that sheep's pen.

A lot of the kids in Rizzardi's gym were brought in by the cops. They were angry or hopeless, and if they weren't violent yet, they were on their way, because violence is the natural expression of those feelings. The cops and Rizzardi, and even Father Sanchez, looked at boxing as a way to channel the aggression that would otherwise come out on the streets. Rizzardi taught kids to bring it all to the ring and leave it in the ring.

Father Sanchez, I don't know if he thought I was a thug or what, but he invited me to come by for confession. That put me off, because I was thinking, OK, you want me to buy into this religion, and we're going to start with a list of all the things *I* did wrong? What about the whole damn world out there and everything that's wrong with *it*? Remind me again who created that.

So I went to confession with a big list I had put together, and I started going through it line by line. "Here's all the things God did wrong this week: The junkie in the dumpster by the high school. I heard he was only twenty-seven and had two kids. Praise be! The pimp who beat up that hooker in broad daylight. Knocked out two of her teeth. Nothing happens but by his will. The kid on the corner, seventeen, with a dozen bullet holes in him after the drive-by. They say God made man in his own image. Well, which one is His image? The one firing the gun and laughing, or the one too full of holes to pick himself up from the blood-soaked gutter?"

Sanchez didn't like that, but I'll give him credit for not losing his temper. He told me it was natural for a kid to be angry, especially if he'd lost his parents. He asked me if I wanted to be free of that anger.

"Be free how?" I said. "By accepting all this? By saying it's all OK and there's nothing anyone can do about it, so why don't we just move on? Fuck that!"

"You have the right attitude," he said. That was not the response I expected. "You want a better world. You just have to focus the negative energy so it works in a positive way."

That was just the kind of thing Rizzardi would say.

"I don't have any money for your tithe," I said. "I'm not a profitable parishioner."

"The church's first concern is you," Sanchez said. "It's what we can do for you."

As soon as he said that, I was done. That's the kind of line the dealers used to recruit guys to sell on the corners. Anyone who comes to you saying they're looking out for *your* interests is lying. I got up and walked out, but Sanchez kept after me for months at the gym.

Every day I'd write down the little things I saw. The robberies and the bullying, the drug use and the prostitution and the general meanness of it all. Then when Sanchez tried to talk to me, I'd tell him it was time for God's confession, and I'd read off the list of all the things the Lord had let happen that week.

After a while, he gave up on me. And I had to stop making those lists, they made me so damned depressed.

It looks like only about forty people showed up to the funeral. I would have expected more in a small town like this. But of course she hasn't lived here in ten years. Maybe with the service coming so quickly after the crash, her old friends didn't have enough time to get back to town.

The mourners are scattered about, three in one row, four in the next. I thought they'd all be bunched up front. Maybe Anna and her friends weren't churchgoers. Maybe they don't feel comfortable here. How sad for her family to see that in the end she mattered to so few people.

That must be her mother and sister in the front row. I can only see the backs of their heads. The mother is short, with straight grey hair cut just above the shoulders. The sister is taller, slim, with blonde hair.

Over on the right is a broad-shouldered guy in a dark-blue suit. That's gotta be Lomax, the FBI guy. What other man would be here alone? If he were Anna's husband or lover, or a local, he'd be seated with a group or talking to someone. When he turns, I see he's holding a paper coffee cup. He's young, with short blond hair and a thick, muscular neck. He has a bit of a cocky look. Someone nods to him, and he flashes a smile as he brings the cup to his lips and takes a sip.

Ten minutes till the service starts. Time enough to duck into the men's room. I walk out of the main sanctuary, through a wood-paneled reception hall with high, lead-glass windows. The restroom signs lead down a narrow hall. I hear footsteps behind me as I push open the restroom door.

I'm standing at the urinal when the blond guy pulls up beside me and rests his cup on the porcelain ledge of the next urinal. I say, "Are you Lomax?" He has a weird, vibrating energy, like he's had too much coffee.

He says, "You work with Ed Hartwell, for the airline, right?" He's flashing his all-American smile right into the white tiled wall. "Hey, I'd shake your hand, but I kinda got my hands full at the moment." Then he laughs.

"Freddy Ferguson," I say. "Been with Ed for a few years now."

"They got you working the passenger list?" he asks.

"Yeah. You too, huh?"

"Yeah, this is the fucking junior beat, man. This is for cadets and trainees."

I say, "You gotta be thorough, though."

And he says, "Yeah, you gotta be thorough."

We go over to the sinks and as I wash my hands, I say, "You guys find any dirt on any of the passengers?"

He says, "You mean other than Obasanjo? Maybe Owen Briscoe. He was mixed up with a bad bunch out in Idaho. Delmont Suggs and his anti-government white separatist militia. Fucking Cracker Jihad. Those guys are gonna go down on a different rap. Weapons trafficking and assault."

"How do you know that?" I ask.

"ATF was watching him for a while last year."

"Alcohol, Tobacco, and Firearms?"

"Yeah." Lomax turns off the water and shakes his hands over the sink. "Suggs only works in the winter. He does avalanche control, firing mortars into mountainsides. The rest of the year, as far as anyone can tell, he supports himself by selling guns. ATF has a problem with that. But this plane crash…" Lomax shakes his head and grins. "That's an open and shut case."

"What makes you so sure?"

He grabs a paper towel and says, "Pfft! D'you see that guy Obasanjo on TV?"

"He looked scared," I say.

"You know what I heard? The kid shit himself in the interrogation." He tosses his paper towel into the garbage and turns to me. "He literally shit his pants! And then he started crying! Well boo-hoo, the kid blows up a fucking plane and he doesn't know why he's in detention."

I grab a towel and dry my hands. "Any idea who he was working with?"

"Who knows?" He tilts his head back and looks into the mirror like he's trying to see up his own nose. In fact, that's exactly what he's doing. "ISIS says they did it, but that's probably bullshit," he says. "They're always looking for publicity. You ready for the big show?"

"Yeah."

The pastor reads from a typed script, and every time he turns the page, the microphone blasts the shuffling sound through the speakers. I'm sitting three rows behind Anna's mother and sister. The mother, Roseanne, keeps her head down as the pastor speaks.

The sister, Julia, turns and looks over her shoulder at me, the same way her sister did in the airport. Christ! I nearly jump out of my skin. The two of them look almost identical. Same blonde hair—only Julia's is real—same blue eyes, bleary from crying all night. But Julia is a little fuller in the cheeks, a little healthier looking all around. Her face shows more emotion. Her mouth isn't set in that stoic look. She's got less mileage on her.

According to the eulogy, Anna was a bright, sensitive girl, loved by everyone. That last part, I might believe. She looks like she got around. Her sister keeps turning around to see the other mourners. She catches me looking at her a few times during the service. But everyone's looking at her. She looks so much like Anna, it's like the woman showed up to her own funeral.

I look around now and then. Lomax is sitting near the back, still sipping his coffee and vibrating. He's *literally* vibrating. I think he's bouncing his knee up and down, like a busy, impatient man who got roped into a pointless meeting, and the motion is making his whole body shake. A couple rows in front of him is a chubby black guy in a suit, and an older white woman in a pants suit. I bet they're from the airline.

The minister says that the eye of God is upon us in our hour of grief, and nothing will go unnoticed. If the FBI thought this was an important part of the investigation, the eye of the federal government would be upon us. Lomax would have a camera mounted somewhere and he'd take the video back to DC and run it through facial recognition software to see if he could latch on to someone who might lead him to his target. Instead, he's on cadet duty, as he put it, sipping coffee and bouncing his leg.

After the service, everyone goes to the reception hall for coffee and sandwiches. People offer their condolences to Julia and her mother. This is the first time I've gotten a good look at the mother, and she seems more than a little tipsy.

The chubby guy introduces himself to them as Marvin something, offers condolences on behalf of the airline, and tells the mom that if there's anything they need—help with meals, errands, anything during this difficult time—the airline will offer assistance. He gives them each his business card. From the looks of old Mrs. Brook, all she's thinking about right now is where she can find another drink, or a place to nap.

I notice a few of the younger folks have their phones out. They're bunching together in little groups, taking photos. Is that a thing at funerals these days? None of the older people are doing it. But maybe some of these kids haven't seen each other in a few years. I take out my phone, turn on the video camera, and take a slow, 360-degree pan around the room. Maybe not the best etiquette, but it'll allow me to pull stills of everyone later, in case I need to follow up on anyone here.

Marvin introduces Julia and her mother to the older woman standing beside him. She's a grief counselor. She says it was nice to speak to them on the phone the other day. She'll be in town for a few days, and after that she can talk by phone at any time. They get business cards from her too. Julia is grateful, she just can't tell them how grateful she is. Yes, they could use some help. And yes, Julia would like to talk. Her mom, though—she looks like she's going to need a Bloody Mary or something to stop her breakfast from turning into a noontime hangover.

Then Lomax introduces himself to Julia. FBI. "I am so deeply sorry for your loss, ma'am. So very, very sorry." He has the sure, confident manner of a good-looking guy who knows how effective his charm is, but the warmth doesn't quite seem genuine. He's on the job, after all.

Why's he only talking to the sister? Why doesn't he talk to Roseanne? Maybe he sees she's too far gone. He says, "I want you to know we are doing everything possible to bring the people who committed this heinous act to justice."

Christ, Lomax, the girl's in shock. There is no justice at a time like this. And stop staring at her goddamn tits. What the fuck is wrong with you?

There really is something creepy about the way he looks at her. Like she's a possession he wants to get back. But she bears it well. Lomax's false sympathy, I mean. Something tells me Anna would have turned her back on this guy if he'd shown such a blatant interest in her at her sister's funeral.

He says something else to her, I don't know what, and then he flashes that smile and gives her a little touch on the shoulder before he moves on. Now Julia and Mrs. Brook are talking to family friends. A young guy with a beard just dumped the remains of a flask into a Styrofoam cup and handed it to the old lady. That got a rise out of her. There's some gratitude right there. She put it straight to her lips.

I wait for the crowd to thin out before I approach the Brooks. I have to be careful what I say, and who hears. The airline rep and the grief counselor are off in a corner. I don't want them thinking I'm misrepresenting the airline, but I need to tie myself into this situation in a way that doesn't put the family off.

"Julia," I say. "Mrs. Brook." They both turn at once.

"Were you a friend of Anna's?" Julia asks.

"No. I mean, I saw her once. I'm with the airline, doing some investigative work. You know, I uh…" God, the way this woman looks at me! She's so unguarded, so open, like her heart is right there for the world to stomp on.

"I'm sorry about what happened," I say. "I really am. I'm uh… I'm up in DC and…" I can't lie to this woman. "Anna was the only one from around here who was on that plane. I mean, driving distance from DC, and I just wanted to come down here to show you… you know, people are thinking about you. People you don't even know. I mean, the world's not all cold." Christ, that's the shittiest lie I ever told, and her fucking eyes are welling up. Then she hugs me.

She says that's kind. That means a lot, because these last few days she hasn't had a whole lot of faith in the world.

Then this family of five comes up and starts telling stories about Anna in grade school, Anna in high school. How smart she was, how accepting, how you could tell her anything. From the sound of it, maybe the minister was telling the truth about her being loved by all.

A young woman in the group, around thirty or so, says, "Remember how she'd run and hide every time she got upset?" She has a bittersweet smile. "And we'd all go looking for her? It's OK, sweet pea! You can come out now."

Julia gets the same bittersweet smile. "That was always the signal. That's the only thing she responded to. How many times did we say those words?"

From the stories they tell, it sounds like Anna was a sensitive kid who toughened up in middle school, around the time the boys started looking at her.

After a few more minutes, it's just the family of five and me and Julia and her mom. Marvin and the grief counselor from the airline have said their goodbyes. The minister is folding up the chairs and stacking them in the corner. Then the family of five leaves. Julia goes to the bathroom, and then it's just me and the mom.

I pull out my phone and pretend to check the time. I want to get a photo of Julia when she comes back, though I can't think of a tactful way to do it.

"Did she go to college?" I ask.

Mrs. Brook looks at me with bleary eyes. "Julia?"

"No, Anna."

"Two semesters," she says. "Lot of good that did her." She takes a sip from the Styrofoam cup, forgetting for the second or third time that she emptied it several minutes ago. Then she stares forlornly into its depths. "Where's Julia?" she asks, as if she just noticed she was gone.

"She went…" I turn my phone in the direction she went, and there she is, in the wood-paneled corridor that leads to the restrooms. She's leaning back against the wall. No, she's pressing herself against the wall, and Lomax is leaning over her, talking. I snap a photo of the two of them.

It's a narrow corridor, and if he had any sense of decency, he wouldn't be crowding her like that. It makes me angry, the way he leans in on her. I can feel her discomfort. Why can't he? She'd push herself right though that wall if she could, just to get a little distance from him.

Then I realize he *can* feel it. I know he can. I've seen this kind of guy before. A guy who thinks it's natural for a woman to shrink from him like that, who's encouraged by her discomfort to press in closer.

She's got her hands behind her back now, and she's looking down, trying to avoid eye contact. He puts his hand up on the wall beside her head and leans into it, closing the space between them and cutting off her exit from the corridor. This is not unconscious behavior. He knows exactly what he's doing. This is the kind of person who makes me truly violent.

"Pardon me, ma'am." I slide the phone into my pocket as I move past the old lady. Six steps, and I'm across the floor. They both feel me coming, like a bull elephant. I grab Lomax by the shoulder and start hustling him back toward the men's room.

He's startled, and he's alarmed at my strength. "What the fuck?"

Lomax is a pretty solid guy. I can tell he works out. Probably in front of a mirror.

"Get out of here," I say to Julia, as I try to push Lomax into the men's room. Only, it's not that easy. The guy is strong, and he doesn't like being pushed around.

I finally shove him through the door, and the first thing out of his mouth is, "Are you crazy?" Boy, he's hot. "What the fuck is wrong with you?"

The fact that he doesn't try to hit me right off the bat— well, if he was a normal guy, I'd chalk it up to him having the decency to refrain from fighting in church, at a funeral. But I know his type. Behind the blue eyes and the blond hair and the all-American frat boy smile, it's not decency that restrains him. It's a cold, hard calculation that says Freddy Ferguson, the heavyweight, just came at me pretty hard out of nowhere, and he's strong and he's angry, and maybe I won't come out of this too well. Maybe it's time to use our words.

There are some people in this world who only understand power, and if you don't show it to them right up front, they'll never respect you.

"You're not talking to a perpetrator," I say. "She's a fucking victim. This is a time for consolation. For respect. It's not an interrogation. You don't intimidate her. You get me?"

I'm ready for him to come back at me with something—not a swing, but a verbal counterstrike, something to show me how tough he is. Instead, his whole look softens into one of concern, and he says, "Are you all right?"

He's got his hands on his hips and his shoulders are relaxed. That's not a fighting posture, not even suitable for defense. And the way he's looking at me, waiting to hear my response, he really wants to know. "What set you off?"

"Just... Goddammit, don't crowd the woman. She's in mourning."

He nods, keeping his eyes on me in a calm, friendly, understanding way. "All right," he says. "Yeah, I shouldn't have crowded her. You're a little sensitive, huh? You know, a lot of cops identify so much with the victims, they get bent out of shape. But you have to keep your head, because losing it isn't going to help you solve anything. Did you know Anna?"

"No. I just..." I swear I saw something in this guy, and I'm studying him hard now, looking for it again, but I don't see it. "I just have a trigger for a certain type of guy."

He nods with a look of understanding. "Well a cop's gotta have instincts, right? Better to be overly suspicious than overly trusting."

"Yeah." You know I'm not a cop. "I guess so." He's got me calmed down, feeling stupid for losing my cool, and grateful for the fact that he didn't lose his.

"Hey." He puts his hand on my shoulder. I don't like guys I don't know putting their hands on my shoulder. It makes me want to hit them. "At least we got out of the office for a day. Tomorrow, we'll be back at the computer." He flashes that million-dollar smile, and I can see why he's so sure of it. It even works on me.

When he walks out, I go to the sink and splash water on my cheeks and look at my reflection in the mirror. The face that held up under all those beatings looks back at me with disdain. I never thought I'd drink, but I do. I never thought

I'd let a marriage go down the drain, but I did. I never thought I'd have my father's temper, but I do. The only difference is the trigger. And the target.

10

When I return from the men's room, Julia's standing at the side of the reception hall. Her mom is beside her in a brown folding chair, starting to nod off.

"You heading out?" I ask.

"I'm taking my mother back home."

"Can you talk for a few minutes?"

She looks doubtful for a second, sizing me up like she's not sure how I'm going to behave. I regret losing my temper with Lomax. Then she says, "You said you saw Anna once."

"Twice, actually." There I go, digging myself in deeper. I can't help it with her.

"What do you mean, you *saw* her?" She pauses for a couple of seconds and then says, "Were you one of her clients?"

Clients? Psychologists have clients. So do hookers. From the looks of her in that airport line, and the goon she was hanging out with, I'm guessing she's the latter.

"No," I say. "Nothing like that. I just saw her at the airport."

"When?"

"Right before she got on the plane."

Julia starts crying. She doesn't even cover her face. "God I wish she hadn't gotten on that plane. I wish she hadn't!" The sight of all that grief pains me.

I put my hand on her shoulder. "Yeah, well, maybe she…" Her stomach and her shoulders convulse, but she's not making any noise. I'm worried she's going to collapse. "Take a seat," I say as I pull a chair from the wall by her mother. The old woman is dozing, her face deeply lined from years of drink.

Julia shakes her head. "I don't want to sit." She wipes the tears from her cheeks and says, "What were you going to say?"

"Was I—I don't know."

"You said maybe she... Maybe she what?"

"Oh. I don't know where I was going with that. You two were pretty close, huh?"

"We *were*. Not as much the last few months, but, yeah. I looked up to her. You said you saw her twice."

"Yeah." I'm starting to feel hot in this suit.

"When was the second time?"

"Right before she got on the plane."

"That was the first time." She looks confused.

"Yeah, well... I guess I saw her twice before she got on."

She gives me a funny look. "What did she say to you?" She's watching me closely. Too closely, like she's looking for clues.

"Nothing."

Still that funny look. "Did you say anything to her?"

"No. Listen, who does she talk to, do you know? I mean, when she's in trouble?"

She's still staring at me, like she's trying to figure me out.

"I mean, does she have any friends you know of? Outside of DC? Anyone in other states?"

"Which states?" she asks. "And why do you keep talking about her in the present tense?"

"Do I? I guess it's just hard to imagine she's really gone."

"You only saw her once."

"Twice."

"And you never spoke a word to each other." Her eyes narrow with suspicion, and then she says angrily, "Who are you?"

"I told you, I'm an investigator."

"What are you investigating?"

"Your sister."

"I thought it was the plane crash."

"Yeah, well..." Fuck! I don't know how to get out of this one. If that prick Lomax hadn't made me lose my head, I wouldn't have fucked this up. And if she didn't keep looking at me like that, with those earnest, probing eyes…

"OK," Julia says in a short, angry tone, "you're violent, and you're lying, and—are you like a pimp or something? Did Anna owe you money?"

"If I was a pimp, do you think that cop would have stood for me roughing him up like that?"

"If you were on the right side of the law, would you be pushing cops around? In church?"

"Justice," I say. "I'm on the right side of justice. Justice and the law are not the same thing. They're on the same road, just not always in the same lane." I make a slaloming motion with my hand to illustrate.

She gives me a baffled look and shakes her head and says, "God you're weird."

"I just want to find out who Anna might go to when she's in trouble."

"When she *was* in trouble," Julia corrects. "The last few months, she was always in trouble. She would talk to the other girls. Not that they could help. But they could listen."

"What other girls?"

She hesitates for a second, then says, "Working girls."

"You know their names?"

"They all have fake names. Cat. Crystal. Misty. You know, like porn names."

"Any of them from Buffalo?"

"Buffalo?" she says, bewildered.

"How about Texas?"

"How would I know?"

"Sorry," I say.

I'm just fishing now, and I'm starting to feel bad about harassing this woman. This is the wrong time and the wrong place for this kind of questioning. I stare down at her feet for a moment, telling myself it's time to go.

When I look up again, to apologize for harassing her, to excuse myself and take my leave, I see she's thinking. Then she says slowly, thoughtfully, "Crystal had an accent."

"Huh?"

"I mean, she was definitely from the South. It *could* be Texas. I never met her, but I talked to her once on the phone."

"You know where I might find her?"

"In a graveyard somewhere."

"What do you mean?"

"What do you think I mean? Why do people go to graveyards?"

"When did she die?" I ask.

"Three weeks ago. That was the last I talked to Anna. She was upset about it."

"They worked together in DC?"

"I think so."

"But you don't know her real name?"

"Jesus, I don't fucking know!"

"All right," I say. "I didn't mean to upset you. I'm sorry. You know I really did... I really honestly did come down here to express my condolences."

"That's kind of you." Her tone is cooler now, a little distant. She's done talking to me.

I give her my card and say, "I'm sorry to grill you like this. I'm just... I'm trying to look out for your sister."

"But Anna's dead," she says. And boy, she gives me a look that goes right through me.

"I'm sorry," I say as I turn to go.

She grabs me by the arm and turns me back toward her, and she looks me right in the eye and says again, in this quiet, fierce, powerful way, "Anna's dead. Say it." And she just keeps staring, right down to the bottom of my soul. There's something about a person who's thoroughly honest, who's straight and true all the way to the core. A person like Ed, and maybe Julia. When they look into you like that, you cannot lie to them.

I don't say a word, but I know my eyes give it away. The look on her face tells me so.

And then she lets me go. She doesn't get hysterical. She doesn't start digging for information. She doesn't ask for anything. She just lets me go.

On the drive out of town, from the middle of Staunton to Interstate 81, I see their faces side by side: healthy Julia in her grief and wounded Anna in her fear. I think about the two of them separated, isolated, and all the wrongs that can't be undone. And maybe, just maybe this one that can.

As I accelerate down the on-ramp to the highway, Julia calls and says, "Butterfly Talent Management. That's what you wanted to know, right? It's in DC. She was Cat. Her friend was Crystal. That's all I know."

11

OCTOBER 3

While I was at the funeral, the news channels picked up on the connection between the schizophrenic passenger Owen Briscoe and the white separatist Delmont Suggs, who had driven him from northern Idaho to the airport in Spokane. Suggs had served early on in the Iraq war. He had special-ops training, carried out a number of dangerous missions, and was wounded twice.

Things started to go sour toward the end of his second tour of duty. Soldiers who served with Suggs said he had become bitter toward his commanders and the US government. They described him as combative and paranoid. Most of his army buddies attributed the changes to the stress of war, several concussions he had suffered, and a falling out with his wife back home. His friends started avoiding him, and he became increasingly isolated.

Suggs was caught trying to ship weapons back to the US that the army had seized from local fighters in Iraq. According to Fox News, the "weapons" were just disassembled parts from a pair of semi-automatic handguns. A number of soldiers had sent home similar souvenirs, often piece by piece, to be reassembled later. The practice wasn't all that uncommon. Suggs just happened to get caught. He was nearing the end of his enlistment, and managed to depart with a censure and an honorable discharge.

CBS reported that Suggs was involved in an operation in which some C4 explosive went missing. The reporter speculated that Suggs may have held on to it somehow.

Then late last night, another story broke. A couple of ATF agents caught up with Suggs unexpectedly, on a road near Kellogg, Idaho. He was in a pickup truck with another man.

Suggs and his friend opened fire on the ATF agents, wounding one of them before escaping into the wilderness.

An ATF spokesman said, "Obviously, if we had known we were going to run into him, we would not have come in with just two agents. Suggs has been on our radar for months. We know he's dangerous."

When Ed called me to check in this morning, he said, "This is exactly what we were worried about, the news announcing to the world that we were after this guy. We knew they were on to Suggs because they started asking the Bureau and ATF about him. I get that they have their mission to inform, but when people's lives are at stake, you need to keep a lid on it. Just for one day. We asked them to keep quiet on this, and they wouldn't. Sometimes I wish these journalists would shut the hell up." I could just see Ed shaking his head.

"He had to know they were coming," I said. "If he's as paranoid as the news makes him out to be, he'd know the Feds would want to talk to him after a plane blew up with his friend on board."

"Maybe so," Ed said. "But the press doesn't need to fan the flames of a paranoid mind, or the hatred of a hater. That's just irresponsible."

Then he added, "Hey, the reason I'm calling is I want you to talk to the guys in the Bureau. Lomax and Rollins. Just to meet them, so you know who you're passing information to."

"What's the point?" I said. "All the action's in California and Idaho. We haven't uncovered anything yet. Anyway, I already met Lomax."

"Well, I talked to Rollins yesterday," Ed said. "There's a coffee shop on Pennsylvania Avenue near the Hoover Building. Ten o'clock, you're going to say hello. It's always good to know who you're working with."

So that's what I'm doing in this place right now. Waiting for the two of them to show up.

At two minutes to ten, Lomax comes through the glass doors with an older guy. Lomax looks like he had a rough night. Maybe a late date, or one too many beers. He's got dark, puffy circles under his eyes, and he's moving a little slow. The guy next to him looks to be in his midfifties. He's a few inches shorter than Lomax. Maybe five foot ten, thin, with a dark red moustache and a ring of reddish-brown hair around his shiny bald pate. He has the indifferent expression of a man who's just going through the motions, and his rumpled brown suit looks like it hasn't been pressed in a while. It hangs off him like a hand-me-down from an older brother. I wonder if he lost a lot of weight recently, if he'd once had enough meat on him to fill out those clothes.

Lomax sees me, and I stand as they approach the table.

"Freddy Ferguson," he says. "Mitch Rollins."

Rollins and I shake hands, and he gives me a quick once-over. Checks out my shoes, the ring finger on my left hand, my shirt, my hair, my eyes. He takes it all in quickly, and I can see the thoughts run through his dark brown eyes as he makes his detective's notes.

"You work with Ed," he says. "Ed's a good guy."

Lomax asks what I want. "A large coffee, black." Rollins wants a quadruple latte. Lomax goes to the counter to place the order while Rollins and I sit.

"He's going stir-crazy behind that desk," Rollins says. "He likes to be out in the field."

"I understand that," I say. "I'm the same way."

"You get a high-profile case like this, and it's all hands on deck." Rollins taps his fingers absently on the table as he talks. His eyes wander from person to person, and I get the feeling he's not all that interested in talking to me. "They throw every spare body into the investigation. There's a lot of wasted effort. A lot of duplicated work. After a while, things settle down. We can do our jobs without all the media pressure. You used to box, huh?"

"I did, for a while. Are you a fan?"

He pulls his cell phone from his pocket, but he doesn't look at it. He flips it slowly in his hand as he watches a woman walk by. "I was back in the eighties and nineties," he says. "I stopped watching after Chavez went downhill."

Everything in his manner shows a lack of urgency that I'm not used to seeing at this level of law enforcement, a disengagement that tells me he's burnt out.

"So what sports do you keep up with now?" I ask. Lomax is over at the counter, sipping coffee and chatting up the barista. She's a young, dark-haired woman. Maybe twenty-five. She's making eyes at him while she fills the steel pitcher with milk. That must be for Rollins's latte.

"Baseball's about my speed," he says with a laugh. "You know, nothing happens for twenty minutes, then there's a burst of excitement, then it all calms down again. You can tune out for half the game without missing a thing."

Lomax returns with the coffee. Though he seems more alert than when he first walked in, he has none of that vibrating energy I saw yesterday. I wonder how many cups it takes him to rev up. Before he takes his seat, he gives me a little slap on the shoulder and says, "We doing OK today? No violent outbursts?" His whole face lights up when he smiles.

"No," I say. "Sorry about yesterday. Sometimes I lose my cool."

"We all do," he says. "You been following this guy Suggs?" Lomax takes two big gulps of his coffee like it's a cold beer.

"Just what I've heard in the news."

"Fucking nut job," Lomax says. "The whole reason I went into this line of work was to go after guys like him. Asshole." The coffee seems to be kicking in. His energy is picking up. He turns to Rollins and says, "Get me off of desk duty, Mitch. Put me out in the field where I can make a difference."

"It's not up to me," Rollins says. He doesn't look at Lomax when he talks. Just stares out the window at the passers-by. "You won't be stuck at your desk forever. It's just timing. Our last investigation wrapped up early, and they don't have our next gig lined up yet. So we got sucked into this bombing mess."

"What did you wrap up?" I ask.

Lomax shakes his head. "Corruption case. Bunch of bullshit. You get a few disgruntled people in an organization making allegations about their coworkers, it's all sour grapes, and then the Bureau gets called in to follow up on it. It's like this whole thing with the passenger list. We know there's nothing there, but we have to look into it anyway, so we can write up the report that says we did our job, turned over all the stones and found no evidence."

With his energy and his athletic build, I can see why Lomax would get antsy behind a desk. It's a waste of his talents. The guy's got the kind of charisma that inspires confidence, and that goes a long way when you're working with people face-to-face.

"Yeah," I say. "You seem like the type who'd rather be in the middle of the action."

"You read that right," Lomax says. "You know what my take on you was? First impression?"

"What?"

"That you're the type who could go either way."

"What do you mean?" I say. "Like just as happy at a desk as in the field?"

"No. I mean like, you could be on either side of the law."

He waits for me to respond, but I'm not sure what to say. I wonder if he got a hold of the same police report Ed saw. It makes sense he'd want to look into me after yesterday.

"Am I wrong?" he says, chiding me with that big white smile. His teeth are perfectly straight, like a toothpaste commercial.

"No. You're not wrong," I say. "I've *been* on both sides. This is act two for me. Act one is what prevented me from ever getting a job like yours."

He nods and says, "You want to cut to the chase?"

"What do you mean?"

"I mean, talk about why we're here. You have any info you want us to dig into? That's what this meeting's supposed to be about, right?"

Lomax is getting to the bottom of his coffee, and his knee is starting to bounce again. Rollins, slouching in his rumpled suit, stares blankly out the window.

Do I have anything I want them to dig into?

The face of Anna Brook flashes in my mind. Not the stoic face from the security line, or the determined face of the woman on her way to the Chicago gate, but the terrified face that looked over her shoulder as she fled onto the gangway. All of a sudden that feeling is back. The sinking, churning feeling in my gut that I felt as a premonition when I first saw her.

Sometimes I can't make myself talk, even when I know it's the right thing to do. It always made Miriam angry. But then, she made me angry too.

"No," I say. "I got nothing."

"Well, I don't either," Lomax says. "So instead of wasting our time…" He stands and drops his business card onto the table. "Just give me a yell if you find something. You ready, Mitch?"

Rollins gets up slowly and shakes my hand again. "Nice to meet you, Freddy."

He doesn't leave a card.

The trip over here from my apartment, plus the twenty minutes we just wasted, plus the trip back to the office— that'll add up to one nice round hour on the bill we send to the airline. It's a line item on a corporate invoice, and an hour of my life that I won't get back. If I tack on an extra twenty bucks for a cab ride up to Second District Police headquarters on Idaho Avenue, will anyone care? The name

Julia Brook gave me, Butterfly Talent Management, is in their territory.

12

Butterfly Talent Management is Kim Hahn's latest DC venture. Before that she ran an outfit called Angels by the Hour, which, according to her tax returns, was in the business of "party equipment rentals." She has a reputation as a fortress of secrecy. According to my friend up at Second District, no one can get information out of her.

She lives on P Street, west of Wisconsin Avenue, near the university. Her neighbors know her from the public hearings of the zoning commission, where she's the voice of preservation for historic Georgetown. No one can build an addition to their house or remodel their storefront without having to answer some pointed questions from her. Outside of the zoning commission meetings, she doesn't talk. Period. The DC cops have an ongoing bet to see who will be the first to get more than two sentences out of her. Whenever they come across a suspect who won't talk even after hours of interrogation, they say they "got Hahned."

She has an office above a coffee shop on N Street. My friend at Second District told me she usually stops in there around four p.m. to pick up an ice coffee before she heads upstairs. So I sit at a table by the barista, nursing a coffee and looking through recent death records on my laptop while I wait for her to show.

At about ten of four, she walks in. She's short, maybe five foot four, and plump, with a big exaggerated bust. She's wearing a black designer skirt suit—I don't know what label—but well cut, elegant, and expensive. She has a black leather purse with a gold snap that matches the suit. The jacket dips down to show her cleavage, centered perfectly between the lapels. If she's wearing a blouse under there, I can't see it. Her black hair is tied up in a bun on top of her head. Her sparse eyebrows are accentuated with pencil, drawn upward above the outsides of her eyes, giving her a look of severity, like she's about to get angry. She has gold hoops in her ears, gold rings on her fingers, a gold watch on one wrist, and a gold bracelet on the other. I can't tell how old she is. Undo the facelift and she's at least fifty. Maybe fifty-five. Boobs like that on a woman her age should be down around her waist.

She picks up an ice coffee, and on her way out the door, she shoots me a sideways glance. She seems to know who to watch out for.

I follow her outside, and she turns immediately to the next door on the sidewalk and pulls a set of keys from her purse.

"Ms. Hahn," I say. "You mind if I ask a few questions?"

She doesn't respond or look at me, just turns the key in the lock and opens the door and goes up the wooden staircase. She doesn't try to shut me out, so I follow her in.

At the top of the stairs, she unlocks the deadbolt and goes into an office. Again, she leaves the door open, and I follow her in.

The place is sparse but elegant: a glass desk with a swivel lamp and a phone, a black swivel office chair, a black leather sofa. A simple rug covers most of the wood floor, off-white with a thick black border. She can't have many people in here or that rug would be dirtier. The walls are decorated with ancient Chinese prints framed in black—spare, ink-drawn scenes of misty mountains and stylized trees. A row of windows looks over the street, and in the far corner, bamboo grows from a round black iron pot.

She sets her ice coffee and her purse on the desk, takes a seat in the swivel chair, and picks up the phone.

"Ms. Hahn?" I say.

She dials and waits.

"I want to ask you about a girl."

She says into the phone, "There's someone here who needs to be removed." Her voice, accented in Korean, is scratchy and severe, like those upward-slanting eyebrows. She hangs up the desk phone, pulls a cell phone from her purse, and thumbs through it while she sips her coffee through the straw.

"Can you tell me about Crystal?"

"Crystal is delicate," she says absently. "Breaks easily." She doesn't look up from her phone.

"You know her real name?"

"You're talking about a person?" she asks. "Or a wine glass?"

"I'm talking about a person. Crystal. She used to work here. Now she's dead."

"Mmm. Not my fault." She sips her coffee.

"I didn't say it was. What about Cat? She also worked for you."

"Cat will scratch you if you get too close," she says.

"Wait, are we talking about a person?"

"Maybe cat broke crystal," she says. "Cats on shelves, always swatting things off." She's still scrolling through messages on her phone.

I take a long breath and let it out slowly, trying not to lose my patience. "Are you interested in helping their families?"

"What help is there for the dead?" she asks indifferently as she lays the phone face-down on the desk.

"So you *do* know them?"

"Did I say that?" Her eyes are a soft, deep brown, but they show an immovable stubbornness and iron resolve.

"Well, you know they're dead," I say.

"*You* said they were dead."

"I said Crystal was dead."

"Mmm. Crystal breaks easy." She picks up her coffee and takes another sip.

"Jesus Christ." I said that under my breath. This woman would try anyone's patience. "OK, look, I'm going to show you some photos." I open up my laptop and the screen flicks on and then right back off. I hit the power button, and the screen lights up again with a message saying I'm running on reserve battery power. OK, fine. Just keep working for a few more minutes.

I click an image in the Gate 76 folder. "Can you tell me if you know any of these people?"

I turn the screen toward her so she's looking at the monitor and I'm behind it watching her face.

The first image is a picture of Anna from the security camera at the airport. I cropped it so it's just her. You can't see the guy holding her arm. This gets no reaction.

"You know her?" I ask.

She doesn't respond. So far, I'm getting Hahned.

I hit the right arrow key, and the next photo slides onto the screen. It's the tall guy, her escort in the security line. I watch her face for a long time, but again, no reaction. "What about him?" I ask. "You seen him before?"

Nothing.

I hit the arrow key, slide to the next photo. Another one of Anna. No reaction.

I hear heavy boots clomping up the stairs, and the narrow wooden steps creak beneath the weight. I assume it's a man. A big, heavy one.

I don't have any more photos related to the investigation—none for her, anyway—but at this point I just want to see if I can get any reaction out of her at all.

I keep hitting the right arrow, every two seconds. Click, click, click, staring at her eyes the whole time. She doesn't react to any of it. I almost want to take her pulse to see if she's still alive.

Click, click, click, a little faster now. She's actually focusing on the images as they slide in. I can see that. But I don't even know what I'm showing her at this point. The passenger manifest, maybe. Or the seating chart. Stills I pulled out of the funeral video, or photos from news articles about the crash.

The guy reaches the top of the steps, lets out a sigh, and says a tired "Goddamn!" Both the sigh and the voice sound familiar.

I keep going through the photos. Click, click, click and then—what was that? Her pupils just flickered. Dilated for a split second, like fear, then contracted, like hatred. The rest of her face shows nothing.

A fat cop pushes the door open. Lester Briggs. I know the guy. He's got his club in his hand, and when his eyes meet mine, he shakes his head and says, "You know you can't be up in here. Come on, let's take it outside."

"Hey, Les."

"Close it up," he says firmly, as he pushes the lid of the laptop down, "and take it outside."

I stand up, and he pushes the computer toward me with the tip of his club. On the way out, Hahn says, "You want something, bring a warrant."

When we get onto the street, Briggs says, "What're you looking for, Ferguson?"

"Information about a girl who used to work for her."

He shakes his head. "Ain't gonna happen, my friend. She don't talk to nobody. Which girl you asking about?"

"Crystal."

"Hmm. She probably get a new Crystal about twice a year. What's she look like?"

"I don't know."

He laughs. "Come on, man, you looking for someone and you don't know her real name or what she look like?"

"She died about three weeks ago."

"Here? In DC?"

"I don't think so. I checked the death records. Nothing matched." Three young women died in DC around the time of Crystal's death. An accident victim and a drug-resistant staph infection, but they both had steady jobs. The third had been an invalid for several years. There may be more. Sometimes the records take a while to appear.

"You check Maryland? Virginia?"

"We're still working on that."

"Stay away from Hahn," says Briggs, giving me a couple of hard taps on the chest with the handle of his club to show he means it. "You talk to her girls, keep it low-key. Don't get nobody alarmed, else my job start getting harder."

I catch a cab back to the office, and a new idea hits me. There were four names on that Chicago flight that I couldn't match to anyone. What if Anna Brook was traveling under the name of her dead friend? That would be pretty easy, wouldn't it? Julia said Crystal died about three weeks ago.

Time to check the death records for those last four passengers. The only problem is, they could have died anywhere.

Heading back to the office, I open my laptop in the back of the cab to get a look at the image that set Kim Hahn off. The screen flicks on for a second, then goes right back off. I try again, and the same thing happens. The battery is too low.

In a few minutes, I'm back at the office. As soon as I walk in, I say, "Leon, we need to look up some deaths."

Bethany glances up from her monitor for a second and makes eye contact. "Hey Freddy."

"You got a name?" Leon asks.

"Melissa Edwards," I say. "Buffalo, New York." The first of those four Chicago passengers.

I put my laptop on my desk and attach the power cable while Leon types.

"Where've you been?" Bethany asks.

"Georgetown. I miss anything?"

"No," she says. "Just the news."

"What news?"

"The Feds are trying to track down that guy in Idaho. He's got a compound somewhere in the mountains, but they don't know where."

"Melissa Edwards," Leon says. "Died two years ago in Buffalo. Seventy-eight years old."

"That's not her," I say. "I'm looking for someone who died about three weeks ago. How about Betsey Renfro, Rocky Mount, North Carolina?"

Leon types in the name and shakes his head. "If she's dead, there ain't no record of it."

"All right," I say. "Tanya DuPree, Oakland, California."

"Who are these people?" Bethany asks.

"Passengers."

"Not from the Hawaii flight," she says.

"No," I say. She waits for me to go on, but I leave it at that.

Leon says, "Last Tanya DuPree to die was in New Orleans, eight months ago."

"All right. Katie Green, Dallas, Texas."

He types in the name and after half a minute, he says, "Katie Green passed away unexpectedly on September 9th in Dallas. Memorial services will be held... Nevermind. You missed it by a couple weeks."

"Let me see that." I look over his shoulder at the monitor. The photo shows a beautiful young woman with brown hair, brown eyes, and a big white smile. She's got a little too much blush on her cheeks, and her eyes show a lack of confidence. They don't quite live up to the smile. I wonder if Katie Green could be our Crystal. Maybe Kim Hahn really was giving me answers, in her coded way. This girl does look a little fragile. She looks like the kind who could be nudged into taking a wrong turn in life. And the date of her death matches up exactly.

OK. So Anna Brook buys a ticket under her dead friend's name. Her friend from Dallas. She goes through Chicago and then on to Austin. But why Austin?

The death notice lists the address of the church where the funeral was held, and the names of the parents and the two brothers who survived her. Her parents live near Dallas, in a place called Heath.

Bethany is looking at me. "What does that mean, Freddy?"

"It means I'm taking a trip to Dallas."

When a case involves the death of a child, it's best to talk to the parents in person.

"Are you going to let us in on this?" she asks.

"I'll let you know if anything comes of it."

Bethany's not satisfied with that answer. I can tell by the way she's watching me, this makes her uneasy. Finally, she says, "OK, I don't know what you're following here, but if you think you're on to something, turn it over to the FBI, OK? Those were Ed's instructions, and that's what the airline is paying us to do. We're not equipped to dig deep on a case as big as this one. We're just looking for leads, and that's it."

"Yeah, well... I think this is a different matter."

"Hey Freddy," Leon says. He's got his back to us, staring at his monitor. "Name Charles Johnston ring a bell?"

"No," I say. "Who's he?"

"A woman from the airline called a while ago. Said you asked who paid for a ticket on that Hawaii flight." He picks up a slip of paper and says, "Charles Johnston from Schaumberg, Illinois, with a Visa card ending in two three eight one. Paid for seat thirty-two B. Anna Brook." Leon turns and looks at me. "What's that about?"

"Look up Charles Johnston, will you?"

I go back to my desk to find a flight to Dallas. As soon as I'm in my chair, Leon says, "Charles Johnston of Schaumberg, Illinois. Independent financial consultant."

"What's he look like?"

"I don't know," Leon says. "No photo. But there's a phone number."

"Give him a call," I say.

As I reach to open the laptop, I see Bethany standing in front of me. She puts her hand lightly on top of the computer, so I can't open it, and she says, "Let this go, Freddy. You don't need to go to Dallas or anywhere else. Whatever info you have, pass it to the Feds, OK?"

She stares at me for a second with those lashless eyes. Why doesn't she wear mascara?

"Come on, Freddy," she says. "Two more days and we'll be through everyone on the list. Then we go back to our normal jobs, where we can actually make a difference."

I sit back in my chair and think it through. What's my interest here? I mean, honestly. It's not the airline, or even the victims. There's nothing we can do for them. It's me wanting to make sure that woman is OK. I don't know what kind of trouble she's in, but Bethany's right. Federal law enforcement has the resources to help her out. And for all I know, she may have had something to do with that plane going down. Why did she get off at the last minute? And why did she look so scared when she saw I was watching her? Was she guilty?

No. I can't see it. She was a call girl. She had no motive to blow up a plane, and from the looks of her, she wasn't in any state to carry out a bombing. She also didn't check a bag. The bomb was in the cargo hold with the checked luggage. Someone else put it there.

But she's in trouble, and the Feds will certainly be interested to know that one person from the passenger list never got on the plane. That's enough right there to get them to talk to her. Why am I holding on to this like it's my own? Bethany's right. She needs the best help she can get.

I look up to see her eyes are still on me.

"All right," I say. "You're right."

She smiles as she walks away. A rare victory over the notoriously stubborn Freddy Ferguson. I think I just made her day.

I take Lomax's card from my pocket and dial his number.

Leon says, "Hey Freddy—no answer for Charles Johnston. No voicemail either."

"Pull his credit reports," I say.

I open my laptop, and now that it's plugged in, the screen comes to life.

On the fourth ring, as I'm typing my password into the computer, Lomax picks up and says, "Errol Lomax." He sniffles like he has a cold.

And then I see the image on the computer monitor—the one that made Kim Hahn's pupils flicker with fear and hatred. It's a photo I took just yesterday at the funeral in Staunton, zoomed and cropped to show a single face. Errol Lomax, with his charming, I-know-how-great-I-am smile and his clear blue eyes, looking downward, tiger-like, at the cowed young woman who's been cropped out of the frame. The laser focus of his eyes shows a flavor of delight I don't like to think about.

"Hello," says Lomax. "Hello?"

I hang up.

13

OCTOBER 4

I booked a flight to Dallas as soon as I ended that call yesterday. And then I did a little digging into Errol Lomax's background.

He grew up in a good neighborhood in San Diego where he went through the public school system. He played football and baseball in high school. In college he played baseball and majored in criminal justice.

He lives in a condo off East West Highway, in Silver Spring, Maryland. That's eight Metro stops from Gallery Place. From there, he can walk three and a half blocks to the FBI building. At least, that's what I'm gambling on, on this sunny, cool October morning. My plane from National takes off at ten-thirty, so I'm willing to burn an hour of my morning trying to get another look at the man who set me off at the funeral the other day. I'm sitting in the back of a cab, in front a place called the ChopHouse on 7th Street Northwest. Around eight-fifteen, he comes strolling down the sidewalk from the Metro station toward the Hoover Building.

He wears a suit, but he doesn't wear it like the other FBI guys. They look professional. He looks like he's going to pick up his date. A cop usually has his suit cut to leave room for his gun. Lomax wears a tapered athletic cut. You can see the bulge of the holster above his left hip.

The guy looks like a Ken doll with muscles: broad in the shoulders and narrow at the waist, with the kind of square jaw and thick neck you learn to look out for in boxing. That usually tells you the guy can take a punch.

He's a half block away, coming right toward me, and I'm trying to see if I can spot again whatever it was that set me off the first time. I thought maybe he just hit a sensitive spot, triggered something that's easy to trigger in me. But he triggered something in Kim Hahn too, and she's not an easy one to move. And what the hell was he doing at Anna Brook's funeral in the first place? The FBI isn't usually in the business of offering condolences.

A car behind us lays on the horn, and the cabbie turns and says over the seat, "I can't sit here. This is a bus lane."

"One more minute," I say. "Then we head to the airport."

Lomax has a kind of jittery air about him, like he's over-caffeinated. He gives every young woman on the street a full up and down look. If he catches their eye, they get the smile. That million-dollar movie-star smile that he can turn on and off at will.

The guy is thirty-two years old and unmarried, so I cut him some slack about the women. Of course he's looking. He could be a little more discreet about it, but maybe he doesn't have to be. Maybe he acts like an arrogant jerk on purpose, trying to spot the woman who isn't immediately turned off by it. That's the one he can jerk around. The doormat he can wipe his feet on.

As he approaches, he's got his eyes on something coming the other way. I turn to look. A young woman, twenty-five or so, in a skirt suit. I watch her eyes, focused straight ahead. They lock on to something for a second. She smiles, then looks away with some effort. I look back at Lomax just as he's turning off his smile. That must be what she reacted to. He stops beside the cab, three feet away, and wipes his nose as he watches her pass. He gives her a quick scan up and down, taking in her whole backside. He's got a stain on his lapel, and one on the cuff of his jacket. When he turns again to continue on his way, I catch a glimpse of his eyes. They're darker than I remember. His pupils are huge black holes rimmed with a thin ring of baby blue. The dark rings below them suggest he didn't get much sleep.

Then it hits me. It's not coffee that's got him wired.

Another horn blares behind us. This time, it's a bus.

"I gotta move," the cabbie says.

"All right," I say. "Let's go."

* * *

Before I get on the plane, I put in a call to Ed.

"How's it going out there?" I ask.

"It's a madhouse," he says. "No one's sleeping. The airline's lawyers want to debrief me every hour, but it takes all day to pry information out of my contacts."

"How are they doing on Obasanjo?"

"They're still grilling him, but if they're getting anything, I'm not hearing about it."

"They got him hooked in with any accomplices?"

"Like I said, I'm not hearing anything. What about your end? Anyone on the passenger list look interesting?"

"Maybe," I say. "I'm taking a trip down to Texas."

"What for?"

"Oh, you know. Just trying to keep the B team busy. Hey, what did you say this guy Lomax was working on?"

"Passenger backgrounds. Same as you."

"No, before that."

"Oh. A corruption case with Mitch Rollins."

"You said you didn't know Lomax when you were at the Bureau?"

"No," says Ed. "But I think the Bureau's got him on their shit list."

"How do you figure that?"

"When an agent gets pulled from the field and planted at his desk running background checks, he's on the shit list."

"Rollins can't stick up for him?"

"Rollins is an old-timer. He was burnt out even when I was there. They're trying to ease him out."

"How do you know?" I ask.

"When you don't take the hint that it's time to retire, the Bureau puts you on a nowhere case with some junior guy who no one else wants to work with."

"You mean like digging into a passenger list in DC when the real investigation is in California and Idaho?"

"Like that, yeah. Or listening to cops rat on cops down in Texas. Rollins is just passing time and collecting a check. He'd be happy chasing overdue library books, as long as he didn't have to get off his ass too much."

My flight is boarding.

"Hey, Ed, I gotta go but... You said the Bureau looked into Anna Brook and wrote her off."

"Who?"

"Anna Brook. A passenger on the Hawaii flight. Remember the blonde? I sent you her photo."

Ed lets out a little sigh and says, "The blonde? Oh, yeah. Sorry, Freddy. With all the chaos out here, it's hard to keep track. Yeah, the blonde isn't a suspect. She didn't even check a bag."

"Any idea who wrote her off?"

"The Bureau."

"No, I mean who? Who in the Bureau cleared her?"

"No idea," he says.

14

The flight to Dallas was smooth and quiet. When I walk into the terminal at DFW, CNN is running a story about Delmont Suggs.

"Suggs drove passenger Owen Briscoe from Northern Idaho to the airport in Spokane. Security footage from the drop-off area outside the terminal shows Briscoe carrying a red suitcase, which was pulled nearly intact from Monterey Bay late last night.

"TSA officials say baggage scans from Spokane show that nothing resembling a bomb or an ammunition box came through the airport on the day Briscoe boarded. That doesn't mean Suggs is off the hook though. He's now wanted for killing a federal law enforcement agent. ATF agents believe he's holed up in a compound thirty miles southwest of Kellogg, Idaho."

The reporter goes on for a while about Suggs's radical political views and his military training, and when he wraps up, the anchorwoman says the network will be running an in-depth report called "Who is Delmont Suggs" later in the day. This is like the old days of network television, where a bit character in a successful show got his own spin-off series. If Suggs is in the clear on the bombing though, that means the spotlight is back on Obasanjo. And the airline can't be too happy about that.

I walk past the newsstands and restaurants, following the signs toward ground transportation. As I near the exits, I pass another monitor. CNN has turned its attention back to the political races. The news anchor, a heavily made-up woman with light brown hair, says the recent airline bombing and all the talk of terrorism have tilted the balance toward the Republicans in a number of states. "The Texas race, however, is still too close to call."

The gigantic Republican incumbent, Jefferson "Jumbo" Throckmorton, former Chief of the Texas Highway Patrol and Director of the Department of Public Safety, is running on a law-and-order platform. CNN shows him pounding the podium beneath the glaring sun in front of a crowd here in Dallas. A few seconds later, his opponent, Patty Rice, with her short, light-brown hair and wire-rimmed glasses, looks more calm and even-tempered in front of an indoor Houston audience. According to the subtitles, she's promising benefits and better wages to the same people Throckmorton is threatening to lock up or deport. The fact that a Democrat even has a chance in Texas tells me something's wrong with the economy down here.

I'm trying to get to the shuttle buses that go out to the rental lots, but there's some commotion up ahead, and a huge knot of people just inside the doors. The crowd is pushing this way, with cops around the edges, and lights and video cameras in the middle. In the center of the cameras a cowboy hat sticks up high above the throng, and there's the man himself: Jumbo Throckmorton. He's got to be six foot eight and three hundred pounds.

He seems to be pushing the whole crowd back by himself. He shakes hands with people while his security detail tries to keep him moving along. The cops in front of him look anxious as they scan the faces and try to clear the way forward. Throckmorton bends his head down to hear the words of an old woman whose hand he seems to be shaking. Then he throws his head back and lets out a booming laugh and says, "Well you tell him he can come say that to my face!"

I'm in the thick of it now, trying to push through to the exit, while everyone else is going the other way. In a second, he's right in front of me. I put out my hand instinctively to greet him. It's not even a conscious action. It just happens. He's got that kind of power. He takes my hand in a crushing grip and shakes it so hard I feel the strain in my elbow and shoulder. How does he greet women? He can't go manhandling them like this.

He mops the glistening sweat from his broad red face, and as he passes, a cop behind him reaches up to his shoulder and says, "Keep it moving, guv. El Paso's waiting." Throckmorton turns, and the smile he had put on for the voters disappears. "We *are* moving," he says. He has a hardness in his look that politicians don't show to the cameras. It's the kind of hardness a cop develops over the years to deal with the kinds of people cops have to deal with. Throckmorton was in law enforcement after all, and worked his way up to the top of the ladder before becoming governor.

The crowd pushes farther into the building, and in a few seconds, I'm past it. I go through the exit, into the warm Texas air, and look for the car rental shuttle.

On the bus, I check my phone. Leon texted to say there's something strange about Charles Johnston's credit reports. Johnston, who paid for Anna Brook's ticket to Hawaii. And there's a text from Bethany saying she has inquiries out to a number of libraries. I don't know what that's about. I write back to say I'll check in with them later.

I pick up a rental, a white Chevy Malibu, and plug the Green family address into the GPS. In a few minutes, I'm heading east on 635, which looks like Dallas's version of the Capital Beltway. After several miles, I turn northeast onto Route 30. Except for this place being a little flatter, and a lot hotter, this might as well be Northern Virginia, or the outside of any other city in the US. It's Exxon stations and Subway restaurants, McDonald's and Motel 6. Malls with big box stores and subdivisions behind high walls to keep out the roar of the highway. Seems like this whole country was built from a box of Legos that only had thirty different pieces.

Who decided to put a city here, I will never know. There are no natural features in or around Dallas to warrant a city.

No harbor or river for commerce, no intersection of major trade roads, no great mountain to admire, no magical oasis to provide shelter from the heat. It's a hot, flat city in the middle of a hot, flat plain. The only things that rightly have a home here are mosquitoes and tornadoes.

Route 30 goes across Lake Ray Hubbard, where men in sports boats plow white furrows through the glistening blue-green waters. I take a right past Costco, onto a road with traffic lights, then right again, past the golf club, toward the south end of the lake.

This is a wealthy area. The homes are big, and the one I'm aiming at is one of the biggest. A giant brick colonial with a circular drive that goes around a big marble fountain. The house is fronted by thick white columns, a two-story front porch, and wings on either side that are bigger than most people's entire homes. I park in front, behind a white Mercedes, walk up four steps and ring the bell.

15

Katie's mother, Marjorie Green, answers the door herself. She's wearing a floral muumuu and a sheer black scarf, like she's vacationing in Hawaii and in mourning at the same time. She's in her midfifties, with a streak of grey in her unbrushed black hair and a few extra pounds around her middle. A faint smell of alcohol wafts about her, and she has a slovenly, careless look, like her clothes just blew onto her and the next good wind might blow them right back off.

"You're Mr. Ferguson," she says with the kind of ill-fitting smile you see on someone who's been on pain meds for too long. They don't remember what actual feeling is like, and when they try to put it on, the absent look in the eyes doesn't match the smile that's trying so hard to be genuine.

And speaking of eyes, her mascara is all smeared. It doesn't look like she's been crying, or that she's aware of the mess. Maybe that's just how she put it on. Three days ago.

"It's a pleasure to meet you, ma'am. I wish the circumstances were better."

"Oh, now, don't you apologize," she says. "Come in, come in!"

"Thank you."

"Would you like some iced tea? Let me show you the house. Do you need to hang your coat?"

It's eighty-six degrees out. I'm not wearing a coat, but she doesn't wait for me to respond. She walks back into the house, and I follow.

"Clara, get the man some iced tea."

"Yes, ma'am."

Clara is a light-skinned black woman wearing an apron. She smiles and gives me a little nod before turning and leaving the room.

"John collects globes," says Mrs. Green. She's already on her way into the next room. "Let me show you."

I follow her to the south wing of the house, into a wood-paneled room with heavy green curtains, leather sofas, and a pool table. It's freezing in here. "John collects telescopes," she says. She touches one gently as she passes, and it turns on its swivel mount.

Mrs. Green swishes around her husband's million-dollar man cave in her flowery muumuu and somehow always manages to have her back to me as she talks. John collects guns and pool cues, bourbons, brandies, more guns, and Persian rugs. John is an avid sportsman, she tells me. He killed that buck himself. He can repair gunshot wounds almost as easily as he can inflict them. John is a surgeon at a hospital in Dallas, and very successful. She married an ATM with a prescription pad, and she's damn proud of it.

Clara hands me a tall glass of iced tea as we cross back through the main hall to the north wing. It's so cold in here, I could warm my hands on this icy glass.

The north side of the house seems to be Mrs. Green's realm. There's a television in every room, and they're all tuned to different channels. Some people don't like to be alone with their thoughts.

Did I know David was in medical school? David! The youngest, who the teachers said wouldn't go far. John Junior is a dentist, but there's no shame in that. "You'll be thankful for someone like him next time you get a toothache. Where is Clara with your iced tea?"

I raise the glass to show her. "She already gave it to me."

"Oh," says Mrs. Green. "So she did. Well where's *my* iced tea?"

Just then the clock strikes two, and Clara, on her way into the room, says, "Here it is, ma'am." I get a whiff of it going by. It's not the same kind I'm drinking. I pick up a photo of a beautiful young girl in a blue satin dress.

"That's Katherine at her debut," Mrs. Green says. "Thank you, Clara. And now you want to talk about Katherine? Is that right?"

"If you don't mind."

"Have a seat," she says.

The sofas on this side of the house have floral prints instead of leather. She sits on one couch, I take the other. There's a coffee table between us. She sips her iced tea, then puts it down on a coaster, and puts on another empty smile for me.

"She was a lovely girl, wasn't she?"

"She was," I say as I replace the photo. "I'm sorry for your loss, ma'am."

"I am too," she says, still smiling. "You know, she was pulling her life together."

"Was she?"

"Oh, yes. You should have seen the clothes she wore. Most women don't have that kind of taste, or a husband who can keep them dressed like that. Not that her husband ever did anything for her."

"She was married?"

"Hardly. She took care of herself. She earned every penny."

"What did she do up in DC?"

"Why, she was a model, of course. Got snapped right up by a talent agency the minute she arrived in town. She used to Skype me from hotels all over the place. The Ritz in New York. From Paris even! She'd give me a video tour of the room."

"Did you know a friend of hers named Anna?"

"Oh, she had so many friends." She lifts her glass from the coffee table and takes a sip. "I told John when she dropped out of college, this is just a phase, I told him. And that guy—oh, that loser! Just a phase. I told him she'd come around, and she did. Left him down in Dime Box and made something of herself."

"You ever go up and see her in DC?"

"We were there three months ago. John spoke at a conference. He wasn't the keynote, but the talk was well attended. People stopped him afterwards to say how well he had spoken." She takes a hard swallow of her drink and puts her hand to her chest. "These were top surgeons. The very best. He's very well respected, you know."

"Did you meet any of Crystal's friends while you were up there?"

"Crystal?"

"Sorry, I mean Katie. Katherine."

"Well, yes. She knew congressmen and lobbyists and lawyers. She was very well connected. We went to the top restaurants after the conference. That's where you see people up there. In the restaurants. Would you like another drink?"

"No, thanks. I'm just wondering if she ever talked to you about a friend named Anna."

"Oh, she talked about a lot of people. What did Anna do?" She swirls her drink and puts on an attentive look that comes more from good manners than genuine interest.

"She worked with Katherine," I say.

"Hmm. What did she look like?"

"About five foot seven. Slim build. Blue eyes, fair complexion."

I can see she's thinking. "What color hair?"

"Probably blonde, but she dyed it."

"Oh, that one," she says with distaste.

"You know who I'm talking about?"

"Yes. Anna. She was down here with Katherine a few months ago." She drains off the rest of her iced tea and says, "I didn't care for her. A pretty woman, to be sure, but some of them get into modeling for the wrong reasons, you know. They want a man's attention, and that's all."

"You have any idea where Anna might be?"

"How would I possibly know that?"

"I have a feeling she might be here in Texas."

"Well, we all have feelings, don't we? When my daughter died, I was in shock. To be honest, I thought she was in the clear. A few years ago, I worried about her. She was smoking pot, you know. Marijuana. And she married that loser Seldin. I told myself girls go through their wild phase too, just like boys. There's a reason all those romance novels have guys with tattoos and motorcycles on the covers. At a certain age, they're exciting and attractive. Until you realize they're never going to do anything for you. They'll still be tattooed and motorcycled at fifty, with a beer gut and grey whiskers and a hangover. And some hourly job, if they're lucky. I told her that. Imagine him at fifty, I said. Is that what you want to be stuck with? It took her a couple of years to figure it out, and thank God he didn't ruin her. If he had had any meanness in him, he could have wrecked her for good. But he was just a shiftless drinker who happened to have looks and charm and knew all the right things to say to a wayward, inexperienced girl. Would you like another drink?"

"Sure." I'm not even done with the first one, but she keeps offering, so I'll humor her.

"So would I." She turns toward the doorway where Clara stands, and yells as if she's not in the room, "Clara!"

"Ma'am."

She rattles the ice in her glass and says, "You know."

"Yes, ma'am."

Mrs. Green turns back to me and says, "She always stopped and saw him when she came home."

"Pardon?"

"Katherine. She'd visit him when she came home. She'd take a couple of days and go down there."

"Down where?"

"Austin. He must have given her some kind of comfort. They never officially divorced, you know. He went soft after she left him. Fifteen beers a day would make anyone soft. He never did have any ambition. But I guess she felt she could be herself around him. There couldn't have been anything physical between them. Not if you see the guy now. But some people, I guess, are like a child's blanket. They soothe you because they're familiar and they're tied in your mind to old memories and simpler times."

Clara returns with a tray, puts two iced teas down on the coffee table, and collects the empties. I smell my drink to make sure it's not the same kind the old lush is having.

"You say he lives in Austin?"

"Just outside. Near a town called Dime Box, which from what I hear is just as exciting as it sounds." She takes a sip of her new drink. "Suits him too. Shiftless beer drinker living in a dime box."

"You know if Anna ever met him?"

"I'm sure she did. She went with Katherine to see him after they left here. Do you know he called to see if she had life insurance? Didn't come to the funeral, but he wanted to know if he was going to get any money. They were still technically married. Did I tell you that?"

"You did," I say. "What's his first name?"

"Travis. And there *was* no life insurance. Who would think to take out a policy on a beautiful child of twenty-seven? A model, no less! It's morbid. I'll tell you what there might be though. There might be a lawsuit. What kind of doctor gives a girl that much oxycodone? John's looking into it. John won't stand for malpractice, or even a hint of negligence. Medical errors have real consequences. People trust their doctors. And just when her life was really getting on track…"

It wasn't oxycodone that killed Katie Green. It was heroin cut with fentanyl, injected by her own hand. It's all right there in the coroner's report.

When I get out of that big frigid mansion and hit the highway, I keep the windows down to bring in as much fresh air as I can. Some people's delusions are pitiful, some are cringeworthy, and some are just plain suffocating. When I first walked into that house, I couldn't put my finger on what made it feel so smothering. But it hits me now. The icy air conditioning, the green velvet curtains, and the dark wood paneling—the place reminds me of a funeral home. Poor Katie, in her debutante's dress, with her hopeful smile and uncertain eyes. What chance did she have, being raised by zombies in that icy morgue?

The air rushing in through the windows is warm and thick, the sun beats down through the windshield, baking the seats, and when the big rigs pass by with their deafening whoosh, they suck all the air out of the car.

There are plenty of ways to get to Dime Box. If you're in Dallas with a reliable car, it's a three-hour drive. If you're a drinker with a reliable thirst, it's just a matter of years. Travis Seldin lives on a narrow country road outside of town. It might still be light when I get there.

16

The first ninety minutes of the drive are uneventful. I stop in Waco for gas and a meal, and a quick check-in using the restaurant's Wi-Fi, sipping coffee and running a background check on Travis Seldin while I wait for the waitress to bring a plate of brisket. The TV is on behind me, with the now-familiar voices of the gubernatorial candidates pressing their cases to the voters. Sometimes elections seem like the price we have to pay to get these people to shut up.

One of the other patrons asks the waitress to change the TV to a sports channel. She's fiddling with the remote when she should be bringing my food. A man's voice comes from the television: "Texas Highway Patrol intercepted a vehicle carrying over two million dollars worth of fentanyl this afternoon—" Click. "—a three and a half point underdog going into next week's game against the Steelers."

"That better, hon?" the waitress says.

"That's more like it."

The results of the background check show up about two minutes before my plate of brisket. Think about that the next time you think there's such a thing as privacy in the Internet age.

Travis Seldin has had twenty-one address changes in his thirty-one years. His life has followed a southwestern drift, from rural South Carolina through Georgia and Alabama to Texas. He backtracked a couple of years ago to Mississippi, but that only lasted a few months. He's been married once, seven years ago, to the late Katie Green of Dallas, Texas. Now he's in a house on a country road eight miles west of Dime Box. He owns a 2004 Ford F-150 pickup.

My food finally shows up, and I continue working as I eat.

I have a text from Leon from several hours ago that I still haven't followed up on. Something about Charles Johnston's credit reports. Leon attached them to an email that he must have sent just after I landed in Dallas. And he sent another text a few minutes ago. *Call me!* There's one from Bethany too, with the same words.

I pull up Leon's email and scan the reports. Charles Johnston, from Schaumberg, Illinois, purchaser of Anna Brook's Honolulu ticket, is supposedly thirty-eight years old. He's had four addresses in the past two decades, all in Illinois and Iowa. It takes me a minute to figure out what got Leon all excited.

I call Leon, and as soon as he picks up, he bursts out, "Yo, this shit ain't right!"

"You mean the addresses?" I ask.

"Yeah. They're all the same," he says. "They're *exactly* the same at all three credit bureaus."

That *is* a problem. Usually, one will say 13th St., with the digits "1" and "3" and the abbreviated "St." Another will have "Thirteenth" and "Street" spelled out. One will be in all capitals, and one will have mixed upper case and lower case letters. But for this guy, they all match exactly.

"What do you think that's about?" Leon asks.

"This kind of thing happens every now and then," I say. "When someone gets careless."

"Hey, I'm gonna put Bethany on. She got some info for you."

Bethany says, "Hey Freddy. How's Texas?"

"Hot. What's up?"

"You saw those reports Leon pulled?"

"I saw them."

"Well I put in some calls to libraries in Illinois and Iowa. Schaumberg, Oak Brook, Freeport, and Davenport. All the places Charles Johnston used to live. You know some libraries keep old phone books around?"

"I didn't know that," I say.

"Well, the credit bureaus say Charles Johnston lived in Davenport, Iowa from 1998 to 2001, but the phone book says he didn't. Not at the address they list. In the directories from 2001 to 2004, there's no Charles Johnston listed at the Freeport address in the credit reports. None at the Oak Brook address from 2004 to 2009, and none at the Schaumberg address now."

"All right, Beth." I take the last sip of my coffee and push my empty plate away. "Thanks for the work."

"What does it mean, Freddy?"

"Right now, it means I gotta go. I'll check in later, OK?"

I leave a twenty on the table to cover the meal and tip, and then head out to the car. I'm back on the highway in a couple of minutes with the AC running. The sun is shining, and traffic is light, but I have a lot on my mind.

See, here's the problem. You can make someone up in all the computers in the world, but you can't go back and alter all the paper records from years ago that are spread all over the country. In the pretech world, it was impossible to completely cover your tracks.

So, how does a guy who doesn't exist get a credit card? There are two ways. One, he goes into the Witness Protection Program. The government makes up a whole history for him, including a credit history. If they're careless, they'll submit the same data to all the credit bureaus. Then you get records that match exactly.

And the other way… Well, that's the one that has me worried. I have a bad feeling Anna Brook has every reason to be as scared as she looked. She's not going to come out of hiding. She can't.

I leave the highway in a town called Temple, and pick up a couple of burner phones from Walmart and some cash from an ATM.

17

The final leg of the drive, from Temple to Dime Box, takes about an hour and a half. The candidates for governor are on the radio, and I've already had enough of them. I switch away from the news station just as a reporter is launching into a story about a major drug bust in Longview. I land on a country station, and the music goes well with the terrain.

This part of Texas is mostly flat, with open fields and farmhouses and occasional stands of trees. Travis Seldin's white clapboard house sits a hundred feet off a two-lane road, behind a clump of trees and shrubs. You can just see the house from the end of the dirt and gravel driveway. It has a sagging wood porch in front and another clump of trees out back. There's no truck in sight.

Maybe Travis is in town having a beer.

And maybe I better go talk to him first. Anna Brook didn't like me watching her at the airport back in San Francisco. I don't think she'd appreciate me walking in unannounced. And in this part of Texas, who doesn't have a gun in their house? If Travis is easy to talk to, maybe I can get him to introduce me. She might feel less threatened if I show up with someone she knows. I continue on past the house toward town.

Dime Box is about what I expected. A few blocks long, a few blocks wide, and a few decades past its heyday, with old grain elevators and faded buildings of brick and wood. There's a barbecue joint and a little market, and down the way, a bar called The Buckaroo with a white Ford F-150 parked in front. The tags match Seldin's.

According to the background check, Seldin got his license back a year ago, after losing it in Mississippi for driving under the influence. He's served a few stints in jail—thirty days for possession of marijuana, sixty for stealing live chickens (who the hell does that?), and ninety for possession of methamphetamine—but no hard prison time. He used to work as a welder but hasn't had steady employment, other than drinking, for the past few years.

In his mug shots, he ages two full decades in the span of six years. He's smiling in the first one. A good-looking, dark-haired guy with obvious charm. In the later photos, he looks tired and worn. Sometimes his hair is short, sometimes it's long, but it's always jet-black. When it's long, he wears it pulled back into a braid, like the Indians in the photos of the Old West.

Before I go in, I plug my phone into my laptop and copy some photos from the Gate 76 folder.

The Buckaroo has a worn wood floor, a few small tables, and a wooden bar with ten stools. It smells of hamburger and French fry grease and spilled beer. If I knew country music, I could tell you whose song was playing when I walked in. Outside, it's just getting dark. Inside, the place is lit with a purple hue from the red-and-blue neon signs behind the bar: Lone Star, Miller Lite, Budweiser.

There's a young couple sitting at a table in back, leaning in close and talking. The four bearded guys at the table near the front are louder. Travis, with his braided black hair, is at the bar. He's got his back to the tables, absently twisting his almost-empty beer glass in little circles and staring at the football highlights on TV. The bartender, a big-boned woman wearing jeans and a light brown ponytail, has a little bit of a paunch, like a man, and a face that looks like it might have been pretty before she wore it out.

At the bar I stand two stools down from Travis and ask for a Miller Lite. I don't like light beer, but if I'm going to spend any time here and draw this guy into conversation, I'd better stick with the watery stuff.

As she slides me a beer, the bartender asks where I'm from. I say, "Washington, DC."

Travis turns his head and gives me a sideways look. The creases in his weather-beaten face show he's had some hard years. He's slouching on his stool, but I know from his arrest photos he's six feet tall. He has a medium build, a thin nose, black eyes, and a week or so of dark stubble on his chin. His loose, faded jeans are stained with black grease and white paint. The belt with the wallet chained to it doesn't seem to be doing its job. I noticed when I came in he was showing an inch and a half of ass crack between the top of his pants and the bottom of his shirt. He wears black jackboots and a black Molly Hatchet t-shirt, and his arms have a few bare patches that haven't been tattooed yet.

"I used to have a friend up in DC," he says. "What brings you to Texas?"

"I'm looking for someone," I say.

"Ain't we all?" His eyes go back to the TV before I can answer.

"Cowboys blew 'em out, didn't they?" I say.

"That's what I kept telling everyone! The Eagles ain't all that. I won three hundred and fifty on that game." He raises his glass to the TV. "Picked the Cowboys by ten."

He drinks the last ounce from his glass and adds, "People were laughing at me. They ain't laughing now."

"You want a beer?" I ask.

He eyes me with mock suspicion and says, "You ain't a Redskins fan, are you?" His eyes are droopy and bloodshot.

"I'm not into football."

"'Cause you know this is Cowboys country."

"Yeah, I know where I am."

"Wait," he says, "let me guess." He gives me a quick look up and down. "You're a wrestler. You look it, man. Big, strong, and all beat up."

"I used to box," I say.

"Is that right? Well, that's a hell of a sport. Thing about boxing is, it's all up to you." He points a shaky finger in my face. "Ain't no teammate gonna come in and pick up the slack when things go wrong. What's it like when you're getting the shit beat out of you?"

"It's like getting the shit beat out of you."

"Yeah, that's what I figured. And that ain't no fun at all. You want a shot of Jack?"

"No thanks."

He turns to the bartender and says, "Gimme a Lone Star and a couple shots of Jack."

I said I didn't want one. Did he not hear me? This guy's already half crocked, and if he starts doing shots, he'll be headed for oblivion. I better get to the point.

"Look, buddy, I'm looking for someone down here—"

"Yeah, you said that."

"—and you might be able to help me."

The bartender slides a pint of Lone Star into Travis's waiting hand and then pulls two empty shot glasses from beneath the bar and turns to get the bottle of Jack.

"I'm looking for a woman," I say.

"Well that's the start of all troubles right there," he says. "My daddy used to say if you go out looking for trouble you deserve to find it."

The bartender pushes a shot to Travis and one to me. Travis picks up the glass, tilts it toward me as if to make a toast and then drinks it down.

"Took me a while to figure out my daddy was right," he says. "Now that," he points up at the TV, where the highlights show Dez Bryant burning a cornerback and a safety for a sixty-yard touchdown, "that's how you juke a guy. He sent 'em in opposite directions. I used to wear that number in high school. Eighty-eight. You got Drew Pearson, Michael Irvin, Travis Seldin, and Dez Bryant. You know which one of them don't fit in?"

He leans in and says in his just-between-you-and-me voice, "I'll give you a hint. One of 'em ain't black." Then he slaps his knee and laughs like he just told the funniest joke in the world.

It takes him a few seconds to get a hold of himself again, and he doesn't seem to care that I'm not laughing. Talking to drunks is my least favorite part of this job. It's even worse than talking to lawyers.

"All right Travis, let me cut to the chase."

He gives me a quick suspicious look. "How'd you know my name?"

"You just said it. You're not Drew Pearson, Michael Irvin, or Dez Bryant. That leaves Travis Seldin."

"Oh yeah."

"Let me show you something." I pull out my wallet and lay my PI license and my driver's license on the bar.

His hand goes straight to his pocket, and he says, "You a cop?"

"Not a cop," I say. "Private investigator. Read the license."

He picks it up with his left hand and looks at it. His right hand stays on his pocket. Whatever's in there is too small to be a gun. I have a guess as to what it is though. His background check turned up a lawsuit in which he was the plaintiff. He's on disability from a shoulder injury. He got a payout, and probably a bunch of prescriptions. Whatever it is under his hand makes a rattling sound when he moves.

I say, "You got pills in your pocket, I don't care."

He lays the PI license back on the bar.

"I didn't come here to mess with you," I say. "I told you I'm looking for someone."

"Sorry, bud," he says. "Can't help you." He picks up the second shot and drinks it.

"She's a friend of your wife," I say. "Your late wife. I'm sorry about that. Sorry you lost her."

That got to him. At least it looks like it opened the door a crack.

"Let me show you something," I say. I pull out my phone and find the photo of Julia I copied from my computer before I came in here.

I give him the phone, and he looks at the image for a few seconds.

"That's not the one I'm looking for," I say. "That's her sister."

"Looks just like her," he says.

"I know," I say. He still seems like he's on the fence, and he's also too drunk to notice he just gave himself away. How would he know who Julia looks just like? "Her sister is worried."

He looks up at me, still a little uncertain, so I throw one more jab at his conscience. "Anna Brook's sister is worried."

He lets out a long breath and says, "All right, buddy. If I can help…"

I take a guess, but I say it like I'm sure of it. "She's at your house."

Immediately, he's defensive. "She ain't coming out," he says, shaking his head. "You ain't gonna get her to leave. Hell, I wish she would. The woman's unstable. I can't even be in my own goddamn home."

"Well I need to talk to her."

"I wouldn't try it," he says. "She might shoot you. Or herself." He picks up his beer with a shaky hand and drinks a third of it.

"I want you to take me to your house and introduce me. I can't just walk in on her."

"No, you can't," he says. "She's running from someone." He twists his beer glass in circles as the bartender clears out the empty shots. "And for all I know, it might be you."

"It's not me," I say. "I already know where she is. If I wanted to get her, I'd have gone to the house and got her alone. I wouldn't have come here and found you."

"Hey Kendra," he says to the bartender. "Another shot."

"You don't need any more to drink."

"Don't tell me what I need," he says. "Fact is, right now you need me."

"I need you standing and talking. The way you're going with the booze—"

"I can't leave yet anyway."

"Why not?"

"I'm meeting someone."

"Can it wait?"

"No," he says. And his hand goes back to his pocket.

The bartender looks at the two of us as she pours him another shot.

"Someone coming to buy those pills in your pocket?"

Travis eyes me suspiciously, so I tell him again. "Look, I'm not a cop. I don't care what you do with the pills. I just need to talk to Anna."

"All right," he says. Then to the bartender, "Another beer too. You want one?"

"No," I say.

"Give him another," he says to the bartender. Then to me, "We got forty-five minutes before this guy shows up. You can't sit forty-five minutes at a bar and not drink."

An hour and fifteen minutes later, we're still waiting for some guy from a town called Snook who's willing to pay $450 for a bottle of OxyContin.

Travis says he can't take the pills himself, because they interfere with his drinking. "Shit nearly killed me one time. And I can't take 'em back to the house, 'cause the girl holed up there is trying to kick the pills. She had it bad the first few days."

I ask him to tell me about "the girl."

"She showed up kinda rattled," he says. "Said she needed sanctuary. That's a funny word, ain't it? Sounds religious. I tell you, after living with her for a week, I think asylum's a better word, 'cause she's about as close to the edge as a woman can get. Got me walking on eggshells 'cause I never know what'll set her off. I try to stay out of there mostly. Hey, how'd you know I had a wife?"

151

"I talked to her mother."

"That woman," Travis says, shaking his head. "I don't care for her and she don't care for me. She don't like the way I drink, but she's just as bad as I am."

He's wobbling on his stool.

"We ain't been together for a while now, Katie and me," he says. "And she died a few weeks ago. That's part of what rattled Anna." He drinks a few ounces of beer and adds, "That and being mixed up with some guy wasn't treating her right."

"Again, I'm sorry about Katie. She looked like a good person."

He shrugs and makes an indifferent face—a drunk who can't connect with his feelings. "Some people you just can't help. I knew when she married me she didn't have no judgment. Funny thing is, when we were married, we couldn't get along unless we were both high. Then we split up, and we could talk on the phone stone sober for an hour at a time. I guess you go through enough hard times with someone, and if you don't come out the other end hating each other, you're friends for life. Don't matter how much time goes by. You saw 'em through their lowest point, and they saw you through yours, and that's a bond that don't ever break."

When I steer the conversation back to Anna, he tells me she's gotten a little better since the first couple of days, when she was so anxious she was shaking and wouldn't eat. She wouldn't leave the house, except with him, and only to the woods, where no one could see her. Travis walked her back there every day, three or four times, like a convalescent.

On the third day, he said, things started to turn. She slept more. She ate a little bit. She stopped shaking. She started walking in the woods on her own and she read the Bible she'd forced him to buy for her. She watched the news and sent him out for papers, but not just the local ones. She wanted the *New York Times* and the *Wall Street Journal*. He had to drive toward Austin or College Station for those. She underlined parts of the news stories and made notes. Same with the Bible. Lots of notes and underlining. She didn't talk much, but she seemed to be thinking a lot. She could be calm for two hours at a time, and then she'd have a fit of panic. She'd shake and pace, and if he tried to talk to her, she'd snap at him.

"I want her out," he says flatly. "Only she ain't got nowhere to go. Woman don't do nothing all day but read the news to get worked up and then read the Bible to get calmed down. You religious?"

"No," I say. "I go to weddings and funerals. That's about it for me and church."

He lets out a little laugh. "Weddings and funerals. You know a wedding's just a funeral for two single people. I ain't a churchgoer either. One of them hardline types talked me into going a while back to heal my soul—which, by the way, I didn't know was aching in the first place. I spent an hour of my Sunday listening to this fella talk about how Satan was gonna roast my soul over eternal fire. Who the hell wants to listen to that kind of talk when there's football on TV? Then he hands me a plate and wants me to put a dollar in it. I gave him a nickel and he got the hint."

He takes a swig of beer and sets the glass down a little too hard as a fat man with a grey beard enters the bar. Travis watches him walk back to the restroom and says, "I get that some people are into it. If faith is what a person needs to get through their day, I ain't gonna kick that crutch out from under 'em. You go ahead and pray your comfort. I'll drink mine. World's big enough for every man to have his church. 'Scuse me now."

He gets up and nearly falls sideways onto the bar. Then he steadies himself and staggers back to the men's room.

"Hey Kendra," I say to the bartender. "I want to settle up. Gimme Travis's tab too."

The bartender hands me a receipt for two Lite beers, along with Travis's receipt, which is a flat sixty bucks.

"He's been on a roll the past few days," she says.

Travis's receipt isn't itemized. "How much did he drink?"

She shrugs and says, "At least twice what the bill says. We comp him 'cause he's a regular. He's been in since ten this morning. Don't let him drive."

As I'm paying the bill, Grey Beard comes out of the men's room and goes straight out the front door without looking at anyone.

Half a minute later, Travis stumbles out of the restroom, trying to walk upright and veering sharply sideways. A couple of guys jump up from their table and grab him before he can knock over their beers. As they steer him back toward the bar, I notice the lump in his pocket where the pills used to be is gone.

I say, "I'm taking you home, pal."

He points to the half-empty beer in front of my stool. "What about that?"

"I don't want it," I say.

He picks it up and drinks it, bracing himself against the bar to keep from falling.

"Hey," I say. "You gotta stay awake. You want some coffee?"

"Another beer," he says.

"No. Let's go," I say. "And remember, my name is..."

"Fray Furgsen," he says. "Pee. Eye. Friend of Anna's sister."

I loop his arm over my shoulder so he can't topple over, and we start toward the door. "Don't pass out," I say.

The TV in the front corner is tuned to the local Austin news. It's on mute, with subtitles across the bottom of the screen. Travis leans heavily on me as we cross the floor. The reporter is talking about a big drug bust in Longview, over on the eastern side of the state. They cut to footage of the suspect being marched from a low brick building to a patrolman's cruiser. It's him! The tall, angular guy who was holding Anna Brook by the arm back in San Francisco. There's his name in the subtitles. Ramón Ramírez.

"Jesus!"

"What?" Travis says drowsily. "Whazzit?"

"That guy! That's…" Wait, didn't he have a record down here in Texas? Looks like he came home and found some more trouble.

Travis starts to slump.

"Come on, buddy," I say. "Let's keep it moving."

18

"Travis, wake up." I give him a little nudge on the shoulder as he snores in the passenger seat.

"Huh?"

"Wake up. This is your house."

He turns and looks. "Yeah it is." Then he closes his eyes again.

"You gotta stay awake for five minutes. Introduce me to Anna. Why the hell'd you drink so much?"

"S'what I do. Why you nag so much? Like a goddamn wife." He folds his arms across his chest, slides his hands under his armpits, and his eyes sag shut as he slumps against the door.

I grab the shoulder bag from the back seat and get out. When I go around and open the passenger door, Travis almost falls out of the car. The shoulder belt stops him, jerking his neck and jolting him awake.

"Goddamn fuck! What the..."

I grab him under the arm and say, "Come on now. You remember my name, right?"

"Freddy Fergis from Redskins land."

"You have the house key?"

He fishes through his pocket as I walk him toward the porch. When he pulls out the key ring, a wad of neatly folded cash drops to the ground. The money from the pills he just sold. I pick it up and give it back to him as he hands me the keys.

"It's the one that don't say Ford," he says.

"Thanks."

When I get him up the steps onto the porch the old wood planks sag beneath us. A flickering spiral bulb hangs above the door, giving off a weak pinkish-blue light. I have to let go of Travis to get the key into the lock, but as soon as I loosen my grip, he starts to fall.

I hook one hand under each of his arms and get him seated on a milk crate beside the door. I slide the key into the lock and give it a turn. As the door opens, Travis topples onto his side with a thud. I watch him for a few seconds to make sure he's breathing, then I look inside. The house is dark, except for a dim shaft of light in the room at the back.

"Anna?" I wait for a few seconds, but there's no answer. "Travis had a little too much to drink." I wait again. "Anna?" The house is silent.

I step inside and feel for a light switch on the wall. I push it up, it clicks, but no light comes on.

I take another step and the floorboards creak beneath my feet. This house must be over a hundred years old.

"Anna Brook? Are you in here?"

I walk through the front room, where I can make out the shapes of a couch and coffee table to the left. I pass an open doorway on the right. The only light in there comes from the green digits of the microwave clock. It's not 4:06, a.m. or p.m.

There's another door on the right, between the kitchen and the back room. A closet.

The front of my foot goes into a fist-sized hole in the floor, and I almost curse out loud as my ankle twists.

One more step, and I'm in the back room. It's a bedroom. The light is coming from a nightlight in the bathroom to the right. To the left is a bed with a body in it.

"Anna Brook," I whisper.

No response.

I wait a moment, and in the silence I hear the slow, rhythmic breath of sleep. She's on her side. I can see her shoulder rise and fall beneath the sheet.

I turn and walk quietly back into the other room, avoiding the hole in the floor. I should drag Travis into the house and throw him on the couch. Or maybe not. Maybe I should drag him onto the gravel driveway and let him sleep there, the bum.

I stop in the middle of the front room and look again. There's trash all over the place. Beer cans and I don't know what. I step back and bump against a small card table. Two bottles tip and rock, but they don't fall over.

No, those aren't bottles. They're candles. And there's a book of matches. What the hell is this stuff all over the floor?

I kneel and light one candle, then the other. They're religious candles, encased in glass. One has a picture of the Virgin Mary, her eyes turned upward toward heaven. The other shows Saint Peter being crucified upside down. There's a dark wood crucifix on the table like the one that loomed over the priest in the church my mother used to take me to in Philly.

The two candles and cross form a triangle, and between them is the Bible, opened to the book of Luke. A few sentences are underlined in pencil. I can just make them out in the flickering light.

You did not give me any water for my feet, but she wet my feet with her tears and wiped them with her hair. You did not give me a kiss, but this woman, from the time I entered, has not stopped kissing my feet. You did not put oil on my head, but she has poured perfume on my feet.

I turn and look at the floor, the coffee table, the couch. They're covered with newspapers. A familiar face stares up at me from the floor. Rashad Obasanjo, with a bootprint stamped across his face. Travis must have stepped on it.

What did he say about Anna? That she reads the newspapers to get worked up and the Bible to get calmed down.

I pick up the paper with the photo of Obasanjo. She's underlined parts of sentences: *had access and opportunity, but no apparent motive... described by friends and family as devout, but no ties to radicals.* The word devout is underlined twice, and the margins are littered with notes in a shaky hand.

I pick up another section of paper from the coffee table and read it by the light of the candles. It shows photos and brief written profiles of some of the crash victims.

She's circled the paragraphs describing Sheldon Brown and his friend Franklin Dorsett, "two successful businessmen on their way to Hawaii to take a break from the pressures of work." Brown owned several car dealerships. Dorsett owned a company that leased equipment for oil drilling. The story doesn't show their photos, but in my mind, I can see them clearly. They were the ones in the VIP lounge in that video the airline sent us. Brown was the skinny, fidgety one. Dorsett was the fat drinker.

In the margin beside those paragraphs, she's written, $2 + 2 = ?$.

What does that mean?

I feel a little vibration in the floor, just a tiny bounce, and then a bright red bead of light appears on the question mark. $2 + 2 =$ a bright red dot of jittery light that travels up my arm and comes to rest on the side of my face.

"Who are you?" Her voice is tense and deadly serious.

She flips the switch beside the closet door, the light comes on, and there she is. Anna Brook, in faded cutoffs and a white tank top.

I put my hands up slowly beside my head as I turn toward her. "Freddy Ferguson," I say. "I'm an investigator."

"Where's Travis?" She has a fierce look in her eye as she holds a black automatic pistol in a two-handed grip with both arms extended. I can tell by the hard look in her eyes she's looking for reasons *not* to shoot me.

I nod toward the front door. "He's on the porch."

The fear rises up in her all at once. "Dead?"

"Drunk," I say. "I had a little chat with him at the bar and—" I turn just slightly and she flinches. The gun is pointed at my chest now, the red bead of light dancing erratically on my shirt as she shakes. She's too wound up to handle that thing. She's going to shoot me without meaning to.

"Can you point that somewhere else, please? The way you're shaking…"

She points it at my crotch and says, "Why were you following me at the airport?"

"You remember that?"

"I had a feeling if anyone came after me it would be you. Who do you work for?"

"A private outfit."

"The FBI?" Her pitch just went up a notch.

"No, I—you're really shaking, you know that? You shouldn't be holding a gun—"

"Raise your hands up as high as they'll go."

I do as she says.

"Turn them around. Let me see the backs."

When I turn my hands around, I see the sharp observation in her eyes as she examines the scarred knuckles, the swollen joints, the pinky that will never be straight again.

"You hit more with your left," she says.

"That's the setup for the money punch."

"Raise them higher," she says. "So your shirt comes up."

I raise them higher so there's an inch of space between the top of my pants and the bottom of my shirt.

"Now turn around," she says. Her voice is shaking. "All the way."

I turn around, three hundred and sixty degrees, nice and slow, and she looks at my beltline to see if I have a gun. Then she looks down at my ankles, checking for the telltale bulge of a pistol.

"Who did you say you work for?"

"A private outfit," I say. "Right now the airline is paying us."

"They pay you to find me?" She takes a step to the side. One more like that, and her foot will go into that hole in the floor.

"They don't know about you," I say. The tilt of her hands changes ever so slightly, and the glowing red dot dances on my liver. "No one does."

"I think someone does."

"Listen, Anna, I came here because I think you might know something—"

"I do."

"I think you're in trouble, and I think it's something bad."

"It is."

She's thin and pale and looks like she's getting tired of holding that heavy gun out in front of her. The red dot keeps getting lower, and then she keeps jerking it back up.

"You're not taking me to the cops," she says.

"No, I'm not."

That seems to surprise her.

"Then why did you—"

"Can I put my hands down?"

"No!" She takes a step to the side and her bare foot goes into the splintery hole. Her ankle twists and as she goes down on her ass, her right hand goes behind her to break the fall. Her knee knocks the gun out of her left hand, and I spring forward to pick it up.

She sits with her back against the closet door, watching in paralyzed terror as I activate the safety on the gun. Her eyes are fixed on me, wide and watering as her throat contracts with a hard dry swallow.

Her foot is bleeding, and the bruises that ring her wrists have faded to a pale greenish yellow.

This is when I take my gamble and see if all the little things add up. The fear and anger in her tone when she asked just now if I'm with the FBI. The fact that Lomax was in San Francisco the day of the crash, just like her. The way he was looming over her sister—her virtual twin—looking at her like a lost possession. Kim Hahn's expression of fear and hatred when she saw his photo.

ANDREW DIAMOND

I crouch in front of her, hand her the gun, and say, "I understand why you don't want to go to the cops. When they find out you weren't on that plane, they'll take you straight to the FBI. And I know you don't want to see Lomax again."

She looks confused as she takes the gun.

"I put the safety on so no one gets hurt," I say. "Now we're going to talk this out."

19

She's sitting on the coffee table, pressing a damp washcloth against the scrapes on her foot. I'm on the couch, drinking a beer to take the edge off my nerves. I don't do well with unstable women, and I don't like guns, and I especially don't like unstable women *with* guns. If I were alone right now, I might want to do what Travis just did and make myself forget about this day.

"You mind if I empty this?" I say, pointing to the gun beside her hip. "It makes me nervous."

She hesitates, looks at the gun, then back at me, and finally says, "Yes. I do mind."

She picks up the gun and puts it in her lap and says, "You know I've thought of using this thing on myself. More than once."

"That doesn't make me any more comfortable."

She gives me a long, curious look and says, "How did you know I wouldn't want to come out? How'd you know about Lomax? How did you even find me?"

I tell her the story. A talk with her sister. An inadvertant tip from Kim Hahn. A tip from Katie Green's drunk mother.

The mention of Katie Green gets her talking. She tells me Katie's overdose really shook her up and made her vow to quit everything. She took the same pills Katie used to take before Katie started shooting: OxyContin, Vicoden, Tramadol. She did a lot of blow too. She tapered off the pills when Katie died. The last one was ten days ago. She stopped doing blow, except for one slip-up the night before the flight from San Francisco.

"And I stopped drinking," she says. "I wish Travis wouldn't keep it in the house."

"How did you know Lomax?" I ask.

"He was my handler."

"Your handler?"

163

"Yeah. Informants have handlers, you know."

"What were you informing about?"

"A couple guys in Dallas," she says. "Rich guys." She hands me the newspaper I'd been looking at earlier and points to the two circled paragraphs. "Sheldon Brown and Franklin Dorsett." Her hand is still shaking.

"What's this mean?" I ask, pointing to her note in the margin. "Two plus two equals question mark?"

"That's what I've been trying to figure out," she says. "There were two other guys on that plane…" She pauses for a second and thinks.

"Who?"

She rubs the crucifix that hangs from the silver chain around her neck. It's an unconscious gesture that seems to soothe her. "I can't remember their names," she says. "They're in one of these papers. The *Austin Statesman* from a couple of days ago."

"Where do you get all these?" I ask, pointing to the papers.

"I send Travis out in the morning."

"Have you been out of the house?" I ask.

"Just to the woods out back."

She tells me she's afraid of going out. There's a trapdoor in the closet that goes to the crawl space under the house. The first few days she was here, she hid down there when she heard noises. The hole we both stepped in goes right through to the crawl space. She tells me Travis dropped his keys through there this morning, and she had to go down and get them. "It's filthy down there," she says. "And there are probably snakes. But sometimes I get so scared that someone's about to come through the front door, I don't even care."

"Have you called anyone?"

She shakes her head. "I don't want anyone to know where I am. I don't have a phone anyway."

"Well I brought you one," I say.

I pick up my shoulder bag from the floor and pull out the cheap Android phone I picked up earlier today at Walmart. "This," I say, handing her the phone, "has one number programmed into it. It goes to this." I pull out the black flip phone, also from Walmart. "They're burners. No one can trace them to you. I brought you some cash too."

I hand her $400 in twenties.

"So you can eat. How'd you meet Lomax?" I ask.

"He came up to DC with those two." She points at the paper again. "Brown and Dorsett. They were in town to meet some Texas congressmen. Frank Dorsett used to keep Katie in an apartment down in Dallas. He knew she was in DC, so he sent Lomax to find her. Lomax found her *and* me, and took us to the hotel where Shel and Frank were staying. It was three nights of drinking and coke and—what they paid for."

She shakes her head as if trying to dismiss the memory. "But the drugs," she says. "It was over the top, even for me. Even for Katie. The reason she left Dallas in the first place was because of Frank. He had a lot of money, and she had a drug problem, and that was his way of controlling her. He'd keep her supplied so she was docile. You ever see a junkie right after she shoots up? You can do whatever you want to her. She's like a rag doll."

She tells me she assumed Lomax was another rich guy who liked to have fun, like Brown and Dorsett. "He did as much blow as Shel, only he didn't shoot it, and he…" She trails off and is quiet for a moment.

"He wanted me to go back to Dallas with them." She shakes her head. "No way. There was no way. I knew what he was like the first time we were together. And, no." She shakes her head again. "He was acting nice that first time. He was pretending. But I knew, and it scared me."

Brown and Dorsett returned to Texas, while Lomax stayed in DC for ten days, trying to persuade Anna to go to Dallas with him. "He took the key I gave to Katie. He'd let himself into my apartment. He was relentless. He told me he worked for the FBI. When I didn't believe him, he showed me his ID. He saw what state I was in. He knew I wanted out of that life. He said if I helped him he'd get me into the Witness Protection Program. I'd have a new name, a new life, and the past would be wiped away."

She rubs her silver crucifix and says, "There's really only one person who can do *that* for you. But I still wouldn't go. Until he brought up Katie. He found my weak spot. He told me he'd get her into rehab. He promised me. He promised! So I said OK. He wanted Katie to come too. She could keep an eye on Frank Dorsett while I kept an eye on Shel.

"He said, 'Shel likes you. Stick by his side. Tell me who he talks to. Tell me everything he says. We can break this case in two weeks with a good informant.'"

"What was the case?"

She unfolds the washcloth from her foot and looks at the blood. The cuts aren't too bad.

"Drugs, I guess. If there even was a case. I don't think Lomax ever told the FBI about me. I did my job, even after I knew it was pointless. Lomax didn't need an informant. There was nothing I could tell him about Shel that he didn't already know. He just wanted to be my handler. He liked to…" She pauses for a second, then says bitterly, "handle me."

She dabs at her foot for a few seconds and her face gets that hard, stoic look again—the look of a strong-willed person who won't be dominated by her feelings.

"Shel was careless," she tells me. "He'd talk right in front of me, with a razor blade in his hand and flakes of coke falling out of his nose. That house was drowning in drugs. It was like quicksand and everyone was sinking. Two weeks went by, then four, and then six. We were all sinking. And poor Katie. She had fled that city for a reason, and I took her right back there. Right back to her death."

This topic is getting her too emotional, so I change it.

"That guy you were with at the airport," I say.

"Ramón?"

"Did you know him?"

"No," she says. "Lomax sent him to get me onto the plane. He introduced us the night before."

"Ramón was arrested today," I say. "Running drugs."

"Oh?"

"You don't sound surprised."

"He wasn't very bright."

"If Lomax wanted you on the plane, why didn't he accompany you himself?"

"He said the flight was sold out."

I think back to the scene at gate seventy-six. There were a dozen people on standby. But that can happen even when a flight isn't sold out. Twenty people show up at the last minute. Eight get seats and twelve don't.

"Did you know the plane was going to crash?"

"No."

"Then why'd you get off?"

"Lomax was waiting for me in Honolulu. I didn't want to see him."

I shake my head.

"What?" she asks.

"Lomax was in San Francisco. He was at the airport after the crash."

She looks puzzled at that bit of news, and I can see as she thinks it through that she's the kind who does a lot of thinking. I don't tell her about her name being checked off with the wrong color ink on the seating chart. If Lomax did that and got the world to believe she had died in the crash, then he could hunt her down later, and when he killed her no one would miss her. But why would he want to do that?

"I *did* try to inform," she says. "I *did* gather evidence. Do you have a pen? Will you take down some names?"

I get a pen and paper from my shoulder bag, and she says, "Midland-Odessa Custom Hauling."

"What's that?" I ask as I write it down.

"I don't know," she says. "But... Martínez Resort Services. And Ramírez Resort Services. One's in Galveston, one's in Corpus Christi."

"What are they?"

"Things Shel talked about with Frank Dorsett, and on the phone... And there's a place in Kerville that rents power equipment, and a place in Rock Springs. Taylor Automotive."

"Was that one of Brown's car dealerships?"

She shakes her head. "He talked about it differently, when he was arguing with Frank Dorsett. And he talked about it on the phone."

"OK," I say. I don't know what to make of this information. "You need to get out of here. You can't hide here forever."

"I know."

"Is Lomax the only thing you're scared of?"

"Isn't that enough?" she asks, offended, and her hand goes right back to the crucifix on her necklace.

"I didn't mean it like that," I say. "I mean, would you come forward and talk to the cops—"

"No!"

"—if we could get Lomax out of the picture?"

"No! How? No!"

"You want to press charges against him?"

"How could I?" she asks. "What evidence do I have?"

I nod toward the bruises on her wrists, and she says angrily, "That's not evidence. Anyone could have done that!"

"You have any witnesses?" I ask.

"No!" she says angrily. "No, I don't have a single goddamn witness. Katie's dead. Shel's dead. Franklin Dorsett is dead. It's my word against his. A prostitute against a federal agent. Who do you think is going to win that matchup?"

"Calm down," I say.

"Don't tell me to calm down. Put yourself in my shoes. You think I want to be here? You think I wanted to go through what I went through?"

"All right, I didn't mean—"

"If you want to help me, go gather evidence. Lomax was doing drugs. The FBI might put him away for *that*. They won't put him away because some prostitute says he raped her. When a woman accuses a man, her character goes on trial. It's not about the facts. It's about her. And I *can't* win that one. I can't."

"Jesus, calm down, will you?"

"I will not calm down. I want him put away. I want *you* to put him away. You did your job well enough to find me. Can you do it well enough to convict him?" She glares at me angrily for a second. "Can you?" she demands.

"I will get you out of here. One way or another. I promise you that."

She gives me a long, penetrating look, and I can tell she's measuring me, trying to figure out how far she can trust me. The truth is, she hasn't given me much to go on, and I have no idea how I'm going to fulfill the promise I just made. She sees the doubt I'm trying to hide, and she's going to call me out on it.

"OK, Freddy," she says calmly. "Then I'm relying on you. Sometimes we have to put our faith in others, don't we?" She gives me another measuring look that shows she still doesn't fully trust me. "Sorry I yelled," she says. "You know I have no one to talk to here. I'm alone all day, Travis is worthless, and I'm going crazy." She looks at the gun in her lap, and I see the thought flash in her eyes.

"Anna," I say.

"What?" Her tone is short, impatient, like she doesn't want to hear any more from me.

"Look at me."

"What?" She says again, with the same annoyed tone.

"Look me in the eye. Just for a second. Please?"

She evades me for a few seconds and then looks at me reluctantly.

"The woman I saw in the airport," I say, "the one walking to the gate for that Chicago flight knew exactly what she was doing. She was getting out. She made a plan, and she stuck to it. That took a lot of courage, and a lot of faith, and a lot of strength. Don't let her down."

"I know," she says softly. "Thank you for understanding that."

20

When you grow up with a guy like Lomax in your house, doing those things to your mother, you develop an instinct, a gut feeling when you see them. And you don't ignore that. Ever.

That's what threw me about him. I'm never wrong about abusers. I can spot them as easily as they spot their victims. What disturbs me is the way he played it off in the men's room at the funeral, so friendly and charming and reassuring. I looked and looked and couldn't find what had set me off. To be able to hide that from a guy like me, you have to be able to hide it from yourself, to turn whole parts of yourself on and off at will. The only people I've met who can do that are psychopaths.

If the guy had me doubting myself in less than a minute, what kind of psych job could he do on a woman he rapes and beats? No wonder she thinks no one will believe her.

I try to get more information out of her, but she doesn't have much to give. She talks a lot about Katie, and when I ask her about herself, all I get is a list of regrets. She's like a woman in the confessional, pouring out her sins to a man who was never meant to play the role of priest. All the things she's done—the selling of herself, the drugs, the lying to her friends and family—it's like listening to the catalog of wrongs I used to bring to that priest every week back in Brooklyn. Only she's not talking about things that happened to other people. She's talking about things she did herself.

I had a premonition when I met her, a sense of dread. She was going to drag me down. I felt it in the whirlpool dream, and listening to her now, I feel it again.

"You wake up one day," she says, "and you ask yourself how you can be doing the things you're doing, how you can be living the way you're living. When did this become normal? When did it even become acceptable?"

Funny she used those words. After my mother died, those were the questions I most wanted to ask her. When did it become normal? When did it become acceptable? Because you and Dad couldn't have started out that way. This is where she takes me. Back to *those* feelings I never want to revisit.

"Is something wrong?" Anna asks.

"No," I say.

"Something's bothering you."

"No. Go on."

She doesn't believe me, but she goes on.

"I started asking myself those questions *before* Katie died," she says. "And every time I dug deep, all I found was shame and despair. It was a whole lot easier to take another pill, do another line, or drink another shot than to face the fact that I did this to myself. That I let it all happen. I can't say that of all the girls I know. Some of them maybe never had a chance. But me…"

She stops and stares blankly at the floor for a moment, then says, "You need something to shock you out of that life. You need to be shaken violently from your complacency before you realize how truly lost you are. For me it was Katie's death and…"

Her eyes go to the crucifix on the table, and then to me, and she says, "It's a shocking thing to be found. It's the most shocking thing you could ever feel, especially after you've tried so hard to disappear." She pauses for a second, then asks softly, "Do you believe?"

I shake my head. "No."

"Why not?"

"How could I believe in a god that would allow his son to be crucified?"

"The Almighty Father," the priest used to say as I sat next to my mother in church. I'd picture a brute like my dad at the dinner table in heaven demanding his food. Only he was bigger and stronger and angrier. And his hands, the hands that made the world, were even more powerful than those giant hands that wrapped around my throat when he got angry and knocked the wind out of me when he was drunk.

I inherited those big thick hands that broke down so many guys in the ring.

"You miss the point," she says. "I mean, that is the point. He said the only way to live in this world is to love each other. And He wouldn't renounce His love for anything. Not even in the face of the most horrible death they could inflict on Him."

In church, I used to look at the man on the cross and think, if that's what God did to his own son, what wouldn't my father do to me?

I can't think about the man who married my mother without wanting to kill him. Even now it makes my blood boil. And that fucking priest telling me God is good and God is great, and the smoke from those candles on the card table, stinging my nose like the candles by the altar…

Anna watches me closely. "That makes you uncomfortable."

I want to throw those fucking candles out the window.

"I don't like the subject," I say.

"But you know the story."

"I know the story. It's just compelling enough to keep God's victims running back into his arms for comfort. If that isn't the model of all abusive relationships…"

I can tell she's offended, even though she tries to hide it.

"You've been to church?" she asks.

"A long time ago."

"With your parents?" she asks.

"My mother."

"What about your father?"

I shake my head.

"No? Well, I understand if you're cynical. Maybe you expected something you didn't get. But you know, I don't really expect anything anymore. It's just… knowing there was one person who cared that much. That makes all the difference."

Here it comes. The story of her life-changing moment, whether I want it or not. These fucking born-agains with their one-track minds are as bad as drunks. I know enough about her type to keep my mouth shut. It's just… she couldn't have picked a worse topic. And the worst thing about born-agains is they really mean it.

God, what's wrong with me?

"I had this revelation—" she says.

She's sincere. She means this. And I'm so fucking full of hatred right now…

"—looking at Him on the cross and understanding that someone cared. I don't know why the realization came when I hit rock bottom. Maybe I wasn't ready for it until then, but that's when it came, and it hit hard. When you understand that one person cares, it changes everything, because then you start to care. It's like you needed permission, and along comes this person and gives you permission to care, and the moment you accept it, everything starts to hurt and everything starts to heal. Does that make sense?"

"It makes sense to you," I say. Why did she have to choose *this* topic?

"Well you're a cold kind of a man, aren't you? You come in here asking me questions, and then you shut me down because you don't like the answers. Well, fuck you."

"Sorry, I don't like sermons," I say. "But you seem to be good at them."

"What the hell are you so bitter about?"

"Excuse me? Have you opened your eyes lately?" She hit the wrong fucking button and I can't stop myself. "Look at this world! Look at *yourself!* You think whoever created all this deserves your praise?"

I feel another Chuck DiLeo coming on, and it scares the hell out of me.

She eyes me coldly and says, "I know your type. You go around keeping score of everything that's wrong with the world, don't you? Do that and you're guaranteed to be bitter, because, yeah, the world is full of horrors. But you asked me about me, and I'm telling you about me. I'm taking responsibility for my life, which is a hard thing to do, considering how shitty I've treated myself. Why are you so tense?"

"When you're all done here," I say, "you can start a church and collect ten percent of everyone's income."

Like that church in Philly. She used to dress up for that. My mother would put on her best dress, and she would get down on her knees, on her fucking knees, like a prostitute, and pray to that bastard like He was going to do something for her.

"What the hell *happened* to you?" she asks with a tone of disgust.

"What was she expecting when she knelt in prayer?" I ask angrily.

"Who?" Anna asks.

"That the all-powerful would help her? Well why didn't He? Was it His will to kill her? Is that how He repays devotion?"

"What are you talking about?" She picks up the crucifix and says, "I don't know what your problem is, but try putting yourself in my shoes for a minute. Imagine there's someone out there who loves you so much, they're willing to take all the punishment that was meant for you."

"You leave her out of this, goddammit."

It was on a Sunday. It was a Sunday when he gave me that beating...

"And why?" Anna muses. "For no other reason than that you were born. You were born worthy in their eyes, so they go through this agony for you."

She folded her body around me, and the shock of the blows raining down on her back went right through her chest and shook my head. He swung and he kicked and he cursed until he wore himself out, and then he left her there on the floor, in the bright yellow dress she had chosen to honor the Lord.

Anna looks at me with clear blue eyes and says, "Imagine what your life would be if you had someone who loved you like that."

"Goddammit, shut the fuck up, you fucking whore!" I'm standing over her with both fists clenched. I'm going to hit her with every ounce of strength I have.

"What's the matter, Freddy?" she asks calmly. "Did I hit a nerve?" She picks the gun up from her lap, clicks the safety off, and points it at me. "Don't even think about hitting me. I won't take any more of that from anyone."

I stare at her for a couple of seconds, filled with shame and hatred for myself as the jittery bead of red light on my heart raises an instinctive panic.

Breathe, Freddy. Breathe. Deep breaths.

She stands and takes a couple of steps back, keeping the gun pointed at my heart.

"You like being a detective, huh? You get to ask all the questions, and you don't have to answer any." She looks at me for a second, then says, "Well let me tell you something. I used to be a stripper. I was the one on stage baring everything while the guys showed nothing. At least, that's how they thought it worked. But most guys are like amateur poker players. They show a lot more than they think they're showing. Let me ask you something, Freddy Ferguson. Do you know what it's like to be looked at like that?"

"Like what? What the hell are you talking about now?"

"The way you looked at me in the security line at the airport. Do you know how intrusive that is? To be put under the glare of that kind of scrutiny?"

"I didn't mean—"

"Tell me, Freddy, what are you looking for?"

"Jesus fucking Christ!" I say under my breath. "I was looking for you, OK? And here we are. I'm sorry I called you a whore. I didn't mean it. I have a bit of a temper, OK?"

"I can see that."

She looks back at the cross on the table and says, "Can I finish what I was saying? Because, you know, it's really rude to cut someone off when they're talking about something so personal."

"All right," I say.

"Try to sound happy about it, will you?"

I let out a long breath of frustration.

"Because I'm sick of people being rude to me. I'm sick of people not listening, and I'm sick of not being heard."

She nods toward the cross and says, "When they crucified Him, His mother had to watch. Mary Magdalene had to watch. I did that to my own mother, and to my sister. I made them watch. And I can't forgive myself for all the hardship I put them through. That's part of the whole program, you know. Forgiveness. But I'm not very good at that yet."

She glaces at the bruises on her wrists and says, "You know, a lot of guys are weird. They want you to piss on them, or pretend you're twelve, or shove a dildo up their ass. I don't judge them. We all have our quirks."

She's drawing little circles on my heart with the laser.

"But I'll tell you where I do judge. Some guys can't get off unless they're dominating you. Those are the real pervs. Those are the ones I won't see twice. And Lomax? Nothing turns him on more than knowing he's really, truly hurting someone."

She looks at the scars above my eyes, the ones that every boxer has, and says, "You look like you've had your fights, and you've probably taken your beatings, just like everyone else. But to be utterly helpless, to be crying and unable to defend yourself, to just have to lie there and take it while you pray for him to finish, that's something no man will ever understand."

ANDREW DIAMOND

No, I think, but a kid understands it. A little kid in the wrong situation knows exactly what that's like.

"Get out of here, Freddy. Get the fuck out of this house. And if you do see Lomax," she says bitterly, "do me a favor and put a bullet in his head."

178

21

At four a.m., I'm sitting on a motel bed in Elgin with the TV on for distraction. I should be tired. This day started back in DC almost twenty-four hours ago. But I can't sleep.

I sent Anna a text two hours ago reminding her she owes me two more names. She had told me she'd find them in the pages of the *Austin Statesman*. So far, I haven't heard anything back.

The TV is murmuring quietly on the wall above the dresser. It's a rerun of the eleven o'clock news, showing the big drug arrest that nabbed Anna's escort on a highway near Longview. That's about 250 miles northeast of here, near the Louisiana border. I turn up the volume.

"The Texas Department of Public Safety announced a *major* drug bust this afternoon, the result, they say, of a lengthy investigation involving the State Highway Patrol and the Criminal Investigations Division. Texas native Ramón Ramírez was picked up just east of Longview, on his way to Shreveport, Louisiana, with two kilograms of fentanyl. Reynaldo Juárez has the story."

The report opens with a voice-over and a shot of several small, taped plastic packets. Fentanyl is sold in micrograms. The street value of this haul was a couple million dollars. A Captain Crunch, or something like that, is praising all of Texas law enforcement, right on up to the governor, for the teamwork and dedication that led to this arrest. No, the Captain's name is Kuntze, not Crunch.

They show the suspect being led from a low brick building toward a police cruiser. Ramón Ramírez has a little swagger. He looks perfectly at home in handcuffs. They don't have to push his head down to get him into the back of the car. He just ducks right in on his own. He knows the drill. According to the news report, he's got a string of minor offenses stretching back seven years. He's served a few stints in jail—thirty days here, sixty there—but he's never been in prison. Whoever he is, he's low-level. Disposable.

I'm wondering how Ramón, the Texas native, wound up in the airport with Anna Brook. The reports Ed sent me about Ramírez seemed a little off. Parts of the record were missing, parts were blacked out, and the cocaine bust that should have resulted in a felony charge was reduced to a misdemeanor. If the guy was an informant, could Lomax have picked him up on the case he was working down here?

The news cuts back to campaign coverage. The two candidates for governor drive their points home through endless repetition to crowds of supporters across Texas. Patty Rice and her benefits for all. The candidate of mercy. Jumbo Throckmorton and his tough stance on crime. The candidate of justice. The world needs all it can get of both.

"What has Patty Rice done for Texas?" Throckmorton thunders at a podium in the middle of a high school football field. His supporters are also on the field. The turnout wasn't big enough to fill the stands. "Patty Rice gave us new regulations when she was in the state senate. She made it more expensive to run a business. She made it harder for the state to turn over illegals to Immigration. She gave away your tax dollars to take care of people who won't take care of themselves."

Patty Rice, on stage at a school auditorium in Arlington, brags she did all that and more. "Jumbo Throckmorton was a good director of public safety," she says. "Yes, crime, and especially drug-related crime, went down on his watch. I give him full credit for that. But the issues facing Texans today—trying to get by in a service economy, trying to earn a stable wage and get decent health care, funding a public school system that will educate kids for better jobs—these are not his issues. Jumbo Throckmorton is a one-trick pony. His answer to everything is jail and deportation. Even the drug trade has moved beyond him. Prescription opioids are killing more Texans than illegal drugs, and Jumbo Throckmorton is not the man to stand up to Big Pharma. He is the property of Big Pharma, of Big Oil, Big Money, big everything. They call him Jumbo for a reason."

I like the sparring between these two. They're like a couple of fighters who really can't stand each other and don't want to miss a single opportunity to land a blow. I can tell Throckmorton is the kind of guy who likes his women in dresses, with long hair and lots of makeup. There's no place for someone like Patty Rice in his world. A woman beyond her childbearing years, with short, feathered hair and pantsuits, who makes no attempt to be alluring but has a relentless focus on issues and getting things done. I can see she gets under his skin, the way she sticks with him, blow for blow. He can't quite shake her off and he can't put her down for the count. Every fighter's had a few opponents like that. You don't realize how much they take out of you until the days after the bout.

I know I have insomnia when I'm watching reruns of political interviews at six a.m. Now Throckmorton's on CNN, up against an unfriendly reporter, a young dark-haired woman whose questions focus on all his weak points: the economy and unemployment, affordable health care, budget cuts, and race relations. It's like Rice handed the reporter a description of the Democrats' agenda and now she's asking the Republican why he's not fulfilling it.

Throckmorton handles it well. He bends every answer back to his talking points, which he delivers in a smooth, easygoing manner that's both folksy and tough. He's like a super-sized John Wayne. The lawman you trust but never want to cross.

When she comes to the topic of immigration, he really hits his stride, talking at length about how much the Latino community has contributed to the culture and economy of the state while throwing in little digs all along the way at the illegals.

Then the interviewer says, "One thing we haven't touched on yet is terrorism, which has been very much in the news lately, with 188 lives lost in what appears to be a terrorist attack on a US airline."

Throckmorton rocks back a little in his seat, wiping his hands on his pants in a subtle show of fatigue.

"You're known for being tough on crime," the interviewer says. "Do you see terrorism as a threat to Texas? And what is the state doing, under your leadership, to combat it?"

"Well, terrorism is a big problem," he says. "While the state plays a part in monitoring and enforcement, the scope of the problem is… it's really a national problem. An international problem. Which is why our federal government dedicates so many resources to surveillance and intelligence."

"Do you think they'll find the people who took down that plane in California?"

"Well, it looks like they already have," he says with a laugh.

"The FBI has a suspect in custody," the reporter says, "but he hasn't been charged."

"All right, look," Throckmorton says, "this case has nothing to do with Texas." He seems a little testy.

"I didn't say it did."

"We're here to talk about pressing issues. About why Texas needs four more years of Jumbo Throckmorton and can't risk the mistake of electing a California liberal like Patty Rice—"

I cut it off there. I've had enough for one night.

At six-fifteen I send an email to Bethany and Leon. Give me all you can on Sheldon Brown and Franklin Dorsett, on Midland-Odessa Custom Hauling, Martínez Resort Services in Galveston, and Ramírez Resort Services in Corpus Christi.

I don't remember falling asleep, but I know I was out by sunrise, when a little unfamiliar buzzing sound woke me. I blinked a couple times, turned away from the window, and went back to sleep.

22

OCTOBER 5

I sleep till ten and am on the road by ten-thirty, heading north toward Dallas. The radio is reporting that Obasanjo's mother and father have been taken into protective custody after receiving death threats. The car rental company where his father works was firebombed overnight. Someone sent a brick through the window, followed by a Molotov cocktail.

The restaurant where Obasanjo's mother works announced it will close indefinitely, in response to threats that its owners fear will be acted on. "We've been getting calls for days," the owner said. He has a deep, gravelly voice. "On the phone, on our Facebook page, on Yelp. After last night, we're not taking any chances. The safety of our employees and customers comes first."

Then it's on to Delmont Suggs. The Feds have located and surrounded his Idaho compound.

I turn the radio off as I near the Dallas city limits. The news is starting to depress me, like those lists I used to make to antagonize that priest back in Brooklyn. My lists of all the things God was doing wrong. Only those things seemed confined to the neighborhood. The drugs and violence and crime were products of poverty. Now the whole country's in distress.

Sheldon Brown's house northwest of Dallas is even bigger than Katie Green's. Stopping at the driveway gate, I can see it's a sprawling stone monstrosity that could have ten or even fifteen bedrooms. I give the car some gas and roll slowly down the road. The driveway is a giant semi-circle with an iron gate at either end. The gates are a hundred yards apart, and they're both wide open. Between them is a high hedge that hides all but the top of the house.

Stopping at the second gate, I see two cars in the drive, up near the house: a big black Mercedes and a white Ford pickup. I turn into the driveway, and the wheels of the Malibu crunch along through the yellow pebbles. There's no one in the yard.

I park behind the Ford. It's waxed to a brilliant shine and decked out with chrome wheels, chrome bumper, chrome mirrors, and when I get around front, I see the big chrome grill. This is a show truck, not a work truck.

I go up the steps and ring the bell, but no one answers. So I take a walk around the side, looking into a couple of ground-level windows as I go. The place is sparsely furnished, but what's there looks expensive. The rooms are so big, it would take a few truckloads of furniture to make the place look lived in.

An iron fence around the back yard turns into a stone wall about thirty feet before it reaches the side of the house. The wall has a stone arch whose black iron gate matches the fence. It's open, so I go through.

Out back is a kidney-shaped swimming pool with a bar at one end and a cave and waterfall at the other. Between the pool and the house is a stone patio with another bar and a grill. Giant French doors with copper mullions lead into a huge back room that looks like a ballroom.

At the near end of the pool, just in front of the cave entrance, a short, shirtless guy with a chest and shoulders carved from gleaming ebony is dragging a net on a twenty-foot pole across the water. He's caught a purple bikini bottom. Or maybe they're panties. He'll have to haul them in before he goes after the four brown beer bottles on the pool bottom. One of the lounge chairs near the far end of the deck is covered with a beige towel. The round imprint in the middle of it and the glass of soda and upside-down novel on the table beside it tell me someone was sitting there just now.

I catch the pool cleaner's eye and nod. He doesn't seem concerned that I'm here. "Anyone inside?"

"Just the usual folk," he says. "They in playing cards." He nods toward the house, then gives me a little up-and-down look, like he's trying to see how much I'm worth. "If they expecting you," he says, "just go on in."

Then I see the body that belongs to that imprint on the lounge chair. She comes out through the back door in a green bikini and makes her way along the edge of the pool back toward her chair. I follow twenty feet behind. She has broad hips, pale, creamy skin, and little dimples on either side of her spine, just above the bikini line. She knows I'm following her.

When she reaches her chair, she picks up the glass of soda and turns around to watch me get an eyeful of her as she sips her drink. Those broad hips have always been a weakness of mine. She has a flat stomach with a smooth, indented line right down the middle, and heavy teardrop breasts that go a little off to the sides, with a wide valley between them.

"You here for the card game?" she says.

"I came to talk about some business."

"Whose business?" she says, and I can tell by the stupid flirty look she gives me that she's not too bright. She's got reddish-brown hair that goes a little past her shoulders, hazel eyes, and a mouth that's too small but somehow still turns me on. She goes on sucking at the straw, real slow, and I'm having a hard time keeping my eyes up on her face. Those hips are like magnets.

"Sheldon Brown's," I say.

"You know he's dead," she says, with a pouty girlish face. "Or don't you have a TV?" She puts her drink down and sits on the lounge chair, knees up and spread a little too wide, with one foot on either edge of the chair.

"You look a little pale to be out in this sun," I say. Usually, no matter how good looking a woman is, the minute I find out she's stupid, the attraction ends. In this case, however, part of me is willing to make an exception. Unfortunately, that part is taking all the blood away from the part of me that does the thinking.

"I'm not trying to tan. Just enjoying the scenery." She's watching the guy across the pool with the twenty-foot pole.

"Kinda hot out here," I say. "Don't you think?"

"Is it? I guess it is. Duluth doesn't get this hot, even in July. Are you a cop?"

"No. What if I was?"

She shrugs. "They usually come by in uniform."

"Who's inside?" I ask.

"The usual hangers-on."

"And you?" I say. "Are you a relative of the deceased?" The line of her legs, from the knees down to the insides of her thighs, keeps sucking my eyes back to the strip of green fabric that just barely covers what I shouldn't be looking at.

"Long-term guest," she says. "You gonna fall asleep?"

"What makes you say that?"

"Your eyes keep dropping."

I run into a lot of people in my line of work, and I've met more than a few like her. Usually, I'm immune to them. She has the scent of boredom all around her, of lazy days spent waiting for some new pastime to fill the empty hours between waking and sleep. Something just memorable enough to make today stand out from yesterday.

"I'm not scared of cops," she says. "Go ahead and ask me a question. Shel's gone. There's no one left to protect."

I turn and look at the guy with the pool net.

"Yeah, he has ears," she says. "Is this top secret?"

"I don't know yet," I say. "Did you know a woman named Cat?"

She perks up. "The blonde? Yeah. She was on the plane too. I guess Shel was taking her to Hawaii." Then she stands and says, "Hey, come inside."

"What's your name?"

"Linnea."

23

Linnea leads me from the pool deck into an enormous kitchen with a cool terracotta-tiled floor. Cigarette smoke and country music and male voices drift in from a room far across the house.

"This way," she says. "No one will see us on the back stairs."

She walks ahead of me up the narrow stairway, and that dimpled lower back, those wide hypnotic hips, and the firm round flesh between them—it's all waving right in front of me. Like I said, usually I'm immune to this stuff. Work is work. But this woman's got something going on, and how long has it been? Last week, I found an unopened box of condoms in my bathroom, and they were expired.

The stairs lead to a wide hallway with dark hardwood floors, long Persian rugs, and side tables with lamps. The walls are hung with paintings every ten feet, and now and then a mirror. We go into the second room on the right, and she shuts the door. There's a big unmade bed with green and white sheets piled in the middle, a low broad dresser strewn with clothing, sunscreen, makeup, ashtrays, hats, and open soda cans. Next to the dresser is a bathroom with towels and damp clothing all over the floor.

She has this big teasing smile on her face, and part of me says I can't be reading this right. I'm not a real good-looking guy. I'm not ugly either, but all those years of getting punched in the face didn't make me any prettier. I'm not charming or stylish or rich. I'm invisible to women. They only see me when there's furniture to be moved, or a flat tire to fix, and the only women who flirt with me are waitresses handing me a check. Her leading me up here and that big smile can't mean what I think it means.

I say, "You know what you're doing, right?"

"What am I doing?" she says.

"I mean, we're on the same page here, right?"

She's standing there in that bathing suit in front of the dresser, and she has those big teardrop breasts, and all my thoughts are headed in the wrong direction. She says, "Why don't you come over here and show me what page you think we're on. I'll tell you if you're right." And then she sucks the tip of her finger in a gesture that comes off as contrived, flirty, coy, and stupid all at once.

So I go over there, and I put one hand on each of those big round hips. I push her gently back until the cool edge of the dresser presses into the firm flesh of her behind, and I kiss her neck.

We're on the same page.

As I'm drawing back from that kiss, she whispers, "Get me out of here."

"What?" I look at her with alarm. "Are you in danger?"

She slides my left hand from her hip up to her breast. "No," she says with a smile. "I'm broke, and I'm stuck, and I'm sick of this place." She puts her arm around my back and pulls me closer. "You could do a girl a favor, you know. A big, big favor. All I need…" She kisses my ear and whispers, " …is a one-way ticket home." Then she kisses the other ear and adds, "Tonight. Can you do that?"

"I can do that."

* * *

A while later, we're lying in bed, talking. She says, "It's nice to meet a guy with a little enthusiasm. These drinkers and cokeheads, they just treat it like they're taking care of business. Their business, not mine. What kind of cop are you?"

"Private."

"What do you want to know about Cat?"

"Did you know her well?"

"No." She gets up and walks to the dresser, takes a cigarette from a crumpled pack of Kools and lights it. "Shel liked her. He met her up in DC."

"What was he doing there?"

"I don't know. The governor flew him up there with Frank Dorsett and another guy to talk to some politicians. I guess they did whatever rich men do in Washington."

"Dorsett's the one with the big beer gut, right?"

"Mm-hmm," she says, taking a drag of her cigarette. "Eighteen months pregnant with a keg of Lone Star."

"Did Sheldon bring Cat down here?" I want to see if her account squares with Anna's.

She shakes her head. "Another guy brought her down as a gift. A guy from DC."

"He was here? The guy who brought her down?"

"Yeah. He came off like a real charmer at first, but he gave me a bad vibe. And she was scared of him. That's never a good sign. She, uh…" She gives me a little uncertain glance.

"Cat? She what?"

"She liked to swim. She was very graceful. A natural athlete. She'd swim laps in the pool, and Shel liked to watch her. Then she stopped."

"How long was she here?"

"I don't know. A month? Two months? It's hard to keep track of time in this place. But she stopped coming to the pool. You wouldn't see her out of her room at all, except when it was dark. And then she only wore dresses. She wouldn't put on a bathing suit, or anything that showed her skin. That guy—he was rough with her. Do you get what I'm saying?"

"I get it."

She takes a drag of her cigarette and blows out a big cloud of smoke. The boredom is back upon her.

"You're from Duluth?" I ask.

"How'd you know that?"

"You said it didn't get this hot in Duluth even in July."

"Oh, yeah," she says. "You have a good memory."

"Speaking of…" I pick up my phone and tap the Expedia app. "You really want to get out of here tonight?"

"The sooner the better." She sits down beside me, and we wait for the list of flights to load onto the screen.

"Where'd you meet Sheldon?" I ask.

"Vegas. You know what a whale is?"

"Big gambler."

"Mm-hmm. You know they get special treatment? Their own tables in private rooms, with their own dealers, so they can get fleeced in luxury away from the pikers."

"I've heard about that."

"Those guys stay at the tables for ten or twelve hours at a stretch."

"Yeah?"

"Yeah," she says. "And guys like Shel, who do a lot of blow, he'll stay for thirty, forty hours straight."

"Were you one of his perks?"

"I guess you could say that. Or a souvenir. He brought me home with him." She reaches for a can to dump her cigarette ash into, but the ash falls on the floor.

"Why are you still here, if he's dead?"

"Why is anyone still here? The house is full of food and booze, and no one's come in to shut it down."

The flight search turns up only four results. "There are no flights to Duluth tonight. There's a six thirty-five tomorrow morning. Stops in Minneapolis."

"I'll take it," she says.

"What's your last name?"

"Johannson."

I type that into the phone, along with her date of birth and an email address where she can receive her electronic boarding pass.

She takes a long puff of her cigarette and dumps the ash into a soda can. It lands with a short echoing hiss.

Six Kools and two Diet Cokes later, I know a lot more about Sheldon Brown.

He was an acquaintance of the governor. Not a friend, but a supporter who attended some fundraising events. He owned a string of car dealerships across the state that benefited from the governor's tax reforms. He was also two years into an increasingly heavy coke addiction. Six months ago, he lost $3.5 million in a single night at one of the big Vegas casinos. He went back to his room, got on the phone, and sold off a $5 million chunk of his car dealerships to cover the debt. Sold it to Franklin Dorsett. Then he lost another $1.5 million over the next two days.

Linnea also mentions that Brown owned a dozen strip clubs. He'd bring in girls now and then from San Antonio or Houston to party for the weekend. Dorsett liked Katie Green, and he liked her best with one or two other girls on the side. "He was a glutton all the way around," Linnea says. "The kind who always comes back from the buffet with two plates, if you know what I mean."

I'm sitting up in bed with my back against the pillows. She's on the edge of the bed wearing nothing, with her legs crossed at the knees and one foot on the floor. "Frank liked to push Shel," she says. "Egg him on, you know?"

"What do you mean?"

"Encourage him to do more blow. Gamble more. Because—well, let's put it this way—a lot of the money Shel lost wound up in Frank's hands."

She looks bored as she bends the matches one by one from a matchbook so they stick out like crooked teeth. Then she adds, "There was another guy, fat and kind of creepy, who came into the house once a week and gave reports."

"About what?" I ask.

"The clubs. He was a bouncer at one of the clubs, a big fat sweaty guy, and he'd come and tell Shel the numbers and Shel would ask if there was any trouble."

She stops and thinks for a few seconds. "The guy didn't like him." She looks up at me and says, "The bouncer. He didn't like Shel, 'cause he knew Shel was using. The last few weeks before he died, Shel started shooting."

"Heroin?"

"Coke. Ever been around someone who shoots coke? They're not like junkies. They don't shoot up twice a day and then lie around all droopy-headed and content. They shoot, they get a rush, then they want to shoot again a minute later when the rush is gone. And they start getting crazy. Like, paranoid, psychotic, out of control. Shel was threatening cops. They'd come in here when the parties got out of hand. When I first got here, he'd tone it down when the cops came, but toward the end, he would threaten them."

"How?"

"He'd say this stuff about how the shit was going to roll uphill, instead of down. How it was all gonna go straight to the top."

"What did that mean?"

She shrugs. "I don't know."

"These were local cops?"

She stops and thinks for a second. "You know, now that you mention it, no. They were State Patrol. Always State Patrol." She puts the matchbook down on the bed and takes the last sip of Diet Coke from the can on the nightstand.

"That's funny," I say. "They're usually out on the highways, not in residential neighborhoods. You have any photos on your phone?"

She gets that teasing smile on her face again and says, "What kind of photos are you interested in? You want one of me?"

"Sure, but—"

"I could tell by the way you were looking at me by the pool. You're not real subtle, you know."

"I'm more interested in photos of Sheldon Brown and Franklin Dorsett. How well do you think Brown knew the governor?"

She lights another cigarette and shrugs as she blows out a cloud of smoke. "I don't know. They knew each other well enough to get on each other's nerves. I wouldn't say there was a whole lot of warmth between them."

"Was he ever here?"

"The governor?" She shakes her head. "No. But Shel took me to meet him."

"Where?"

"A country club. A fundraiser. Once at the governor's mansion in Austin. Wait a second." She picks her phone up from the dresser and scrolls through some photos. "Here." She comes back to the bed and turns the screen toward me.

It's a photo of Brown and Dorsett with Jumbo Throckmorton. They're all standing in front of a bar, dressed in tuxedos. Dorsett is red-faced from booze. Brown's pupils are dilated, but it could just be the dark interior. Throckmorton towers over the two of them.

"Where was this taken?"

"Galveston. He pinched my ass about two seconds after I took the photo."

"What were you doing in Galveston?"

"The governor."

"You slept with the governor?"

She laughs. "Well, we didn't sleep. It was just an in-and-out kinda thing. He left his wife at the party to entertain. Told her he had to take a call upstairs."

"Why didn't you tell me this before?"

"Why didn't you ask?"

"I guess I got kinda distracted."

"Well, aren't you a smart detective?"

"Was he a perv?" I ask, ignoring her jibe.

"The governor?"

"Yeah."

"Not at all. But whoever named him Jumbo's got a funny sense of proportion. They got the throckmorton part right though. He hangs a little crooked."

"You have any more photos like this?"

She shrugs. "I can send you all I got. You decide what's interesting."

"Well, I have one for you," I say. "That guy Cat was with? I just want to make sure we're talking about the same person." I pull up the photo of Lomax on my phone, and when I show it to her, she recoils and puts her forearm across her breasts, as if to protect herself.

"I fucking hate that guy!" she says, and she eyes me like I'm the devil.

"But this is the one?" I say.

"That's him."

"What do you know about him?"

Her eyes narrow and her nostrils flare, and she says, "I'm glad I'm not Cat. That's what I know about *him*."

"What was he doing down here?"

"Same thing everyone else was doing. Living it up. Milking money out of Shel while he self-destructed. Why do you ask so many questions?"

"I'm a detective, remember?"

"Yeah. You said that."

"Did you have a sense of anything different about him? About Lomax?"

"I told you—"

"No, I mean, did he ever try to get you alone—"

"I avoided him," she says flatly.

"Wait till I finish the question. Did he try to get people alone so he could ask them questions?"

"I don't know." Her eyes narrow again. "What are you getting at?"

"Did he ever ask you to..." There's a fine line here that I'm not sure I should cross. I want to know if he ever asked her to inform. Because I want to know if he was actually doing his job while he was in this house, or if he just got caught up in the drugs and the drinking and the sex. The problem is, if I start asking whether he acted like an undercover cop, she's going to pick up on it. Her ditzy flirt routine out by the pool was pretty convincing, but after talking to her, I see she's a lot smarter than I had thought. Exposing the identity of an undercover federal agent would be cause for revoking an investigator's license, and it's not something Ed Hartwell would ever forgive.

She sees my hesitation and asks, "What? Did he ever ask me to what?"

"Did he ask you questions about Brown and Dorsett? About the drugs, or the guy who came in with the weekly reports from the strip clubs, or any of that?"

She looks at me closely and I can see her mind going. "What are you asking me? If he was a cop? Is that what you're asking?"

Shit. She said it, not me.

"That's not what I asked. Just answer the question I *did* ask."

"OK, mister investigator. The answer is no. No, he did not ask me about any of that, and if he asked anyone else, I never heard of it. He *did* ask me if I wanted to snort a line with him. He *did* ask me to sit on his lap, and then he asked if I liked having a big dick up my ass. He was *that* kind of guy. Especially when he was doing coke.

"And every morning, he'd come out of Cat's room all shiny and fresh. He was the kind who trimmed his nose hairs every day, and kept his hair combed, and brushed every speck of lint off his jacket. A control freak with a perfect tan, and a big ego who could ooze charm when he wasn't totally self-absorbed. Poor Cat. To have a guy like *that* obsessed with you…" She shakes her head. "I'd rather be dead. And if I don't do something with my life soon, I probably will be."

The Lomax I saw in DC the other day, with the stains on his lapel and cuff, seems to have slipped a little from the one she described. And I wouldn't say he looked shiny. He looked jittery and worn with those dark circles under his eyes.

"You'll be out of here tomorrow," I say.

"It can't be soon enough," she says. "I've had enough of this nowhere life."

"What'll you do back home?"

"I don't know," she says. "Duluth is just another nowhere, but at least it's not here. And I have family there. Hey, I'm gonna wash up. You sticking around? Or do you have to go?"

"I can stick around for a few. I want to wash up too."

When she goes into the shower, I find her wallet and take a photo of her license, just to make sure. Linnea Johansson of Duluth, Minnesota. The names on the credit cards match the license. I find her phone and copy her number, and I put my number into her contacts while I'm at it.

When it's my turn to shower, I take everything into the bathroom with me: clothes, phone, wallet, keys. Afterward, she gives me a little kiss goodbye and tells me to keep in touch. I give her a card and tell her my number's in her phone.

She says, "You're sweet, Frankie. Thanks for the roll!"

24

I don't see anyone on my way out but I can still hear the voices, more of them than before, coming from a far corner of the house. The country music seems like it's been turned up a notch or two. There's a yell, five or six voices together, when someone sweeps up the pot with what must have been one hell of a hand.

It's still hot outside. I start the car, and on my way down the driveway, crunching along that yellow gravel, I see a state trooper rolling slowly down the road past the iron gate. I turn his way and come up behind him. He's going about half the speed limit in a black-and-white Dodge Charger with red and blue flashers on top. License plate says 8-TA. I wonder if he's an old Cowboys fan. Troy Aikman—TA—wore number eight. I pass him and he follows me for a while, no lights or sirens. After a few minutes, he disappears.

I have Franklin Dorsett's address in the GPS. He lives about ten minutes from here, in a neighborhood where the houses are only two or three times normal size. That must be where the regular millionaires live.

Dorsett's house looks good from the outside. In front is an acre of dark-green lawn, manicured bushes, and neatly mulched beds. No cars in the driveway. The stone porch has flowers in giant urns on either side. A lawn jockey holds a lantern beside the front door.

I ring the bell a few times but get no answer. Through the front windows I see an empty hallway. I go around the corner and look in, but that side of the house is in the late-afternoon shade, and I can't see much. Around back, where the sun is still shining, I can see into the kitchen. There are crumpled paper towels all over the counter, Chinese food containers lying on their sides, and Lone Star beer cans scattered around the sink. If the guy's so rich, why's he drinking beer out of cans?

There's not much to see here, and there doesn't seem to be anyone around. I go back to the car and head out along the freshly paved asphalt driveway.

My phone rings just as I'm turning onto the street. It's Miriam, and she launches right into a fight without so much as a hello.

"What did you tell Lenny?"

"Excuse me?"

"You told him a *lion* was coming to his birthday party?" She's outraged. "A lion? And a panda? In our house? What's that supposed to mean?"

"He wanted the animals to come to his birthday," I say. "That's why we went to the zoo. To invite them."

"OK, first of all, we're taking him to Chuck E. Cheese's—"

"He said the party was going to be at home—"

"I'm talking," she says. "OK? Don't interrupt me when I'm talking. The party is going to be at Chuck E. Cheese's, with *people*, not lions. Three friends and their moms."

I can hear Lenny crying in the background. Miriam says, "Lenny, go back to your room, sweetie. Mommy's talking."

"Why's he crying?" I ask. "Did you tell him he can't have the animals over?"

"Freddy!" I hate that exasperated what-is-wrong-with-you sigh.

"Look," I say, "I went to four toy stores to find a stuffed elephant, a gorilla, a panda, a lion, and a cheetah. I told him they were all coming. We even made a seating chart. His heart's set on it."

"Well, why didn't you tell *me* about this?"

"Didn't Lenny explain it?"

"He's four," she says. "He doesn't explain things. What am I supposed to think when he tells me half the zoo is coming to his birthday party?"

"OK, well now you know."

"You need to be clear about these things, Freddy. How was I supposed to know you did all that?"

"Why didn't you talk to me?"

"Why didn't *I* talk to *you*?" she says. "Oh my God, *you're* the one who never talks."

"I'm talking now," I say.

"You're yelling!"

"No I'm not."

"Yes you are!" she says.

"Why do you have to contradict everything I say?"

"Why are you yelling at me?"

"I'm not yelling, goddammit!"

"Listen to yourself!" she screams.

"OK," I say, taking it down a notch. "You want to know why I don't talk to you? *This* is why. Every time I say something, you contradict me."

"No I don't."

The red-and-blue flashers come on behind me. It's Troy Aikman again. I didn't see him sneak up on me, but it looks like he wants to have a talk.

"Hey, Miriam. I gotta go. I got some trouble here."

"Freddy, you—"

I hang up before she finishes her sentence. We'll pick up this argument next time, just like we always do. The divorce has just been a continuation of the marriage, only now it takes place on the phone. Every time I start wondering if there's a way to divorce yourself from a divorce, I remember the wedding vows. Till death do you part.

I pull over, and the trooper walks up beside the car. He looks nothing like Troy Aikman. He's short and stocky, around fifty years old, with black hair shaved close beneath the sides of his cowboy hat. He wears reflective, wrap-around sunglasses, and his scalp shines with sweat. He tells me the registration decal on my license plate expired a few days ago, on September thirty-first. I want to tell him September only has thirty days, but he doesn't look like the kind who's interested in trivia.

I tell him the car is a rental. He says he doesn't care. If the registration's expired, it can't be on the road. He takes my license and goes to his cruiser to run a check. A few minutes later, he comes back and asks if I'm a cop. I tell him I'm not.

"Step out of the car, Mr. Ferguson." He tells me to stand behind his car, and he pops my trunk, pulls my suitcase out, and opens it up. It's one of those little black deals that has wheels and fits in the overhead bin on the plane.

He goes through all my clothes, dropping each piece on the ground after he examines it. Then he tells me to pick it all up and repack it. I know when a cop's looking for an excuse to make my day a whole lot worse, so I don't protest.

He says, "You know it's a crime to carry a concealed weapon in Texas without a permit?"

"I'm not carrying."

"I didn't ask you if you were carrying."

Fucking prick. Then why'd you open your mouth?

"I asked if you know the law," he says.

"Yes, officer, I know the law."

"You down here on business?"

"Yes."

"What business?"

"Investigation for a corporate client."

"Where's your gun?"

"I'm not licensed to carry in the state of Texas."

"Smart ass." He puts his boot up on the bumper of the Malibu. "You leave the force in bad standing?"

"What?"

"A retired cop can carry a gun, long as he leaves in good standing. It's the law."

"I'm not a cop."

"And you never were?"

"Never was," I say.

"Not a Fed?"

"No, sir."

He looks at me a little differently now. Kind of nods and tries again to size me up. "What were you doing at Sheldon Brown's house?"

"Talking to a girl."

He lets out a long, wheezing laugh that almost doubles him over and makes his face and neck flush a deep crimson. It takes him a few seconds to collect himself. Then he wipes the sweat from his brow and says, "Talking, huh?"

"Yeah."

"Well, I hope you had yourself a nice little talk. What were you doing at this house here?"

"Dorsett's house?"

"I was wondering if you knew his name."

"Seeing if anyone was home."

"Any luck?"

"No sir." I see a tow truck coming down the road. I think he's serious about not letting me drive with expired tags.

He says, "If your corporate client needs help, tell them they can talk to us. Texas Highway Patrol is always happy to help."

Yeah, you seem pretty happy to be helping me.

The tow truck pulls in ahead of my Malibu and starts backing up.

"When you leaving?" the cop asks.

"I have a flight in a few hours."

"Call an Uber. You'll make the airport in plenty of time."

As I reach for my phone, the tow truck driver hauls a pair of chains off the back of the truck and says to the cop, "Hey, Tommy!"

"Hey, Bill. Take her to the impound lot."

I have both phones in my front right pocket: my personal Android and the little burner flip phone. As I pull the Android out to call an Uber, the flip phone falls to the ground. The cop looks down at it, then up at the phone in my hand, then back to the one on the ground. I want to grab it, but I don't want to set him off.

He sees I'm uneasy. He squats down and picks up the flip phone and says, "You need two, huh?"

I don't respond.

"That was a question, son. A simple affirmative would do."

I say with a sigh, "Yes, sir. I need two."

He hits a button on the phone and says, "You only have one number in the contact list? Must be someone special, huh? You mind if I give 'em a call?"

I picture Anna answering a call from this guy, mister warmth and good cheer. What if he tells her he's a cop? She's terrified of being taken into custody, because in her mind, it'll lead right back to Lomax.

I start to tense up, ready for a fight.

He says, "That's a mighty big fist you got there, son. I wouldn't go swinging it." Then he adds, "You know what kind of problems we have to deal with out here? We get these guys running drugs. They send a car up ahead to call back and give reports on where the cops are. Now you don't look like the type to be mixed up in that kinda thing, but I wouldn't be doing my duty if I didn't make sure."

The more pissed off I get, the more he seems to like his job.

"I'm going to give your friend a call here—"

"Please don't." What if he hears the fear in her voice and understands there's something wrong? What if he decides to send someone by to check on her? I can just see the cop at her front door. *Something wrong, ma'am? You look scared. What's with all the newspapers about that plane crash? May I see some ID?*

Would it come out that she had a seat on that flight and didn't board? Would she plead with him not to turn her over to the FBI? How would *that* come off?

"What's the matter, son? You look mighty uneasy all of a sudden. You don't want someone on the other end of that phone to know you're in custody?"

She's on the edge, and so am I. Give her a nudge in the wrong direction, and she might shoot herself.

"I'm not in custody," I say. "This is a traffic stop. Gimme that phone, you redneck bastard!"

He chuckles and shakes his head and says, "Now that is no way to talk to a lawman."

"Give me the goddamn phone."

"Wrong tone, buddy. That sounds like a threat." He's all business now.

Fast as lightning, he grabs my right hand, gives it a twist, and spins me around. I drop the smart phone, and he's got me up against the hood of the cruiser. He pushes my head down, kicks my feet apart, and puts one of my wrists in the cuffs. I let him cuff the other one without resistance.

I spend the next ten minutes in the back of his car. He cuts the engine and the air conditioning and stands outside chatting with the tow-truck driver. When the cop returns, I watch the little white Malibu being dragged nose-up down the road, like a fish on a line. My suitcase is still in the trunk.

The cop says, "Whooo-wee! It's hot in here! Don't know how you stand it without the AC."

He starts the engine, picks up the radio, and tells the dispatcher he's bringing me in for processing.

We're still sitting there on the side of the road when he takes the flip phone from his pocket and says, "Let's see who we got on the other end of the line here."

"Hey," I say in the most reasonable tone I can muster. "I'd appreciate it if you left her alone."

"Her, huh?" He turns with a knowing smile. "Got yourself a lady-friend on the side? That one you were talking to at Sheldon Brown's ain't enough for you?" He lets out a laugh and says, "You do a lot of *talking*, huh? You got some kinda stamina, dontcha pal?"

He hits the button to dial the number, I hear a little click over the hum of the air conditioning, and then her voice comes through the speaker.

"Hello?"

"To whom do I have the pleasure of speaking this fine afternoon?"

"Who is this?" she asks in an uncertain voice.

"Who is *this*?" asks the cop. "That's the question." When he turns to look at me, his holster makes a creaking sound against the fake leather seat. He gives me a smile and says to Anna, "You know I got a little magic phone here with just one number in it, and I'm wondering what makes you so special you can't be on the regular phone." He lets out his wheezy laugh as he turns and faces forward again.

Her voice goes a full octave higher, and I can hear her heart in her throat. "Oh my God, who is this?"

"Look, lady, you're friend here ain't too bright. Whatever he's trying to hide between you two, he already blew it. You want to stay out of trouble, I suggest you move on. Find yourself a fella that's got his shit together." Then he hangs up the phone and eyes me in the rearview.

As we pull away from the roadside, he tosses the phone onto the seat beside him and says, "I noticed you don't wear a ring. You take it off when you travel?"

"I'm not married."

"Then why you gotta go sneaking around with the ladies?"

I say, "Hey, what's it mean, shit rolls uphill?"

"Come again?" he says.

"Shit rolls uphill. Is that a Texas expression?"

He laughs his wheezy laugh and says, "You got it backwards, son. Shit rolls downhill in Texas." He slows for a left turn, which he makes through a yellow light changing to red. No turn signal. Fucking cops.

I say, "I thought I heard Sheldon Brown say that once."

The cop's eyes move from the road back up to the rearview mirror. He gives me a long, hard stare and says,

"That don't sound like the kind of thing Sheldon Brown shoulda been saying to anybody. You know what I think, pal? I think you got better places to be than Texas."

25

After a long drive, he hauls me into a station with half a dozen highway cruisers parked out front. Inside, he cuffs me to a bench in the main office and leaves me sitting for a long time. My friend Troy Aikman, or whatever his name is, lets me know his shift ended thirty minutes ago, and he's processing my disorderly conduct on his own personal time, as a service to the community. I ask him what I did that was disorderly, and he tells me now would be a good time to shut up, seeing as our previous conversations didn't go so well.

I've been listening to the cops' chatter and watching the guys they've been bringing through here in cuffs. There's been one drunk, one reckless driver, and five drug arrests. One was for possession, four for possession with intent to distribute. The one they busted for possession was all bent out of shape about his money and whether he was going to get it back. It sounded like the cops relieved him of a lot of cash.

Every cop coming into this place and every one going out stops to say hello to Aikman. The only exception is the barrel-chested Latino cop with the long, skinny legs. While Aikman stands at a counter making small talk with the female officer on the other side, the Latino cop silently fills out paperwork. They're standing five feet apart, but they don't acknowledge each other.

The female cop asks Aikman which guy was picked up coming out of Franklin Dorsett's place. Aikman turns and points to me. The Latino cop turns and gives me a thorough looking over.

The female cop says, "He says he's an investigator?"

"That's the story," Aikman says.

"He show you a PI license?"

"Nope."

"We'll get him on the transport." She pushes a paper across the counter for him to sign. He signs it, says he'll see her tomorrow, and walks away. Doesn't say a word to the Latino, but on his way out of the building it's goodbyes all around.

The Latino cop stays at the counter with his back to me, flipping though papers on a clipboard and occasionally checking his phone. A female cop opens a door over on the far left side of the room and says, "Bring 'em on."

A burly cop unlocks me from the bench, then he and his buddy march me toward the open door.

The Latino cop turns and says, "That one goes to 3A."

The cop on my right repeats, "3A."

They take me twenty feet down the hall, through a door on the left, and leave me cuffed to a chair in a small room with a desk and an overhead camera.

A few minutes later, the Latino cop comes in with a cup of coffee. He introduces himself as Lieutenant Alfonso Jiménez, then he goes behind the desk, puts his coffee down, stands up on the chair, and pastes a sticky note over the lens of the camera. He fiddles with something else up there while he's at it. The microphone, I think.

He pulls a pen from his shirt pocket, takes a seat behind the desk, and gives me a long look and says, "So you're an investigator?"

"That's right."

"Who you working for?"

"We've been through this already."

"I wasn't part of that conversation," he says. "So let's go through it again. Who are you working for?"

"The airline."

"Which airline?"

"The one that crashed."

He nods and says, "The plane Sheldon Brown was on. You were at his house?"

"I was."

"Part of your investigation?" He watches my face closely.

"You could say that. I might be off on a tangent here. I don't know yet."

"You find anything interesting?"

"Just a girl. You guys always get this many narcotics busts through here?"

This guy has a stare that takes in everything. "That's an interesting question," he says. "You work for the airline directly, or someone else?"

"Right now a guy named Ed Hartwell." I lean toward him and pursue the line of questioning he interrupted. "Because, you know, what's odd is that Highway Patrol doesn't usually pick up a lot of drug dealers. The dealers are on the city streets, not the interstates."

"That's a nice observation. Hartwell, you said?" This guy's got a face like a poker player. Doesn't give away anything. I like him.

"Yeah," I say. "He's a private investigator up in DC. Former FBI."

"How former?"

"What's that?"

"How long's he been out of the FBI?"

"A little over four years," I say.

He taps the pen gently on the desk in a quick steady rhythm, but he hasn't taken any notes yet. He doesn't even have a pad to write on.

"Hey," I say, "when you get those guys down to lockup, do you ever have to separate them?"

"'Scuse me?" He stops tapping the pen.

"I mean these guys you're picking up for distribution. If they're in rival gangs, do you have to sort 'em out down at lockup? Or you just throw them all in one big cell and let them fight it out?"

"They sort themselves out," Jiménez says, and he never takes his eyes off my face. "You're full of questions, aren't you?"

"I thought Highway Patrol was just speeding tickets and accident scenes and overweight trucks."

"It's a lot of that," Jiménez says. "You got a number I can reach Ed Hartwell?"

"Yeah, but I'm interested in a guy you picked up yesterday. Ramón Ramírez. Where'd they get him again?"

Jiménez lays his pen on the desk and leans back and takes a long hard look at me. Finally, he says, "Longview."

"Another drug bust for the Highway Patrol."

"A big one," Jiménez says.

"I want to talk to that guy."

Jiménez frowns and shakes his head.

"Why not?"

"You watch the news today?"

"No."

He watches me for a moment and I wait for him to continue.

"He died overnight in holding."

"How'd that happen?" I ask.

"Balloon full of fentanyl burst in his colon."

"No," I say, shaking my head.

"No what?"

"That doesn't make any sense."

"Really?" The way he's looking at me, I can't tell if he thinks I'm stupid, or he doesn't like me, or he just doesn't trust me.

"Yeah, really," I say. "Why would he have swallowed a balloon with a few grams of fentanyl when he's carrying two kilos in his car? You swallow a balloon if you're expecting a body search. Like if you're going through airport security. Not when you're driving a car with two kilos of the shit in the trunk."

Jiménez takes a deep breath and leans back in his chair. He lets out a little frustrated "Goddammit" under his breath, and then just sits there quietly, looking troubled.

"What's Ed Hartwell's number?" he asks.

I give him the number. He doesn't write it down, but I can see him make a mental note. Then he says, "You want some coffee? Water or anything?"

"Some water would be nice."

He leaves the room, leaves his empty coffee cup there on the table, and I'm alone for the next twenty minutes, listening to the buzzing of the overhead fluorescent light and the echoing conversations of the cops in the hall.

When Jiménez returns, he unlocks my cuffs and gives me my wallet and smart phone. He says, "Call an Uber, or Lyft, or whatever you use. I can't drive you anywhere."

He gets back up on the chair, pulls the sticky note off the camera, and fiddles with the mic.

I rub my wrists. "I'm free to go?"

"You're free to go. Your buddy Ed Hartwell seems to know the right people." If Trooper Aikman had said those words, he would have spoken them with bitterness. But Jiménez seems more relieved than annoyed.

I check my phone. There's an Uber just a few minutes away. Jiménez says he'll walk me out. On the way out, we pass a wall of photos of officers who have fallen in the line of duty. Jiménez stops and points out a young white guy, no more than twenty-six or twenty-seven. "This guy was shot by a crazy man. Execution-style while he sat in his cruiser. Only lately I've been thinking the guy who shot him might not have been crazy."

I look at the face in the photo. He doesn't look like a cop. A little too gentle in the eyes. I could see him managing a pharmacy or a movie theater.

As we exit the station through the double glass doors, Jiménez says, "There's two more who aren't up on that wall."

"Who's that?" I ask.

"A patrolman named Manuel Martínez, and a captain named Brandon Robertson."

The names sound familiar. A green Toyota Prius pulls into the lot and heads toward us.

"Were those recent?" I ask. "You didn't have time to put the photos up?"

The driver of the Prius rolls down the passenger window, leans his head toward us, and says, "Airport?"

"They *were* recent," Jiménez says. "They might never make the wall. But I want to make sure they get their due." And then he hands me the flip phone and tells me to have a nice flight.

When I'm in the car, he leans his head through the window and says, "What kinds of contacts does Ed Hartwell have in the Bureau?"

"Plenty," I say. "Why?"

He nods and says, "I took a card from your wallet, and I put in one of mine." Then he tips his hat and walks away.

* * *

I get to the airport just before my flight boards. Inside, I make the gate in no time, since I don't have a bag. It's still in the trunk of that rental car.

After the stewardess finishes the safety demonstration, she tells everyone to turn off their laptops and put their phones in airplane mode. I shut off the smart phone, and I'm about to turn off the flip phone when I notice the little exclamation point up in the corner of the screen. It's a text from Anna. The timestamp says 6:43 a.m. That was the unfamiliar buzzing sound that woke me at the motel this morning. I open the message. *My password is JULIA*, it says. *And the names of the other two passengers on the Hawaii flight: Manuel Martínez and Brandon Robertson.*

26

OCTOBER 6

When I got back to DC last night, I called Anna, but she didn't answer. I called again this morning, three times, and texted too. No response. That asshole cop must have spooked her. I wonder if she blocked this number.

I've been sitting outside Lomax's apartment since six-thirty, waiting for him to appear. If he comes out on foot, I'll recognize him. If he's driving, he'll be in a silver 2016 Chevy Impala. That's what he's got registered, anyway.

A little before ten I see his car drive up from the underground garage. That's him behind the wheel.

He drives out Wayne Avenue, past Sligo Creek Parkway, then turns right on Bradford Road. This is a middle-class residential neighborhood. He parks in front of a small yellow house with a spotty lawn and a pink girl's bicycle leaning against a concrete birdbath. He sits there for a while, looking at his phone, as a FedEx truck makes its way down the street.

The truck stops halfway down the block, at a house that's for sale. The driver gets out, dashes up the walkway to the porch, and drops a flat box in front of the door. He stands there for a few seconds, punching the keys on his hand-held tracker, then returns to the truck and drives off.

Lomax opens his door just as a guy in painter's overalls comes around the far side of the for-sale house carrying a ladder. Lomax eyes him for a few seconds, then closes his door and stays in the car. The guy with the ladder crosses the front yard and goes around the corner of the house. He returns without the ladder and fetches a bucket of paint, a brush, and a rag, and carries them back to where he left the ladder.

Lomax waits a couple of minutes, then gets out of the car. He walks up to the porch, picks up the package, and carries it back to his car. When he drives off, I follow him, keeping about a hundred and twenty yards behind. The painter is out front, wiping his hands with a rag. He looks toward the street just as I pass, and he gives a little nod to someone behind me. In the rearview mirror, I see a blue Dodge Dart fifty yards back. I follow Lomax, and the Dart follows me, straight down Bradford, right on Manchester, left on Wayne.

When we get back to the big buildings in the center of Silver Spring, I figure Lomax is headed home. He'll go straight to East West Highway and turn left. I turn left on Fenton and keep my eyes on the rearview, waiting for the blue Dart to follow. But it doesn't. It continues straight down Wayne, following Lomax, with two cars in between.

I make a few turns and come up toward Lomax's building from the opposite direction. From a block away, I see his car go back into underground parking. The blue Dodge Dart is a block farther up the street, coming toward me. We both pass the building at the same time, me going north and the Dart going south. The Dart has a dashcam. The driver is black and the passenger is white. They're both clean-cut.

OK, what the hell was *that* all about? I stop a couple blocks past Lomax's building and sit there, tapping my fingers on the dashboard for a few seconds.

Then I head back up to the house where Lomax picked up the package. I park out front and walk around the side where the painter went. He's standing at the foot of the ladder, typing something into his phone. He looks Salvadoran or Guatemalan, with copper-tan skin, dark hair, dark eyebrows, and a mustache.

I walk up and tell him I live in the neighborhood. I was just passing by and my house needs painting. Can he give me a business card? He hands me one that says Delgado Brothers painting. I don't like the look he gives me. It's not a mean look. It's the look of a guy who takes notes on everything he sees. Like he's getting all the details down, in case he has to describe me later.

An hour later, when I walk into the office, Bethany says, "Hey, Freddy. Where you been?"

"Out," I say, as I head to my desk. "You make any progress on those names I gave you? Brown, Dorsett, Midland-Odessa Custom Hauling?"

Leon doesn't even look up from his computer. "Still digging," he says. "This shit's like a maze."

"What's like a maze?" I ask.

He looks up and says, "One business owns another owns another. Like those Russian dolls you keep opening up and finding more dolls." He turns back to his monitor.

"How was Texas?" Bethany asks.

"Hot. Can I use your computer?"

"What's wrong with yours?"

"It's still in Texas."

She gets up from her chair and lets me sit. I can feel her eyes on me, even though I'm looking at the monitor.

"You not feeling chatty today?" she asks.

"Sorry, Beth. I got something I want to look into here."

I look up the owner of the house in Silver Spring. The guy is ninety-six. I call the realtor, a cheerful-sounding woman, and pretend to be a concerned neighbor. I tell her the owner, Mr. Kowalczyk, should have his mail forwarded, so people don't steal it. She says his mail is being forwarded to his daughter up in Gaithersburg. Mr. Kowalczyk is in an assisted living home up there, two minutes from his daughter's house.

I ask her about the painter. Is he reliable? Does he do good work? She says she doesn't know about the painter. Kowalczyk's daughter must have hired him.

I can't get ahold of the daughter. No one answers the phone, and she has no voicemail. Maybe she rejects calls from unknown numbers.

The painter's card says Roberto Delgado. He and his brothers have been proudly serving the DC area for six years. At least, that's what their website says. But the Wayback Machine over at the Internet Archive says different. The Wayback Machine takes snapshots of every site on the Internet every few months. You can go there and see what Yahoo looked like in 1998. But you can't see a snapshot of Delgado Brothers's website from six months ago, because it didn't exist.

This is another one of those data problems, like the one where all the credit bureaus had the exact same addresses for our friend Mr. Charles Johnston. Somebody downtown has been slipping up.

What kind of package would Lomax be picking up at a house that isn't his?

Ed Hartwell told me of a case a couple years ago that some of his former colleagues at the Bureau helped to crack. A guy was selling drugs through the dark web. Coke, fentanyl, ecstasy, OxyContin. You go online and place an order through a site that looks like eBay. The buyers and sellers are rated on a five-star system, so you know if the person you're dealing with is reputable. This seller has a couple hundred five-star ratings, with lots of comments about the purity and quality of his goods. The FBI and the DEA thought he was operating out of California, but they weren't sure.

They had one agent posing as a buyer online. He had a hundred or so transactions under his belt, and a good buyer rating. He spent a lot of time in the user forums answering questions: how to cut fentanyl so you don't kill your customers and don't piss them off too much, which ecstasy was the best, whether the cocaine with the pinkish hue was worth buying.

The agent was placing two or three orders a week, having it all sent to different addresses in the DC area. The packages would always show up on time, but they were postmarked from different places in Colorado, Missouri, Louisiana, and Kansas. The Feds couldn't track the source.

Finally, they got a break. The postal service told the FBI that a lot of drugs were coming through a post office in Columbia, Missouri. All the packages were being sent to houses that were for sale, and every package had a different name on it.

The FBI looked into it and found the realtor who was the selling agent for all of the properties. Any mail that showed up at the houses, he carried in and left on the kitchen counter. If a special package showed up—say, for example, a few ounces of cocaine, or a couple hundred ecstasy tablets— the guy would look up and down the street for cops before he took it home with him. If there were any cops around, or anyone who looked like they might be watching, the guy left the package on the counter and tried again the next day.

If the cops ever did show up at one of those houses and found the package, what could they do? It wasn't the realtor's house. The package didn't have his name on it. How could they tie it to him?

Each package might contain ten different orders for ten different customers in ten different states. The realtor repackaged the orders into ten parcels and handed them out to guys who got paid a couple hundred bucks a day to drive around to other towns and drop the parcels one by one into neighborhood mailboxes.

The dealer—who was, in fact, based in California—had hooked up with realtors in several states and was paying them a hefty fee for their distribution services. Eventually, they all went down. But the FBI guys who worked the case were impressed with the ingenuity of the scheme.

Lomax, I assume, had also heard the story. Seems like he didn't want to have a realtor in the picture. And he wouldn't need one for a FedEx package. Their tracking system tells you right when they're coming, and FedEx packages don't get forwarded like regular mail so you can just sit outside and wait.

So what's in the package? And who would want to follow him?

My phone chimes as a few new emails come in. One of them is from that cop who questioned me in Dallas yesterday.

27

The email from Alfonso Jiménez has no text, just links to some old news stories in the *Austin Statesman*.

The first is about a woman named Wilma Juarez. There's a video of her from a year and a half ago in front of the statehouse, screaming at lawmakers, reporters, and passersby. When she pulls out a cigarette lighter and tries to light her skirt on fire, the cops arrest her. It's really kind of pathetic seeing a woman try to immolate herself without gasoline. She was clearly distraught.

The article says Juarez wants to sue the State Patrol because they intercepted a car loaded with drug money, which her husband was driving. When the car failed to make it to the border, the cartel sent someone up from Mexico to pump thirty bullets into her husband. She wanted to sue the State Patrol for the money they stole, plus a few million for the emotional distress of losing her husband in such a violent way. Juarez was undocumented, and by drawing all that attention to herself on the steps of the statehouse, she got herself deported.

I dig a little further and find that the local stations in Austin got a lot of play out of the story. They actually covered it with a straight face—mostly, anyway. They interviewed a captain from the State Patrol about Wilma Juarez's story, which he dismissed. The cop said the woman was out of her head with grief. When the reporter asked if it was true the car was loaded with drug money, he said the seizure amounted to $20,000.

If it had been a major bust, he said, they would have invited every camera crew in Texas to come film the piles of cash. "People tell us all the time we're not doing enough to earn their tax dollars," he said. "Believe me, when we have a big money bust, that's a win for us. We let everybody know."

But the cop looks uneasy. I don't know why. They aren't throwing him any hardball questions. He looks like the kind of guy who puts his heart into his work. Maybe he doesn't like the way the media is making fun of the woman he described as distraught. I rewind the interview to where the cop first appeared. There's his name on the bottom of the screen. Captain Brandon Robertson. One of the cops on the Hawaii flight.

The second article in Alfonso Jiménez's email is about an incident that occurred a little over a year ago, just south of San Antonio. A guy walked up to a State Patrol car parked beside a highway diner where a trooper sat drinking coffee and, without provocation, put a bullet through the trooper's head. One of the cooks had just finished his shift at the diner and was leaving the parking lot when he witnessed the shooting. He aimed his car at the assailant and knocked him down.

When the police interviewed the assailant in the hospital, he admitted shooting the patrolman and said it was retaliation for the cops stealing money from his cousin. A lot of money. The article wrote the guy off as delusional, and noted that he had a long history of drug use.

It went on to give some background on the cop who had been killed—a guy named Moses Tate. He was an eight-year veteran who had been written up once for being too lenient on speeders. The article included a number of quotes from Tate's best friend on the force, Manuel Martínez, who vowed to investigate the matter thoroughly. There's a photo of Martínez in the middle of the article. He's an earnest-looking guy in his early thirties.

I scroll back to the top of the page and check the date of the article. August 29th of last year. That's thirteen months before Manuel Martínez perished with his wife and kids on the flight to Honolulu.

The last two articles in Jiménez's email are brief, just a couple of paragraphs each. One describes the conclusion of the investigation into the shooting of Patrolman Moses Tate: it was the act of a delusional individual whose many run-ins with the law left him with a bitter resentment toward cops, and whose mind was deranged by years of heavy drug use. The other article describes the execution-style death of Wilma Juarez's husband. He really did take thirty bullets just hours after he was released on a bail bond.

I call Alfonso Jiménez down in Dallas.

"Why'd you send me this?"

"Because you asked all the right questions and your boss is connected to the FBI. Now let me ask you something. That guy Juarez, the drug runner who got all shot up, he had a number of priors. Why would they let him out on bail?"

"I don't know," I say. "Who put up the bond?"

"Your buddy Ramón Ramírez," he says. "Why would a cartel bother bailing someone out and then shoot him thirty times over twenty thousand dollars?"

"I'm not familiar with the cartels," I say, "but I hear that's how they operate. Big displays of violence keep everyone in line."

"Uh-uh," says Jiménez. "It cost them fifty grand to bail him out. Why would they spend fifty thousand to make a point about twenty thousand?"

"So what are you thinking?"

"That's just it," he says. "I don't know. But Brandon Robertson was a friend of mine, and he was talking to the FBI. I think he knew something."

"About what?"

"I don't know," he says.

"Do you know who he was talking to? Was it a guy named Lomax?"

"Doesn't sound familiar."

"How about Rollins?"

"Mitch Rollins," he says. "That's the guy."

"He's Lomax's boss. Anything come of it?"

"No. Nothing. Robertson was upset about it."

"From the video I saw, he looks like the kind of guy who took his job seriously."

"Yeah. He was."

"Hey, I want you to do me a favor," I say. "Can you get me a credit card statement?"

"Maybe. Does it have to be evidence-worthy? Because you'll need a warrant for that."

"No. I'm just looking for a lead. I got a Visa card, belongs to a guy from Illinois named Charles Johnston. He used it to buy a plane ticket for a passenger on that Honolulu flight, and I'd like to know what else he bought."

"Give me the number," Jiménez says. "I'll see what I can do."

28

I'm not able to get much background on Mitch Rollins. He's been with the Bureau for close to thirty years. He's married, and his kids are past college age. He lives on the other side of the Potomac, in one of those neighborhoods in McLean that was affordable when he moved in, back in the late 1980s. Now you need two incomes to buy into an area like that.

A couple years ago, when the house was nearly paid off, he took out a $300,000 second mortgage. Last year, he took out a $200,000 home improvement line of credit. I take a drive over Chain Bridge and head up Dolly Madison Boulevard, past CIA headquarters in Langley. Rollins lives near a public elementary school, in a neighborhood of luxury cars and perfect lawns. A quick drive by his house shows me it hasn't had any obvious improvements in at least a decade. And there's a For Sale sign out front.

When I call the number on the sign, the realtor tells me her seller is motivated. She's a gossipy type, so I chat her up for a while. Seems Mitch and his wife are getting divorced. She hints at money troubles. Maybe that's why Rollins is hanging on to a job he no longer cares for.

Just as we're wrapping up, another call comes in. I thank the realtor for her time and pick up the second call.

"Hey Freddy?" It's Julia Brook. Something's up. I can hear it in her voice.

"Julia? Where are you?"

"Fredericksburg. I'm on 95, heading up to DC."

"What for?"

"I want to pick up some stuff from Anna's apartment." Her voice is high and tense, with an unsteady quaver.

"You mind if I join you?"

"That's why I was calling," she says. "Can you meet me there?"

"Yeah. You sound nervous. You all right?"

"I don't know, Freddy." The line is quiet for a few seconds, except for the background noise of the car on the highway. "You know, I went into work this morning. At the florist."

"Yeah?"

"And there was a letter. It arrived a few days ago, but I hadn't been in until today."

"OK."

"It was from Anna." Her voice is trembling.

"What'd it say?"

"Nothing. It was her phone. She put it in a regular envelope with ten stamps across the top and mailed it. The screen is shattered."

"Does the phone still work?"

"It does. I charged it and turned it on, but it has a passcode and I can't get in."

"You sure it's Anna's?"

"I'm pretty sure. It was her handwriting on the envelope. There was no return address."

"Where was the postmark from?"

"San Francisco. I tried unlocking it, but—"

"Is it an iPhone or an Android?"

"Android," she says. "What difference does it make?"

"If you guess the passcode wrong too many times on an iPhone, it erases itself. Androids don't do that."

"Freddy, why would she send me her phone?"

"She wanted you to have it."

Because something told her she might not come back from that trip. I believe what Anna told me, that she didn't know about the bomb. But she did believe Lomax was waiting for her on the other end of that flight, or at least she thought he was, and she was scared to death of him.

"Freddy..." Her voice breaks. "I have to pull over."

"Julia?" No answer. "Julia!" She doesn't respond, but I can still hear the background noise. I wait, and when the highway noise dies down a bit, I can hear her sobbing. After a minute or so, she picks up again, and she sounds even more rattled.

"Freddy, someone just called this phone. Right before I called you."

"Who?"

"I don't know. But he said, 'I knew you weren't on that plane. You know I'm going to find you. It's just a matter of time.' And then he hung up. I think he thought I was Anna."

"You sound just like her. What number did he call from?"

"999–999–9999."

"That's not a real number."

"No shit!" Now she loses it. "Freddy, where the hell is my sister? What the fuck is going on?"

"Meet me at Anna's apartment," I say. "Call when you get close. And if you start freaking out, pull over. Don't kill yourself on the way up here."

It takes her a couple seconds to respond. "OK, Freddy." There's no life left in her voice.

"And turn that phone off. All the way off, OK?"

I don't want the phone sending her location information back to Google and Uber and the phone company, and God knows how many other places. From there, the Feds can get it. Lomax can get it. Like he said, it's just a matter of time.

29

It takes Julia an hour and a half to get from Fredericksburg to Adams Morgan. I'm waiting with the property manager when she arrives wearing jeans and a white cotton blouse, with a black leather bag looped over her shoulder. It's almost five p.m., and the Indian summer air is starting to cool. She's calm now. Serene, as people often are after all the emotion has been wrung out of them. The property manager, a sturdy Salvadoran guy in his thirties with thick hands and thick black hair, says, "Wait, you're Anna's *sister*, right? You look just like her." How often does she have to hear those words?

He offers his condolences in the elevator, and Julia gracefully accepts. He wears the same silver crucifix as Anna. He says these terrorists are bad people, and God will punish them. You don't honor the Lord by killing his children. They'll realize their mistake when they have to explain themselves to Him. Their hell will be their understanding of what they've done, and when it dawns on them, their grief will be deeper than Julia's. I can see his words don't comfort her, though they seem to reassure him. I step in front of him on the way out of the elevator, because I want to get a look at that deadbolt before he opens the door.

My little toothpick fragment is gone. As he slides the pitted key into the lock, I ask him if he's been in the apartment since Anna died. He says no.

"Who else has a key?"

"No one," he says. "Unless Anna gave her spare to a friend. You can't duplicate these. Not at the hardware store."

I ask him if Julia can keep the key for a few days. He says sure, gives us his card, and leaves.

The main room of the apartment has a light oak floor and cheap rug with a grey-green Persian pattern, the kind of thing you might find at Lowes or Walmart. There's a sofa with one end table, and another table by the windows, covered with books, candles, and unread mail. To the right are a small kitchen and closet. To the left is the bedroom. The door is open. The queen-size bed is neatly made in white.

Julia seems to know exactly where to go. I follow her into the bedroom. She slides open the top drawer of the dresser and stares for a second. Then she looks at me.

"She kept a journal," Julia says. "Look."

In the front right corner of the drawer, which is packed with women's underwear, there's an empty rectangle that looks like it once held a stack of books. I put my hand into the empty space and feel around through the clothing. When I look up again, she's staring into my face, calm and determined, and she says in a tone that tells me there can only be one answer to this question, "Are you going to tell me now? Where's my sister?"

I examine her for a moment, trying to gauge her mood, how volatile she may be. I don't want another encounter like the one I had with Anna.

She seems calm. A little worn out, even, like the shock of that phone call took everything out of her. Her eyes show the same quiet intensity they did at Anna's funeral, when she asked me why I kept speaking of Anna in the present tense. She knew. And she knows now.

"She's alive," I say.

She swallows hard and puts a hand on the dresser to steady herself. She takes a few deep breaths through her nose and nods. I wish I had that ability to calm myself.

"Where is she?" Her voice is barely above a whisper, and it's quavering. Her body starts to tremble.

I shake my head and say, "I can't tell you."

"Why not?" She's trying to keep a lid on it, but her anger is rising.

"Because if whoever's after her gets to you, I don't want you to be able to tell him."

The anger drops and the calm determination returns. "Him," she says. "You know it's a him. Who's after her?"

"I don't—"

"Don't you lie to me, and don't evade me either. I know you're not a liar, Freddy Ferguson. I saw that in your eyes at Anna's funeral. Where is she? Who's after her?"

"You remember that FBI guy at the funeral?"

She has to think for a minute, so I give her a little prompt. "The one who was leaning in on you when he talked. His name is Lomax."

"Him?"

"Yeah, him. Did you recognize his voice when he called Anna's phone today and threatened you?"

"He..." She cocks her head a little, looks down at the floor, thinking. "No. Maybe it was him. I don't know. I wasn't in the best frame of mind at the funeral, so I don't remember much. To be honest, what I remember most about that day is you."

"Didn't he give you the creeps?"

"He did, kind of. I mean, that's not the kind of attention you want at your sister's funeral. But I put it out of my head. Why is he after Anna?"

"I don't know yet. That's what I'm trying to figure out."

"Did she tell you?"

"I'm not sure she fully understands it herself. She gave me some leads. I'm still digging into them."

"Is she OK?"

"She's safe, for now. But if it comes out that she wasn't on that plane, the FBI will pull her in for questioning, and she thinks Lomax will..." I stop short.

"Will what?"

"You know what line of work your sister was in. It's not hard to get into a bad situation. You don't have many people to turn to, and the ones who are supposed to look out for you aren't much better than the ones who are trying to hurt you. You're the property they rent out at night, and they just want to make sure their property doesn't get damaged. But if it's a cop, a federal agent damaging your goods, well… What can you do about that?" I remember the look of hatred in Kim Hahn's eyes. What *could* she do?

Julia pulls a pair of red lace underpants from the drawer, then another just like it, in dark blue. She examines them as if she's trying to make sense of her sister's life. I take a seat on the bed and explain what I've been able to piece together so far.

"Lomax was working on an investigation in Texas that involved Sheldon Brown and Franklin Dorsett."

"Who are they?" Julia asks.

"A couple of rich losers. Brown and Dorsett got a trip to DC to meet the Texas congressional delegation. That's usually a political favor. For what, I don't know yet. Maybe they wanted the Texas congressmen to introduce some legislation that would benefit their businesses. Or maybe they were just networking.

"That was a few months ago. Apparently, Lomax kept an eye on them while they were up here. More than kept an eye on them. They did some partying with your sister and her friend, Katie Green. Sheldon Brown took a liking to Anna. So did Lomax. Dorsett seemed to like Katie. Crystal."

Julia looks down at the floor as she tries to take all this in.

"Brown liked cocaine," I say. "From what I hear, he was rolling in it. Lomax got caught up in it somewhere along the line. You ever been around cokeheads?"

"No. I mean, I've seen people use it a couple of times."

"You know how they get?" I say. "It inflates their self-esteem and makes them feel invincible. It distorts their character. Some aspects of their personality become magnified. Other parts wither and disappear. That guy Lomax is a frat boy at heart, a pretty boy who's used to having his way with the ladies. He carries a badge and a gun, and walks around like he can do whatever he wants and get away with it.

Pump a guy like that full of coke, inflate his sense of power, and the power becomes a high he can't get enough of.

"When Brown and Dorsett went back to Texas, Lomax followed. Part of the investigation, I suppose. He took your sister and Katie Green with him. He told Anna he wanted her to be an informant for a federal investigation, and her assignment was to get information out of Brown. But cops don't get involved with their informants the way Lomax got involved with her. At least, they're not supposed to. He probably never even told the FBI about her. She was his little toy. She eventually figured that out, but by then she had no one to turn to."

"What was he investigating?"

"According to the FBI, some kind of corruption. According to your sister, it was drugs. Brown lived a pretty lavish life, and he took a lot of risks. The state cops seemed to know about him, but they never locked him up. Can I have the phone?"

"Anna's phone?"

"Yeah."

She picks up her bag from the bed and slides out the phone with the shattered screen. When she hands it to me, my thumb hits the button beneath the screen and it lights up.

"I thought you turned this off," I say.

"I did."

"You sure?" I show her the screen.

"I'm sure," she says. "Maybe it pressed against something in the bag."

The phone is sending GPS data out through a clear four-bar connection to the nearest cell tower, telling whoever wants to know that it's sitting right here in Anna's apartment.

"You can't get into it," Julia says. "There's a passcode."

"You look worn out," I say. "You want to get something to eat?"

"OK. I just… I want to lie down for a few minutes. Do you mind? That phone call creeped me out… And the drive, and just… everything. This is all just overwhelming."

"Take a rest if you need to. And then we'll get something to eat."

I take the phone into the living room. Julia shuts the bedroom door.

30

A guy who really likes to hurt women wants to find a woman who's really hurtable. He doesn't get much satisfaction beating up a drunk who's not going to remember it the next day. He wants to inflict some trauma and see it register. That's where he gets his kicks. Anna Brook, for all her strength and all her problems, has a lot of soul in those blue eyes, and the depth of a spiritual seeker. There's plenty there to hurt.

From the time we spent talking, I have an idea what's on this phone. Lomax told her she was an informant, and she believed that, at least initially. Her job was to gather evidence, and if she went out of her way to mail this phone to her sister, there must be something on it. And she went out of her way to text me her password along with the names of those two Texas cops.

I hit the button on the bottom of the phone, and the home screen image of a blue sky with cottony summer clouds appears behind a web of shattered glass, like a window to freedom barred by a spider's deadly trap. Then the keypad appears. What's *Julia* on a numeric keypad? J-5, U-8, L-5, I-4, A-2.

58542. Open sesame.

The first thing I do is put the phone in airplane mode, so it stops sending out location information. Then I check the photos.

She has quite a few of her apartment. And there's Katie Green, with the pretty face and the eyes that lack confidence. She's sitting at a picnic table with blue crabs and beer bottles and wooden mallets. Then come a few more of the apartment, including the couch I'm sitting on right now. I keep scrolling. There's one of Anna in the mirror, wearing only white satin underpants, with her arm covering her chest. She must have taken this some time ago. She looks healthy, at least ten pounds heavier than she is now. Her skin is glowing, smooth, and clear. Her hair is honey blonde, not the faded flaxen color I saw at Travis's house down in Texas. Her face shows a sharp appraisal of her reflection, but she's not looking down at her body. She's looking up at the eyes that show a mixture of intelligence and doubt.

I keep scrolling. She gets thinner over time. Katie Green starts looking strung out, the vulnerability in her eyes replaced by the hollow, absent look of the junkie. And then there's full-figured Linnea standing in a white bikini and sun hat, sipping a piña colada beside the shimmering blue water of that pool in Dallas.

There are more women inside Sheldon Brown's house. Then two men in the kitchen, looking hungover. The thinner one, the guy in the white collared shirt with the brown hair and eyes, that's Sheldon Brown. The one with the checkered shirt and big beer belly is Franklin Dorsett. Brown looks worn from too much partying. Dorsett eyes him with a calculating look, like he's overseeing the downfall of the man whose empire he will inherit.

There are photos of messy bedrooms, and big tables covered with liquor bottles, ashtrays, playing cards, white-dusted mirrors, and mirrors licked clean.

Then comes a series of Anna in the mirror, her face thinner now, tired and careworn. Her skin has lost the glow of the earlier photos. Her hair is paler, drier, more brittle-looking. I can see the outline of her hipbones pressing through her black stretch pants.

In the second photo in the series, she's removed the stretch pants. Her legs are thin. I zoom in and study the bruises on her thighs. What did Linnea tell me? That Anna, who liked to swim, had stopped going to the pool and stopped baring her skin.

In the next photo, she takes her shirt off. The bruises on her ribs and stomach would be hidden by a dress. She turns around. More bruises on her lower back and buttocks.

I keep scrolling. There's no photo of Lomax anywhere. She knew better than to try that.

I check the videos on the phone, but there are none. Strange that someone who took so many photos has no videos.

I poke around a little more and find an app called File Explorer. I open it up and see the phone has an extra storage card. It contains a single folder called *vids*, which is filled with hundreds of videos. Usually, when a phone has an extra storage card, the video app is automatically set up to use it. But on this phone, it's not, which makes me wonder if that storage card came from somewhere else. Like maybe Anna slipped it into this phone right before she mailed it.

Each video has a preview image, the opening frame, and they're almost all black. I pick one from about a month ago and hit play. The screen is dark, and at first there's no sound. Then I hear her muffled voice.

"I'm changing."

There's a click, maybe a door opening, and the voice of a man, far away. "Keep your clothes on." The door closes.

"I thought you wanted—"

"I said keep them on," and then he sniffs. "I'll take them off."

They exchange a few quiet words I can't make out. Then there's a sudden thud, a loud creaking, and what sounds like fabric rustling across the phone's mic. What just happened? I listen for a few more seconds before it hits me. The phone is under the mattress. One of them just sat on the bed.

"Where's your phone?" That's Lomax talking.

"On the nightstand." That's Anna.

For a few seconds, all I can hear are muffled noises and the mattress rustling against the mic. Then two little clicks. I bet that's Lomax taking the battery out of her phone and then dropping the phone and battery onto the night table. She knew he'd try to control that thing, so she got a second one and hid it from him. She's a good informant.

There's the creaking sound again, maybe Lomax sitting down on the bed, and then some vague noises. Kissing? I don't know. In a minute, she protests. He's too rough in taking off her bra. There's a loud slap. He tells her to shut up, and she does.

I listen for fifteen minutes. He hits her a number of times, and does some things quietly that make her yelp. At one point, I go to check on Julia in the bedroom because I don't want her to hear this. She's asleep.

Lomax grunts a lot, and Anna makes almost no noise until the end, when he does something that really hurts her.

I spend the next few hours skimming through these sound-only videos while Julia sleeps in the other room. No one in that house would have let Anna take a video of what really went on there. But she figured out a way to gather evidence without anyone knowing. Let Lomax control her personal phone, and she would hide the secret second phone and record audio.

In some of the recordings, she's walking through rooms full of people, or she's out by the pool, probably at night, among the sound of music and drunken partiers. The phone must be in her purse, or stuffed into her dress. In one, I can hear her heartbeat, quick and urgent, like an animal on alert.

In a recording from inside the house, I hear the clink of ice in glasses and the tapping of the razor blade on the mirror, the snorting and everyone talking over everyone else. A woman says, "Do that in the bathroom, Shel. No one wants to see that." That was Linnea. She told me at the house she didn't like being around people who shoot coke.

Another snort, and then Lomax says, "You're up."

"I don't want any," Anna says.

"Come on!" Lomax coaxes her the way you'd lure a reluctant dog with a treat.

"No," says Anna.

"What, all of a sudden you're Little Miss Clean?"

"I don't want it," she says. "I've had enough."

"You haven't had any."

"I've had enough for one lifetime. Really," she says wearily, "I have."

"Hey, Shel," Lomax says. "Got an extra needle? Little Cat here doesn't want to damage her pretty nose."

Shel sounds excited to have someone to shoot with. Anna says she won't do it. Lomax says she will. I don't know how that turned out. The recording ended too soon.

A number of the recordings don't include her voice at all. She must have left the phone hidden somewhere in the room and then walked out. The sound quality is poor in all of them, and most contain little of interest.

There's one, though, that's pretty revealing. It's a poker game, with the occasional shuffling of cards. There are only two people in the room, though now and then others pop in and out. One person snorts an occasional line. One opens a can of beer. It's Sheldon Brown, the cokehead, and Franklin Dorsett, the drinker.

In one hand, Brown loses a strip club in San Antonio to Dorsett. Three hands later, he wins it back. Brown tells Dorsett he's getting fat, and then taunts him. "Linnea says you're more interested in eating and drinking than screwing."

Dorsett says that understanding your priorities is one of the benefits of age. Anyways, he adds, food and beer are better vices than cocaine. Sheldon Brown disagrees, then bets $50,000 on what turns out to be three tens. He wins that hand and tells Dorsett he needs a minute in the bathroom. Dorsett says why can't he just do it at the table? I can just picture him watching Brown shoot up with the same interest a trainer shows in his developing fighter. Both want to make sure their man is progressing.

There's a moment of silence, and then Brown moans and gasps like he's having an orgasm. Then he goes quiet again.

"How's that feel?" Dorsett says, and I can almost hear a grin in his voice.

For a couple of minutes, they don't talk. One of them burps a couple of times, probably Dorsett, as he shuffles the cards.

Finally, Sheldon Brown says, "I gotta get that damn monkey off my back." His voice is shaky and agitated.

"Yeah, you do," Dorsett says. "You in for another hand?"

"Yeah. Gimme a... gimme a... minute."

"How 'bout ten thousand for the ante?"

"How 'bout OK?"

Someone comes in and says, "Anyone seen Cat?"

It's Lomax.

"What the hell you been doing to her, Chuck?"

Chuck? Is that Lomax's undercover name?

"Me?" Lomax says. "I thought you were the one roughing her up."

"I don't treat 'em like that," Brown says. "Just in and out. No need to get rough."

"How do you know what you do?" Lomax asks. His voice is filled with arrogance. "You're so full of coke, you're like Jekyll and Hyde. You talk too loud, gamble too much, and fuck too hard."

Dorsett lets out a loud laugh, and adds, "Yeah, Shel was just telling me he's got a monkey on his back."

"I said I have to get that monkey *off my back*. That's what I said. You want a taste?"

Lomax says OK, and I hear the razor tapping against the mirror, then two big snorts.

"Where's Cat?" Lomax asks again.

"What's the difference?" Dorsett asks.

"I'm looking for Cat," Lomax says, and then he sniffs loudly a few times.

"No," says Dorsett. "I mean, what's the difference between having a monkey on your back and wanting to get a monkey off your back?"

Brown says, "The difference is, you're talking about blow, and I'm talking about that goddamn ape Throckmorton. He's squeezing me too hard."

"What's he want?" Lomax asks.

"More. Always more. Fucker. Next time you see him, Chuck, tell him to grow some balls and come here himself to collect his money."

Dorsett laughs. "What're you gonna do, Shel? Shoot him?"

"You're damn right I am. Fucking overfed bastard. You tell him, Chuck. Tell him to come down here. I'll shoot his fat ass and throw him on the grill with some barbecue sauce. Serve him up to his own patrolmen next time they come by."

"That's not the kind of message I'd take to the governor," Lomax says. "You can tell him that yourself, tough guy."

"Sometimes I think you're a little too friendly with him," Brown says. "Sometimes I think you're the kind of guy who might bend over for a big man like that. Maybe you like doing favors for a big powerful guy. You like to feel that kind of power, Chuckie?"

Dorsett says, "Watch it, Shel."

"Damn, you're a mean-looking son of a bitch," Brown says with a taunting laugh. "Didn't know such a handsome fella could look so mean."

I hear furniture shuffling around. A chair goes over. Someone is hitting someone, and there's a lot of grunting. Dorsett says, "Calm down. Calm the fuck down, you goddamn psycho!" He's struggling, like he's trying to restrain Brown or Lomax. "Go find Cat, will you? He's high as hell, Chuck. You know there's no sense arguing with him when he's like this."

Lomax says something I can't make out. Sheldon Brown is laughing. "I make you mad, pretty boy?"

"Get out of here," Dorsett says. "Go find Cat." It sounds like he shuffles Lomax out of the room. "You're gonna get yourself killed, Shel, if you don't watch that goddamn mouth of yours."

I skim through a few more recordings without finding anything of interest. Then I come across one that I wish I didn't find. The phone is under the mattress again. Lomax is getting rough with Anna. He's charged up, sniffling, like he's just done a few lines. She tells him she'll do what he wants if he stops hitting her. He curses and tells her to shut up. Then she's choking. He's strangling her, and she must go unconscious, because he starts shouting at her frantically to wake up. I can hear him slapping her. "Wake up! Wake up, you stupid bitch! What the fuck is wrong with you? Wake up!"

And then the bed starts creaking rhythmically, and I hear him grunting.

He didn't wait for her to wake up.

I have to turn the phone off.

31

Julia woke up hungry around eight p.m., so we walked down Columbia Road to 18th Street and had dinner at an Ethiopian restaurant. She told me her father had been a metal worker in a machine shop just north of Staunton until a job accident left him unable to work. The family got by on his disability and the money her mother brought in from housecleaning.

Her dad was a restless, pushy kind of guy. "And impossible to please," she said. He started drinking after he went on disability, and was controlling toward their mother and Anna but not as much toward Julia. Their mother seemed frustrated and bewildered by her lack of opportunity and a life that didn't turn out the way she had imagined. She picked up her husband's drinking habit. When he died ten years ago, she went on a binge that hasn't let up.

"It leaves you with a sense of defeat," she told me, "to see your parents give in to a life that demeans them. It upset Anna more than it upset me. I don't think she ever dealt with it. Not in a healthy way. She did too many things too young, and no one intervened to stop her."

Julia came out of college with a lot of debt. "Anna paid hers off," Julia says, "because she only went for two semesters. I don't know how I ever will."

As the waiter lays the food on the table, she asks me where I grew up, and I say Philly and change the subject. Then she asks how I became a private eye.

"I worked in a fish market in New York," I say. "And when I moved down here, I worked in a fish market again. It was the only job I could get. One of our regular customers was a private eye. I used to talk with him two, three times a week. He knew about my boxing career.

"One day, he wanted to confront a guy who was blackmailing one of his clients. But he was scared. The blackmailer was this big Harley-driving redneck out in Calvert County, Maryland. A mean-looking guy covered in tattoos. The PI brought me along to intimidate the guy. He had dug up some dirt on Mister Harley and basically said, you keep blackmailing my client, and we'll expose what we know about you. We had a tense conversation in the guy's garage and we came to an understanding.

"That's what got me interested. The chance to put guys like that in their place. The PI brought me on for a three-month probationary period and started training me. Small-time investigators like him chase insurance cheats, crooked employees, cheating spouses, and other lowlifes. I understand those people, and I like them about as much as I liked the smell in the fish market.

"Eventually, I took the courses and got my license. And then I met Ed Hartwell and took a step up."

Julia listens politely to all this, but the whole time the questions she wants to ask about her sister hang heavy in the air. She's patient and quiet in a way that really gets to me. I can see the burden on her mind, but she doesn't ask me to lift it.

On the walk back to the apartment, she says, "Do you always hold on so tightly to your dates?"

I didn't notice until she said it, but I'm holding her by the elbow the same way that goon in San Francisco was holding her sister. I'm scanning the street with every step, wondering if Lomax is tracking her sister's phone and has it pinpointed there in Anna's apartment. Is he nearby, watching for her? Julia looks so much like her sister, he might go after her by mistake.

"Is this a date?" I ask.

"It might as well be," she says. "What else do we have going on? And what are you looking for? You don't seem like the type who checks out other women when he's already got one on his arm."

"Just looking out," I say. "When were you planning on heading back to Richmond?"

"Tomorrow."

"You can't spend the night at Anna's."

"Why not?"

"It's not safe."

"Where am I supposed to go?"

"I have a place lined up for you. I know a US marshal who lives in Northeast." A good friend of Ed's. I called him while Julia was sleeping and set it up.

"Well, I want to clean up before I go."

"That's fine."

And she leaves it hanging there in the air, unsaid. I know she's dying to know, but if I tell her where Anna is, someone could pull that information out of her.

We're both quiet for the last couple blocks of the walk. With her arm in mine, she leans on me, all sweetness and warmth, asking nothing. I don't know if she gets it, if she understands how seductive her simple presence is to someone who's always on his guard against the scammers and liars and losers and thieves. In my world, everyone's working an angle. Everyone's trying to rip everyone else off. No one rests their head on your arm just because they like you. No one does that because they're sweet. Except this one, who has no guile in her eyes and doesn't shy away from a direct look because she has nothing to hide. All my defenses were built against dishonest people who are out to screw everyone they can. I have no defense against the honest wishes of an honest heart. All she has to do to break me down is leave me alone with my conscience.

Finally I say, "You want to talk to her?"

And she says softly, matter-of-factly, as if she knew this was coming, "More than anything."

I'm going to regret this. I know it.

* * *

I made Julia give me the key before we left the apartment, so I could lock it and do the toothpick trick again. When we get to the door, the sliver of wood is still on the deadbolt. Even so, I ask her to wait in the hall while I do a quick check of the apartment.

She watches me and says, "You're nervous, huh? Am I really in so much trouble?"

"Your sister is. I just want to make sure whoever's after her—"

"Lomax?"

"—doesn't get you by mistake."

The apartment is clear.

I give her the flip phone and say, "There's only one number in the contacts. Call it. Talk in the bedroom, so you can have some privacy. I'll be in the other room."

She shuts the door, and I go to the kitchen for a glass of water.

When I get back to the couch in the main room, she opens the bedroom door, looking disappointed and a little concerned.

"She's not answering."

"Yeah. I was afraid of that. You know, she's very uneasy right now. Just keep trying. If it rings enough times, she'll know it's important." At least I hope she will. We didn't part on the best terms, and she hasn't answered since that damn redneck cop called her.

Julia nods and whispers, "Yeah," then shuts the bedroom door.

I want to look at Anna's phone again, but instead I'm straining to hear what's happening behind that door. Several minutes pass, and I hear Julia sigh. How many times has she tried? Six? Ten? Is she going to give up?

Finally, I hear the burst of emotion in her voice.

"Anna? Oh my god!"

* * *

I spend the next two hours catching up on work. Leon sent about a dozen emails with info on Sheldon Brown, Franklin Dorsett, and the businesses Anna told me about. Most of them belonged to Brown, though Dorsett seemed to be slowly taking them over, just like Linnea said. Other than a big chunk of an oil-drilling services company, which he inherited, all of Dorsett's assets once belonged to Brown. He probably won them in card games, or bought them on the cheap after Brown needed quick cash to bail himself out of gambling trouble in Las Vegas.

In all, there are many more companies than the few Anna had mentioned. The chain of ownership for most of the businesses was hard to trace. Leon found they belong to a handful of holding companies, which in turn are owned by other holding companies, some of which are registered offshore. But with help from a paralegal over at Baker/Watson, Leon managed to dig up the legal documents that tie every one of them back to Brown and Dorsett.

Bethany, always the librarian, has organized electronic copies of the paperwork into a searchable archive. That's one step toward the evidence that might eventually get Anna out of hiding.

The last email in my inbox is from Bethany. "I don't know what you're after, Freddy. Maybe you'll let us in on it soon? But thanks for giving us a break from the endless background checks of the passenger list. BTW, how does this tie in?"

I open the attachment, which is a list of donors to a super PAC called Healthy Texas. A dozen of the top fifty donors are companies owned by that maze of holding companies that Leon traced back to Brown and Dorsett. Their contributions come to over a million dollars. Way to go, Bethany!

Who is Healthy Texas trying to put into office? I look up their ads.

Jumbo Throckmorton.

During all this time Julia only came out of the bedroom once. She pulled a Bible from the table where Anna stacks her mail. That was about twenty minutes into the conversation.

She took the book back into the bedroom and began to read some vaguely familiar Psalm, changing the pronouns halfway through from male to female.

She shall call upon me, and I will answer her. I will be with her in trouble. I will deliver her, and honor her. With long life will I satisfy her, and show her my salvation.

Those words bring back the sight of the altar, the smell of candles and incense, the sound of hymns, and the swaying of the priest's robes in the aisle. And my mother, in her Sunday dress, smelling of soap and shampoo, who called and called and called upon Him, never to be honored or delivered.

As I finish scanning through all the stuff Leon and Bethany sent, Julia ends her long conversation and comes from the bedroom buzzing with energy.

"She told me to tell you she was there to delay them," she says.

"What?"

"She said Lomax brought her to San Francisco to delay two guys named Brown and Dorsett. They were stopping there for a day between Las Vegas and Hawaii, but Lomax wanted them on a different plane, two days later. So he brought Anna to Brown's hotel room with a half ounce of cocaine and told her to keep him busy."

"Hey!" I point to the smart phone in her right hand. "Why are you holding that?"

"I just got off the call."

"You didn't call her from *your* phone, did you? I gave you the flip phone."

"She wouldn't answer. I knew she'd answer if she saw my number in the caller ID, so I dialed from—" She cuts her answer short when she sees my anger rising.

I'm about to lose my temper but... I don't. And I don't know why. I was going to yell at her for making a stupid mistake. If Lomax is looking for Anna, he'll be watching the phones and email accounts of her mother, her sister, her friends, maybe even Kim Hahn, looking for contact. I was going to blurt out that she was an idiot, and then I'd spend the next three days regretting that. But something stopped me, and I'm glad I kept my mouth shut. How horrible would she feel if I told her she had just put her sister in more danger? And who's to say Lomax even has the ability to look at the emails and phone records of her friends and family? That requires a warrant from a judge, or at least an administrative warrant, and if he's on some solo mission to hunt her down, he's not going to expose his plans by filling out the legal paperwork.

The fact that he hasn't shown up here yet, despite the GPS signal from Anna's phone—that makes me think he doesn't have access to her accounts. But I'm not going to bet on that. I'm certainly not going to risk Julia's life on it. He's been here once already to pick up Anna's journals. He called her phone too. He may have been calling it for days, and now that he finally got an answer, he might come by again. I don't want Julia to be here when he shows up.

"Do I really need to go to that marshal's house?" Julia asks.

"Yes. You do."

"I want to shower before we go."

"Make it quick. It's already past midnight."

She goes back into the bedroom and takes some clothes from Anna's dresser. In a minute, I hear the bathroom door close. Then I look again at the list of businesses Sheldon Brown was hiding in those holding companies. They're spread all over Texas. I can hit a bunch of them in one big loop if I head west from Dallas to Odessa, then down to San Antonio and the Gulf Coast, back up through Houston to Dallas. That'll be a few days of driving.

I book a flight to Dallas on my phone, leaving in eight hours.

This has been another long day, and I'm wearing down. It's quiet in here, dead quiet, and I'm wondering why that's wrong. Then I hear the shower go on. She's been in the bathroom for fifteen minutes, and she just turns the water on now? Christ! What does "make it quick" actually mean to a woman?

I tilt my head back and let out a breath of frustration and tell myself to be patient. Usually when I tell myself that, I become *less* patient. But maybe I'm losing my fire, or just getting old. Or maybe the intensity of that encounter with Anna the other night took more out of me than I thought. I can't quite muster the emotion to get pissed off over a fifteen-minute delay. Tonight I will be patient. Twenty minutes and we'll be out of here.

I take Anna's phone from my pocket, take it out of airplane mode and check for recent calls. None. No texts either. I tap the email app and look at what's come in since the day of the crash. Nothing but spam.

My eyes are burning. The splashing of the shower is like rain in the quiet night, and the little humming noises Julia makes in there are like the ones my mother used to make when she'd wash her hair. The moisture seeping beneath the bathroom door carries the scent of her shampoo.

I close my eyes for a minute. Just one minute...

32

The sound of Anna's phone ringing jolts me awake. I couldn't have been asleep more than thirty seconds. The shower is still running. It's that same number again. 999–999–9999. And there's a shadow beneath the door. He's out in the hall, listening to it ring. He knows the phone is in here.

I get up off the couch. My mind is foggy, and my body is heavy and slow. I walk quietly into the kitchen and find a three-inch paring knife. There's probably a bigger one in the drawer, but I don't want to risk opening it and making a sound. Wake up, Freddy! Shake it off.

And then—the phone! I left it on the couch.

I consider going back for it, but it's still ringing. If I pick it up and bring it with me, the ringing will lead him right to me. I don't want that. I'd rather surprise him. I could turn the ringer off, but... No time. Stay put, Freddy.

The phone quiets down and then I hear the key slide into the lock. I turn off the kitchen light.

If he's opened the door, he's done it too quietly for me to hear. His first step into the apartment has to be on the bare wood floor. The next step will be on the rug, and I won't be able to hear that one. But so far, I hear nothing from him. The bedroom door is open just a crack, and the sound of the shower comes through just loudly enough to mask his quiet footsteps.

I'm straining to listen, and then I hear the click of the hallway door shutting. Is he in?

For a few seconds, there's silence, then a little sigh, like he let out his breath. I wonder if he's high. If he's on coke, he might be more violent, or just more rash. His senses might be more acute, his reflexes quicker. That could put me at a disadvantage. As if a knife against a gun isn't disadvantage enough. I should have gotten her out of here earlier.

There! That creak must be the bedroom door. He hears the shower. He has her right where he wants her. Maybe that puts him at ease, knowing his job won't be too hard.

I look out through the kitchen door. The main room is empty, and Anna's phone is gone. That's a big chunk of evidence, and I need to get it back.

The bedroom door is open. I cross the main room, and just as I reach the bedroom, the light inside gets brighter and the shower gets louder. I come in three steps behind him as the steam billows out through the half-open bathroom door.

Julia's half-mumbling, half-singing in there. He's got the door all the way open, and I'm four feet behind him now, the sound of the shower masking my steps. He lets out a laugh and says, "You stupid cunt!" Then he rips open the shower curtain.

Julia shrieks as I plunge the knife into the lower right side of Lomax's back. He screams and jerks awkwardly back, his right hand going to the wound as the back of his head smashes my face. For a split second, everything goes black. My legs wobble, and I see stars. In the ring, I developed an instinct to stay upright after blows like that.

We stagger backward. I'm in the bedroom and he's in the bathroom doorway. I get him in a sleeper hold, with my right forearm pulling on his windpipe, and my left arm pushing from behind like scissors. I press his left side against the doorframe so he can't reach his gun.

Of course, that's the first thing he does. Goes for the gun. When he can't get it, he balls up his right fist and swings back at my crotch. I'm standing a little to his right, and he lands a good hard shot that makes me buckle forward. As I slide to the left to avoid another one of those, my grip on his throat weakens. That kind of blow takes some of the starch out of you. As I move left, my hip hits the knife in his back and he screams. I still have a hold on his throat, but this guy is all muscle. Strangling that thick neck is like trying to choke a tree.

He takes a swat at me, his right hand coming backward over his shoulder. I see the big thumb sticking out, and I let out a yell when it goes into my eye. That hurt worse than the crotch shot, and it makes me mad. I put every ounce of strength into the chokehold, cutting off the blood flow as well as the oxygen, and he finally starts to wilt.

I keep the hold on for a few seconds after his legs give out, after he's sagging and I have to support his weight. Only when I let him go do I notice Julia standing there, holding a thick white towel in front of her, watching horrorstruck, with big wide eyes.

"Put some clothes on," I say.

I drag Lomax into the bedroom and drop him facedown on the floor. I take his gun, and I find Anna's phone in the pocket of his jacket. I put the gun and the phone on the dresser, and then give him a good hard kick in the crotch. Not very sporting, but then neither is beating up women.

I pull him up onto the bed, facedown, so the knife wound doesn't bleed all over it, and I give him a few hard left hooks under the ribs. His body doesn't react to the blows. It's like hitting the heavy bag: a big lump of inert matter. Then I work the right side the same way. He might not feel these now, but he'll feel them when he wakes up. And no one will be able to see his bruises in the morning. It'll be our little secret. That's a trick my daddy taught me. Hide the evidence, so the crime is invisible.

Then there's a hand on my shoulder, someone behind me.

"Stop it, Freddy! You're going to kill him." It's Julia.

"That's right," I say. "I am. Put some clothes on, for Christ's sake."

"Freddy, stop!" She's not used to seeing this kind of thing.

"Put some clothes on and open the hallway door."

She wraps the towel around herself and opens the door. I pull the knife out of Lomax's back and throw it in the bathroom sink. Then I grab him by the shoulders and drag him out and down the hall, facedown to keep his blood off the carpet. I lug him down the back stairs and into the alley, where I prop him up next to the dumpster, just like I did with Chuck DiLeo. As he comes to, I give him a kick in the gut, one under the ribs, and one up under the chin that knocks him senseless. He slumps over sideways and I'm about to stomp that pretty face of his into hamburger meat when a police car rolls past the end of the alley with its flashers on.

I know what this is about.

I give Lomax another boot to the side of the head—hopefully good for a three-day headache—then walk back toward the building. Only I can't get in the back door. I go back to Lomax and fish the keys out of his pocket. Anna's apartment key, and probably his own too.

On the way out of the alley, I wipe the blood from my face onto my shirt. He smashed my nose pretty good with the back of his head when I stabbed him.

When I get around to the front of the building, the patrol car is there with its flashers on, and the cop is just getting out—a tall, skinny black guy with a moustache. I know him. D'Andre Tomlinson.

"You get a call about a domestic disturbance?" I ask, wiping the blood from my hands onto my black pants.

"Yes, I did."

"That was me," I say.

Tomlinson looks me up and down, then calls for backup on his shoulder radio.

"There's a woman up there," he says. "The neighbor heard her scream."

"That's right."

"She OK?"

"She's OK." I press the buzzer for 204. "Ask her yourself."

"What happened?" Tomlinson asks.

"Who's there?" Julia asks through the speaker.

"Officer Tomlinson, Metropolitan Police. Everything OK up there?"

She doesn't answer.

"You wanna buzz me in?" Tomlinson says.

The buzzer goes, and we go in. I explain to Tomlinson that Julia came to get some things from her sister's apartment. She asked me to meet her because she was scared. Her sister was a prostitute and might have had an angry pimp. Someone came into the apartment with a key, maybe her pimp coming to collect money. He went after Julia and I had to hurt him.

When we get inside, he asks Julia what happened. She tells essentially the same story. She came to get some of her sister's things. She was in the shower. A guy came in and ripped open the shower curtain. He and I fought.

I go to the bedroom while she and Tomlinson continue to talk. I grab Lomax's gun and Anna's phone from the dresser. The gun goes under my belt. The phone goes into my pocket. Then I check the sink. The knife is gone, and there's no trace of blood in the sink, but there are drops on the bathroom floor, on the bedroom rug, and a couple big smears on the white bedspread.

Tomlinson comes into the bedroom to have a look as Julia buzzes in the second cop. Tomlinson examines the bloodstains and I can see him do a quick calculation in his head. Definitely not enough there for a murder. More like a bloody nose or a split lip.

"You hit the guy?" he asks.

"In the nose," I lie. "He's a bleeder. And I put a gash above his eye too." That's also a lie, but I have to account for the blood.

He looks at the drying blood beneath my nose, then says, "Let me see your hands."

I show him my hands, which bear the marks of many hard blows, along with a few scrapes and bruises from the work I just did.

He shines his flashlight in my left eye and asks, "What'd he put in your eye?"

"His thumb."

"Why were you outside?"

"I chased the guy. He got out after he put his thumb in my eye."

"Why would you chase an intruder?"

"I wanted to kill him."

"OK," Tomlinson says with a nod. He knows me well enough to take that statement at face value.

"What's the guy look like?"

I describe Lomax, and Tomlinson seems a little suspicious.

"That doesn't sound like a pimp," he says.

"Maybe it was one of her clients."

Tomlinson seems uneasy about it all. He says, "Where's the owner of the apartment?"

"She's dead," I say. "She died in a plane crash."

That does nothing to quell his doubts. "Stay here, Freddy. I want to talk to the woman."

He leaves me in the bedroom and I hear him talking to Julia and the other cop in the main room. I can hear little snippets of what she says. But I don't hear anything that contradicts what I've said. She's surprisingly calm.

After a few minutes, Tomlinson returns to the bedroom, seemingly more at ease. "Any idea where the guy went?"

"He took off, straight down Lanier just a couple of minutes before you showed up." Another lie. "Listen, that woman out there, Julia." I point to the main room. "I'm worried someone might come after her again. You know Carl Harrington?"

Tomlinson shakes his head.

"Former US marshal," I say. "Lives in Northeast. He's expecting her. Tonight. You think you can drive her over there? She's pretty shaken. It might make her feel better to ride over in a police car."

Tomlinson says he'll take her, and she agrees to go.

I'm impressed at how naturally she plays along with it all. She's obviously not over that little scene in the bedroom, but

I don't have to coach her on anything. She keeps her emotions in check, knows what to say and how to act, just like her sister in the airport in San Francisco.

33

OCTOBER 7, 8, 9

After touching down in Dallas, I picked up a car, along with my old suitcase and laptop from the rental agency. They had retrieved the white Malibu from the impound lot. I've mapped out a big loop through the heart of Texas so I can take a look at some of the businesses Sheldon Brown and Franklin Dorsett were running.

By ten a.m., I'm heading west into the center of the state. Dallas-Fort Worth to Abilene is only three inches on the map, but in that space there's a lot of flat, hot country that never got the word that summer's over. It's a mix of open fields, scrub brush, and low-growing trees.

I've driven the length of Virginia, from Arlington down to Bristol. It may not look like it on the map, but it's a big state. You don't really get a sense of *how* big until you drive it end-to-end. New York is big too. So's Pennsylvania. But Texas is the size of an entire country. I know from previous visits that the southeast part of the state is nothing like the far west, which is nothing like the panhandle. Texas is lush, humid, almost tropical. It's barren and rocky. It has high stony hills lined with evergreens, and then it's dead flat all the way to the horizon. Mostly though, the place is just huge. I can hop in my car at the crack of dawn, drive as fast as I can till the sun goes down, and when I get out of my car, I'm still there.

After a few hours beneath the bright sun on miles of flat, open highway, I finally hit the eastern edge of Abilene. A little detour on a two-lane road takes me up to Green Grass Septic Service, an outfit that pumped $65,000 into the Healthy Texas super PAC. The address is in a strip mall off Route 351. Driving in, I see a payday loan store, a Mexican restaurant, and a barbeque joint. My first thought is, how can two restaurants survive with the smell of those septic trucks? Wouldn't it drive their customers away?

I don't see a sign for the septic company, so I drive around back. There's a Highway Patrol car cruising slowly across the lot, but no septic trucks. The white metal door at the rear of the building has a little square window, and the sign above it says Green Grass Septic. I guess they don't need a fancy office. I don't suppose they get a lot of walk-ins.

I park my car and walk up to the door, which is locked. I look through the window, cupping my hands to block the reflection of the glaring sun. It's one of those windows with crisscross metal wires running through it in a diamond pattern, like they're worried about someone punching out the glass and stealing all the sewage. I can't see much inside: a desk and a phone, a chair, a couple of filing cabinets, and a calendar on the wall that says March.

The police cruiser drives back from the far end of the lot, slowing as it approaches me. I turn to watch, and the cop, a burly guy with a thick mustache, gives me a long look. Not a mean look. Not even a what-are-you-up-to look. It's more like he's taking notes. So sometime in the future, if it ever comes to that, he'll remember my face and where he saw it.

I make a note of the car. A black-and-white Chrysler 300 with license number 70707. Easy enough to recall.

My next stop is Odessa, about two and a half hours to the west. I don't want to do that drive straight, because it's well past noon and I haven't had lunch. I also have something on my mind. Something that's been troubling me since last night. I leave the highway in Sweetwater for gas and food and a quick phone call.

I don't know if Lomax knows that was me who beat his ass last night. I snuck up on him and choked him out from behind. He never did see me. But I'm assuming he put two and two together. I had already assaulted him once for getting too close to Julia, and I had called and hung up on him the day before my first flight to Dallas. He must have seen my number on the caller ID. Anyway, who else would have been in Anna's apartment with her sister? Who else would have beaten him up?

I don't care if he knows. I'm not scared of the guy, and I'm not worried about him telling anyone. What could he say? That he was just innocently stalking a woman in the shower when some guy came in and beat the crap out of him? I wonder how he's going to account for his injuries when he goes back to the office. He can hide the stab wound and most of the bruises, but if a law enforcement officer shows up to work moving gingerly and in obvious pain, his coworkers are going to ask what happened. He can't just say it was nothing. Lie to a detective, and he'll be on your case in an instant. Maybe Lomax will come up with a story. Or maybe he won't go into work at all for a while.

What really has me worried, though, is that Julia called her sister from her own phone. Lomax can't monitor Julia's phone without a warrant, but he could still have a back channel, a friend at the telecom or the NSA who he trades favors with.

I find a Mexican restaurant in town and order lunch. While I'm waiting for my food, I call Leon back at the office. He's the last person I want to send out to tail someone, but he'll have to do.

"Where you at, Freddy?"

"Texas. Listen, I need you to do me a favor."

"What's up?"

"I want you to go to Silver Spring and find out whether or not a guy is in his apartment."

"For real?" He sounds disappointed. He doesn't like being away from the computer. "Why don't you send Bethany?"

"I wouldn't send any woman around this guy."

"He dangerous?"

"Probably not in his current condition," I say. "I just need you to tell me if he's home, and what kind of shape he's in."

I'm hoping he's not working today. Not looking at Julia Brook's call history.

"Yeah, I gotcha."

"Don't sound too enthusiastic, Leon."

"I won't."

After a chicken burrito and iced tea, I'm back on the road.

I find Midland-Odessa Custom Hauling just off Route 20, on a narrow highway south of Midland. It's a gravel lot with a single cinder-block building with one serviceable tanker truck and another that looks like it hasn't moved in years.

A middle-aged man wearing cheap boots, overalls, and a cowboy hat sits in a rocking chair in the shade of the lone tree by the building's front door. He has a mouth full of tobacco, and eyes me lazily with the drowsy indifference of a basset hound that wants to get back to its nap.

"Where are the trucks?" I ask.

He points his thumb back to the two filthy heaps in the lot and says, "Which one you interested in?"

"Where are the rest? Out on the road?"

He points his thumb again and says, "That's it," and then he squirts a mouthful of spit into the dust.

"I'll keep looking," I say.

When the Healthy Texas super PAC was out raising money, Midland-Odessa Custom Hauling was good for $61,000. If they sold the two trucks, the building, the land, and the redneck, they couldn't get $61,000.

By now, I know what I'll find when I visit Taylor Automotive in Rock Springs, and Southern Equipment Rental in Kerrville, which happens to be my next stop. That's a few hundred miles down the road toward San Antonio. The sun is already setting, and there's no way I'm going to drive that far tonight.

I pull into a gas station to fill my tank, and there's that patrol car I saw back in Abilene. Number 70707 is just on its way out as I'm rolling in. The cop driving it gives me the same long look he gave me in the lot behind Green Grass Septic.

After I fill the tank, I sit in the station lot for a while, looking for motels on my phone. Leon calls.

"Hey, man, that dude is fucked up."

"What?"

"That guy Lomax you asked me to check on."

"Was he home?"

"Yeah, he was home limping around like he got hit by a truck. Dude looks like he's on some heavy pain meds."

"You got a good look at him, huh?"

"Yeah, man. I walked right up and knocked on his door."

"Why the fuck did you do that?"

"How else could I tell if he was home?"

"Dammit, Leon!"

"I picked up a pizza at Domino's on the way. Got my Domino's shirt and knocked on his door. You know I used to work at Domino's?"

"Yeah, Leon. I know."

"He said he didn't order no pizza. I said the hell you didn't, you gotta pay for this shit, motherfucker."

"Way to keep a low profile, Leon."

"He told me to fuck off."

"That sounds about right," I say. "Did you eat the pizza yourself?"

"Me and Bethany."

"Well good work, Leon. I'm glad you didn't get shot."

As soon as I hang up with him, I get a call from Bethany.

"Hey Freddy."

"What's up, Bethany?"

"I got a call from a cop down in Texas asking about you."

"Alfonso Jiménez?"

"No. A guy named Chester Dixon."

"What was that about?"

"I'm not sure," she says. "He asked if you worked here, for how long, what kind of work you did. I just told him you've been here four and a half years."

"That's it?"

"That's it," she says. "He called Ed too and asked the same questions. How's everything going down there?"

"All these companies are fake. They're all fronts. They don't do any real business."

She's quiet for a moment, then she says, "OK, Freddy. So what's it all about?"

"What's what all about?"

"Come on," she says. "We've gone way off track here. Ed asked me what I'm working on and I said research. I don't like to lie, and I'm not going to cover for you forever. What's going on?"

"Nothing."

"It's not nothing, Freddy. You sent Leon out of the office to spy on someone. Leon!"

"Let me get back to you." I hear her huff of frustration as I hang up. Under any other circumstances, I'd tell her. I would. But the thing is, when this gets back to Ed, he'll tell me to turn it over the Bureau. And I promised Anna I wouldn't do that.

I got myself in a bind here, but I'm going to stick to my word.

I head back out on the road, and as the stars spread out overhead, I tell myself I'll take the first decent room I can find.

* * *

Twenty minutes later, I'm checked in to a cheap chain motel. The room is clean to the point of sterility, with spotless starched white sheets and white textured walls that have a cold bluish tint beneath the fluorescent lights. The endless miles of Texas highway, the glaring sun, and the bareness of the sterile room make this feel like the loneliest place in the world. I can't just sit in here. Even with the TV on, it's too empty.

I walk to the restaurant two parking lots away. It has a 1970s feel to it, with laminated wood tables, and booths upholstered in brown and orange vinyl. There's something empty and oppressive about this place, but I can't put my finger on it until the waitress apologizes for the radio being broken. It's the silence that makes this place so weird. Public places are never this quiet.

An older couple is finishing their meal two booths away. I hear the man clear his throat and the scraping of his spoon on a bowl. Little noises in this strange oasis of silence are amplified until they become harsh, like the glaring white fixtures of the bathroom in my motel.

I don't know why I ordered chicken when I had that for lunch. The whole meal tastes like it was cooked two days ago. The chicken is bland and chewy. The green beans came from a can. The potato is dry. I leave it there, half-eaten, and return across the parking lots to the motel.

Back in the room, I check my email. Nothing. No texts either. No missed calls.

I don't use social media, so I have no Instagram to check. No Twitter or Facebook or anything else to fritter away my time. I swipe through the apps looking for some distraction, and then give up.

I kill the lights and lie on the bed listening to the whoosh of cars outside, and I ask myself what good happened today. What is one thing I can be happy about? This is an exercise Miriam used to make me do when I complained too much.

Well, Lomax is stuck at home. That's one thing. Even if he did have some way to trace the calls from Julia's phone, he's in no shape to make a move. Not today anyway.

I find the flip phone and text Anna. *You OK?*

She doesn't respond.

I fall asleep to the sound of traffic on the road outside.

* * *

The next morning, as I'm finishing a cup of coffee in the room, there's still no text from Anna, but I do get one from Ed.

Got a call from a cop in Texas about you. Dixon. You know him?
I text back, *No.*
Second call from him asking about your character, Ed writes. *This related to that traffic stop & disorderly conduct the other day?*
I write back, *I don't know.*
Ed: *What are you doing down there anyway?*
Me: *Long story.*
Ed: *Busy now. We'll talk later.*

* * *

The drive to Kerrville takes a few hours. I call Anna twice along the way, but she doesn't answer. I leave messages telling her I'm back in Texas. "Call me, will you?"

The rental place in Kerrville is a low, flat-roofed building with windows all along the front. It actually has some equipment to rent. It's the closest thing I've seen to a legit-looking business so far. But it's small-time stuff: post-hole diggers, chain saws, lawn aerators. Nothing that would add up to a $70,000 campaign contribution.

From here to Corpus Christi is a good long drive. The most direct route goes through San Antonio, where the traffic barely moves. I swear I catch a glimpse of that patrol car on Route 37, just south of the city. 70707. Seems like a hell of a lot of territory for one cop to cover.

It's dark before I reach the bay in Corpus Christi. I call it a night at another cheap motel at the north end of town.

I asked Leon to check on Lomax again, and he was a little more subtle this time. He found a spot with a view into Lomax's apartment and then hung around for most of the day. He said Lomax was moving around a little better, but he never got dressed or left the apartment.

Before I go to sleep, I text Anna.

She doesn't respond.

* * *

At 4:12 a.m., I wake up in a sweat.

I had that dream again. I'm standing on the rocks above the sea. Anna is swimming in ten feet of crystal blue water above a sunlit, sandy bottom. She is lithe and graceful in her blue bathing suit. And then one by one, the bruises appear, big dark spots on her arms and legs. The sea floor drops out beneath her, the waters darken, the whirlpool opens and begins to pull her down.

I dive in after her, and as soon as I hit the water, I'm scared for my life. Again, she turns her body forward and swims with the current into the depths, while I struggle against it, trying to get back up to the light. I push against the swirling waters with all my strength, but I can't make it back to the surface.

In the last second before the terror wakes me, I see her swimming downward with her hand outstretched to retrieve a pearl that shines like starlight from the blackest depths of the sea.

* * *

I sleep through the alarm at six a.m., and again at seven, and finally make it out of bed at eight. I have breakfast in the motel lobby—coffee and toast from the buffet—and then get in the car to take a look at Martínez Resort Services. They provide contract workers to hotels: maids, cooks, groundskeepers. When I get there, the office is empty, except for a stack of mail on a table. I go around to a few hotels, but when I talk to the managers, none of them has heard of

Martínez. They were good for $44,000 when the super PAC came calling.

Ramírez Resort Services—clever name, huh?—in Galveston. Same story. $46,500.

I don't need to check out the waste hauling outfit in El Paso, or the machine shop in Amarillo. I'm not driving to Beaumont or Plainview to look at another shell company. Everything in this state is nine hundred miles from everything else, and after three days on the road, I've had enough of Texas.

I know where the money's going—into a hard-bought election for the incumbent governor, the law and order man who's making Texas healthy by keeping drugs off the streets. But where's it coming from? Why would Sheldon Brown and Franklin Dorsett need these fronts when they both had legitimate businesses that *were* making money? Was Brown moving enough drugs through his strip clubs to warrant all this? Or was there another source that needed to be covered up?

I'm pondering these questions at a roadside diner halfway between Galveston and Houston when I get a call from Ed. He says the FBI now has serious doubts about the involvement of the baggage handler, Obasanjo, and so does he.

"Why's that?" I ask.

"You know what happens when you get a real terrorist in interrogation?" he says. "The kind who's capable of putting a bomb on a plane? At some point he tells you he did it. Because terrorism is an ideological thing. Those guys believe they're right no matter what. In the end, they'll answer to a God who already put his stamp of approval on whatever they've done. In their minds, they have nothing to hide. They're proud of what they did.

"But this kid was terrified when they brought him in. You saw how scared he was when they paraded him in front of the cameras. He had no idea what hit him. If he'd planted that bomb, he'd have known they were coming for him. A Muslim with access to the plane's cargo hold? He'd have known they were coming, and he would have gone down in a shootout, as a martyr. Or he would have confessed and made himself a hero of the cause. But he's standing his ground, just like he did a year ago at his battery trial. The kid stands on principle, says he didn't do it, and they can't dig a single contradiction out of him, no matter how hard they push. Everything he's said checks out. Besides, he has no motive and no mental health issues."

"Yeah, well, what are they supposed to think, with ISIS claiming responsibility?"

"ISIS would claim responsibility for a solar eclipse. Anything for publicity."

"What about the missing TSA agent? What's his name? Welcher?"

"That's what I called to tell you about," Ed says.

"They find him?"

"Dead in his car, behind an auto repair shop that was scheduled for demolition. The foreman of the wrecking crew found him."

"They know what killed him?"

"Alcohol and oxycodone."

"So what are they thinking? He played a part in it, then had some regrets and took his own life?"

"He probably played a role," Ed says. "That bomb didn't go through any other TSA checkpoint. And maybe he had some regrets. But he didn't take his own life, though the Bureau will tell the press he did."

"How do you know he didn't kill himself?"

"For one thing, he wasn't much of a drinker. According to his girlfriend, he was a one- or two-beer guy who took a shot of bourbon every now and then. For another, the prescription he got when he injured his back last spring was for Vicodin, not oxycodone. They found the bottle still full in his trunk."

"So they think it was staged?"

"Seems that way," Ed says. "They'll tell the press it's a suicide. If the bomber thinks we bought his ruse and we're on the wrong track, he might get overconfident and slip up. If we tell the press it's a murder, he'll know we're onto him. He'll be more cautious."

"When did Welcher die?"

"The night of the crash."

"So who's the suspect now?"

Ed lets out a long breath. "Maybe Welcher. Maybe someone else."

"But who?" I ask. "Who else do they have?"

"No one," Ed says. "They have no one."

"They going to release Obasanjo?"

"Not just yet. The press will jump all over the Bureau if they release one suspect without picking up another. And the public wants a lynching. With all this media coverage, the pressure on the Bureau is horrendous. Somewhere out there, the perpetrators are sitting back and watching it all unfold on TV."

"Hang in there, buddy."

"Where are you?" Ed asks.

"Just north of Galveston."

"What the hell are you doing down there?" I can hear someone in the background calling his name.

"It'll take me a while to explain."

"Freddy, I have to go."

"Yeah, OK. I'll talk to you later, Ed."

As soon as we hang up, I call Anna Brook, but still there's no answer. I'm starting to worry about her. Maybe it's time for another visit to Dime Box.

I ask the waitress for my check and as she walks off to get it, that cop pulls up in the lot outside. License plate 70707.

34

The guy who steps out of the cruiser is big, six five at least. Seven feet with that ridiculous cowboy hat. He takes a look at my car, and then glances up toward the diner. He's got a folder under his arm.

When he comes inside, he scans the booths from left to right until his eyes land on me.

I can't tell what he's thinking as he approaches. When a cop wants to mess with you, you usually know it. This guy's trying to size me up, but he's not being confrontational. He seems a little tentative.

Finally, he says, "Freddy Ferguson?"

I stand and shake his hand. "That's me. You are?"

"Chester Dixon, Texas Highway Patrol. You work with Ed Hartwell?"

"How'd you know?"

He called the rental agency after he copied the license plate number from my car, then he traced me back to DC and Ed's agency.

"What case are you working with Ed?" he asks.

"A case for the airline. The one that crashed."

He nods like I was just confirming what he already knew.

"What brings you to Texas?"

"I got off on a tangent."

He nods again and says, "Anything you need help with?"

"Maybe. For the moment, I'm keeping it to myself. I have a client to protect."

"You had a little run-in up in Dallas," he says.

"Yes, I did. You want to have a seat?"

We sit on opposite sides of the booth. He lays his folder on the table and says, "You and I've been doing the same grand tour of the campaign money factory."

"Seems like it."

"None of those businesses are legit."

"What got you looking into them?" I ask.

He says his friend is a tax auditor in San Antonio. "The guy spent a few weeks putting together a file of things that don't look right. He asked me to go out and take a look."

Dixon tells me he works in Longview, where Ramón Ramírez was busted.

He says, "Your friend Ed isn't easy to talk to."

"He is, usually," I say. "But he's in the thick of a big mess right now, and he doesn't have a lot of time."

"He's former FBI, right? How close are his ties to the Bureau?"

"That's funny," I say. "You're the second cop to ask me that. You know a guy in Dallas named Alfonso Jiménez?"

He shakes his head.

"Jiménez sent me some news stories the other day. I couldn't quite make sense of them." I tell him about Wilma Juarez, the woman who tried to light herself on fire in front of the statehouse, her complaint about the money that was taken, the arrest of her husband, and how the cartel eventually pumped thirty bullets into him. I tell him about the cop who was shot in the head while sipping coffee in his cruiser because some kid thought he had stolen millions from his cousin.

Dixon just nods and strokes his mustache. "Well, it's nice to know someone else has their eyes open."

"What do you mean?"

"I mean I've been looking at those same stories."

"What's in the folder?" I ask.

He slides it across the table, and I see the same documents Ed sent me days ago: Ramón Ramírez's record of petty crime, with the redacted arrest reports. I don't bother going through it all again. But I ask Dixon why some of the record is blacked out.

"Was he an informant?" I ask.

Dixon nods.

A couple years ago, State Patrol picked up Ramírez with $3,000 worth of cocaine. He said he was delivering it to a party. They held him for about an hour. That much coke, along with his string of priors, should have gotten him locked up for a long time. The state cops told Ramírez they'd forget about the incident if he'd be willing to inform. The guy didn't bat an eye. All he said was that if they wanted him alive, he had to complete the delivery. So they let him go, and they followed him. He pulled up to Sheldon Brown's mansion, where there was a party going on. He was in and out in two minutes, like he walked in, dropped the drugs on the table, and left. The cops followed him from the house, pulled him over a couple miles away, and did a thorough search to make sure he didn't still have the coke.

They kept an eye on Ramírez for the next few months, and they hauled him in every now and then, but all he ever had to say was something big was coming down the pike. He never had any real news. It was always something's coming, something's coming, something's coming. He did give them accurate information about some people on the street, so they weren't ready to write the guy off completely.

Then one day he collars this cop at a gas station on Route 37. State Patrol. Tells him a burgundy Lincoln Continental will be coming past in a few minutes carrying cash down to South Padre Island, where it'll go by boat back to Mexico. The cop calls a couple buddies, and they're ready for the Lincoln, thinking it's carrying maybe ten thousand bucks.

When the cop puts his flashers on, the Lincoln takes off. The other two cops are waiting down the road. They pick up the chase, and the passenger in the Lincoln starts shooting. The cops shoot out the tires, and the Lincoln goes off the road. Then the passenger comes out shooting. The cops kill him, and the driver surrenders. In the trunk, there's a huge chest of cash.

Normally a bust of that magnitude unfolds over months. Lots of planning goes into it, and lots of people in the department know it's coming. That's not how this one happened. Three cops responding to an unexpected tip lucked into a big pile of money, and no one else knew about it.

Chester Dixon started getting suspicious because when cops shoot a guy to death on the side of the road, they usually file an initial report immediately. It may not be complete, but it gives a sketch of the timeline, the events, and who was there. An investigation later will flesh out the details.

But this time the initial report took five days to appear, which told Dixon there was some wrangling inside the department as to what the report should say. Cops usually like to play up busts like that for publicity, so everyone can see they're out there protecting the public. But this one was just a blip in the news. A ten-second mention on local TV about a couple of dealers who tried to run and got shot. They were carrying $20,000 in cash, according to the news reports, and no one thinks about it after that.

The driver who surrendered was Wilma Juarez's husband. A few days later, Ramón Ramírez showed up with money from the cartel to bail him out.

"Texas doesn't usually give bail to guys who shoot at cops," Dixon said. "To be fair, the driver didn't actually shoot. It was the passenger who had the gun. But still, I didn't like the smell of that."

A few months later there's a second bust, again on a tip from Ramírez. Only this time he gave the cops a couple days' notice and they got to plan it out. So more people in the department should have known about it. People in the Criminal Investigations Division should have known about it.

But no. It's the same three cops, only a smaller highway. And it's the same blip in the news, only this time the cops killed everyone in the car, and they were a little more generous about the money, telling the press they took in a hundred thousand in cash. The governor even went on TV to praise the Highway Patrol for their work.

Dixon drums his fingers on the Formica tabletop and gazes out the window with a troubled expression. For a few seconds, he says nothing as he considers the next part of his story.

"I went through the academy with a cop named Manuel Martínez. He was friends with a guy named Moses Tate, who was involved in both busts. Martínez told me a different story." Dixon leans in. "He said there was a lot more than twenty thousand in the trunk of that burgundy Lincoln, and a lot more than a hundred grand in the second car. He didn't get to count it, but he did get a look at it. There were rumors going around that it was twelve million in the Lincoln, and six million in the other car. Those are major busts. Those are front-page headlines and lead stories on the evening news. I can tell you, none of that cash showed up in the evidence lockers, except the hundred and twenty thousand that was reported on the news. And I can also tell you it's unlikely the cartels would spend fifty thousand dollars to bail a guy out so they could shoot him for losing twenty thousand. If he had lost millions, they'd do that for sure."

"Manuel Martínez," I say. "He was on the plane."

"Yeah," says Dixon. "Funny we keep crossing paths, huh? Hey, can you give me the contact info for that guy in Dallas? Alfonso Jiménez?"

"Yeah. He seems to have a few pieces of the puzzle. And you have some, and I have some. Maybe together we have enough to connect the dots for a grand jury."

I give him Jiménez's contact info, and we exchange cards as the waitress returns with my check and a pot of coffee.

She looks at me and says, "You still want to settle up, sugar? Or does your friend want something to eat?"

"You hungry?" I ask Dixon.

"No. Just coffee."

"Go ahead and add it to my tab," I say.

She nods and pours him a cup. When she leaves, I ask, "Why was Martínez going to Hawaii? And there was another cop on the plane too. A guy named Brandon Robertson. What were they doing?"

Dixon says they won the trips as part of a program Jumbo Throckmorton instituted to honor top lawmen. Robertson boarded the flight with his wife, Martínez with his wife and two children.

"Who decides which cops are honored?"

"The governor," he says.

"You said you're up in Longview, right?"

"Yeah."

"Were you in on that big bust the other day? Ramón Ramírez and his two kilos of fentanyl?"

"No. They had me over on the other side of the county."

"They don't trust you on a bust like that?"

"They don't trust me on something that looks like a setup," he says. "That guy was too low-level and too stupid to be trusted with two million dollars worth of anything. And look how he died. You don't swallow a two-gram balloon when you're driving down the highway with two kilos in the trunk. I'm not surprised someone wanted the guy dead. I'm just surprised that it looks like it was someone on our side of the law. He was arrested before noon. He died after midnight. If he had swallowed that balloon himself, it would have gone through him by then."

"You think someone put it there after he was in holding? Like, put it in his…" I don't like *that* image.

"You have a better explanation?" Dixon says. "I'll tell you another thing. I sometimes patrol near the Louisiana border. The Louisiana cops ask me why we're not catching guys running drugs into their state. I hear the same thing from patrolmen working the borders of Arkansas, Oklahoma, and New Mexico. We don't catch guys running drugs *out* of Texas, but we do catch the money coming back *in on its way to Mexico*. Those two big busts I told you about probably aren't the only ones. I have a feeling there have been more, and they never made the news."

"That's a lot to think about for one day," I say.

"Well, think about it."

I nod and start to pull out my wallet to pay. "I need to head out."

Dixon stands and extends his hand. "It was good talking to you," he says. "Real good. I'm going to give your buddy Alfonso Jiménez a call. And hey—your FBI friend—can he get the ear of someone in the Bureau?"

"I think so."

"Good. 'Cause the fucker Martínez talked to was worthless."

"What fucker?"

"Rollins, or something like that. An old do-nothing burnout of a cop."

I'm getting close to the point where I can walk back into Travis Seldin's house, lay out the case, and show enough evidence to convince Anna to come out of hiding so she can get the help she needs. I keep thinking of her disappearing down that hatch in the closet floor, like she's climbing into her own grave. I know a lot of people died in that crash, but right now all I care about is making sure the one who didn't die comes out of this OK. It's been too long since I've heard from her, and I'm getting nervous.

I need to see her—tonight, if possible—but I'll never convince her to leave while Errol Lomax is still at large. Even if I had an airtight case and all the evidence in the world—and that could take months—he has a hold on her through fear that no amount of reason can outweigh. I looked for him in the alley the other night, after the cops took Julia to the marshal's house. He was gone.

Looking back on it now, I wish I had killed the guy.

Anna Brook has one thing right in that religion of hers. Someone is going to have to die to set her free.

GATE 76

35

Fifteen minutes after I leave the diner, I get a call from Alfonso Jiménez in Dallas. I tell him I just met someone he should talk to. I give him a rundown of our conversation and Chester Dixon's contact info.

When I finish, he says, "I got your credit card statement."

"Yeah?"

"I'll email it to you."

When traffic on Interstate 45 backs up a few minutes later, I get a chance to look at the statement. There are only two charges on the card, each of them two days before the crash. One was for Anna Brook's ticket. The other was from an army surplus store in San Francisco.

I call Ed to see if he can check on that one. He actually sounds happy about it.

"I've been in this office for days," he says. "Talking to investigators, talking to lawyers, eating stale sandwiches."

"Well here's an excuse to get some fresh air," I say. "Take a little walk outside."

"Hey, while you're on the phone," he says, "were you following Errol Lomax?"

"I followed him once or twice back in DC. And once or twice we just kind of wound up in the same place."

"You need to back off," Ed says.

"Did he tell you I beat his head in?"

"You did what?"

"I beat the shit out of the guy."

"Why the hell would you beat up a federal agent? Are you crazy?"

"Yeah, Ed. I actually think I am. You know how some things set me off. Like when a guy walks in on a woman in the shower with bad intent. Like in that movie *Psycho*. You ever see that, Ed?" I don't tell him I've had Leon tailing Lomax too.

"What are you doing back in Texas, Freddy?"

"This place keeps sucking me in."

"Stay away from Lomax."

"No, Ed. I can't back off of this one."

"You have to," he says.

"Why?"

"Don't ask that question. The airline is paying your salary so stick to the case. It has nothing to do with Lomax."

"Listen, Ed—"

"Sorry, Freddy, this one's not negotiable. Back off. You hear me?"

I say nothing.

"You hear me, Freddy?"

"Yeah, Ed. I hear you. Call me back when you find out about that credit card purchase."

36

The drive up to Dime Box doesn't go as I had hoped. Traffic on Route 10 west of Houston sets me back an hour and a half. In Columbus, I make the mistake of turning onto the part of Route 90 that runs through town, where Patty Rice is holding a rally in front of the Santa Claus Museum. The road is choked with security vehicles and either I'm not following the cues right, or the cops are directing people in circles. That costs me another hour.

I do enjoy the irony, though, of listening to Rice's address on local radio live from the Santa Claus Museum. Patty the promiser, with her platform of handouts for everyone. I picture her in a bright red suit, throwing candy canes to the crowd.

A big chunk of her speech is about numbers: how many dollars the state allocates per student in the public schools, the projected rise in health-care costs, the number of bonds the state will need to float to cover infrastructure improvements. After a while, it starts to sound like an accounting presentation. But every number comes with the promise that she'll increase it.

Jumbo Throckmorton, meanwhile, is live on the other end of the AM dial. He's up in Amarillo, telling the locals how he's been sticking it to the bad guys throughout his career and how he's going to keep sticking it to them.

"Can we talk about something voters care about?" Throckmorton says to the cheering crowd. "Can we talk about how every major industry in the state of Texas supports my campaign? Do you know why that is? It's because I understand how organizations run. Not Patty Rice. Businesses don't want a tax-and-spend liberal who's going to regulate the legals to death and turn a blind eye to the illegals. She's a Californian posing as a Texan, and we don't need any more of her."

One thing I'll give the guy: he knows how to connect with his audience.

By the time I get to Dime Box, it's dark. From the end of Travis's gravel drive, I can see the porch light burning, but there's no light coming from inside the big front window. I want to check up on my witness, but I haven't heard a thing from her in days, and I have no idea what state of mind she's in. If I walk in on her in the dark, she might shoot me.

So I head to The Buckaroo, where I find Travis on his stool, talking to one of the locals about when it's going to rain. He does a double take when he sees me. The local takes the opportunity to excuse himself and avoid more of Travis's drunk talk.

"How's Anna?" I ask.

He eyes me kind of funny, and then I remember what state he was in the night I drove him home. He might not remember I was at his house.

"Who?" he says.

"You don't have to protect her. I already talked to her. How's she doing?"

He's a little bleary, but not as drunk as he was the first time we talked.

"She ain't so good," he says.

"Is she eating?"

"Yeah, she eats. She's nervous all the time."

"If I stop by to see her—"

"I wouldn't," he says. "Not till daylight. She's like to snap."

"Has she been talking to anyone?"

"Just me. And the shit she says don't make no sense. The cops are out to get her. The FBI's out to get her. Only one who loves her is Jesus."

"Well, that's something," I say. "I'll stop by tomorrow. You tell her, OK?"

"What's your name again, mister?"

"Freddy. Tell her Freddy's gonna stop by."

As I walk out, I hear him order a shot of Jack Daniels. He's going to forget. I know it.

.

37

I check into a motel in Elgin after a late dinner—the same motel I stayed in the night I met Anna Brook. It's about thirty miles west of Travis's house, still in the flatlands. The hill country is farther to the south and west.

The news channels are all running stories on the missing TSA agent, Timothy Welcher. Fox says he died of drug and alcohol poisoning. He was thirty-two years old, unmarried but had a steady girlfriend. He grew up in San Diego. Same age as Lomax. Same neighborhood, in fact. I do some digging online and find that he and Lomax played baseball together in high school.

Both Fox and CNN are calling Welcher's death a suicide. Then CNN shows a photo of a face I haven't seen in a while. It's the garbage collector from San Francisco International with the big ears. The Feds are asking for help in locating him.

I give Ed a call.

"How are you holding up?" I ask.

"I'd be doing better if I could get out of here."

"You didn't make it to the army surplus store?"

"No. They open at eight tomorrow. It's crazy out here. I'm having trouble connecting with my sources."

"What's going on?"

"Internal problems. The Bureau's all bent out of shape about something."

"I see they got the Cambodian guy up on TV now."

"Yeah" he says. "TSA didn't like those videos of him in the terminal. They would have released his photo earlier, but they thought they had him. By the way, I told them that tip came from you."

"Thanks, Ed. They still don't know who he called? Right before the flight took off?"

"No. Like I told you before, it was a burner phone out in one of the long-term parking lots."

"That phone spend any time in Texas?"

Ed's quiet for a couple of seconds. "How'd you know that?"

"Dallas area?"

"Yeah."

"Why'd you ask me to stay away from Lomax, Ed?"

"What's that got to do with anything?"

"What was it you told me when you first mentioned Lomax and Rollins? You said something about them being on a nowhere case, with cops ratting on cops?"

"So?"

"So, Ed. Go down to that surplus store first thing tomorrow and let me know what you find."

I don't usually tell Ed what to do, but I can see he doesn't get what's going on. Why would he tell me to stay away from Lomax? And why are his contacts in the Bureau all bent out of shape? I'm thinking about that painter at the house in Silver Spring who wasn't really a painter. And the blue Dodge Dart that, when given the choice to follow me or Lomax, followed Lomax. I'm thinking about Timothy Welcher, the dead TSA agent, and how his girlfriend said she overheard him talking to someone outside the apartment the night of the crash. She didn't recognize the voice, but Welcher seemed comfortable with the guy, like he knew him. And then he never returned.

What kinds of things get the FBI bent out of shape? One is when some private eye starts following the same guy they're following. They don't want the amateurs messing up their work. Another is when an agent brings shame upon the Bureau. When he comes into the Hoover Building all jittery, with dilated pupils. Or even worse, when he's somehow wrapped up in a crime they're busting their asses to sort out. They don't like that kind of situation one bit.

While I'm mulling all this over, I get a call from Chester Dixon. It's well past midnight.

"Ferguson!"

"Hey, Chester. How'd you know I'd be awake?"

"If you weren't, I would have woken you up."

"You sound excited."

"I just had a long talk with your friend Alfonso Jiménez in Dallas. Did you know the State Patrol up there was protecting Sheldon Brown?"

"Yeah. I had a talk with a girl at Brown's house. She told me they used to come by to tell Brown to quiet down. I also had a little run-in with them myself. They seemed to be watching the place."

"Well," Dixon says, "Jiménez didn't like that. And remember what I told you about those two drug busts? How there was a lot more money involved than was reported in the news?"

"Yeah."

"Well, guess where that went?"

"I'm guessing Midland-Odessa Custom Hauling. Green Grass Septic. Taylor Automotive. What kind of evidence do you have?"

"Jiménez has been working on a couple of cops in Dallas, and they're ready to talk. And I got another little tidbit for you, though I'm not sure how it fits in. Remember our friend Ramón?"

"How could I forget?"

"All that stuff edited out of his records, or just plain missing?"

"He was an informant, right?"

"Yeah. For the state. But when his associates figured out he was the one leaking information, he begged the cops to get him out of Texas. So they passed him off to some Fed who took him somewhere else."

"Why'd he come back to Texas?"

"I don't know," Dixon says. "Why do criminals do half the shit they do? Because they're fucking dumbasses. If the guy knew how to make an honest living, he'd have done that and saved himself a life of trouble."

* * *

After I hang up with Dixon, I give Anna a call. She doesn't answer. I leave a message telling her I'll stop by tomorrow.

But my nerves are on edge and I can't sleep, so I turn on the news. CNN is reporting that a source inside the FBI says the Bureau may be releasing Rashad Obasanjo soon. There are already protesters outside his parents' house in Oakland, and Obasanjo's family is under protection. The threats against his family have increased since the alt-right news sites started reporting earlier in the day that "the terrorist" would be freed.

CNN has a reporter embedded in the crowd of protesters at the Obasanjo house. He keeps looking behind him as he describes the scene and the general air of tension. "This crowd feels like it could turn at any moment," he says. On the right edge of the screen, someone is waving a burning t-shirt on a stick, and farther back, the cops are moving in on three people fighting beside a burning garbage can.

I turn the TV off. What a state we're in...

* * *

I don't remember falling asleep, but around three a.m. I wake up in a sweat. This time, it's the other dream. The one that's haunted me for years.

I'm eight years old, and I walk into the living room of our apartment in Philadelphia. Mom is lying dead on the floor. She's on her side, facing away from me, with her head resting on her arm, while Dad sits on the couch watching the baseball game and drinking beer like she's not even there.

That's not how it really went down, but I've had this dream a thousand times, and it always leaves me with a heavy feeling of dread that saps my strength for days.

I finally told Ed about this a few weeks ago. After all these years, he's the first person I've ever told. He could see the weariness and sickness on my face on the mornings I woke up from that dream. He had seen it for a long time. A few weeks ago, at the beginning of the Smithsonian case—the case that took me out to San Francisco—he finally pulled me aside and asked me straight-up if I had a drinking problem. "I've seen you come in to work too many times looking like that."

"I don't have a drinking problem, Ed. I have a problem with a past that will never change."

I didn't go into detail. I just told him I had this dream, and it upset me.

"You want to talk to someone about that?"

"That's the thing, Ed. I can't."

"Well then, you're stuck."

"Yeah, Ed, I'm fucking stuck. And it cost me a career, and it cost me a marriage, and it's going to keep on costing me forever and ever."

I can't get those images out of my head. My mother crumpled on the floor. My father on the couch, utterly indifferent.

I can't stop sweating, and I feel trapped. It's 3:16 a.m., and the whirlpool is pulling me down.

In a panic, I call Miriam.

"What is it?" she says. "What's wrong?" The fear in her voice wakes her husband, who says something in a groggy voice with a thick Serbian accent.

"It's nothing," I say. "Calm down."

"It's nothing," she says to her husband. "Go back to sleep." Then she says to me, in a quiet voice, "What's the matter, Freddy? Why are you calling me in the middle of the night?"

"Were you ever afraid of me?" I ask.

"What?"

"Were you ever afraid of me?"

"Well," she says, "you can be moody. That's not easy to live with."

"No, I mean, were you ever afraid I would hurt you?"

"No, Freddy. Never."

"My temper didn't scare you?"

"It scared me all right, but I never feared for my safety."

"You never thought I'd hit you?"

"No!" She says it like the question is shocking and offensive. "Freddy, if you didn't hit me after all the things I did—after Lenny in particular—I couldn't see you ever hitting any woman. What brought this up?"

"I had a little run-in the other day."

"With a woman?"

"Yeah. She said some things that got to me, and I said some things I regret. I swear I was going to hit her. I don't know what stopped me."

"*You* did, Freddy. *You* stopped you."

"It scared the shit out of me."

"Well that's a good thing," she says. "It means your moral compass is working. You're not your father, Freddy. Don't you understand that? You're not him."

"I don't know that for sure." My mouth is dry. I can't stop shaking, and I can't stop sweating.

"Well I do. Your father was an alcoholic. You don't drink more than two beers a week. Have you ever been drunk?"

"A couple times," I say. "But I have his temper too."

"And you have restraint. He didn't."

"I didn't have restraint with Chuck DiLeo."

"Well maybe he didn't deserve it. Freddy..." I hear her shift the phone to her other ear. "I antagonized you from the beginning of our relationship to the end because I just wanted you to open up. You are the most frustrating, exasperating person I have ever met. Ever! Some of the things I said to you—well, if anyone had said those things to me, I would have hit them. I would have punched them right in the face. And I know you loved me, Freddy. I know you did."

"Yeah, well… How's little Lenny doing?"

"Good," she says. "I cleared up the birthday party, so we're back on. Sorry for the confusion."

"Thanks."

"He's really excited," she whispers, and I can hear the happiness in her voice. "And I love your idea of having all the zoo animals. While you're comparing yourself to your father, you should ask if he ever would have done anything like that for you. Give yourself some credit, will you?"

"Yeah, I know. This job just gets me bent out of shape sometimes."

"Freddy?"

"Huh?"

"You gonna talk to someone?"

I'm not sure if that's a dig or real concern. "I'm talking to you," I say.

"I know you are. It's a few years too late, but it's a start. Maybe all that work I put into you will pay off someday for somebody else."

"Yeah, maybe. Hey, um… good night, Miriam. Thanks for listening."

"Good night, Freddy."

I don't really hate her. I could never hate her. I just don't like to admit how much she hurt me, or how badly I let it all go wrong.

38

OCTOBER 10

I had so much buzzing through my head last night, I was up till dawn.

I slept till eleven and could have gone on sleeping if I didn't force myself to get up. According to the mirror, I look like shit, even for me. Five days without shaving, and there are dark, puffy bags under my bleary eyes.

After I wash up and get the coffeemaker going, I turn on the TV and flip to ESPN. I can't stand any more news. Beach volleyball is a much nicer way to ease into the morning. Four good-looking women enjoying a day of sport. Though I never could figure out why the sand doesn't stick to them when they fall.

My phone vibrates with a text from Ed. The damn thing's been in silent mode since I hung up with Chester Dixon. Ed's text says to call him ASAP.

When I call, the first thing out of his mouth is, "Who the hell is Charles Johnston?"

"No one," I say. "Why?"

"Don't fuck with me, Freddy. Who is he?"

"He's no one. Literally. He does not exist."

"I went to the army surplus store this morning. The purchase on that Visa card, you know what it was?"

"An ammo box. And I bet it was a metal one, with a metal clasp, just like the one that held the explosives on the plane."

"You knew I was going to say that, didn't you? And you know what else? That photo you sent me the day after the crash? The tall guy in the security line? He's the one who made the purchase. The clerk described him exactly."

"Pretty convenient he's dead, huh?"

"He's dead?"

"Yeah, look up Ramón Ramírez in Texas. He was all over the news for a couple of days." I can hear Ed tapping on the keyboard of his laptop.

"He's dead all right." Ed lets out a little sigh. "We finally get a step ahead of everyone, and the guy dies in custody on an unrelated case."

"You're not ahead of anyone," I say. "And it's not an unrelated case."

"It says here it was a drug bust in eastern Texas."

"You could call it that," I say. "Or you could call it the Witness Elimination Program. Whoever's running this show deserves a prize for thoroughness and efficiency. Whoever it is really knows how to get things done. I have a feeling he'd make a good governor. You know how you get away with a really big crime?"

"What are you talking about, Freddy?"

"You spread out the work so everyone's doing one little piece. There's a piece here in this part of the state, and another piece three hundred miles away, and a piece in California, and a piece in DC, and no one thinks to put it all together."

"Freddy?"

"The only problem is, some of the jobs you need to do require someone who's willing to take big risks, and a guy like that—maybe he's a little unhinged. Maybe he's not thinking straight anymore because maybe he can't."

"What are you talking about?"

"Listen, Ed, I've been holding out on you."

He doesn't miss a beat. "This have anything to do with Lomax?"

"It does," I say.

"Well I have some news for *you*," Ed says.

"What's that?"

"Lomax failed a drug test. The Bureau didn't tell him. They just put him back on desk duty doing background checks on passengers from the Hawaii flight. The Bureau brought in a couple guys from the Chicago office to follow him. Guys he doesn't know."

"Like a black guy and a white guy, driving a blue Dodge Dart?"

"I don't know," Ed says. "But the fact they're following him, instead of just sticking him in rehab means something's off. He picked up a package at a house in Silver Spring the other day."

"Yeah," I say. "A house that was for sale."

"You followed him?"

"I did."

"That must have been what the Bureau was hot about. That's why they told me to warn you off. Last night they sent Lomax down to Dallas to follow up on a case he was working down there."

"The corruption case? Highway Patrol and Department of Public Safety?"

"That's the one. Only there is no case."

"Oh, there is," I say. "Trust me."

"No, there's not. Lomax and his supervisor did a preliminary investigation and—"

"And they wrote the whole thing off. I know."

"How'd you know that?"

"Why'd they send Lomax back to Dallas?"

"So he'd think he was in the clear," Ed says. "So they could search his apartment, his office, his computer, and his car. You know what they found? That package he picked up in Silver Spring?"

"What?"

"Sixty-two thousand dollars in cash. They found it in his freezer, stuffed into Lean Cuisine boxes."

"Lomax eats Lean Cuisine?"

"I don't know."

"They know what the money was for?" I ask.

"No. Why were you following him, Freddy? You don't usually get off track unless you're on to something."

"Well I'm on to something all right."

"Listen," Ed says. "There's nothing the agency hates more than when one of its own agents goes astray. They don't know yet if it's drug money or—"

"It's not drug money," I say. "It's payment for services rendered."

"What services?"

"The Witness Elimination Program, Ed. Ever hear of it?"

"No. What the hell are you talking about? Just say it!"

"Lomax was investigating the Texas Department of Public Safety and the State Highway Patrol, looking into tips from a couple of cops."

"Yeah?"

"Well, he found something."

"That's not what the report says."

"I know that's not what the report says. Lomax and Mitch Rollins wrote the report. Did you know Mitch Rollins took out a second mortgage and a line of credit on his house? He spent it all but he never did any renovation work. He was up to his ears in debt. *Was.* I have a feeling he paid that off recently. Lomax and Rollins found plenty to report about, but they were paid to keep it quiet."

"And when did you have time to dig all this up?" Ed asks. "You're supposed to be working on the airline case, not corruption in Texas."

"It's the same case, Ed. There were two cops on that plane, a patrolman named Manuel Martínez and a captain named Brandon Robertson. They both had evidence of wrongdoing. They both talked to Rollins. Somehow word went up the ladder that these two knew something. And then the governor himself put them on that plane as a reward for their good work.

"There were two other guys on the plane, Sheldon Brown and Franklin Dorsett, a couple of high rollers who liked to party. They were laundering money and filtering it into the governor's re-election campaign. Some of it was drug money that came in through Brown's strip clubs. The State Patrol was turning a blind eye to it. Some of that money even came directly through the State Patrol. Cash seizures from drug runners. The two cops, Robertson and Martínez, had evidence. Maybe not enough to seal the case or even to get an indictment, but enough to get an honest cop nervous. Enough to make him want to investigate. That's why they called in the FBI."

Ed's quiet for a moment then says, "So how does this all connect?"

"Brown was going off the deep end, using a little too much of the product he was moving through his clubs. Dorsett was egging him on, pushing him to gamble more and do more blow and then relieving him of his businesses when he needed quick cash. Dorsett milked him till he was just about broke. And I think maybe Brown started to snap. He was talking about blackmailing the governor, telling cops that shit was going to roll uphill, all the way to the top. Throckmorton twisted Brown's arm to pump more money into his campaign. I think he may have crossed a line somewhere and pissed Brown off. Brown wanted some of his money back.

"So with the two cops and Brown and Dorsett on that plane, you have all your incriminating witnesses in one place. At least, all the ones you know about. The only people outside that plane who had all the pieces, who could put together the whole story, were Rollins and Lomax. They had talked to all four of those guys. Lomax spent a lot of time with Brown and Dorsett. They didn't know he was a cop. He was a guy who liked hookers and blow, just like them. Am I making sense to you, Ed?"

He's dead silent.

"Lomax was in San Francisco the day of the crash. He had gone there with a woman and some drugs, to delay Brown and Dorsett. They were going to Hawaii on a flight two days earlier than the cops, Robertson and Martínez. Lomax's job was to stall them for a couple days, to make sure they got on the same flight as the cops.

"You know that ammo box that exploded in the cargo hold? We can trace that to Lomax, at least circumstantially, through the credit card. Charles Johnston, the cardholder, doesn't exist. He's a government-created identity, with a government-created credit history, custom-made for undercover work. Lomax was called Chuck down here in Sheldon Brown's house. Chuck as in Charles, as in Johnston.

"Ed, I've been on the airline case the whole time. Obasanjo had nothing to do with it. Delmont Suggs had nothing to do with it. Welcher probably did. He knew Lomax from high school. Lomax either sweet-talked him or twisted his arm to get that ammo box onto the plane. But Welcher's dead, so we'll never know. Convenient, right? And Ramón Ramírez, a Texas informant turned federal informant under Lomax's supervision. He bought the ammo box. But he's dead too.

"You see the pattern here? This is a highly efficient, highly effective Witness Elimination Program, and all the bloodhounds in all the federal agencies, and all the reporters in all the news organizations were put on the wrong trail with that Obasanjo bullshit. Because everyone is ready to believe a Muslim will blow up a plane for Allah, but no one's ready to believe a governor will do it to hold on to power."

"I can't believe what you're telling me," Ed says. "No one's going to buy those allegations without a mountain of evidence. You've got to have evidence."

"That's the same thing the girl said. I *have* the evidence. That cop named Dixon in Longview—the one who called you the other day—he has a file with part of the story. Another cop named Jiménez in Dallas has another part. Jiménez even has a couple of patrolmen willing to testify about Sheldon Brown's protection detail, about money from some big busts never making it into the evidence lockers. And Dixon has an accountant in San Antonio who's traced the money through Sheldon Brown's businesses to Throckmorton's campaign. The FBI has $62,000 in unexplained cash pulled from Lomax's own freezer. Lomax, who failed a cocaine test! I got a girl in a bikini up in Duluth who can tell you where he picked up *that* habit. Why'd you ask me to back off of Lomax, Ed? It's because those guys out in Silver Spring, the fake house painter and the two in the blue Dodge Dart were already following him, and they didn't want me to blow their surveillance. They already knew their guy was crooked.

"And I got another thing for you, Ed. The icing on the cake. I have a witness down here—"

"Down where?"

"Texas. I'm in Texas, remember? I have the lynchpin of the case down here, the person who can tie it all together—"

"You mean that skinny blonde woman?" Ed says.

"What?"

"Anna Brook?"

"How do you know about her?"

"Haven't you been watching the news?"

"No."

"It broke twenty minutes ago," he says. "Turn on CNN, Fox, MSNBC, anything. That's all they're showing. The whole Bureau's in meltdown. I thought she was just crazy, but everything you're telling me…"

I flip to CNN and there she is. Anna Brook, holding up a copy of this morning's New York Times, pointing to the headline and the date. The tagline at the bottom of the screen says, "Shocking development in crash case."

She looks shaky and worn, like she's inches from her breaking point. She says she was supposed to be on that plane. She knows why it crashed. "Check the passenger list," she says, and she holds her license up to the camera. "Anna Brook of Quarry Road, Washington, DC. That's me."

It looks like she made the video with the Android phone I gave her. And all those newspapers that were spread all over the house with all her annotations—she's been working on the case herself this whole time.

"If you doubt I'm who I say I am…" She raises her left shirtsleeve and shows a red birthmark about the size and shape of a small bee. "Ask my friends. Ask my family. I was supposed to be on that plane, and I know why it went down. It wasn't Rashad Obasanjo, and this isn't a terrorism case. It was Errol Lomax, the FBI agent who was supposed to protect me. And this is a case of power, pure and simple. This is about a crooked man who wants to hold on to his power."

She moves the camera closer to her face and looks directly into the lens and says, "Sorry, Freddy. I won't make it another day down here, or anywhere else. I had to let the world know, before they came and got me."

"You're in Texas?" Ed says.

"Ed, I have to go. I have to pick her up before she snaps."

"Looks like she already did. Freddy, listen. They had Lomax under surveillance down in Dallas. They were going to pick him up on his way out of the airport."

"What do you mean, they *had* him under surveillance?"

"He slipped away. They don't know where he is."

It takes a few seconds for *that* to sink in.

"When did he arrive in Dallas?"

"This morning," Ed says.

"When did they lose him?"

"A few hours ago."

Dallas to Dime Box is a three-hour drive.

I think about that decision I made, letting Julia call her sister. I let my emotions get the better of me that night. I knew I would regret it. Why the hell did she have to call from her own phone?

"Ed?"

"Yeah?"

"Can an agent get access to phone records if he has no warrant. If there's no case. I mean, say he just wants to know who's calling who, out of curiosity?"

"If he has contacts inside the telecom, he might be able to get some info as a favor. Or he could get it unofficially from the NSA, if he has connections."

"Ed, I have to go. I have to pick her up before he does."

I turned off location services on that Android phone before I gave it to Anna. But the telecom still knows her general location because it knows which cell towers she's connecting to. Depending on when he left Dallas, Lomax might be there already.

How many houses are on that little country road west of Dime Box? Four or five in a three-mile stretch? He can go from house to house at his leisure. He's a presentable guy when he wants to be, good looking and well dressed. I can see him walking right up to someone's front door. A little knock, a pleasant hello, and that thousand-watt smile of his. He'll go into some bullshit story just to get the person talking. Anna will be hiding, of course. But he's a cop. If he walks into a house and something isn't right, he'll sniff it out.

Would Travis tip him off? It's hard to read a guy like Travis in the morning. The queasiness of a hangover can mask the normal signs of fear and nervousness, like a strong odor masks the scent the hounds are following. Maybe Travis can pull it off and get him to go away. Or maybe Lomax is all coked up. Maybe he'll just shoot his way in and find her cowering in the corner and blow her brains out. Maybe he'll spare her for half an hour, so he can have one last go with her, for old-time's sake.

How far is it from here in Elgin to that little road west of Dime Box? Thirty miles? I can make it in twenty-five minutes. Maybe twenty.

That gun I took from Lomax is in my suitcase, along with some ammo I bought on the way to Dime Box after I talked to Chester Dixon. My hands are shaking as I load the magazine. Part of it is fear for Anna. Part of it is anger at myself for not finishing Lomax when I had the chance. And part of it is that old feeling welling up. The same feeling Chuck DiLeo once got on the wrong side of.

39

Heading east on highway 290, I'm doing eighty-five, ninety miles an hour. I've called Anna three times. She doesn't answer. I leave messages, warning her that Lomax might be on his way. "Hide in the woods," I say. "Or if Travis is there, have him take you to The Buckaroo. He won't shoot you in front of a crowd."

That was the wrong thing to say. She's scared enough as it is. I don't need to put images of a shooting into her head.

Now I have the phone to my ear, trying to get a hold of that cop Jiménez in Dallas. He's not answering, so I put in a call to Chester Dixon over in Longview. He picks up on the third ring.

"You know any cops between Austin and College Station?"

"Freddy?"

"You know any cops anywhere near a place called Dime Box? I mean cops who aren't crooked."

"I know one in College Station," he says.

"You trust him? You know for sure he's not wrapped up in all this shit we talked about?"

"I trust him. What's going on?"

"I need someone in Dime Box, ASAP. Worst case is, I have a Fed here coming to kill someone."

"Coming to kill who?"

"A witness. A star witness for our case. Turn on the TV if you have one nearby. You'll see her. The guy coming after her is well trained," I say. "He knows how to use his weapon. I don't think I can take him out myself. How far is College Station?"

"Almost an hour, if you go the speed limit. A lot less with a heavy foot and your flashers on."

"Send your guy with backup, and make sure they make it in less. This is it, Dixon. It all goes down now."

"I'll send him," Dixon says. "Hang tight."

I give him the address. The GPS says I'll be there in sixteen minutes.

I call Anna again. No answer. Shit! Does she still not trust me because of that mocking redneck cop up in Dallas? Is she too scared to answer? Is she hiding? Or is she dead?

I call Julia Brook. She picks up on the fifth ring.

"Julia, she knows your number. She'll answer if she sees it's you."

"Freddy?"

"Hang up and call her right now. And then call me back. I want to know if she's alive, and if so, where is she? Tell her to get out. Tell her the woods or The Buckaroo, and then call me back and let me know where I should meet her."

I just did it again. Said the wrong thing and alarmed her. "*If* she's alive?" She says it like her heart is in her throat. "Freddy, what's—"

"Hang up and call her. The number's still in your phone, right? Find out where she is, and call me back."

I hang up.

Thirteen minutes to the house.

Chester Dixon calls back. His friend is on the road with three more cars to follow. "They started out near Cooks Point, about ten miles closer than College Station. How far out are you?"

"Twelve minutes," I say. "How far are they?

"Twenty-five," he says. "But they might be able to make it in less."

"All right," I say. "I gotta go."

After almost missing the turn up Highway 21, I gun it straight through the fields of Lincoln, across Highway 77, and through the flatlands. Now I have to slow down so I don't miss that last turn onto Travis's road.

I switch on the radio while I wait for Julia to call back. The news station is saying CNN, Fox, the *New York Times* and a number of other outlets have already got hold of Anna's friends in Staunton, and they've all confirmed it's her in the video.

The station plays some snippets from an impromptu news conference that took place just a few minutes ago.

"Is the FBI taking the video seriously?" a female reporter asks.

"Until we can disprove allegations, the Bureau takes all information seriously in an investigation like this."

"Do you think one of your own could have been involved?"

"It's too early to speculate on that. The woman in the video appears to be distraught. We are investigating."

"Where is Errol Lomax?" asks another reporter.

"Lomax is in Texas."

"Are you questioning him?"

"We will question him once we've located him."

"You don't know where he is?"

"We know he's in Texas."

That's as much as the press can get out of the Bureau.

Then the local news switches back to election coverage. Jumbo Throckmorton, addressing a crowd in Lubbock a little while ago was helped offstage by his aides after suddenly appearing pale and stricken. The aides went to work immediately to quash speculation he'd had a heart attack.

"The governor is suffering from exhaustion," his campaign manager says. "It's been a long and difficult campaign, a fight the whole way through. And the last few weeks have been unusually warm. All those rallies out in the heat have taken their toll. This isn't a sudden thing. The governor just needs some rest."

I think back to that interview with Throckmorton on TV, how his body language changed when the reporter mentioned the plane crash. What if he really didn't know what he was getting into?

I try to picture it from his perspective. He's protecting Sheldon Brown, who's dealing from his clubs, and

Throckmorton is squeezing money out of him at the same time. He's forcing Brown to launder the cash his cops rake in on busts they're not even reporting.

A lieutenant and a patrolman get suspicious about what's going on. They call in the Feds to have a look, just as Sheldon Brown starts going off the deep end, shooting coke, complaining about the governor shaking him down, threatening both Throckmorton and his cops.

Rollins and Lomax figure out what's going on. But Rollins is deep in debt and past caring about his job. He lays out all he knows to Throckmorton, and then offers to get rid of the witnesses and bury the findings of the investigation in exchange for money.

Throckmorton probably pictures a sensible plan. He sees Dorsett falling off a boat in Hawaii. Brown ODs on coke in Vegas. Martínez and Robertson, who knows? But it's a series of unrelated tragedies, spread all over the map. Just the daily goings-on in a world full of troubles. No one would ever connect the dots.

Throckmorton thinks his problems are solved, until he wakes up one day to see how it all went wrong over Monterey Bay. Maybe he didn't know Lomax was coming unhinged, that the drugs were making him psychotic. Put coke in the wrong person and he thinks he's invincible. He thinks he's so far above everyone else, he can't make mistakes. He's not just sloppy. He's reckless.

Jumbo learns a little too late it's not just his mistakes he has to worry about, but all of his associates' as well. They're all liabilities. It's only a matter of time before they screw up, and when they do, it'll all come back to him. Just like Sheldon Brown said. Shit rolls uphill.

So the governor's aide wasn't lying when he said this was not a sudden-onset sickness. Old Jumbo had probably been dreading this for quite a while, wondering how long he could keep a lid on it all. And the dread must have kicked into high gear when that plane went down.

No, it wasn't a sudden thing. Old Jumbo had it coming.

Four minutes to the house. There's Travis's road. Two lanes of faded blacktop coming out of a clump of trees. I slow down and bear left.

Three minutes and still no response from Julia. I look up ahead as far as I can see, which is a half mile or so before the road bends at another clump of trees. There are no other cars in sight. Nothing behind me either.

Two minutes to go. Finally, Julia calls.

"Where is she?" I ask.

"In the house."

"Did you tell her to get out?"

She hesitates for a second, and then chokes out her words. "She won't go, Freddy."

"What do you mean, she won't go?"

Another little pause, and then the words of the concerned and baffled sister: "She says she wants to see him."

40

The front wheels slide sideways on the gravel as I swing into the driveway, kicking up a cloud of dust that blows onto the porch. The car skids to a stop and I get out, gun in hand, and dash up the steps calling her name. If she's in there, I want her to know it's me.

Inside, I see her through the bedroom door. At least, her arms and legs. She's on the end of the bed, feet on the floor, arms hanging down between her knees.

"Anna!"

"Hey, Freddy." Her voice is emotionless and flat. She holds the gun in both hands.

"Come on, we have to go."

"You go," she says. "I'm staying."

"I think Lomax knows where you are."

"Good for him. He always did know how to get to me." I study her face for a moment, trying to see if she's had a psychotic break.

"Come on," I grab her under the arm and pull her up onto her feet. "We have to—"

I didn't see it coming because I wasn't expecting it from the left hand. She hit me hard with that gun right beside the eye, and it hurt. I can't help my reflexes after all those years of training. I throw her on the bed before I even know what I'm doing. She points the gun at my face, the glow of the laser light dancing on my cheek.

"What's the matter with you?" I ask.

"I've had enough," she says coldly. "Today it ends."

"Yeah, what the hell do you think I came down here for? We leave now. The FBI knows about Lomax—"

"Nobody *really* knows about Lomax."

"—they know, and they're going to lock him up. The State Patrol will be here if he shows up."

"The State Patrol?" she says bitterly.

"Not the ones protecting Sheldon Brown," I say. "I mean ones we can trust. I have some guys coming from—"

We both turn at the sound of tires crunching gravel in the driveway. The front door is wide open, and we see Travis's truck pulling up out front. He gets out and examines my car. Then he pulls a gun from his waistband and walks up the front steps yelling, "Anna!"

Jesus, you idiot! Don't announce yourself when you *know* there's a stranger in the house.

"Back here," she says.

When he sees me, he stops in his tracks. His eyes go right to my gun. His arm hangs by his side the whole time, with his gun pointing down at the floor. His eyes are bleary from the breakfast he just drank, and he wavers on his feet. This guy isn't prepared for anything.

"I've seen you before," he says.

"Christ, I talked to you last night!" I say.

Then he says to Anna, "This ain't the guy, is it?"

"Travis—"

"She was on TV," Travis says. "CNN. Saw her at the bar when they switched from Fox Sports—"

"Shit!" Anna leaps from the bed at the sound of a car door slamming. "That's him!"

He must have come in slowly along the drive. Travis heads straight out the bedroom door, across the creaking floor of the living room, with me following and Anna bringing up the rear.

"We're three on one," I say. And we could coordinate something intelligent, but Travis goes straight through the front door firing two shots without even aiming.

"Get the fuck off my property, bastard!" He thinks he's dealing with some trespasser who's going to back off after a threat.

A second gun goes off outside and Travis curses. I go to the wall between the front door and the window. If Lomax makes it into the house, I'll be behind him when he comes in.

Travis fires four consecutive shots from the porch, and four more come back from the driveway. The first two of those are wild, making me think Lomax is off his rocker. One comes through the wall just beside my knee, and one goes through the window behind me. The third or fourth shot hit Travis somewhere bad. He staggers back into the doorway, groaning. I can see him through the crack between the hinges.

Then I feel a bounce in the floorboards beneath my feet. That's Lomax leaping onto the porch.

A blast goes off behind the door, two feet from my face, and Travis thuds backward onto the old wood floor, dark blood spilling from the back of his head like wine from a ruptured gourd.

I look back across the room to see where Anna is, but she's gone.

Lomax has to step over the remains of Travis Seldin to get inside, and as he does, I fire two shots through the wooden door, both about chest high. If either of them hit him, he didn't make a sound. As soon as he's past the door, he swings his arm around and fires, and I let off a shot at the same time. But he slips in Travis's blood, almost going down, and we both miss. My shots wouldn't have mattered anyway. He's wearing a vest. That's why the bullets through the door didn't hurt him.

On his way up, he sends a grazing shot along my right thigh, and I pull my trigger the instant his face is in front of my barrel. Only nothing happens. The slide of my gun is jammed open. Quick as lightning, I swing a left up under his chin and catch him hard. It stuns him for a split second, long enough for me to land another hard blow between the eyes with the useless gun. I drop it and grab his left wrist, his gun hand, with my right, but not before he gets another shot off. That one was point blank along my right side, grazing my ribs and burning the cotton of my shirt.

When I push his left hand out, his gun goes off again, sending a bullet through the wall above the doorway. I'm trying to push him backward so he'll trip over Travis, but he's strong.

I know his right hand will be coming because of the way he shifts his feet. I brace for it, and as his fist comes across, I swing a hard left hook at the side of his face.

His blow lands just as I break my hand on the side of his head. His punch buckles my legs, but I know the one I threw hurt him more, because it hurt me plenty, and I feel some of the strength go out of his left arm. I'm pretty sure I broke the cheekbone under his eye, and the way he's blinking, I can tell his head isn't clear.

I take my eyes off him for a split second to look around the room. Where's Anna? Did she go back to the bedroom? Did she leave? Is she in the woods? This guy's on drugs, and he has a gun, and I can't hold on to him much longer.

Just my luck to bring a fist to a gunfight, and then break it. Lomax's strength comes back quickly, and his eyes are dilated like a crazy person's. I'm down to one good hand, and that one is locked around his left wrist, to keep his gun away from me.

What am I going to do? I want to push him back over Travis, but if I want to knock him to the floor, I'll have to let go, and he'll shoot me as he goes down. But I have no other option. It's my only...

He sees my eyes flick up toward the ceiling behind him, but he can't see what I see. The red bead of laser light dances on the plaster. It's coming up through the hole in the floor. As I start pushing him back, that grazing wound across my right thigh starts to feel more like a gouge. My pants are wet with blood, and I'm losing strength in that leg.

But still I'm stronger than him. I slam my forehead into his nose, then throw a left elbow into his teeth just as his head snaps back from the butt. That nudges him back a step. His nose is broken, and I see a flash of doubt in his cocaine-dilated eyes. I can tell he's never been pushed to his limit in a fight. But I've been there many times.

He takes a swing at me with his free right hand. I twist my head away. His fist glances off my temple, and I counter with another hard left elbow to the mouth. His teeth are streaked with blood. I have his left wrist locked in a death grip, and with my forearm across his chest, I push him back another step.

He digs a right hook into my ribs, but I've got him going backward, and his feet are in no position to give leverage to his punch. He looks at my face, he sees the punch had no effect, and I see his confidence drop another notch.

I look him in the eye and think, *If I have to throw you down to get you over that hole in the floor, I'll do it, even if you shoot me in the process.* He sees my determination. He's breathing hard, starting to gasp, and he's pouring sweat. That makes his wrist slippery. He's twisting it, trying to get it loose, but he can't. He blinks in confusion as my grip begins to cut off the circulation to his hand.

I evade his head-butt, and when he throws a right hook at my crotch, I twist, and his blow lands on my hipbone. He hesitates, not sure of his next target, and I think, *You finally get it, you fucking psychopath! You didn't think you'd run into someone stronger than you, but you did. You didn't think you'd run into someone more determined, but you did. You can't intimidate me. You might shoot me. You might even kill me. But I will get you to her. I will.*

I can see the fear in your eyes, and you can see the anger in mine. Let that be your parting image of this world. All that anger. You can take it with you into the next life, because I'm done with it. I'm fucking done!

His body starts to twist with another right hook aimed at my ribs. I smash my forehead into his nose, and his blow lands weakly against my side as the blood gushes from his face.

"You're losing and you know it, Lomax."

He's breathing heavily and shaking. He spits his blood into my left eye, but I can still see out of my right. And then he begins his final mistake.

I see what you're lining up for. I'm a boxer, you idiot. I see you shifting your weight onto your left leg. I was trained to watch every move, remember? Your gun is stuck and your fists don't hurt me, so what do you have left? A knee to the crotch. I push him back another step closer to the hole while the red bead of light dances on the ceiling.

He lines up again, puts his right hand on my shoulder, shifts all his weight to his left leg—a mistake because it puts him off balance—and as his right knee comes up, I push with all my might against his chest and send him backward, letting go of his wrist so he can fall.

"Now, Anna!"

I see the fire from the muzzle of his gun as he goes down on his ass. Two quick shots, just as two more come up from beneath the floor. One of his bullets thuds into my right side, sending me down. The second tears a burning gouge through the top of my left shoulder.

For a second, there's silence. Then someone shrieks. I'm on the floor, on my side. Lomax has keeled over sideways, with his leg bent awkwardly beneath him. He shrieks again with the agonized cry of an animal in distress. He's bleeding heavily, and the whole room smells like shit. She hit him in a bad place.

I try to sit up—my fighter's instinct to rise from the canvas—but the movement sends a jolt of pain through my body, and blood gushes from the hole below my ribs like toothpaste from a tube that's just been stepped on.

I hear the crawlspace door slam shut outside, and the footsteps coming around the corner of the house. Then Anna comes in, stepping through the pool of Travis's blood, pale and shaking and out of breath. She's got her gun out in front of her, the red dot dancing across the floor until it lands on Lomax's twisted face. His gun is six inches from his hand, but he can't even reach for it. His yells have turned to whimpers. Anna kicks his gun away, looks him over, smells the shit, and winces. She looks at Travis, dead in a heap by the door, and then she sees me on my side, still breathing and bleeding heavily.

"Are you OK?"

Lomax tries to get a word out. A call for help maybe, but it sounds like the cry of a wounded cow.

"Not you, fuckhead."

She's looking at me, but I can't respond. A look of anguish comes over her face.

Lomax's breath is fast, shallow, panicky. Every now and then he holds it for a second, and then lets out a deep, roiling moan, like a woman in labor. Anna stands over him with the gun and points the laser into his eye.

"Do you ever wish it would just end, Lomax?" she says. "Have you ever been in so much pain, and you know the only person who can save you isn't going to lift a goddamn finger to help, and all you can do is pray and pray and pray for it to end?"

He lets out a desperate, high-pitched, gurgling moan.

"They say suffering brings you closer to God," she says. Then she slides the magazine out of her gun and pushes the bullets out one by one onto the floor beside his head.

"That's the one thing you did for me, you bastard. You brought me closer to God." She flicks the last bullet out of the chamber and lays the gun on the floor.

"Go ahead and pray, Lomax. You don't have to do it out loud. I just want to know you're doing it."

She stares at him for a few seconds, waiting. The hot blood is running out of me, from the hole in my right side, from the tear in my leg, from the raw red trench gouged through the top of my left shoulder. It all runs down into a sticky, slippery pool around my broken left hand.

I hear the wailing of the sirens and the crunch of tires in the gravel drive. The red lights pulse through the dusty window shards like the beating of a shattered heart. Staticky voices crackle on the radios outside, and the cloud of dirt the cruisers kicked up comes blowing in through the open door.

The paleness of Anna's skin in the darkening world makes her float like a vision above the horror and the gloom and the blood and the stench. She kneels beside Lomax in his pool of filth, and she takes his hand, and she says calmly, "Don't be afraid. I'll show you how."

And the world fades to black as she begins.

"Our father, who art in heaven, hallowed be thy name…"

41

I hear voices around me, urgent shouting, and the chopping blades of a helicopter.

My mother, in her yellow Sunday dress, walks down a sidewalk in Philadelphia, carrying a bag of groceries. She is pregnant, about to burst. She stops, puts the bag on the pavement, leans against a building, and grimaces through a hard contraction. The other pedestrians pass by as if she isn't there. When she picks up the bag again, her legs are wet with broken water. She plods on until the next contraction forces her to stop.

Then hushed voices give instuction. Scalpel. Suction. OK. There.

A metal instrument clangs against a metal tray, and then I fade into a darkness where there is no time.

Fade back in. I'm in Travis's house. The police and paramedics have left their debris: bloodstained nitrile gloves, paper wrappers, soiled gauze. Travis lies in a pool of blackening blood just inside the door. My father walks in drunk and laughing.

"Jeez, Travis, you really tied one on, didn't you?"

He tears the plastic wrapping from the neck of a whiskey bottle and unscrews the cap. "This'll get you going," he says. He kneels down and pours the booze into Travis's open mouth. It goes out the back of his head and warms the pool of blackened blood to a bright healthy red.

My father pats Travis's cheek. "Come on, buddy, drink up. What the hell'd you do to yourself? You look like shit."

I want to kill him. The filthy, ignorant brute. I want to kick his fucking brains out. But I can't move. I'm pinned to the floor. The big steel pins go right through me, like an insect in a museum exhibit.

"All right, then," Dad says. "We'll go to the bar." He drags Travis out by the feet, leaving a long, thick smear of blood.

"Goddamnit!" I yell. I try with all my strength to break free from this paralysis, and then...

My eyes open to fluorescent lights in the ceiling of a large, quiet room. My throat hurts. "Shh..." I feel a hand on my shoulder as I try to sit up. A man's voice says, "Not yet." He's a chunky, dark-haired guy in light-blue scrubs. "You're good, buddy. Go back to..."

The world goes black again.

Then I'm in the office. Leon's desk is mostly bare, and so is Bethany's. All their personal items are gone, and the keyboards and mousepads have been straightened and cleaned, as if in preparation for some new person. The frames on the walls that held Ed's diploma and his certificates of recognition are empty. Outside the window, traffic goes by at the normal speed, but it's silent, as if the windows have been soundproofed.

I sit at my desk and check my email. There are hundreds of messages, but they're all blank. My phone is a blank white screen.

And then Anna Brook walks in wearing a blue satin dress, like she's going to a party. She's back to her normal weight. She has color in her cheeks, and she looks healthy. Her hair hangs limp and slightly curled, like she hasn't washed it since swimming in the sea. Her right hand is closed in a fist as she approaches, but she's smiling.

She sits in the chair beside my desk and says, "Freddy, I want you to find something."

"What?"

She holds out her right hand and opens it. Inside is the pearl she dove after in the whirlpool dream, when she chose to swim downward with the current instead of struggling up against it. It glows like the moon in her palm.

"This," she says.

"But you've already found it."

"I know," she says. "But you haven't."

42

"For thine is the kingdom, and the power, and the glory forever."

I awake in a hospital bed. Pale white sunlight streams in through the window to my right, surrounding Anna in a halo. She is seated, holding my hand in hers, as she raises her head from prayer.

It takes a few seconds to remember why I'm here. I look down to the end of the bed, to make sure both legs are still there. I wiggle my toes, to see if they work. I know exactly where I was shot, because that little bit of movement makes the swollen, oozing wounds ache. My right thigh. My right side, just below the ribs. The burning muscle above the left collarbone.

My left hand is in a cast that extends almost to the elbow. Julia is sitting on that side, in a beige cushioned chair. I have to look twice to make sure it's her. Did she come all the way from Virginia? How many days have I been here?

Her posture is straight, legs crossed one knee over the other, and she's holding a newspaper. She smiles and says, "Hello, Freddy." I smile weakly back, then turn my head the other way. They stuck the IV needle into that sweet blue vein at the top of my right forearm. The one the junkies usually blow out first.

Anna is looking at me with a softness in her gaze I haven't seen before. Her face is calm, serene almost, like the face of her sister that day in DC after she had cried herself out. The trauma of the past few months is etched into her eyes in a way that will never be undone, but it doesn't seem to rule her. I can still see in her face traces of a stoic patience and an unbroken will.

She watches me for a few seconds before she speaks. Her voice is smooth and sure, warm and concerned.

She asks how I'm feeling, and I tell her I feel as good as I look.

"Do you remember what happened at the house?"

"Yeah. Up until the cops arrived."

"You want to see something?" She nods to her sister. "Show him the headline."

Julia folds the paper back to the first page and holds it up for me to see. "Obasanjo Freed. Governor Arrested."

I turn back to Anna, and she says, "They got a few words out of Lomax after his surgery. Enough to figure out that he passed the bomb through Welcher's checkpoint. They have another FBI guy in custody in DC. Mitch Rollins. If you thought this was a media circus before, you should see what's going on now."

But this is small talk. She has something else on her mind. I can feel it, the way she's looking at me. The way she's holding back.

"What is it?" I ask.

"It's that…" She takes a few seconds to search for the words. "Some of those things you said at Travis's house that night. I don't think you really meant them."

"I'm sorry I called you that," I say. "I lost my temper."

"That's not what I mean," she says. "I mean the way you talked about the world. Like there's nothing in it but evil and suffering. That it's irredeemable. You didn't mean that."

"I did," I say.

"No," she says. "I don't think you understand yourself."

"I manage to get by well enough," I say, trying to shake her off.

But she has that probing, challenging, you-can't-avoid-me look in her eye.

She says, "You know, I really started to doubt everything after that talk with you. I looked back on my life, and there was so much to regret. And I looked around me in that little house, and it all seemed so hopeless. And I looked forward, taking your dark view of the world, and I saw nothing worth sticking around for. I almost gave up, Freddy.

"I *almost* did. But I couldn't let you win any more than I could let Lomax win, because I knew you were wrong. I mean, there was no point going on if you were right."

She leans toward me and brushes the hair back from my forehead. "Answer me this, Freddy. What is it you believe so deeply that you won't renounce it even in the face of death?"

"I don't know, Anna. What?"

"That's your religion, the belief you will not live without. And you know what that is, Freddy. You know who you are. You put your life on the line for a person you didn't even know. Why did you take an interest in me? Why did you follow me through that airport? Did I look like someone who was worth your while?"

"It was instinct," I say.

"It was none of your business, but you couldn't leave it alone, could you?" She pauses for a second, then says, "You and I aren't as far apart as you might think. We both want a world that's fair and just, and we're both pretty tuned in to the ways it's not. We both want people to treat each other with respect and decency. You come at it from your angle, and I come at it from mine."

"Why didn't you kill Lomax when you had the chance?" I ask.

"Why should I have?"

"After all he did to you?"

"After all he did to me..." She trails off and lapses into thought. I turn to look at Julia, who's sitting with the newspaper on her knee, watching her sister think.

"I don't believe in an eye for an eye," Anna says. "I don't believe that revenge is justice. It's just paying back one wrong with another. The only real justice is to not let injustices happen in the first place.

"I shot him because I was scared. Because I wanted to end his power over me and make sure he'd never hurt anyone

314

again. I fully intended to kill him. And then when I saw him there on the floor, I could tell he was terrified. He was in a lot of pain, but I think the terror was worse than the physical suffering. And I thought, Ah! Now you're down here with me. You're in a dark and lonely place. You can't find your way out, and no one is coming to rescue you."

She pauses for a moment, and I see in her eyes some of the darkness she must have felt when she hid in the crawlspace beneath the knotted floor of that broken-down shack. She looks at me and says softly, "Suffering is a kind of understanding life inflicts on you against your will, and you don't come out of it the same person. You're deeper, because it forces open depths you wouldn't willingly explore. I actually pitied him there, bleeding all over the floor of that filthy little house, and part of me said, OK, Lomax. Let's see how you deal with *this*. Let's see who you really are, down there at rock bottom, without your power and your confidence and your certainty that it'll all work out. Maybe sometime in the months between now and your execution, a conscience will emerge, and your hell will be your own regrets and the past you can't undo. If you think enough of yourself, maybe someday you'll get down on your knees and ask forgiveness. And when you find the person generous enough to give it to you, you'll finally understand how much it all matters."

She stops again and looks at her sister, taking in the healthy, youthful face and the bright eyes unmarred by anguish and abuse.

"You know he'll never rape again," Anna says. "He can't even use the toilet like a normal person. He's got a bag attached to him now, and he'll be wearing it on death row while he thinks about all the people he killed."

"And the one he didn't," Julia says.

"And the one he didn't," Anna says. She turns back to me and adds, "And the one who took an interest in her when he didn't have to, because… God only knows why." She studies my face with calm curiosity.

It's a funny thing when someone looks at you like that. When they see right through to the bottom of you, and you know it, and you know there's no point in hiding or lying about anything anymore.

"Somewhere along the line," she says, "something taught you not to ignore a sight like me, and it must have been a hard lesson, because most people turn their backs on trouble. But you just dive right in."

"It's my job," I say.

"It's the job you chose. And you chose it for a reason."

I can see in her eyes what she's thinking. You tipped your hand, Freddy Ferguson. You tipped it that night at Travis's house when you blew up and called her a whore. She hit that nerve dead on, and you reacted.

What was it she said about guys? They're like amateur poker players. They can't really hide what they think they're hiding. Somehow, it all comes out between a man and a woman, doesn't it? And it took one who's been around a lot of guys to crack me, because when you get right down to it, only the damaged truly understand the damaged.

She doesn't push or prod. She doesn't dig for more. She just says softly, "Maybe someday you can tell me about it."

And I want to.

I want to tell her everything.

Because… Well, didn't I say it?

Didn't I say right from the get-go I had a premonition about her?

ACKNOWLEDGMENTS

Many thanks to Kristin Mehus-Roe and Ingrid Emerick of Girl Friday Productions for their help in editing this book, and to Dorian Box, author of *Psycho Tropics*, for his suggestions on improving a key chapter. Thanks to Meredith Tennant for proofreading, and Lindsay Heider Diamond for her cover design.

ABOUT THE AUTHOR

Andrew Diamond's novel Impala won the 24th Annual Writer's Digest Award for genre fiction and the Readers' Favorite Gold Medal for mystery. Amazon.com editors picked it as a best mystery/thriller of the month upon its release in September, 2016, and IndieReader chose it as one of the best indie novels of the year.

If you enjoyed this book, please leave a review online. We indie authors have only our readers to recommend us.

CPSIA information can be obtained
at www.ICGtesting.com
Printed in the USA
BVHW072045170720
583829BV00003B/595